Sue Limb read English at Cambridge. Following an early career as a teacher, she became a free-lance journalist and then a writer and broadcaster. She is the author of several radio scripts including *The Wordsmiths at Gorsemere*. She co-authored a biography of Captain Oates before turning her hand to fiction: *Up the Garden Path* was published to critical acclaim in 1984. She is married to the composer Jan Vriend and lives in Gloucestershire.

Also by Sue Limb

UP THE GARDEN PATH
LOVE FORTY

and published by Corgi Books

THE WORDSMITHS AT GORSEMERE

published by Bantam Press

LOVE'S LABOURS

or

Further Up The Garden Path

Sue Limb

CORGI BOOKS

LOVE'S LABOURS

A CORGI BOOK 0 552 12873 2

First publication in Great Britain

PRINTING HISTORY
Corgi edition published 1989

This book is set in 10/11pt Plantin by County Typesetters, Margate, Kent

Corgi Books are published by Transworld Publishers Ltd., 61–63 Uxbridge Road, Ealing, London W5 5SA, in Australia by Transworld Publishers (Australia) Pty. Ltd., 15–23 Helles Avenue, Moorebank, NSW 2170, and in New Zealand by Transworld Publishers (N.Z.) Ltd., Cnr. Moselle and Waipareira Avenues, Henderson, Auckland.

Made and printed in Great Britain by
BPCC Hazell Books Ltd
Member of BPCC Ltd
Aylesbury, Bucks, England

For Jan

FAIR PRINCESS, WELCOME

'Oh, look, Dick! Down there! There's a river – it must be the Thames.'

Dick couldn't quite share Izzy's enthusiasm for peering down on things from a height of several thousand feet. Ever since their Jumbo had lumbered into the air above San Francisco the previous night, he'd had a feeling that the top of his head was going to fly off, leaving his private fantasies dangerously exposed. Even now he was smoothing his scalp down anxiously and all too aware of how eggshell-thin even his thick skull was.

Izzy, of course, was in her element. Further up was her idea of heaven. When they took off from San Francisco she'd burst into tears of ecstasy.

'Oh, look, Dick! All the lights down there! It's just as if someone's spilt a whole jumble of necklaces onto something soft and – you know, black. Onto something like . . . er, black velvet. Jewels on black velvet!'

Dick had pretended to take a quick peep. But he didn't like to think of jewels and black velvet at times like this – or indeed, at any time at all. They made him feel faint. And he didn't want to feel any fainter than he already felt, up here. He had teetered on the verge of consciousness for the last thirteen hours or so, and now, above London, Dick was sure that these were his last moments on earth – or rather, above it. Still, if the plane crashed, at least he wouldn't feel so inadequate any more. And if he died, at least he'd stop feeling faint. He had put on clean underwear just in case.

Izzy seized his hand, in anticipation of the descent into Heathrow. Had it really been a heath, once? She was overcome by a rush of sentimental geography. Heath, marsh, moor, wood, hill and watermeadow. Kingcups in the mud. Black and white cows hock-deep in billowing grass. A distant spire quivering in the haze: larks up above. Tears burst from Izzy's eyes.

FASTEN SAFETY BELTS. NO SMOKING.

Chimneys smoking in a deep wooded vale, and a cuckoo calling from an oak. Oh England, England! Izzy looked down on the patchwork of tiny green fields. Now she had seen the endless wilderness of North America, she realized how small and intricate England was. She gazed down upon her native land with a jeweller's fascination.

'It's like being a god, isn't it, Dick?'

'What is?'

'Oh come on, you know – flying up above the clouds. Oh, doesn't England look lovely and green! Isn't it marvellous to be back!'

Dick wasn't altogether sure. San Francisco had been all right, actually. The Americans apparently hadn't noticed what a berk he was. In fact, they'd treated him with great respect, queueing up to talk to him at parties and clamouring for him to say something in English English.

Given the shortage of straight men in San Francisco, Dick had enjoyed considerable social success. He was certainly straight. So straight, he was almost panelled. It was exactly this oaken quality that had appealed to Foxy La Speranza. Foxy La Speranza was the name of a person, in case you're wondering – not a disco or a sandwich. Foxy was small, passionate (her Italian origins, no doubt) and determined. She needed an impassive, grainy background upon which to rest her dew-spangled wings. That's the way she thought of it, anyway. She was a bit of a West-Coast poet, you see. So she descended on Dick, spread her wings, and basked.

Soon she was installed upon his Futon. This, in Dick's view, made the Futon ever more uncomfortable. It was bad enough tossing and turning all night long as hard bits of Oriental wadding invaded the spaces in his back normally occupied by his kidneys. When long Italianate fingernails traced spirals over his shoulder blades at 3a.m., just as he'd finally got off to sleep, it was far worse. Not that Dick wasn't flattered and grateful for Foxy's attention. But he was also acutely embarrassed.

No one had ever found him attractive before. Izzy's solitary act of seduction, all those millennia ago, had been conducted in an unmistakable atmosphere of charity. Modest Dick found this quite appropriate and not at all unacceptable. So to be positively desired by Foxy was unusual. And to be desired by Foxy in the apartment he shared with Izzy, had been extremely disconcerting.

They had often all watched TV together. Foxy's finger-nails had toyed playfully with the dull fur on his chest. Foxy's legs would be tossed proprietorially across his knees. And how odd it had been for Dick to discover that if Foxy were to trot off to another lair, leaving Izzy and himself watching TV in a companionable silence, well, that would be all right by him. But then, to retain perfect sangfroid in the presence of a woman one adored, whilst being fawned upon by a woman one didn't, would tax the sensibility of a greater man than Dick. Of which he was sure there were many.

'Look! We're banking now, Dick – we must be going to make our approach. Isn't it exciting! England! Hot buttered toast! Dickens! Cricket!'

She was having an acute attack of nostalgia. It had started with a solitary shepherd on some chalk downs overlooking the sea. He'd seen the Spanish Armada sailing up the channel, and before Izzy knew where she was, Queen Elizabeth I was sweeping down some golden steps to the sounds of lutes and citterns. Izzy had dawdled agreeably in Georgian England for a few moments, sipped tea with Dr Johnson, been chased through a box hedge by a mad king, got lost in a Victorian fog and finally managed a brief appearance at a village cricket match, pre-First World War. Ah, the poignant echoing crack of ball on bat! The fading applause! The scattering of seats and muslin skirts at the first prickling of mild summer rain! Luckily, Izzy did not get as far as 1914.

Dick gritted his teeth as the world tilted sideways and houses and trees appeared suddenly to be growing on the walls. He didn't like the way these pilots took liberties with your sense of the perpendicular. Indeed, the whole experience of flying seemed to his primitive soul to offer a monstrous challenge to the gods. Whereas Izzy, flying close now to the earth, her eyes glittering with tears of joy, might have passed for Aphrodite herself scorching down over Berkshire.

Actually, Izzy had had a pretty quiet year, for a goddess. Just as well, really, after the previous one. She'd gone to San Francisco having promised herself that, whatever else happened, she wouldn't get involved with any married men whilst she was there. Imagine her chagrin when the opportunity to exercise this elegant restraint never even presented itself. The Chinese proprietor of her local supermarket had begun to smile at her after the first three months, but this was the limit of her transatlantic conquests. Mind you, given the deep misanthropy of Mr Dung, it was perhaps more impressive than all Izzy's previous conquests put together.

Her American pupils worshipped her, of course, but most of them had been the offspring of the wealthy middle class, and too full of scrambled eggs and smoked salmon and cocaine and philosophizing. Izzy had missed her London roughnecks, dear old 4C. She wondered where they were now. They would just have left school after their final exam. Where was her erstwhile favourite, Roger Razebrook, known to his peers as Razors? Running a successful racket somewhere? Or already in prison? She wished she wasn't so mesmerized by criminal chic – or Razors' version, anyway. It was the movies. They'd corrupted her.

As for San Francisco, well, she'd enjoyed the sheer blue and glitter of it, the chasms of streets, the palms, the ocean. She'd enjoyed watching the kids roller skating in the park. And the Chinese restaurants had been pretty good. Izzy had spread a little, sideways, she had to admit it. But what can a girl do who's not in love? Eat, that's what. Hashbrowns, brownies, muffins, jelly, mountains of fruit. Buying great bagfuls of oranges just to squeeze for juice. Already it seemed like a paradisal dream. There had been a serpent in

10

the paradise, though. Foxy La Speranza.

'Would you fork-split my muffins for me, Dick honey?' she had whined, one memorable morning of fog and foghorns and melancholy when all Izzy wanted to hear was some low jazz.

Izzy had felt bad about feeling bad about Foxy. Dick deserved to be loved. She couldn't manage it herself, so why resent Foxy doing it? Perhaps it wouldn't have been so bad if Foxy hadn't been quite so scenic: so petite, so deft, so dazzlingly dressed, so (by Izzy's standards) rich. She was a designer, though Izzy couldn't remember of what. Whenever Foxy had launched into her long-drawn-out mosquito whine, Izzy had suffered from wilful inattention. Though Izzy was a good-natured person, she couldn't help wishing that Foxy had designed herself a better voice.

Had she been jealous of Dick? Surely not. At least, not jealous of Dick in the sense of wanting him herself. It was a shame that they couldn't have been celibate together, that's all. But, of course, Izzy wouldn't have denied Dick a moment's pleasure . . . it was just such a shame that he hadn't been really in love with someone nice. Then, she, Izzy, could've rejoiced unstintingly. Well, almost.

The plane levelled out and dropped towards earth.

'It dropped then!' said Dick in a sort of desperate gasp, holding his hair down.

'That's right, Dick. We're coming in to land. Look, there are trees just below us.'

Dick went pale. *Trees just below them?* He didn't like the sound of that, at all. They were obviously going to fall short of the runway. He could see the piece now, in the local paper, complete with an unflattering photo of himself. 'Mr Richard Barnes, aged thirty-two, previously of Worksop, who died in last week's Heathrow tragedy. Mr Barnes was a pupil at Witherthorpe School. . . .' His mother would be stoically silent in her flowered pinafore. She'd lay on a splendid funeral tea, he was sure.

'It's a shame they used that photo of him with the beard,' she'd say, poking the fire.

'Aye,' his Uncle Norm would affirm, sucking his pipe. 'I never did like that thar beard o'his. Mind you, once th'lad took off for London, it were inevitable really.'

Ruin and Desolation, Dick was sure, were to be his lot for having deserted Derbyshire. If only he had lived! A sentiment which would be echoed by the local paper. He had started painting again in California – perhaps inspired by the light so beloved of David Hockney, whom Dick hoped, in vain, that he resembled. This imminent aircrash was a shame, really. If only he'd lived, he could've produced a series of drawings and paintings entitled *The Desertion of Derbyshire*, starting in dark thickets of woodcut, back-to-back houses in fog and soot, and ending in watercolour blue. He had lain beside the swimming pools of California. The gods of Derbyshire would have their revenge.

A brief sideways glance brought Dick an appalling glimpse of treetops so near you could practically see the nests. He gulped, closed his eyes and waited for death. He was blushing furiously. It was so embarrassing, dying in public like this. Dick couldn't help feeling it was somehow his own silly fault. Er, – sorry, God, he murmured in the depths of his heart.

BONK! BONK! KER. . . .BOINNNNGGGG!!
WHEEEEEEEEEE! ROARRRRRRRAH!

'Crikey!' gasped Dick. Not a very distinguished Last Word, but all he could manage as the stricken Jumbo tossed to and fro. The jets roared one last ferocious scream. Which bit of him would die first? Dick hoped it would be one of his edges, so he could get used to it gradually, like slipping into a hot bath.

An angel whizzed down.

'We're home, Dick! Home!' it whispered in his ear. 'Open your eyes!'

Dick obeyed. Izzy was beaming at him with wet cheeks. The plane had not crashed after all, just landed. Dick released his scalp, sighed wearily and reconciled himself to more life.

I GIVE THEE THY LIBERTY

It wasn't until they found themselves in the booking hall
for the Tube that Izzy realized she had no idea where she
was going. Dick purposefully bought himself a ticket for
King's Cross, an act which threw Izzy into a slight panic.

'Dick! Where are you going?'

'Home,' he faltered guiltily. 'To see my Mum. To, you
know, show her the photos and all that. Where are you
going, Izzy?'

Where indeed?

When she'd last lived in London, it had been with
Michael and Louise Tristram in Muswell Hill. Izzy
blushed fleetingly at the memory. Dick saw her blush and
blushed himself. He never missed the chance of a bit of
extra embarrassment. He thought perhaps his question
about her destination had been indelicate. For aught he
knew, Izzy was off to an assignation with some smart
fellow in – oh, Mayfair.

'Oh, I, er, I'm just going to Maria's for now,'
improvised Izzy. It sounded like a lie, as did most of what
Izzy said. Dick suspected that she was lying to protect the
identity of her secret admirer. 'You know, Dick – erm,
Maria and Gwyn have got a flat in Canonbury Square.
Quite convenient for school.'

She bought a ticket for Highbury.

'How are they getting on, now?' enquired Dick, warily.
He did not relish gossip about the married. For a start, it
made him seem even more unmarried. No doubt there are
many bachelors of thirty-two who feel that they enjoy a
sublime state of life, but Dick had known from about the
age of eight that his only chance of happiness would be to

marry. He had been desperate for matrimony ever since his schooldays. It's a bit of a waste of being a bachelor if you have no capacity for the fast and loose. Dick, being slow and stuck, ached for his dear little wife, but where was she? Not, alas, at his side. That was all too clear. Of course, he would never adore his dear little wife with quite the fervour Izzy had inspired in him, but what of that? Marriage was about safety: and Dick felt about as safe with Izzy as a wandering blow-lamp in a firework factory.

'I didn't hear from Maria all that often, actually,' pondered Izzy as they boarded their train. 'But she and Gwyn seem to have settled down into some kind of life together. It's really inspiring, isn't it, Dick? When you think what the situation was eighteen months ago. When she walked out on him and moved in with me, she wouldn't even hear his name mentioned. For *months*. Ah well. It just shows that human beings are capable of . . . well, you know. Change and development. And learning and things.'

Dick was silent. He was especially fond of the ideas of change and development, since they were precisely the excuse Foxy had offered when at last she'd tired of his Futon and sidled off up the hill. 'You see, Dick honey,' she'd sighed, staring deeply into his glasses and holding his hand meaningfully across the immaculate white tablecloth of the Water Lily Café, 'it's not that I don't think you're truly wonderful: in fact you're the most beautiful person I've ever seen on the face of this glorious globe.' (At this Dick had winced as if struck.)

'It's just that we all have to move on on the journey of life, sweetheart. I feel a deep need to step back from life, to meditate and consider. To develop myself as a person mentally and spiritually.' Once it had dawned on him that he was being discharged, Dick had felt such a profound cheering-up taking place inside him, that he had to keep pushing the smile back down his throat and shore up the façade of piety and sobriety with which it was appropriate to listen to her sermon. Before dessert he could stand it no longer and had had to run to the men's room for a burst of uncontrollable smiling. Ah, the insanities of San Francisco.

'Yes, Izzy,' he said, at length. 'It's a good thing, personal development. In fact, I'm thinking of developing myself one day.'

'Oh yes, Dick, you should, you should. I mean, we can't stay teachers all our lives, for a start, can we?'

'Can't we?'

'Oh no! I mean, what sort of teachers would we be if we'd only been in schools for the whole of our lives?'

'Are you thinking of – you know, giving up, then?'

'Well, not now, of course, I mean, just, you know . . . eventually.'

'What would you do instead, then?'

'Oh, you know – anything. Sort of thing. Work in the media, for instance.'

Dick was rather frightened by the media. It sounded a bit fierce, like electricity.

'You mean, be a journalist, like?'

'Maybe. Or TV. Or local radio.'

'I like the sound of that. I like the sound of local radio.'

Izzy sighed. She had been with Dick too long. The train rattled comfortably along the familiar London line: Acton Town, Hammersmith – had there really been a smith there, once? *The smith a mighty man was he, with arms as thick as iron bands.* For a moment Izzy was tempted back into her sunlit tour of Olde Englande, but was distracted by an exquisitely beautiful black man who got on and sat opposite her. Izzy wondered how big the bags under her eyes were. It was so long since anybody had found her beautiful, that she wasn't even sure she could be it any more. Maybe she'd feel better in a couple of days, when she'd caught up on her sleep and had a nice long bath. Then she'd put on her dancing shoes and skip out onto the summer pavements.

'I wouldn't mind working in local radio myself, in fact,' mused Dick.

God, it would be marvellous to see Maria. Izzy realized

15

she had been without wit for an entire year. The other thing about England was that all her best friends lived there. Dick was all right, a good sort, but Izzy couldn't begin to open her heart to him. Mind you, there had been times when she'd regretted opening her heart to Maria because what it revealed was – well, so revealing. There was something about Maria that often made Izzy feel faintly guilty, but nevertheless she needed Maria's bracing tongue and critical eye. She was particularly looking forward to seeing Maria now, because she was aware that she had been less than usually wicked in San Francisco. She was also faintly worried about Maria. Izzy hoped Gwyn was behaving, these days. Maria had been through too much in the past. She deserved a break.

Izzy hoped Michael Tristram was behaving, too. But there was something slightly different about the quality of her interest in Michael's misbehaviour. Not that his wife Louise hadn't also been through hell and deserved a thundering great load of happiness to be dropped on her front doorstep. But when Izzy thought of the possibility of Michael's misbehaving again, there was a tiny spear of pain in her heart. Not that she was remotely in love with him any more. That was really ancient history. Ah, the old days of frisson and tremor, of snatched phone calls, watched clocks and wildly beating hearts! Not that she would ever, ever go in for that sort of thing again. Apart from being wrong, it was so desperately uncomfortable.

What I need is a husband, thought Izzy. One of my own, I mean. But where could they be found, these days? Izzy longed to marry the black man sitting opposite, and settle down to a life of music and cricket and a delightful throng of coffee-coloured children with beautiful big kissable lips. Alas, he got off at Hyde Park without even asking for her phone number. Izzy thought how particularly pleasant it would be to be able to introduce her husband to Michael. Especially if her husband were taller than Michael and had more hair. How odd! She still wanted to hurt Michael slightly. Not much. Just a brief sting.

She shouldn't permit these thoughts to surface. It was because she was light-headed with jet lag. Michael was a father, again, now. Izzy would soon see the new baby girl. She could imagine how beautiful Louise would look, transformed by motherhood as many of Izzy's friends had been. Izzy was sure Louise would glow. And the baby would nestle into Louise's arms, feeding quietly, its head smelling of new bread. Drifting towards sleep, Izzy was not altogether surprised to see a blazing star shining down above the scene. Louise's maternal glow brightened around her head to a golden shimmer. A donkey looked on over her shoulder . . . no, wait, it was Michael, with an unexpected grey beard. As the mother leaned over to put the baby down in the manger, Joseph gave Izzy a brief wink.

'Mind you, not all local radio is all that good, I reckon.'

'Gosh! Dick! I was asleep in a Christmas card!'

'Sorry!'

'It's OK. Where are we? Green Park? Let me rest my head on your shoulder, Dick, just for a couple of minutes.'

Dick leapt in a startled way, brushed his shoulder in a frenzy of shame, and received her sleepy head with a sigh.

At King's Cross they parted. Izzy felt a sudden rush of sentimental regret.

'How long are you going to be up North, Dick?' she asked anxiously.

'Oh, not – you know, just a couple of days. Er – then I'll have to come back and look for somewhere to – to live.'

'Somewhere to live,' echoed Izzy. For a second she was tempted to wonder if they should househunt together. 'Maybe we should . . . get together for a meal or something when you get back,' she concluded, following some deep instinct not to househunt with him after all. Then she flung her arms around him and gave him a big hug, which made her feel better and him worse.

'I must go and get my – my train,' he muttered into her dark tangle of hair. 'Maybe you should get a taxi. With all these cases.'

'Yes, Dick. Good idea. Got any English money?'

Dick had thought ahead and changed some currency before he left California. He gave her ten pounds, a last fevered stare, pushed her towards a taxi and was suddenly gone.

Soon she was on Maria's doorstep. At least, she assumed it was Maria's. The address was the same as the one in her address book. She'd always loved the eighteenth-century elegance of Canonbury Square. Too bad it was invaded by the roar and fumes of traffic. She consulted the array of bells. Jenkins and Shadwell appeared to occupy Flat 2. She rang and almost immediately Maria flung the door open. She looked cross.

'Hello!' she barked. 'What – *Izzy*! What have you done to your hair?'

'Only grown it,' ventured Izzy.

'It makes you look completely different.'

'Don't you like it?'

'Well, I'm not sure. I'll have to get used to it.'

'Can I come in, Maria? Only I've just got off the plane.' Izzy drooped pathetically over the threshold.

'Just got off the plane? Why didn't you ring? Go on upstairs – first door on the right at the next landing. Honestly, Izzy! You're impossible!'

Izzy staggered upstairs with her heavy cases, Maria scolding her every inch of the way. After all Dick's acquiescence and veneration it was quite pleasantly bracing. Izzy truly began to feel that she had crossed an ocean and come home.

I THAT HAVE BEEN LOVE'S WHIP

Maria's flat was dark and cosy, and overlooked the square.
As usual it was immaculately tidy – the one characteristic
Maria and Gwyn shared. Izzy fell into the sofa and sighed
deeply. Remote parts of her being were still buzzing away
in mid-air.

'I'll get you some tea,' said Maria. 'Camomile be all
right? That's supposed to put you to sleep.'

'What I need is a tea to keep me awake.'

Maria disappeared to the kitchen. Izzy's glazed eyes
travelled luxuriously along the mantelpiece, recognizing
some of Maria's possessions: the brass candlesticks, the
eighteenth-century clock. Maria's father was an antiques
dealer, and over the years his frequent gifts had provoked
many a matrimonial row. Gwyn, a bit of a working-class
hero, saw his father-in-law's gifts as the relics of privilege.
But Izzy found objects from the past soothing. The stately
tick of the clock and the glimmer of old brass mingled with
a sudden darkening of the sky outside and a freckling of
raindrops on the windowpane. This was undoubtedly
England. Izzy snuggled into the sofa, and when Maria
arrived with tea and toast, Izzy was nearly asleep.

The smell of toast revived her. Maria watched as Izzy
gorged. She had only had plastic airline food in the past
twenty-four hours.

'Didn't they feed you in San Francisco, then?'

'Honestly, Maria, it was so strange out there! I wish
you'd come to see us.'

'Money problems.'

'I know. Isn't it terrible! I had to borrow ten quid from
Dick, just to get here.'

'How is Dick? Did he blossom in San Francisco?'

'Oh, no. Not really. Although he did have a – well, a bit of an affair out there.'

'What, Dick? Really? How grisly.'

'No, not all that, in fact, she was quite – well, quite attractive really.'

'For God's sake wipe that honey off your chin, Izzy.'

'Sorry – got a tissue? – Thanks. What a pig I am. That was lovely.' Izzy leaned back, yawned and stretched, as perfectly at ease as a cat on a warm windowsill.

'You must be exhausted, Izzy. Do you want a kip? You can use our bed. Don't worry, Gwyn's in Manchester.'

'Manchester? What for?'

'Oh, a seminar on water. Gwyn's very active now, you know.'

'He was pretty active before.'

Izzy thought wryly of a certain night last year when she'd had to frogmarch a drunk, desperate Welshman through the streets of Earl's Court and put him to bed in a seedy hotel, to protect Maria from his dramatic urge for reconciliation with her.

'No, I mean politically active. He's actually standing for the Council next May.'

'Really? Well, it's his thing, isn't it? Good old Gwyn.' Izzy yawned again.

'Izzy . . .' There was something about Maria's tone of voice that caught at Izzy like a dozen little hooks. She was jolted out of her jet lag and instantly wide awake. She smelled danger.

'What is it, Maria? Are you all right?'

'Oh yes. In a way, never better. But in a way, well, my life's a lot more complicated and difficult than it used to be.'

Izzy sighed. Maria's life had seemed pretty definitively complicated and difficult before.

'How do you mean? Is Gwyn . . . is Gwyn . . . er, is Gwyn all right? I mean, are you and Gwyn all right?'

'Oh yes. I think we've discovered where we ought to be.

We've got a companionate marriage.'

'A what?'

'A companionate marriage.'

'Wait a minute – isn't that what that king had? The one who had to abdicate? The one who married that American woman – the divorcee?'

'Edward VIII and Mrs Simpson?'

'That's right. It was on telly – remember?'

'That was a morganatic marriage, Izzy.'

Maria got up and began to rearrange the books in the bookshelf. There was something odd about her, Izzy realized: something different. Something missing.

'You're not smoking!'

'Ah yes. That's another thing. It's all part of it, Izzy. I've had a change of heart. And mind.'

Izzy was overawed. Maria's heart and mind were wild, aggressive organs, it seemed to her; in a state of permanent flux. Each new discovery irrevocably the truth. Izzy had not the faintest inkling of what to expect next.

'You see, Izzy,' muttered Maria, biting a nail, 'I've gone Green. Changed my mental outlook. I have espoused the environmental cause.'

'What?'

'I've joined the Green Party.'

'Oh, the Greens! I like them! Greenpeace! My heroes! Save the rainforests!'

'That's right.'

'Oh yes. They're wonderful, the Greens. They make me feel awfully guilty, though. We ought all to be . . . you know, doing that sort of thing all the time, oughtn't we?'

'Saving the planet, you mean? Yes, we ought. Want to join, Izzy? I've got a few application forms, here.'

A *few*? How many times did Maria want her to join, for goodness sake? Izzy gulped. There were times – she was beginning to remember them now – when faced with Maria's certainties, Izzy could only flutter helplessly like a gay little flag in an Arctic gale.

'Of course I'll join.' She scrabbled in the depths of her

handbag. 'Oh wait. How much is it? I've only got a few quid left. Dick only lent me a tenner.'

'It's all right. I'll take a cheque.'

'Er – well, I haven't got a new chequebook, yet,' faltered Izzy. 'Not – not a British one, you know.' She squirmed under Maria's laser eye. She felt she was behaving suspiciously – evasively, even. She seized the form.

'At least I'll fill it in now.'

She scribbled her name: IZZY COMYN. So far, so good.

'Oh help! I haven't got an address yet!' She didn't even have an environment, dammit.

'I don't even know where I'm going to live, Maria.'

'That's all right. Put our address down for the time being. You can sleep on our sofa till you find yourself somewhere.'

'Oh thanks! All right.'

Izzy filled in the form. She had joined a political party for the first time in her life. It made her feel nervous and slightly sick.

'So, Izzy. Who's the lucky man of the moment?'

Why did Maria have to snarl whenever she asked this kind of question?

'Nobody,' boasted Izzy. 'I've been completely and utterly chaste for a whole year.'

'Well, well,' grinned Maria. 'But then, I suppose, it *was* San Francisco.'

'No it wasn't – I mean, it wasn't for lack of interest,' lied Izzy. 'I just didn't feel tempted, that's all.'

'We'll see what London can offer, then,' said Maria prophetically. 'I bet you anything you like that by the middle of next term you'll be madly in love with some gangling idiot.'

'It's all very well for you,' said Izzy with, almost, a snap. A snip, perhaps. 'You're safely married to your gorgeous Celt and being all cosy and companionable with him. It's all right for you, Maria.'

'If only you knew,' said Maria, rearranging a few more

books. 'You haven't even the faintest idea, Izzy.'

'Of what?'

'Of my situation.'

'Well, then tell me.'

'I'm not sure I should. I'm not sure you can take it.'

'Of course I can take it!'

Izzy wished Maria wouldn't treat her like a child. Somehow it only confirmed her childlike tendencies. If Maria really wanted Izzy to grow up, she was going about it entirely the wrong way.

'Well . . . I was telling you . . . about my change of heart.'

'Yes, you said. You've gone Green.'

'It's not just that. Ever since you've been away, Izzy, I've had a chance to think about things.' Maria was looking out of the window in a strangely evasive way. Maria didn't usually look past people out of windows. She usually pinned them to the wall. 'I began to think about the way I'd felt when you were involved with Michael.'

'You disapproved – well, naturally.'

'Was it really disapproval? I wonder, sometimes.'

'Oh yes. I remember what you said. About him being married, and everything. How I was wronging another woman, and stuff.'

'Oh, I know what I said. But was that what I really meant?'

'What then?'

'Jealousy.'

'What?'

'I was jealous.'

Izzy's mind spun like a kaleidoscope of scattered shards of light. She remembered how well she'd got on with Louise, Michael's wife, once she'd moved in. She'd neglected Maria, certainly. She'd wallowed in her new friendship with Louise. Louise hadn't tried to improve Izzy. She had just laughed at her. And all the while, poor Maria had been feeling left out. It reminded Izzy of her little-girl friendships far away and long ago:

'You're *my* best friend! Not *hers*!'

'Oh dear,' she began. 'I'm very sorry. I must have been a bit, er, insensitive. I hadn't really – I mean, I just shot off and enjoyed getting to know Louise. I suppose it must have seemed very – I mean, you must have felt . . . after all, you'd just left Gwyn. You must've—'

'Oh shut up, Izzy! For God's sake!' Maria jumped up and folded her arms very resolutely, tucking her chin down like someone looking into the eye of a storm. She became very still.

'It's you I've been in love with, all along, Izzy. Yes – you.'

IMMURED, RESTRAINED, CAPTIVATED, BOUND

Izzy blinked. She opened her mouth automatically but seemed to have neither wind nor words to draw on. Maria, in love with *her*? Had she heard right? Had her ears or brain twisted a perfectly normal statement into a crazy piece of gobbledegook?

'Did you say. . . .' she could not finish it.

'Yes. I'm in love with you, Izzy. Sorry to be so inconvenient. But I'm gay.'

Izzy had a violent desire to be in Yorkshire. Why hadn't she followed Dick's example and fled to her Northern mum? It wasn't that she was appalled, or anything. It was just that she was so tired, just now: it was, oh, all so difficult, and demanded such – hang it, she was appalled. Maria, her best friend, gay. Actually, that concept was quite easy to get used to. Having just returned from a year in San Francisco, Izzy could take it all in her stride. Maria gay was no problem. It was Maria besotted that made her hair stand on end and her flesh creep.

'Don't worry,' said Maria, moving to the furthest chair and perching on its arm. 'I won't jump on you or anything.'

'Can we have – could we – have some more tea?' asked Izzy weakly. She wanted a nice ordinary practical ritual to set between them.

'You want to escape from all this emotion, don't you, Izzy?' Maria flung her head back and scratched her scalp energetically. 'So do I. Believe me. But I had to tell you. You must see that.' Izzy thought for a while.

'Er . . . why did you have to tell me, Maria?'

'Well, it's a fundamental truth about me, Izzy. There's no getting away from it.'

Izzy hoped there was. It wasn't that Maria was a woman. Izzy would feel just as queasy and uneasy if Maria had been a man. Although, if she *had* been a man, it would've been different, of course. Or would it? Izzy was sure that Maria wouldn't really have been her type – not for falling-in-love purposes – even if she'd been a man. That was quite a useful thought, actually. Reassuring. Izzy was pleased with it. She would say it in a minute. It might cool things down a lot.

'And don't be afraid that I'll expect you to reciprocate,' Maria went on. 'I know how devoted you are to the Unfair Sex.'

'There's no need to sound so – oh, I don't know.' Izzy floundered. 'If you really want to know, I don't think you'd be my type even if you were a man.'

'Well, thanks a lot.'

'I don't mean it like . . . well, I don't mean to be rude.'

'Who'd want to be your type anyway, Izzy?'

Izzy felt increasingly rather hurt. She'd arrived back from San Francisco, flown to the side of her best friend, and now all this. Somehow it was all assumed to be her fault. She couldn't do anything right. All she wanted was a friendly gossip, and, increasingly desperately, twelve hours sleep.

'What does Gwyn think of all this?'

'Ah,' Maria looked a bit shifty, and stood up. 'I'll go and put the kettle on,' she mumbled. 'Come with me – if you like.'

Maria's revelation had given every little phrase an unfortunate echo of innuendo. But Izzy went with her to the kitchen. It was Maria's usual kitchen: spotless and orderly. Izzy was sleepless and dishevelled, and felt that she contributed to it about as much as a crumpled old bag of sprouting potatoes.

'Gwyn,' began Maria, opening tins and setting out spoons, 'is another problem. Because you see, Izzy, I have another epoch-making discovery to reveal to you.' Izzy boggled. Just how many epoch-making revelations can a woman take, in one afternoon?

'What is it?' she gasped.

Maria shut the cupboard door with a brisk slam.

'I want a child,' she said, in a rather demanding tone. Then her eyes slithered sideways towards the window, where the sun was staging a comeback upon some mangy marigolds in a windowbox.

'At least, I think I do.'

'Oh, Maria, that's marvellous!' Izzy seized at this straw. The more Maria could be encouraged to get pregnant, the better things would be. A baby, or even better, several, would cement Maria and Gwyn's marriage, Izzy was sure, as it must already have cemented Louise and Michael's. Of all this afternoon's revelations, this was by far the best.

'What's so marvellous about it?'

'Well, a baby would – would be so lovely. I mean, it would make you so much more . . .' Izzy faltered, on dangerous ground.

'Preoccupied?' enquired Maria, as the kettle boiled. 'Drained? Exhausted? Depressed? Suicidal?'

'Oh, no, Maria – don't be so negative! I love babies. I'll help you with it.' Although Izzy didn't want to offer her services too expansively. She wanted to twinkle briefly over its cradle, like the Good Fairy, and then zoom off, leaving Maria set deep into motherhood like a pebble into concrete.

'And Gwyn'll be marvellous. He'll make a perfect father.'

'I'm not so sure. He's highly irresponsible.'

'Oh, no, Maria – just, you know – spontaneous. He's a terrific bloke, really – you don't know how lucky you are.'

'And you don't know what you're talking about.'

'Er . . . are you actually, um, you know, trying? If you know what I mean. Sorry to be so . . . whossname.'

'The fact is, Izzy,' said Maria, carrying the tea tray back into the sitting room, 'we've been trying for three years.'

27

Izzy gasped. She'd assumed it was easy, getting pregnant. 'Ah well, they say it takes longer if you've been on the pill.'

'Look, Izzy, I don't really want to talk about this baby business, if you don't mind.'

Izzy was disappointed. She'd nearly managed to relax again. She wanted above all to talk about this baby business. She was sure it was just what Maria needed. But Maria wanted to talk about that other business. Izzy began to squirm again. How fast could she drink her camomile tea and be out of here? And why the hell had she suggested another cup of tea, anyway? She took a reckless sip, and scorched both sausagey lips.

'Ow! Er, what do you want to talk about, then?'

'You and me.'

Izzy's toes curled up inside her tennis shoes. Her feet had turned into turtles – terrified ones.

'What about it?' sighed Izzy.

'There's no need to sigh! You really know how to make me feel like a worm, Izzy.'

'I don't, do I?' Izzy was astonished. She'd always felt it was Maria who made *her* feel like a worm.

'I just wanted to say that it needn't change anything,' said Maria.

'Of course not.' What nonsense. It *had* changed everything.

'The trouble is, and I know it's inconvenient of me, but people who are in love want to talk about it – at least once.'

'Well, of course.'

But they had talked about it once, already, surely? This was twice. Izzy dived into her camomile, and burned another layer of cells off her tongue. She had to escape, to fly to some neutral ground. And then – the phone rang.

'Damn,' said Maria and went out to answer it. Izzy looked round desperately, but there was no potted plant into which she could empty the boiling camomile: only some cut flowers in water, and the vase was already full. She must cool this tea down somehow. Izzy spat surreptitiously into the teacup, but she felt desperately short of saliva. Her mouth was as dry as the desert. Even thinking about chocolate cake had no effect. But wait! There was the vase, full of water. *Cold* water. Instantly Izzy had whipped the flowers out and tipped a generous helping of vase-water into her cup. Too late, she saw the green slime slop through and swirl round in her cup. Out in the hall, Maria put the phone down. Izzy jammed the flowers back into their vase as the door opened and Maria came back in.

'Just smelling these flowers,' said Izzy, burying her blushes in pollen.

'They don't smell.'

'Er – they don't, do they? Never mind.'

Izzy hoped that Maria wouldn't notice the curl of green slime on the surface of her tea. But Maria was engrossed in The Situation.

'That was Gwyn,' she sighed, and ran her fingers through her hair. 'He sends his love and hopes he'll see you soon. He asked if you were as luscious as ever. Oh, God!'

Maria stared distractedly at the hearth rug. Another wave of raindrops hit the windowpane. Izzy had to escape. To escape she had to do two things: think of an excuse, and finish her tea. She could perhaps have left her tea, if it had not had green slime on it, but now . . . she had to finish it. To leave one's tea undrunk and beslimed is not a kindly act, arousing both horror and incomprehension in the hostess's breast.

Izzy braced herself. She closed her eyes, nostrils, and ears. She snapped her navel shut, bunched up her toes, and sloshed the tea down without even tasting it.

'Good God, is that the time? I must go,' she cried, leaping up and stifling a wave of nausea.

'But I thought you were staying?'

'Oh ah er yes – in general, I mean, of course, but I did promise to go er – to go round and see the baby as soon as I got back.'

'What – Louise's?'

29

'Oh no!' gasped Izzy. 'Not Louise's.'

Very silly that had been; and rash, to provoke several kinds of jealousy simultaneously in Maria, who had already suffered so much that afternoon, and was within easy reach of the four-and-a-half pounds of *The Oxford Dictionary of Quotations*. Izzy ducked at the mere thought. It would be a distinguished end, though – to be brained with literature.

'No, not Louise's baby – my cousin Debra's.'

'Who?'

'My cousin Debra. You've probably never heard of her.' Since Izzy had just invented her, this was a pretty safe bet. 'She moved down to London last April. She had a new baby last week. A boy. Called Scott.'

'Oh,' said Maria, helpless beneath the torrent of fiction falling from Izzy's lips. Not that it seemed particularly like fiction. Everything Izzy said always sounded like a desperate invention, so it was actually quite hard to tell when she really was lying.

'How much does he weigh?'

'Who?'

'This baby.'

'Oh – six pounds, two-and-a-half ounces.'

'I see. A wimp.' Maria seemed grimly satisfied.

'I'll probably stay at Debra's, just for tonight,' said Izzy as breezily as possible, seizing her handbag.

'Where does she live?'

'Mitcham.'

'Where's that?'

Izzy's heart nearly stopped.

'South of the river,' she shrugged. 'You know. I'll ring you tomorrow.'

'You're running away,' Maria burst out. 'I knew it! I knew you wouldn't be able to take it.'

'Don't be silly, Maria.' And suddenly, absurdly, crazily, guiltily, Izzy kissed Maria on the cheek, and then ran like hell.

'I'll ring!' she called from the stairs, and rushed out into the welcoming rain.

WARBLE, CHILD

Soon she was in leafy Highgate, walking towards the Tristrams' house in Muswell Hill. She was feeling better. She felt proud that she had joined the Greens. She wished Maria had given her a badge to wear. She would get Michael and Louise to join, too. She couldn't wait to see Louise again. They'd been over to visit her in San Francisco at Christmas, when Louise was in the fifth month of her pregnancy, and radiant. Her red-gold hair had stood on end in the wind, Izzy remembered, on the beach by the ocean. It had looked like a crown of flames streaming upward, as if she was some sort of beautiful fecund angel. And it would be great to see funny old Michael again, though Izzy did rather wish that she'd managed to have another boyfriend since him. Ah well. Time would make it all easier.

If only her legs weren't so empty and tired. Here she was at last at the flight of steps leading up to their front door. It seemed a long way to go. Izzy paused for a deep breath, feeling as if she'd arrived home. Here, in this house, last year, she'd been perhaps her happiest ever. Her furthest from lying and desperate improvisation. She should've come here straight from the airport, only she'd been obscurely worried about Maria – worried by something under the tone of her recent letters. Ah well. At least the obscurity didn't trouble her any longer. Now it was all horribly clear. She staggered up the steps and rang the bell. There was a shuffling within and the door opened.

A stranger stood there: a fat woman with a white moon-face, and wearing dark glasses. Her hair was scraped back beneath a headscarf, and she wore a filthy dressing-gown. Izzy gaped at her.

'Oh – Izzy!' cried the woman in Louise's voice.

'Louise!' Izzy fell into her arms, and prolonged the embrace to hide her embarrassment. What on earth had happened to Louise? She looked dreadful.

'Be careful, Izzy,' said Louise, emerging from the hug. 'I'm covered with sick. Only milky baby-sick, but still . . . come in for a minute.'

Come in *for a minute*? Now what sort of welcome was that, for the prodigal lodger who'd come home across half the globe? Izzy began to realize that she might have arrived at an inconvenient moment.

Wailing came from the kitchen. Izzy followed Louise timidly through the door to find Michael holding a crying baby. Jack was also red-faced and roaring. Michael looked frazzled and cross. His eyes were bloodshot and he looked balder than ever.

'Izzy!' he cried pathetically, 'Look who it is, Jack! Your favourite person! Say hello to Izzy.'

'Shan't!' cried Jack, pulling a face, and he ran out into the garden, slamming the door behind him.

'Oh well,' sighed Michael. 'Very rude, of course, but it does reduce the density of bawling. Dear Izzy! Welcome home!' He placed a brotherly kiss on her cheek, and showed her his baby, who resembled a wrinkled beetroot.

'Isn't she adorable!' cried Izzy. 'Can I hold her?'

She took the small damp parcel and peered into its furious red face. The screaming increased to a hysterical pitch.

'Oh dear,' faltered Izzy, not really liking the smell of stale milk very much, either. 'She doesn't want me. Do you want your mummy, little darling-poo?'

'No thanks!' said Louise firmly, 'I'm putting the kettle on for a cup of tea for you, Izzy. And then I'm going to have a wonderful two minutes of peace in the lavatory. Excuse me for a moment.'

Louise slopped out and Izzy handed the baby back to Michael. The cross little creature didn't think much of him, either, it seemed. Izzy sat down, awkwardly, and wondered if she could possibly put her fingers in her ears without Michael noticing, or being offended.

'What's her name?' she asked.

'What?'

'What's her *name!*' she shouted, above the din.

'Rose,' replied Michael, walking up and down with the hypnotized compulsion of a bear in a zoo, the baby howling on his shoulder like a demented violin. 'O Rose, thou art sick,' he added grimly.

'What's wrong with her?'

'It's called three-month colic. Every afternoon, they suddenly start all this screaming, and it goes on for about four hours.'

'Why?'

'Nobody knows.'

Conversation seemed impossible. So much for all the anecdotes about San Francisco. So much for gossip and scandal. So much for a comradely cup of tea whilst the baby snoozed picturesquely in the background. Rose was evidently not background material. Rose was a Prima Donna.

'There is a Rose, you know,' said Michael, 'a real rose, I mean – a horticultural one – called Rose *Horrida*. We call her that, sometimes.'

'Oh no, bless her.'

'And Rose *Foetida*.'

Izzy could see his point, however.

'What's up with Jack?'

'Oh, God knows. Sibling rivalry. Nose out of joint.'

'I'll go and see him.'

Izzy escaped to the deliciously quiet garden. Jack would be down in the shed, she was sure. The garden had a neglected look – as did Louise, Michael, and indeed the whole establishment. Izzy could hear Jack moving about in the shed. She knocked on the door.

'Jack?'

'What?'

'Can't I just say *hello*? I haven't seen you for a whole year.'

33

When Michael and Louise had come to San Francisco, Jack had been left behind with Grandma in Godalming. Izzy peeped round the door. Jack was staring into a cardboard box. He sniffed sorrowfully.

'What's wrong, Jack?'

'It's her. She won't stop crying.'

'I expect it's only because she's got a tummy ache.'

'Well, I wish she wouldn't. It's horrible.'

Izzy could not but agree. Perhaps the most tactful thing would be to change the subject. Izzy slipped into the shed.

'What have you got in this box?'

'My toad.'

'Your *toad*?'

Izzy felt a qualm. She had not, so far in her life, had much contact with amphibia. Jack held the toad up to her. It sat quite quietly in his hand. It was a beautiful shade of honey, with mottled sandy-coloured markings.

'It's – it's rather beautiful.'

The toad eyed Izzy with a golden gleam. It did not declare its passion for her, but was silent and grave. Izzy could see the charm in its cold-bloodedness.

'What do you call him?'

'Mr Jackson. Like in that book, you know. The Mrs Tittlemouse one. Only I think he might be a female really because he's rather big and fat.'

Izzy felt a vague tremor of fellow-feeling. She'd also had rather enough of sexual uncertainty, for one afternoon.

'So she's a big blowsy blonde, really,' she said. 'You should call her Mae West.' This was lost on Jack. To him Mae West sounded like a place. Or a time.

'What does Mr Jackson do?' asked Izzy, beginning to tire of the toad's Buddhist calm.

'He sheds his skin. And he eats maggots. And he does poos. And sometimes you can see the bits of dead maggots in the poos.'

'How interesting.' Izzy sidled backwards towards the door. She suddenly remembered that somewhere in her digestive system was a strand of slippery slime from

Maria's flower-vase. She could almost feel it coiling about, snakelike, in her stomach. She needed more tea – and a lot of cake and biscuits, if that could be arranged. She had ingested enough Natural History for one day.

'Izzy!' Louise was calling her from the back door: a source of possible cake.

'Coming!'

'Earl Grey or Night-Time Bouquet?'

'Earl Grey, please!'

Izzy picked her way back through the weeds. Last year, Louise's garden had looked like a perfect English meadow. This year it looked like a bombsite. There were old bottles and nettles and plastic bowls among the feathery wild flowers. Izzy needed Earl Grey and she needed it bad.

Earl Grey. You can trust a tea named after an English aristocrat, thought Izzy, with rather less than republican fervour. She was a bit frightened of tea called Night-Time Bouquet. It sounded a bit hellebore and henbane-ish. It hinted of toads in sheds and sick roses. But Earl Grey was clear and strong as daylight: no nonsense and apple pie order. Earl Grey would pull Izzy up by her bootstraps. And she realized, as she climbed up the three steps into the kitchen and nearly fainted, that her bootstraps were her only hope.

BUT HAVE YOU FORGOT YOUR LOVE?

The baby was still crying, but dimly, elsewhere in the house. Louise had washed her face and taken off her dark glasses. The sick-stained dressing-gown had been replaced by a baggy jumper and voluminous skirt, within which Louise's post-natal bulges were decently minimized. Her hair was still pulled back, though. Izzy wished she would release it. Louise looked as wrong as a lion without its mane.

'Michael's taken Rose upstairs so we can have five minutes peace,' said Louise, sitting down heavily at the kitchen table, which was more than usually littered with half-eaten old dinners, used tissues, empty cans and plastic spaceships. Izzy looked anxiously for a bit of carbohydrate going begging, but all she could see was a torn cardboard box which had once contained some rather undistinguished shop cake. To Izzy, however, even the cardboard looked fairly delicious. Louise poured the tea and sighed.

'My God, Izzy, the tiredness!' she said. 'I'd forgotten about the tiredness.'

'It must be dreadful,' Izzy sneaked another two spoonsful of sugar into her tea, in case there was nothing to eat.

'And I'm so fat!'

'So am I,' Izzy tried for a little solidarity. But Louise appeared not to hear her.

'*She's* not, of course. *She's* sylph-like. Oh yes.'

Izzy felt a pang of alarm. Had Michael . . . oh, no.

'Who's sylph-like?'

'The bleeding nanny.'

'Oh, you've got a nanny?' Izzy wondered where the nanny was. Why hadn't she taken the little screamer out in the pram, then, so her parents could have a few minutes peaceful chat with their old friend?

'It's her day off,' explained Louise. 'I dread Thursdays. Where the hell are those god_lam bleeding biscuits?'

Louise never used to talk like this. This was post-natal expression.

'In the cupboard?' suggested Izzy, leaping up with more than mere helpfulness. The cupboard was bare, though.

'There's nothing here – except a pack of trifle sponges.'

'Right. I'll have them.' Izzy was rather distraught at Louise's use of the personal pronoun. Louise fell on the packet, tore it open and devoted herself to solitary crunching.

'Do you mind if I have one, too?'

'Good God! Izzy, I'm terribly sorry. Of course. Help yourself. I've become a completely selfish cow. It's this breast-feeding lark. It's a killer. Do you know, you burn up more calories than a mountaineer going up Everest?'

'Do you really?' Izzy was amazed. It had always looked a relatively peaceful operation, on the Christmas cards. She was also amazed by the gorgeousness of the trifle sponges. They exploded drily in her mouth and then melted into a divine sugary fluff. Izzy was surprised that any of them ever got as far as being in a trifle, at all. Well, none of this packet would.

'Is the nanny good?'

'Oh, wonderfully good. Sensationally gorgeously effing marvellous. Everyone tells me how lucky I am. And Rose becomes a meek little mouse when she's around.'

'But isn't that good?'

'Good, but galling. And I tell you what else is galling, Izzy. It's having her pussy-footing around my bleeding husband all day.'

'Pussy-footing?'

There was only one trifle sponge left. Izzy sat on her hands, and felt heroic.

'She fancies him like mad, the rotten little tart. She's forever flirting and skirting around him and passing him the salt and making his toast for him and putting the milk in his tea for him. One day she'll follow him into the lavatory and wipe his blinking bum for him.'

'This doesn't sound like you, Louise.'

'It isn't me. I've turned into a maternal virago. My hormones are locked into some appalling post-natal whirlpool. I say the most ghastly things. It's bad enough having her twinkling and tweeting around Michael and driving him mad with desire, but the fact that I'm in this state makes it a hundred times worse.'

'What state?'

'What state? Come on, no need to be tactful. I look appalling. I'm still nearly eleven stone. I lumber about like some god-forsaken tanker about to spill my load.'

'Poor Louise! – but does she really drive Michael wild with desire?' Izzy enquired rather anxiously.

'Who knows? He's trying so desperately hard to be good. And of course he's completely shattered as well. I think even Michael finds it hard to be a philanderer on less than five hours sleep.' Just then Michael put his head round the door. Rose's bawling had modulated to a slight snicker.

'She's just been sick again,' he reported.

'Oh God,' Louise closed her eyes. 'Where?'

'I pointed her at the bath. I think most of it went in.'

'At least she's calmed down a bit.'

They fussed and fretted over the bundle. Tiny claw-like hands waved above the stained shawl.

'I think she'll be asleep in a minute.'

'I'll walk her up and down a bit now, Michael. You have a word with poor Izzy.' Louise leaned Rose on her shoulder and creaked wearily to and fro. Michael collapsed onto a chair beside Izzy.

'Hello, old thing,' he smiled ruefully. 'How goes?'

'Oh, I'm all right,' Izzy finished her tea. There was a nice syrupy bit at the bottom of the cup.

'We are, as you see, more or less totally defeated by the tiny Empress. We are her slaves. *N'est-ce pas*, Louise?' Louise almost smiled.

'Willing slaves, though?' ventured Izzy. 'She's lovely. And this stage won't last long. Soon be through it. She'll soon be borrowing the car, Michael.' This rather facile optimism fell to the floor unacknowledged.

'Look,' Izzy thought she'd better put her cards on what was clearly already a somewhat overtaxed table. 'I was wondering . . . you see, I haven't fixed up anywhere to live, yet, and I wondered – might it be at all possible for me to kip here for a day or two? I haven't slept for thirty hours,' she added, dramatically, hoping for some sympathy. Perhaps they wouldn't mind if she crawled off to bed right now.

'Know the feeling,' observed Michael. 'We haven't slept for two months.'

Izzy withered silently at her tactlessness.

'I'm very sorry, Izzy,' whispered Louise – the babe being evidently on the brink of sleep – 'but Melanie has your old room, now.'

'Melanie?'

'The nanny.'

'Of course! But I don't mind. I'll kip on the sofa – anything.'

'Oh dear, Izzy. This is awful. I'm afraid we're being terribly inhospitable, but Michael sleeps on the sofa, these days.'

'You see, my dear,' Michael yawned. 'I have to go to work. And the nights are so ghastly, with her Majesty screaming for her grub every couple of hours, that quite frankly I have abandoned the matrimonial bedchamber and fled to a nomadic life on the sofa. Good practice for the park benches, later.'

'Couldn't you stay with Maria, Izzy?'

'Well, I've just come from there. A really strange thing happened, you know. She told me she was in love with me.' Michael and Louise peered at Izzy in a mystified way, as if she was speaking some foreign language.

'What? Is Maria gay?'

'So she says. I'm afraid it scared me off, rather.'

'Bound to. Well, well.' Michael rested his head on his hand. 'Hard to imagine finding the energy to be in love with anybody, these days.'

Izzy was silent. She must sleep. Being with other tired people made it worse. Anywhere would do – under the kitchen table with the Lego and stale crusts, perhaps. Or in the garden shed with Mr Jackson the toad.

'Poor Izzy,' pondered Louise. 'It is a problem – Wait! What about Aunt Vinny?'

'Aunt Vinny!' cried Michael with a triumphal whoop. 'Perfect! Louise, you're a genius! By my standards, anyway.'

'Who's your Aunt Vinny?'

'She's this extraordinary eccentric lady who lives in Worcester Road – off Westbourne Grove, you know. She married money.'

'How clever.' Izzy had the distinct feeling that she would marry poverty.

'Yes, well, the thing is, she's got this garden flat, you see, Izzy. She's trying to let it.'

'Not trying all that hard, mind you,' added Michael, nibbling a few crumbs. 'She doesn't want to advertise. She wants to do it all through personal contact.'

'Well, how much is the rent?'

'You can never tell with Aunt Vinny. If she takes a fancy to you, it could be next to nothing. Tell you what, Izzy – no time like the present – I'll ring her up.'

Louise reached for the phone, and soon it was all arranged – Izzy was to go round there right now, since Aunt Vinny was apparently at leisure and eager to make her acquaintance. Despite her weariness, Izzy was glad to go, since her presence here was evidently a burden and there seemed no prospect even of a camp bed or dog basket.

'I shall snatch an hour's sleep, now Her Majesty's

gone off,' said Louise. 'Good luck, Izzy. She'll adore you.'

'Oh dear,' Izzy rifled through her handbag. 'I've got hardly any money left.'

'I'll take you to the bank,' said Michael. 'And then deliver you to the tube. A ride in the car is a treat, these days.'

Jack went along for the ride, too. Izzy was duly delivered at Highgate Tube with forty crisp new pound-notes in her threadbare old purse and a sketch map of Aunt Vinny's whereabouts in her hot little hand.

'Thanks, Michael,' she gave him a kiss on the cheek. Michael turned and fixed her for a moment with a strange tormented gaze.

'We must have a proper talk sometime,' he said ominously.

'Oh yes, that would be lovely,' trilled Izzy guiltily. ''Bye, Jack!' And she leapt out of what was becoming another slightly hot seat. What did Michael mean? Was he having an affair with the nanny? Did he want to unburden himself to her? Or worse? Just keeping awake was burden enough for her at the moment. The escalators at Highgate were out of order, as usual, so she had to walk down the seemingly endless staircase, down, down, down into the groaning bowels of the earth.

AN EXCELLENT DEVICE

There were several Rolls-Royces parked in Worcester
Road, which was worrying. The houses were tall and
elegant and painted cream and white. Lack of sleep, and
transatlantic trauma made Izzy feel rather unworthy of her
surroundings. She was sure she didn't smell too good,
either. She paused in the shelter of a tree, whipped out
her *Rive Gauche* and gave herself a quick blast on the
neck. A passing dog paused, and howled. *Too much, as
usual*, thought Izzy, trying to scrub the excess scent off
with a tissue soaked in saliva. Why did she never have
enough saliva, these days? Was it the hole in the ozone
layer? A front door opened nearby and someone clattered
down some steps. Izzy pocketed her tissue furtively and
tried to look rich and nonchalant.

'Ya!' called the person. '*Ciao*, then, Bianca!'

'*Ciao*, Henry!' yodelled a young harpy from the door.
Henry leapt into his BMW and roared off. Izzy wasn't
quite sure if Worcester Road was going to be right for her.

Aunt Vinny was tall and vivid. She peered down at Izzy
with glittering eyes of jet. Her cheekbones were slightly
slanty and her hands heavily bejewelled. She wore a black
velvet jacket and an eccentric little beaded cap. It was
impossible to judge her age – it could have been anything
from a raddled forty to a radiant seventy.

'Ah, Isabelle. Do come in! I've heard so much about
you.'

Crumbs! Just what had Aunt Vinny heard? Surely
not . . . *everything*? But Izzy's speculations were cut short
as she surrendered to the effortless opulence of her
surroundings. The deep mahogany and rosewood shine of

the furniture; the pall of antiquity on the yellowing faces staring out from the ancestral oil-paintings; the genteel shade of grey in which the curtains hung, in generous folds of mist. *It would've taken me a lifetime to discover a grey like that*, thought Izzy, in despair at her own deep-seated vulgarity.

'Would you like a drink, Isabelle? Or may I call you Izzy?'

'Oh, please *do*!'

'And do call me Vinny. Short for Virginia. Never liked Virginia. Too imposing,' grumbled that most imposing lady.

'I never liked Isabelle, either.'

'Virginia and Isabelle. Sounds like a school story from the 1920s. Very Angela Brazil!' Aunt Vinny brayed briefly and then fumbled with some glasses.

'White wine all right?'

'Lovely. Thanks.'

This was quite reckless of Izzy, considering her lack of sleep and food. But what the hell. Izzy had less than the usual quota of reck. They sipped their wine, and Izzy thought she detected, behind the rather forbidding façade, a familiar twinkle in Aunt Vinny's eye.

'I've got some salted almonds in a secret box!' she hissed, suddenly. '*Shall* we?' Ah, yes. Greed.

'Yes, please!' cried Izzy in piteous need.

Aunt Vinny flew to a little Chinoiserie cabinet and took out a rosewood box – the sort that in Izzy's favourite sort of film would invariably contain a rewritten will, or at the very least, a series of incriminating love letters. But the serried ranks of salted almonds within were treasure of a different kind.

'Oh!' groaned Izzy, 'they're scrumptious!'

'Go on, have another handful! Nature's bounty, my dear. Why did God create almond trees and salt if not – *et cetera*.'

This was a novel view of God, and quite an attractive one.

'Well, Izzy,' said Aunt Vinny, sitting up very straight and peering disapprovingly at Izzy's neck, almost as if she could still see the faint traces of teenage lovebites, flotillas of raspberries upon the cream. 'I'm afraid I have to warn you that I'm a very old-fashioned person.'

Izzy endured a paroxysm of guilt. She had always known she was not old-fashioned enough. Even now she was wearing a Mickey Mouse T-shirt. She felt as if Aunt Vinny's eyes could penetrate beneath her modern garb and see into her very heart, with all its naughty modern susceptibilities.

'I don't suppose I am a very easy person to live with, either,' Aunt Vinny went on. 'My niece tells me I am too severe on young people. But I tell her that life is not worth living without some principles.'

Aunt Vinny tossed another handful of salted almonds into her mouth and crunched them with the fury of an industrial machine. Izzy sipped more wine, and began to feel faint.

'Oh, I quite agree,' she murmured spongily.

Aunt Vinny gazed for a moment into space: alert, and, it seemed, listening.

'What is it, Rupert?' she whispered suddenly.

Izzy looked round for the small and unpleasant dog which the name suggested, but there didn't seem to be an animal of any sort in the room. Perhaps Izzy had imagined it. But Aunt Vinny still looked odd: staring and attentive, her eyes fixed on empty space.

'My dear, you're quite right,' she said to the air. Then she turned to Izzy.

'Rupert likes you.'

'Oh,' stammered Izzy. 'Well, er . . . well, good.' Benevolence was always welcome, after all.

Aunt Vinny's eyes travelled comprehensively over Izzy's T-shirt, jeans, and shoes, and then returned to her face. She gazed into Izzy's eyes.

'What do you make of it?' she asked suddenly. Izzy jumped.

44

'Of what?'

'Of death, dear. What *is* death, do you think? Just another vibration? I'm sure of it, you know. Aren't you?'

'Well – yes, I think you might well be right.' This wasn't exactly the landlady and prospective tenant interview Izzy had been expecting. She staggered on, gamely, however. At least she had a bit of death to draw on.

'My father died a few years ago.'

'Oh dear! I am sorry to hear it. Although you may have evidence – *has he been in touch since, dear?*' Aunt Vinny leaned forward eagerly, her black eyes a-gleam.

'Er, not exactly. Not yet, anyway.'

'Dear Rupert has,' Vinny hissed ecstatically. 'My Rupert is ever with me, Izzy. We have conversations many times a day. I never do anything without consulting him.'

'Is Rupert your. . . .'

'My husband, you see. He died ten years ago. Fell off a mountain. So sad. I knew he would. A passionate climber, but blind as a bat and terribly clumsy. But enough of Rupert. Is your mother still alive?'

'Oh, yes. Very much. She still lives at the farm. Where I grew up. In Yorkshire.'

'How delightful!'

'Yes. But we sold the land to the farmer next door.'

'Fascinating. Rupert will be most interested. He may be able to trace your father, my dear. Establish a channel. Unless the thought of that upsets you.'

'Oh, no! I'd love to . . . establish a channel.'

'Izzy, I have been an absent-minded old coot. I haven't shown you the flat. Come!'

Aunt Vinny called her to heel. Izzy obeyed. They went downstairs and Izzy found herself in a rather warm brown hall. There was a sitting-room, a bedroom overlooking the garden, an immaculate bathroom, and a tiny kitchen. Izzy was particularly taken with the bedroom. She longed to prostrate herself on the embroidered coverlet and give up her soul to the Gods of Sleep.

'Will it do?' asked Vinny sharply.

'It's utterly gorgeous!' drooled Izzy, perhaps too modernly.

'My dear,' Aunt Vinny laid a finger on Izzy's arm. 'I find myself in a quandary.'

Oh, Lord. Here it was. The declaration of passion.

'The thing is, my dear, I did rather want a married couple down here – properly *married*, I mean. Not a young girl on her own.' Aunt Vinny hesitated. Izzy, charmed at being thought a young girl, was yet aware that the delightful flat, complete with enticing bedcover, was slipping away from her grasp.

'You see, I have such a horror of people breaking in. The world is such a dreadful place, these days. I thought, if there was a husband down here, he could intercept the burglars. Bash them on the head with a polo stick, sort of thing. And I find it very hard to open jars of jam, these days.'

Izzy stared at the bed. Every bone in her body longed for it. She would've murdered for it. For a split second she was tempted to bash Aunt Vinny over the head with a polo stick herself, and sink into a wonderful slumber before giving herself up to the police in the morning.

'Oh, that's all right,' she heard herself say. 'I *am* married.'

'My dear! But that's wonderful! Louise never said.'

'Louise doesn't know. I'm . . . I'm very recently married, you see.' Aunt Vinny would never guess just how recent.

'Splendid! Splendid! So you're a bride, Izzy! Many congratulations!'

'Thanks. I – I didn't really go into it all with Louise and Michael. The baby was crying all the time, you see, and—'

'Frightful, frightful, yes, poor little thing. But where were you married? Haven't you just got back from America?'

'Yes. In . . . San Francisco. We were married there.'

'How dazzling! But my dear . . .' Vinny's face darkened

46

momentarily. 'He's not . . . not an *American*, is he?'

'Oh, no. British to the bone.'

'It's not that I have anything against Americans myself, but Rupert is very anti.'

'Of course.'

'And what's his name?' Izzy hesitated on the North Face of Untruth, all ten fingernails slipping on the scree.

'Dick!' she exclaimed, finding a toehold at last. 'Dick Barnes. He's a colleague from school. A pottery teacher.'

'Dick! How sweet! He sounds an absolute brick!'

'Oh, yes. Dick's a brick. I think you'll like him,' stammered Izzy, bright scarlet as the momentous implications of her lie began to unfold. Would she have to produce Dick? Would she have to cohabit with him? Would she – oh Lord – have to *marry* him indeed? Mind you, to gain the haven of that bed, Izzy would've agreed to marry, well, almost anybody. Even certain parts of Dick. His hands, for example, were capable and strong. Indeed, had Dick ever offered Izzy his hand in marriage, she would've accepted – as long as it stopped right there.

'And where is Dick now?' Izzy's mind went blank. Where was Dick?

'Ah, well, he's – he's gone to see his mother. Up north.'

'Oh, I love the north! I have a delightful nephew who went to school at Ampleforth! It has such – well, integrity. Where exactly?'

Where was it? Where was it? It had bags of integrity, and Izzy was sure it ended with an *op*.

'Er – Glossop – I mean, Workshop – *Worksop*.'

'Isn't that in Derbyshire? Or is it Nottingham?'

'It . . .'s Nottingham, I think. Geography was never my strong point.'

'But you stayed in London?'

'Yes. To househunt, you see.'

'Well my dear, the flat's yours, if you want it. I'm sure we'll get on. And Rupert likes you. That's the main thing.'

'Well . . . well, thank you – both,' said Izzy meekly.

'And now I suppose you'd like to ring Dick and tell him

you've found a place? There's the phone.'

Even if Izzy had had Dick's mother's phone number, such a call, with its desperate hints and monstrous enigmas, would probably give Dick a nervous breakdown.

'No! I mean, er, I can't phone now.'

'Please do, my dear. But really.'

'No. Thanks everso, but I can't ring just now, because, well, because Dick's mum has her meetings on Thursdays.'

'Meetings?'

Now, what meetings could not be disturbed by the ringing of the telephone?

'Séances – er, sort of thing.'

The minute Izzy saw Aunt Vinny's face light up, she knew she'd made a major mistake. Séances had simply been near the surface of her mind, for obvious reasons. Of all the fictitious eccentricities Izzy's fictional ma-in-law could've been victim to, this was the most inconveniently fascinating. And Vinny was enthralled.

'Why my dear how absolutely wonderful! I must meet her.'

'Yes, you absolutely must,' gulped Izzy.

'Does she come to London often?'

'Oh – er, now and then. Not – not very.'

'We have a group that meets on Monday evenings, in Belsize Park. She *must* come. Is she mediumistic?'

'Medium what?'

'Does she have the gift? Can she communicate?'

'Oh – off and on, I think,' faltered Izzy. 'Yes and no. It depends on the weather, I think. I'm sorry I'm so vague, but I'm afraid I don't really know many of the details.'

'Never mind, my dear. I can ask Dick all about it in due course. When do you expect him?'

'A couple of – well, a couple of days, I should think.'

'Splendid. Well. When would you like to move in?'

'To tell you the truth, I mean. . . . I know this is probably a bit unusual, but, well, could I move in right away?'

'You mean this week?'

'I mean, well . . . now. Today, to be honest. You see, I've got nowhere to sleep tonight. We just got in from San Francisco this morning, so I've missed a whole night's sleep. I'm a bit – you know.'

'Dear me, how unpleasant for you! Of course. The bed's made up, in fact. I was expecting my other nephew to call – but he never arrived. So do please make yourself at home. Where's your luggage?'

'At a friend's. I can collect it tomorrow. All I want to do now is sleep.'

'Of course. Please do! I won't disturb you any longer, my dear. Sleep well.'

Vinny went back upstairs. But on the turn of the stair she paused and said something in a low voice.

'Sorry?' called Izzy.

'It's all right, dear. Rupert was just reminding me that I hadn't mentioned the rent to you.'

He was a down-to-earth emanation, this Rupert.

'Oh no. That's right. How much is it?'

Aunt Vinny mentioned a sum of money so vast, Izzy thought for a brief moment she must be talking in Escudos or Lire.

'Is that all right?'

'Of course. Fine,' croaked Izzy, waddling towards the bedroom. She would've given her last sou for that bed. And it wouldn't be long before she'd have to.

'Splendid. Sleep well! Sweet dreams!'

Izzy crashed onto the bed, crawled under the covers and groaned aloud. It seemed to have taken her about three weeks to find somewhere to lie down. And now she was jolly well going to sleep for another three weeks. She just hoped that Rupert wouldn't materialize in the night and make any extra-terrestrial extra-marital suggestions.

BLUSHING CHEEKS BY FAULTS ARE BRED

Izzy slept. An endless and delicious sleep. At times she drifted to the surface and rolled about like an old Coca-Cola can in the sunlight. Then she was vaguely aware that she was not in her San Francisco room, with its white blinds, wood floor and radiators that hissed and chugged with steam. She knew she was back in England – but she wouldn't let her attention get too preoccupied with the details. Izzy asleep knew that Izzy awake would have quite a lot to contend with. So she slept on, and eventually had an erotic dream about a certain slightly ghoulish ex-Cabinet Minister of the Tory persuasion. She awoke thinking, *Everyone's wrong. He's absolutely delightful.* For several seconds afterwards she felt quite sorry it had only been a dream. It was time she fell in love again, for real.

Now, where was she? Westbourne Grove. She grinned when she remembered. She'd always liked its racy feel and late-night shops. Lots of action. But the memory of the rent soon wiped the grin off her face. It was going to be a desperate struggle, even shared between two – if indeed she and Dick did somehow share it, and they had to, really: she was up to her neck in it already. Well, if they lived on bread and cheese, they might be able to afford it for a while. Although cheese was rather expensive. Izzy wondered if Dick had any hidden assets he could liquidate, but this speculation did not detain her long.

She must get cracking. Informing Dick of his sudden promotion was the first priority. Although how to contact him was a problem. Izzy got up and showered lingeringly, postponing her problems in a cloud of steam, and washing her hair with soap. Her shampoo, together with all her clothes, was still at Maria's. Too late, Izzy noticed that there were no towels in the bathroom. Her own were in Canonbury. She'd really have to face Maria, today. But first there was the problem of how to get dry.

'I know,' steamed Izzy, 'I'll run round the flat and sort of dance about a bit. That'll be good exercise and I'll soon be dry.'

So, damp and gleaming as a Titian Venus, she bounded from the bathroom stark naked singing *Ta ra ra boom-de-ay*.

Even as she performed her first high kicks, there was a clatter of feet on the stairs and a tall young man with fair hair burst very familiarly into her sanctum. Izzy screamed. He froze.

'Oh my God – I'm terribly sorry!' he stammered.

'No – it's all right – excuse me—' Izzy bolted for the bathroom and locked the door.

'Do forgive me,' he persisted, politely, without.

'It's all right. Really. I shouldn't have—'

'But it was inexcusable of me. I was looking for my Aunt Vinny. I had no idea there was anyone in the flat. I usually stay here when I come to see her, you see. I have a key.'

'Oh. You must be her nephew, then.'

'Yes. Charles Armstrong. Delighted to make your acquaintance.' He smiled at the door. Izzy wished she could get another look at him. And the feeling was more than mutual.

'I'm Izzy. Isabelle, that is. Comyn.'

There was a tremulous pause.

'Come in?' A rather excited note crept into Charles' voice. 'Did you say . . . *Come in?*'

'No – at least – that's my surname, you see. Comyn. With a Y.'

'Ah yes. Of course. Sorry. Silly of me. Well, look, I must leave you in peace. If you'd just tell Aunt Vinny I called.'

'Oh yes. Shall I say you'll call again soon?' asked Izzy,

still unaccountably covering her nakedness, as if there were no door between them.

'On Tuesday perhaps.'

'Right. Oh, wait a minute. Could you just tell me – what day *is* it today?'

'Saturday.' Charles sounded rather surprised.

'Thanks. Gosh. I slept through Friday, then. Jet lag, you see. I've just got back from San Francisco.' Izzy felt somehow like prolonging a conversation which she knew had to be concluded.

'Really? San Francisco? Sounds exciting.'

'Well, it *was*, really. Very exciting. I'll tell you about it sometime,' promised Izzy. 'I mustn't keep you now.'

'No, of course. I'll look forward to that, then,' concluded Charles, withdrawing reluctantly, and wondering if a second interview with Izzy, about the excitingness of San Francisco, could possibly be as exciting as the first. He thought not, probably.

'Cheerio, then?'

''Bye!'

It was a bit like those lovers in Shakespeare, talking through the wall, thought Izzy, with a giggle, examining the bathroom door for a chink. Pyramus and Thisbe. She heard Charles going upstairs, then through the hall. The front door slammed, and his footsteps, fainter now, echoed on the steps outside. There was the dim roar of what Izzy supposed to be an expensive car, and he was lost in the distant hum of London. Izzy wiped the bathroom mirror clean of steam, and peeped in. She looked quite pretty today, really, even if she was nearly thirty. She sang as she climbed into her smelly old in-flight clothes. But then she had to ring Maria and her song shrivelled slightly.

She paused nervously by the phone. There was a note beside it, and a key. *Izzy*, it said, *Hope you slept well. See you soon. Vinny.* Izzy pocketed the key, and found Maria's phone number. The dreadful scene with Maria was still festering in her memory. Izzy squirmed. She needed her luggage, though. She dialled Maria's number. *Please, God*, she urged, *make Maria be out and just Gwyn in. Please, please do this little thing for me, God, and I will try even harder to be good*.

''Ulloa? Gwyn Jenkins here.'

Oh thank you thank you thank you God you are a darling.

'Hello, Gwyn! This is Izzy.'

'Izzy, darlin'! How are you? How was the West Coast, mon? Brought any psychedelic souvenirs back for me, 'ave yew? An' when can I clap my tired old eyes on your scrumptious little body again?'

'Er, well – I need to come and get my luggage, Gwyn. Is Maria in?'

'Noa, noa, never yew mind about Maria. She saw you on Thursday, right? 'S my turn now. C'mon over, babe. Jump in a cab, now. I need your advice about my career.'

'Yes, well, but – where is Maria? Is she likely to come back soon?'

'Look, Isabelle, you're perfectly safe with me, girl. Doan't insult me with these hesitations, darlin'. I'm like your brother, right? You're my little sister.'

'Don't be silly, Gwyn. I just want to know if Maria's – well, likely to show up or not.'

''Fraid not, babe. She's gone off to Camden on some feminist foray or other. Said she'll be back by suppertime.'

Izzy consulted her watch. It appeared to be mid-morning. So she was safe.

'What a – er, what a pity. I'll miss her. Never mind. It'll be nice to see you again, Gwyn.'

'That's more like it. I'm pantin' for a kind word from your delectable lips, Isabelle. This place is a desert of meaningful puritans, if you get my drift. Now get your arse over here and give me the doape on San Francisco, darlin'. I'm parched for a bit of depravity.'

Izzy thought she'd better leave a note for Aunt Vinny. The only piece of paper she could find was Vinny's note to her, so she wrote on the back: *Your nephew Charles Armstrong called. He said he'd probably come again on*

Tuesday. Thank you for the key, and for all your kindness.
Izzy.

Was that too crawling? Or not quite crawling enough? Izzy had not had a landlady on the premises for several years. She left her note on the beautiful little rosewood table in the hall, and went out into the mêlée of Westbourne Grove. On the way up to Islington (by tube – an economical gesture, by way of an offer of thanks to God), she admired the name Charles Armstrong. It was so absurdly English-historical. Like trumpets lifted above a coat of arms. Armstrong. Fortinbras. He probably even had a coat of arms of his own. He ought not to be in Westbourne Grove. He ought to be in a historical romance (of which Izzy's Mum had devoured several hundred). He ought to be fighting hand-to-hand under the Plantagenet flag at Agincourt, a henchman of King Harry. He ought to be hesitating on horseback under an oak, and turning to wave one last golden glove at the maiden in the tower. He ought to be leaping into moats. He ought to be . . . crumbs! This was Highbury and Islington. Izzy ought to be getting off. Time passes fast in timeless, sunlit Olde Englande.

BREAK OFF, BREAK OFF

'Gwyn!'

'Darlin'!'

Izzy was swept off her feet into a wild Welsh hug that knocked the breath out of her.

'Oh, my ribs! Stop it! Please, Gwyn!'

'Lovely scrumptious creature! You're lookin' even more sensational than usual, darlin'!'

'Don't be silly, Gwyn! I look awful. I haven't changed my clothes since Wednesday – or was it Tuesday?'

'I doan't care! Remember what Napoleon wrote to Josephine, mon.'

'What?'

'*Battle won. Home next Tuesday. For God's sake don't have a bath.*'

'Ugh, Gwyn! How disgusting!'

''Twasn't me, darlin'. 'Twas Napoleon.'

Upstairs, Maria and Gwyn's flat seemed a lot more cheerful than on Izzy's previous visit. While Gwyn made some coffee, Izzy wondered how much Maria had told him of her epoch-making changes of mind and heart. Did Gwyn know that his wife was – but Izzy abandoned the thought. Gwyn carried in a steaming tray.

'Here you are, babe,' he grinned. 'Chocolate cake. When I knew you were coming, I just popped out and got one.'

'Oh no! How marvellous! But it's awful – I'm not supposed to have any.'

'Says who?'

'Oh, I just sort of promised – well, I promised God,' she giggled.

'Stroll on down! You're not Born Again or anythin' like that are you, babe? You didn't get lured from the broad path of misdemeanour by some jumped-up West Coast TV evangelist, did yew?'

'No, Gwyn. Don't be silly.'

'Now lissen, Izzy, doan't trust any of these religious bloakes – from God downwards, right? It's all sublimation, see? Under all that beatin' of breasts an' wringin' of hands they're as filthy-minded as the next man, girl. Worse. I read another one's been caught with his trousers down last week.'

'Oh well,' sighed Izzy. 'If God hadn't meant us to have chocolate cake, he wouldn't have created – where *does* chocolate come from, Gwyn?'

'Round the corner in the Greek deli, darlin'. Now get stuck in. This cake is one o'the wonders of creation. It shows the marvels o'man's hand.'

For a while they ate and drank and twinkled at each other as some invigorating jazz rock belted out of Gwyn's speakers.

'Right then, Isabelle. Give me the goods. What acts did you commit on the St Andreas fault? What did you inhale on the Golden Gate bridge? An' who with?'

Izzy delivered to Gwyn the blameless outlines of her Californian sojourn, and insisted that she had inhaled nothing but ozone.

'Dear, dear, Isabelle, I'm very disappointed with you, darlin'. Or were you – keepin' yourself for some lucky bastard back here? Wasn't me by any chance, was it, sweetheart?'

'No, Gwyn. I'm waiting till you're a Cabinet Minister.'

'Cross your heart and swear to die, like?'

'I promise. If ever you get to be Cabinet Minister, Gwyn, I'll be your secret floosie. I'll wait outside Number Ten in a taxi with drawn blinds whilst you wrestle with the Budget.'

'Sod the Budget! I'll be right there in the taxi, wrestlin' with you, darlin'. On the way down to our love nest in Brighton.'

'I expect I'll be the ruin of you, Gwyn.'

'I devoutly hope so, Isabelle. *Cabinet Minister resigns in sex in taxi scandal. Curvaceous English mistress Izzy tells all.*'

'I hope the gutter press will offer me a six-figure sum for my memoirs.'

'Bound to, darlin'. Depravity of truly heroic proportions will become more an' more of a rarity as this miserable century crawls towards its close.' Izzy sank into a chocolate-flavoured chuckle.

'It's noa joke, Isabelle!' warned Gwyn. 'This Council business is just the beginning. The Tory stranglehold is losing its grip, babe. I could be sending the Ministerial limousine round for you well before I'm forty.'

'How long's that? Six weeks?'

'You cheeky little thing! Listen, power's a great aphrodisiac! You know who said that? Henry Kissinger. Or his wife. I forget which.'

Izzy couldn't remember much about Henry Kissinger. But she liked his name.

'Kissinger,' she drawled languorously, licking the chocolate off her lips. Gwyn went quiet, watching her intently. She caught on his eyes like barbed wire. A weird spiral of feeling went through her. The room was suddenly terrifyingly still. All their flirtatious badinage fell away, like a regatta scattered and appalled by the slow emergence of a nuclear submarine, water streaming off its deadly sides.

There was a sudden movement, and Gwyn seemed to be on top of her. Izzy blinked and ducked, but it was too late. He pinned her to the sofa in a crushing embrace, his breath roaring in her ear. Izzy struggled feebly.

'Izzy, darlin'!' he panted. 'Darlin'! You turn me on too much, babe!'

'Gwyn—' Izzy protested, but he stopped her mouth. Izzy had never been seriously kissed by Gwyn before, only in public or when he was drunk. She had underestimated him in his sober and sex-crazed stride. He was deft, determined, immensely strong. She was frightened, and tried to struggle, but his grip was like iron. She decided to wait until the end of this kiss, and then protest when she got her mouth back. But she didn't get her mouth back. The kiss didn't end. This was mad. She had to escape.

Izzy struggled again, but by now she realized she'd lost a lot of ground. She seemed to be losing a lot of clothes, too. His dexterity was extraordinary. Izzy began to feel the draught in surprising places. How could he immobilize her and undress her at the same time? His strength was phenomenal. But then, Gwyn's style of lovemaking owed quite a lot to rugby football, at which he had had many years of practice. These rogue thoughts flitted through her head, accompanied by a rising panic, as she sank under the scrum.

I've got to get him to stop, or it'll be too late. Izzy's struggles redoubled themselves, to the frenzy of an ant beneath an elephant.

I should never have mentioned Lloyd George, thought Izzy. *Or was it Kissinger? And, oh God – GOD! What'll he say? First all that chocolate cake, and now this!*

Gwyn's lips left hers for a magic moment. No doubt he now considered himself safe. His mouth moved to her ear, into which he stuck his tongue.

'Isabelle!' he whispered, all aflame, 'Isabelle, you beautiful creature! I've longed for you, girl, longed for you for ever!'

The terrible pleasure of his words spread over her like Golden Syrup. A sickening-sweet, paralyzing mess.

'No!' cried Izzy at last, 'Stop it, Gwyn! I can't!'

'Yes you can, darlin' – in fact, you *are*.'

'No, Gwyn! You must stop! Listen! It's very important – I'VE GOT HERPES!'

''S all right, darlin'!' Gwyn's breath boomed in her brain. 'So have I.'

Only a final desperate act could save Izzy now.

'Please God!' she prayed. 'Give strength to my knee.'

Gwyn went reeling backwards with a roar of anguish. His flying fist hit the eighteenth-century clock, which slithered along the mantelpiece, then plunged and smashed on the tiles below. Gwyn fell into the armchair groaning and cursing whilst Izzy leapt up and pulled the bits of herself back into order.

'Oh, Gwyn! I'm really sorry – but I had to.'

'What the hell you think you're playin' at, Isabelle?' he choked.

'I told you not to.'

'You asked for it, girl. Jesus, Jesus, Jesus!'

'I did not! I was only kidding about that Lloyd George stuff. But Gwyn – what are we going to do about the clock?'

'Sod the clock!' he groaned, still bent double in the armchair. 'What are we goin' to do about my Crown Jewels?'

'You're all right,' said Izzy nervously. She hadn't done a lot for Maria's chances of getting pregnant this week, that was for sure. She made for the door, trying to ignore the pale green colour that had spread over Gwyn's face.

'I'm sorry, Gwyn. Really—'

On a sudden, extremely dangerous impulse, Izzy flitted across the room and kissed him briefly on the cheek.

'Doan't add insult to injury, you daft bitch!' he roared. Izzy skipped to the door, with an incongruous sense of déjà vu.

'I'll go, then' she faltered, and seized her cases. 'I'll ring, and things. This was silly, Gwyn. We mustn't ever – you know – again.'

The only answer was a deep groan. Grabbing her luggage, Izzy struggled down the stairs and burst out into the sane sound of traffic. A taxi approached. She hailed it. *God must have sent it*, she thought, sinking back gratefully into the leather seat. She had resisted temptation for the first time in her life. It felt awful.

I DO NOTHING IN THE WORLD BUT LIE

Getting in touch with Dick proved tricky. Since Izzy did not know his parents' initials, or his address, Directory Enquiries were not terribly helpful. There were several hundred Barnes entries in his area, and after the first six, Izzy gave up in despair. Where would Dick go, when he returned to London? Would he seek her out? The only people who knew of her whereabouts were Michael and Louise. Maria and Gwyn didn't, thank God. If she gave them her address, then they would be in a position to pass it on to Dick. But they would also be in a position to come round and offer her their bodies and souls. Izzy had had rather enough of that. On the other hand, she did need urgently to get in touch with Dick.

'When's your husband coming?' enquired Aunt Vinny, on one of her slightly too frequent trips below stairs. Izzy began to wish that this basement flat had no connecting staircase with the rest of the house. Not that Aunt Vinny intruded, exactly: she always paused on the stairs and shouted, 'Coo-ee! Are you decent?' before thundering down. Perhaps she had been talking to her nephew. She always brought something useful, too: an iron, a spare key, some lavatory cleaner. But she was understandably anxious to meet Dick. Since he was the man who was going to open her jam jars and brain her burglars for her, he already had a special place in Aunt Vinny's heart.

'When's he actually coming, do you mean?' faltered Izzy, seizing the dustpan and pursuing some crumbs.

'He's having to see all his relatives, you see,' Izzy went on, face hidden in the carpet. 'Telling them all about San Francisco and things. Most of them haven't been any further than – er – Manchester.' Izzy hoped Manchester was up there somewhere. She was rapidly developing a rather patronizing attitude to her new in-laws. Quite convincing, really.

'Is he one of a large family?' enquired Aunt Vinny, perching ominously on the arm of the sofa. 'Do leave those crumbs, Izzy. My girl's coming tomorrow. She can nip down and do an hour or so for you.'

'Oh no – I mean, really, thank you, but – it's all right.'

'Now don't argue, my dear. It's included in the rent. And she's excellent.'

Izzy hated the thought of domestic help. She'd have to tidy up for hours every time the wretched girl was due.

'Has he got lots of brothers and sisters?' enquired Aunt Vinny remorselessly.

'Oh yes,' said Izzy. The more siblings Dick had, the more excuse for his late return. 'Lots. Four brothers and three sisters, actually.'

'Good heavens! How unusual.'

'Oh, it isn't unusual up there. Big families are traditional in W—' Izzy forgot the name of Dick's home town. '—where he comes from.'

'How delightful! What do they all do?'

Izzy felt faint. Her brain scuttled around for famous Northerners. Alan Sillitoe, George Formby. . . .

'Alan and George work – work in the mill.'

'Really? Are there still mills up there?' Izzy panicked. *Were* there still mills up there? 'I thought all the cotton mills were a thing of the past.'

'Oh, cotton, yes, of course,' Izzy desperately wished she had taken a serious interest in the recent economic history of Britain.

'It's not a cotton mill. It's a . . .' What other sort of mills were there? Her brain went into mill overdrive. *Millstone grit*, it shrieked. *The Mill on the Floss. Mills and Boon. Dark Satanic Mills.*

'A coffee mill.'

'A coffee mill? How odd.'

61

'Yes, it is a bit odd, isn't it? It's a – a new project apparently. It's for that decaffeinated coffee, you know. They, well, they sort of, er *mill* it to get the caffeine out. I don't understand all the details,' she concluded modestly.

'What about his sisters?'

'Ah, the sisters,' she began, falling quite arbitrarily into a dark and meaningful tone of voice. 'Yes. Margaret. Margaret's a bit of a character.' Izzy fixed desperately on the only Margaret she could think of and shamelessly drew on her. 'She fell in love with this marvellous chap, when she was quite young, only her parents wouldn't let her marry him, because he was divorced.'

'But how fascinating! Poor thing! What then?'

Izzy had the misfortune to tell such enthralling lies that everybody always wanted more.

'Then she – married a very nice chap, and they had two children, but it didn't work out, and the marriage broke up.'

'How tragic! Why?'

'I'm . . . I'm not sure.' After all, in real life one wasn't always sure of things. Why not in fiction?

'So what does she do now?'

'Oh, she opens things, and – I mean, she – she opened a fish and chip shop.'

'I'd like to meet Margaret. She's obviously a woman with grit.'

'Oh yes. Bags of grit.' Millstone grit, probably.

'She's been through a lot.'

'She certainly has.'

'It sounds a terribly close family. Is Dick's father still alive?'

This was a real dilemma. On the one hand, if Izzy killed him off, Aunt Vinny couldn't entertain any hopes of meeting him. Not in this world, anyway. Although with Aunt Vinny's spectral inclinations, even a dead Dad might excite her social appetite. Dick had never mentioned his Dad.

'Ah, Dick's Dad. Don't ask!' (Izzy wished she had thought of that useful little phrase a lot earlier.) 'It's all very mysterious. Dick's Dad is . . . elsewhere. He's never mentioned.'

'My dear Izzy, you have married into a most extraordinary family!'

'Yes, I have.'

'And do they accept you?'

'Oh, they, er, well – I am from Yorkshire, you know, originally, so what with the traditional Yorkshire–Lancashire thing, well, it's been a bit, er sticky at times.'

The first truth to drop from Izzy's lips for twenty minutes, and it sounded like a lie.

Suddenly the front doorbell rang. It was Izzy's. Aunt Vinny's was a genteel tinkle: Izzy's, as befits one lurking in a basement, was a deep croak. Izzy's flat did have its own separate entrance, but nobody seemed to notice it or use it. Everyone seemed to come down from the main hall above. It was slightly, well – public.

'Ah. Someone to see you. I must fly.'

Aunt Vinny leapt to her feet and they both went upstairs. Izzy wondered who on earth could be ringing her doorbell. She prayed urgently that it would not be Dick. She had to see Dick alone, first, to brief him. He could not be turning up on this rather public doorstep unaware that he was married to Izzy and that he had a psychic mother and a sister who was full of grit. *Let it not be Dick, please, Lord* prayed Izzy. The Lord had been rather good to her, so far. *If it's not Dick I will resist temptation again if that's what you want, Lord.* Glory Hallelujah! It was Michael.

DID NOT I DANCE WITH YOU?

'Michael! How marvellous to see you!'

Izzy gave a little leap and clapped her hands, like a child beholding a particularly exciting birthday cake. Michael was encouraged. He had hoped that his arrival would not be unwelcome. For some months now he'd been anticipating Izzy's return with increasing tender-heartedness. Not in an unwholesome way, of course. Erotic memories had not been ransacked, in her absence. Not often, anyway. No. He simply wanted to lay his battered, tormented head in her lap, and be stroked into slumber, like a superannuated old tomcat.

'Did you say Michael?' called Aunt Vinny from within. Michael and Izzy exchanged a glance. Aunt Vinny was probably the most charming person they both knew. But all the same, surely she would benefit from the occasional trip to Harrod's? Michael greeted her heartily, and hoped she would now withdraw decently as befitted a landlady. Izzy also prayed for her speedy removal. It was only natural that Vinny should mention, in due course, Izzy's marriage. This would be news to Michael, to say the very least.

Aunt Vinny was not yet very practised at being a landlady. She was more used to the slightly more sociable and dominant role of aunt.

'Michael! How lovely to see you! Isn't this exciting! Let's all have a cup of tea!'

They were stuck. They could do nothing but follow her dumbly to her drawing-room, Michael covering his irritation with charm and Izzy wondering how soon he would have to get to grips with the idea of her marriage. Aunt Vinny settled them and then went off to make the tea.

'How are you, Michael?' asked Izzy in a strange voice, half-public, half-private. She wasn't sure if Vinny could hear them from the kitchen. Was there time for a quick briefing? A whispered warning? Or would Aunt Vinny hear the whisper, and be offended? Izzy had a terror of offending her.

'How am I? Don't ask. It should be apparent to the most casual observer that I am more or less totally destroyed. But listen, Izzy—' he lowered his voice, 'that Welsh clown is trying to get in touch with you.'

'What – Gwyn?'

'Yes. He rang this morning and asked if I knew where you were.'

'You didn't tell him?'

'Certainly not. I do possess a few tattered shreds of tact, believe it or not.'

'Thank goodness!'

'What have you been up to, Izzy? He sounded tormented, I'm glad to say. Got him simmering nicely, have you?'

'Shut up, Michael. Don't be so beastly. It was just – we had a – a row yesterday.'

'A row? What about?'

'About – about politics,' concluded Izzy, squirming at the sex and violence which seemed to dog her innocent footsteps.

'*You?* Having an argument about politics? My dear, tell me more. Your year in America must have had a fairly radical effect upon your furry little brain.'

'Michael! Don't be so damned patronizing!'

'Sorry, but *politics*? Pull the other one, old girl. I bet you don't even know who the Chancellor of the Exchequer is.'

'Yes I do! He's – he's – well, I can't remember his exact name, but it sounds like a tree. Or was that the last one? Oh God!'

'Listen, dearest, this scenario of Isabelle Comyn as political commentator simply does not convince. I know what a liar you are.'

'Oh Michael! Hush!'

'My theory is, Gwyn was driven into a frenzy of desire by

65

your divine reappearance on these shores, and swept you into his bed. Though appalled, you were too nice to say no.'

Could Aunt Vinny hear this? Izzy almost burst with shame and agitation.

'Michael! How dare you? *Shut up!* I am *not* too nice to say no.'

'You always were when I knew you.'

'You conceited pig! I hate you!'

How had they managed to get so hostile, so soon? Izzy was desperate to shut him up, and haunted by the sense that she should've used this precious couple of minutes to brief him *vis-à-vis* her marriage to Dick. Then he could have been helpful. Instead he was being maddening. What right did he have to say such things? She heard the kettle come to the boil, out in the kitchen, and feared she might soon do likewise.

Aunt Vinny swept in with the tray, beaming with delight. Michael was her favourite nephew-in-law, and Izzy was rapidly becoming one of her most cherished young things.

'So splendid to have a little party like this! I want you two young people to get to know each other better!'

Michael grinned. 'Izzy knows me far too well already, Aunt Vinny.'

'Yes—' added Izzy. 'I've been a friend of Louise and Michael for ages.'

'Of course! Silly of me! That's how you got in touch with me in the first place, of course.' Aunt Vinny handed round the tea and biscuits. 'But you must beware of Michael, Izzy: he can be quite a ladykiller, you know.'

'Can he? I'd never have believed it,' smiled Izzy. 'He's always seemed terribly tame and well-trained, to me.'

'How dare you blacken my character, Aunt Vinny? I'm a model husband.'

'Speaking of husbands, Michael,' Aunt Vinny passed Michael a gingernut, 'what do you think of Izzy's marriage?'

The gingernut flew from Michael's fingers and embedded itself in the rug. Izzy cringed. Michael went pale.

'Izzy's – did you say, marriage?'

'Oh, didn't you know? I'm terribly sorry, Izzy – have I spilt the beans? Do forgive me.'

'So you've finally managed to hook some poor devil, have you, Izzy?' asked Michael in misery.

'As a matter of fact, Michael, I have,' Izzy was aware that she'd recently been fantasizing about this very situation – introducing her husband to Michael. The husband: the idea of the husband: it was the same thing. In this case, in fact, the idea of the husband was more real than the real thing. Izzy tried to enjoy the moment as much as she had in the fantasy. Michael was certainly suffering nicely.

'Who is it? Some West Coast charlatan? An ancient hippie? A Born Again dentist?'

Izzy was aware that her husband's identity was not exactly a trump card. More of a frump card, actually.

'It's Dick,' she admitted, with the hint of a shrug.

'Dick!' Michael made it sound like an oath. He was astonished. '*Dick?* Surely not. Nobody in their right mind would marry Dick, for God's sake.'

'Don't be so rude, dear,' Aunt Vinny was uneasy. She was already devoted to the idea of Dick. She was also devoted to Michael, and up till now had absorbed his prejudices effortlessly. Michael ignored her.

'Well, stroll on down!' he shook his head in amused disbelief. 'You married Dick. Well, I suppose it solves the problem of what to do about him.'

'Really, Michael! I won't have you being so rude to Izzy. Dick sounds wonderful. I can't wait to meet him.'

Aunt Vinny was bound to be plagued, however, by misgivings. What were the origins of Michael's scorn? Was there something not quite right about Dick? Aunt Vinny resisted the idea of a drooling, smelly and hunch-backed Dick. Although Izzy was clearly soft-hearted, that would be going a little too far.

'Dick's all right, Michael,' ventured Izzy. She wasn't sure what tone of voice was appropriate. She had never defended her husband's honour against attacks by her ex-lover, before. 'He's a real – a real brick.' She borrowed Aunt Vinny's vocabulary, and with it, she hoped, the power of class. 'He's loyal, and faithful—'

'But Izzy, we all know there's more to marriage than certain canine virtues. Can he supply the excitement you thirst for, my dear?'

'Marriage isn't about excitement, Michael,' said Aunt Vinny sternly. 'It's about kindness, and sharing responsibility.'

'Quite right!' Izzy was grateful for the support. 'And anyway, I *don't* thirst for excitement.'

'Oh yes you do, my dear.'

'I do not!'

'You should have seen the fellow she used to go round with,' he said, turning to Aunt Vinny with a sepulchral sneer.

'Was he exciting?' enquired Vinny eagerly. Izzy was certainly proving a most fascinating tenant.

'Dazzling!' grinned Michael conceitedly. 'A dashing man-about-town. Brilliant. Charming. Everything Dick isn't.'

'Oh no he was not, Michael!' growled Izzy, dangerously near to melt-down. 'He was a married man, Aunt Vinny, and he led me up the garden path.'

'My dear! You poor thing!'

'He told me that he was unhappily married, and he kept promising that he'd leave his wife and marry me—'

'He didn't!' exploded Michael. 'He never promised to marry you!'

'How do you know so much about him, Michael?' enquired Aunt Vinny.

'He used to play squash with me. Knew the fellow like an open book. I won't have Izzy maligning him.'

'Ah, but I don't think you knew him as well as I did, Michael,' seethed Izzy. 'I can assure you that under all that charm he was an utter swine.'

'Not entirely without attraction, though, was he?'

persisted Michael. 'I remember you saying that you'd never been so madly in love in your life.'

Izzy couldn't believe that Michael could be so vile. Telling Aunt Vinny their most sacred secrets like this! Scornfully. Izzy would've thrown the teapot at him if it had been hers.

'Ah, well, I may have thought so then, Michael,' she said between clenched teeth, 'but it all seems totally absurd to me now. And with Dick,' she glared balefully at him, 'I have discovered a far far superior sort of love. And what's more—' she added spitefully, 'he's a *much better lover*.'

Michael winced, but Aunt Vinny did not notice. She was hoping Izzy would continue.

'I must say,' she purred, ' – have another biscuit? No? Nor you? – I must say, Dick sounds more and more like the real thing, Izzy. You should forget this other worthless fellow.'

'I have.'

'Dick is clearly the stuff of which really sound marriages are made, my dear. I can't wait to meet him.' Aunt Vinny's doorbell rang. 'Excuse me one moment.'

She went out. Michael and Izzy glared at each other in silence. They heard Vinny open the street door. She found a solid, bespectacled young man there: bearded and slightly muddy at the edges, but no trace of a hunchback. He hesitated.

'Is – is – iz – Izzy in?' he said at last. 'Tell her it's Dick Barnes.'

'Dick!' shrieked Aunt Vinny, at which dynamic syllable Izzy uttered a demented little squeal and for an instant thrust her fist right down her throat. 'Do come in! Your wife's just been telling us how wonderful you are.'

BY MY SOUL, A SWAIN

It hadn't been a terribly comfortable day for Dick, so far. His train had stopped a few hundred yards short of King's Cross station and stayed there for an hour-and-a-half. 'It's the signals,' a surly guard had reported, with an irresponsible shrug. Signals were not, he implied, part of the railway service of which he was a paid functionary, but some random act of the gods, like hailstones or lightning. At this news, a few thrusting young executives immediately leapt out onto the track and scurried off, anxious not to lose a moment of frenzied competition in the money markets. Dick stayed behind with the women, the elderly, and the idle – aware that he had opted out of the Darwinian struggle and would soon become extinct.

Out in the noisy Euston Road, afterwards, Dick breathed in deep lungfuls of carbon monoxide and turned his attention to Izzy. Where was she? He longed to know, at least. A year spent in close proximity to her, had not, in the least, diminished her dazzle. If only he knew that she was living in, say, Fulham, he could gaze wistfully at the map of London in his *A-to-Z* every night before going to sleep. Now, who would know where she was? Maria, of course. Dick took out his address book and braced himself. He had Maria's new phone number. But he was deeply afraid of Maria. She was so sharp and keen. So clever. So contemptuous. So quick-witted. She made him feel as squeamish as an unshuckled oyster upon a pin.

There was the other place, of course. Where Izzy had gone to live last year. Muswell Hill: Michael and Louise's house. Dick had gone to their party and even talked to Michael, but he still couldn't conquer his appalling embarrassment. Why, Izzy had even been in a – a ménage à whossname with them. Or so it was said. Dick could hardly believe it, even now. Perhaps Maria had been kidding him. You never could tell with Maria.

Dick entered a phone box, and hesitated between embarrassment and fear, a dilemma which he had to face every day. Fear of Maria won, and he found himself dialling the Muswell Hill number after all, and trying not to breathe too heavily into the mouthpiece. Dick often seemed to have too much breath. It was another inconsiderate emanation of his. And since the thought about ménages it had begun to roll and billow like the Atlantic.

It was all over very quickly, however. A woman had answered: a stranger. Dick did not recognize her or need to identify himself. She simply gave him Izzy's new address and phone number. Dick did not need to write it down. It was instantly engraved on his memory, in the golden archive which also held every detail on Izzy's passport, at which he had once gazed for a whole hour whilst she slept. He had his own photograph of her, now – one he'd taken on a California beach. She was lying on her stomach, propped up on her elbows, reading a book. It had been a French book by someone called Colette. Just Colette. A bit rum, that, Dick had thought. Surely only good-time girls abandoned their surnames? Ah well – it only added to the peculiar piquancy of the situation. Dick fished the photo out of his wallet and stared at it with renewed anguish.

He'd had to lie flat on his stomach to take the photo. He remembered the feeling of sand under his arms, and how he'd had to lie there for ten minutes afterwards, thinking hard about the Industrial Revolution, before it was safe to get up again. There she was, captured for ever in all her majesty. Slick lips and slanty eyes, with the ocean all behind her, as if she'd just been cast up out of it. Dick's entire phone booth steamed up. His hands shook. His throat went dry. His ears popped. He had to ring her up, just to hear her voice again. He dialled;

though his heart was hammering so loud, he could scarcely hear the far-away sound of Izzy's phone, ringing.

The phone rang then clicked, and then a housewifely voice burst upon Dick's ears 'COURSE I SAID TO HER NO WAY, IRENE, THAT'S JUST NOT ON. AND IF IT WAS DOWN TO ME, I'D TELL HIM STRAIGHT – THAT SORT OF THING JUST WON'T WASH. Dick replaced the receiver hurriedly. His second attempt to contact Izzy produced a mind-numbing electronic shriek and·then profound silence. Crikey! Had he broken the phone? For a moment he thought he'd better ring the operator and report the fault, but the phone was too sick even to report itself sick. Dick fled guiltily from the phone box. He was sure his breath had done it. He would just have to take a chance and go and see Izzy at her new place. And he would buy some mints on the way.

It was easy to find: soon he was on the doorstep. Izzy's new flat. It seemed awfully grand. Timidly he rang the bell. The door opened. Dick cringed, but a handsome woman of uncertain years beamed at him. Dick felt as near to encouragement as he ever dared. All the same, an Extra-Strong Mint had paralyzed his tongue.

'Is – is – iz Izzy in?' he enquired. 'I'm Dick Barnes.'

'Dick!' shrieked the woman, her face breaking into an astonishing smile, 'Do come in! Your wife's just been telling us how wonderful you are!'

I SMELL FALSE LATIN

Do come in. Dick followed her, but only literally. Had she said something about his wife? His *wife*? He must have misheard. Unless there was another Dick Barnes somewhere: a married, wonderful one. Dick found himself in a drawing room of surpassing elegance. Yes. He was definitely in the other Dick Barnes's shoes. Then who should bounce up at him but Izzy, her face – unless his eyes deceived him – *radiant with delight.*

'Hello, darling! How are you?'

She threw her arms around him and kissed him rapturously on the beard, nose and ear. Dick was beginning to wonder if he'd got fantasy and reality seriously mixed up. He was dumbfounded, but submitted to her embrace without a word. If he spoke, it might break the spell. Indeed Izzy didn't seem to want him to speak. She seized his hand so very urgently that Dick divined that he should simply hold on tight and say nothing.

'I've just been telling Aunt Vinny and Michael about our wedding in San Francisco!' she trilled. Dick's heart gave a palsied leap. Half-a-bathful of adrenalin shot up the back of his legs with such ferocity he was afraid he might drown. He tried to grin. A grin must be appropriate, surely. If he had somehow married Izzy without noticing, a grin would conceal the surprise. And if this was, as he suspected, some sort of tasteless mickey-taking, a dignified grin would protect him from ridicule.

'We had the most wonderful honeymoon in the hills, didn't we, Dick?'

There was a sudden silence. Dick seemed to be required, now, to assent. He reached for his tongue. It had gone.

'Most – wonderful. Aye.'

'Oh, I'm sorry – Dick, this is Louise's Aunt Vinny – she's very kindly offered us her garden flat. Downstairs. Isn't that wonderful?'

It was all a bit too wonderful, actually. Dick suspected he was lying in a hospital somewhere, violently ill, and this was an anaesthetic dream out of which he would soon awake. All the same, he struggled to make sense of his surroundings.

'What – a flat to live in now, like?'

'Yes! It's lovely! I'll show you in a minute.'

Michael got up and offered his hand. 'Congratulations, Dick, old man,' he smiled. 'You're a very lucky fellow. The envy of millions. The man who tamed Izzy Comyn. Who brought her ashore. What a catch!'

Perhaps the plane did crash after all, thought Dick. Perhaps I am dead and this is heaven.

'Oh, do sit down, Dick,' said Aunt Vinny. 'I'm longing to hear how your family are. Izzy has told me all about them. How's your mother?'

'Fine, thanks,' said Dick warily, sitting down upon the kind of chair he had only previously seen in costume dramas on TV.

'She's evidently a very gifted person.'

Dick floundered. 'Gifted? Who?'

'Your *mum*, stupid,' hissed Izzy, giving his shoulder a playful tap.

'Aye, well,' Dick shrugged. 'She's, well – you know. I wouldn't say gifted, exactly.'

'I suppose she takes it all for granted, does she?' persisted Aunt Vinny. 'Lives a very ordinary life.'

'Oh yes. Very ordinary.' Dick felt safe for a split second.

'All the same, it must be a very inspiring thing, to have a gift like that.'

'A – um, gift?'

'I was telling Aunt Vinny,' hastened Izzy, 'about your Mum and how she's psychic. You know. Does séances and things.'

Dick was struck dumb. 'Séances?'

'You know, Dick. Those meetings she goes to. Table-tapping and stuff. Messages from the beyond.' Dick stared. 'You *know*, Dick.' Izzy gave him another, slightly more dislocatory, tap on the shoulder. Izzy's eyes seemed big with fear.

'Oh, that,' he responded at last to her silent plea. 'That's right. She's always been – er – psychedelic,' he faltered.

'Psychic!'

'Yeah, well, you know. We never took much interest in it ourselves.'

'And how's Margaret?' pounced Aunt Vinny.

For a moment Dick thought she must be talking to somebody else. But she was looking straight at him and obviously expecting an answer. Now, this was a new dimension in social confusion. He could take references to his mum's psychic powers. After all, he did have a mum and for aught he knew, she might indeed have psychic powers. But this – Margaret? Who was she? He looked anxiously at Izzy, desperate for a sign.

'Is she still running the fish and chip shop?' hissed Izzy. Dick clutched at this straw.

'Oh yes. Very much so. Fish and chips. Yes.'

'And has she found a new boyfriend yet?'

New boyfriend. Now what did this mean? It must mean, surely, that this Margaret was an ex-girlfriend of his. Dick shrugged. In a world where Izzy could somehow miraculously be his wife, there was plenty of room for an ex-girlfriend. Several.

By now he had begun to accept his total lack of information. It was only a monstrous exaggeration of his ordinary everyday struggle to make sense of life. Perhaps, like Rumplestiltskin, he had slept through a vital week or two. Perhaps he'd been in a coma for a while, sort of standing up, and no one had noticed. Dick wouldn't put it past himself. He would embrace this Margaret or ex-Margaret with enthusiasm. Had she got a new boyfriend yet?

'No,' he admitted at length. 'I think it'll be a bit longer before she's ready.'

'Well, quite. Poor thing!' Aunt Vinny clearly sympathized. He was obviously doing OK. He relaxed a little. Became expansive.

'Mind you, I felt a bit of a brute, having to finish with her like that.' Dick was beginning to enjoy himself. 'She were so mad about me, like. But it wouldn't do.'

A horrid silence fell. Aunt Vinny went pale. Izzy went red. Dick stalled. He'd said something dreadfully wrong, but he hadn't the faintest idea what. He faltered, and crashed down into panic again. Back to normal, in other words. His brief moment of relaxation was over. But at least he'd managed one, today.

The silence deepened. It was a shocked, sick silence. Dick looked at his shoes, and envied them. They did not have to use their tongues.

'Not *that* Margaret, Dick,' spluttered Izzy at last, 'the *other* Margaret. Your *sister*!'

'Ah. That Margaret.' Dick fell silent. He had run out of adrenalin. Michael stood up with a deep sigh.

'Fascinating though this saga of crypto-incest is, dear people, I must be on my way.'

'Lovely to see you again, Michael,' said Izzy, with a hint of suppliance. They must part friends.

'And lovely to see you so charmingly married at last,' sneered Michael. 'I know a lot of chaps who'll breathe more easily to know you're safely out of harm's way, Miss Comyn – or is it Mrs Barnes?' He hurt her with his eyes. Izzy was surprised that Michael could still hurt her like this. But he had been provoked.

Michael withdrew, and even Aunt Vinny began to clear up and give vague signs of departure.

'You two lovebirds will want to be alone,' she cooed as she went. 'Don't mind me. I'm going to have my bath.'

She went upstairs; they went down. Izzy led Dick into a very smart flat. The dream was still going on. There appeared to be only one bed – a double one. Dick nearly fainted. Was this real? *Were* they married? Him and Izzy, alone together in this inescapably matrimonial flat? Dick's whole being tingled with excruciating happiness. Tears burst from his eyes and bespangled his beard. Izzy turned to him: her glorious face uplifted to his. It was Dick's moment of supreme joy.

'My God, Dick, what a nightmare!' she whispered. 'I think I'm going to be sick!'

TO LOCK THE LITTLE GATE

Michael drove home with a sour and angry feeling flooding through him even to the fingertips. Married! To that clown! It was as if she'd done it on purpose to vex him. For a moment he experienced again the sense that Izzy was, in some parallel life, his teenage daughter. Or rather a rehearsal for one. In a mere thirteen years he would be experiencing the horrors of the real thing. Earlier, probably. Girls would become teenagers at the age of nine, by then. He struggled to imagine Izzy as a married woman and somehow couldn't get to grips with the concept at all. His chest felt knotted with rage. How could she have said those things about him – and in public? Michael and Izzy had never had much in the way of rows, so the recent interview was as strange as painful.

Pursuing his violent feelings to their source, Michael discovered that it was Izzy's remarks about Dick being a much better lover that really stuck in his gullet. Surely she couldn't be serious? She couldn't have . . . *meant* it? What, Dick? Michael sank suddenly into complete misery, holed beneath the waterline. Yes. It was true. He'd always feared it. He'd read all the books, he'd taken on board the whole philosophy, nobody had been more passionately opposed than he to the brutal world of machismo. Of wham-bam. Michael had prided himself on his exquisite lingerings. On his atmospheric slownesses and curlicues and refinements. On his breathings upon pulse-points. And all the time – she'd been bored!

The little cow! If he'd known how publicly she was going to spurn him, to hurl into contempt his pathetic attempts to give her and the rest of her fellow she-devils pleasure, he'd never have bothered in the first place. He'd have released the stone-age thug that slumbered beneath his Fair Isle pullover and fallen on her like a ton of rock. Michael hoped there was a stone-age thug slumbering there, anyway. You couldn't be a real man these days unless you were ready for anything – ready to look angry in the right brand of jeans, to drive your car at 90 mph down twisting mountain tracks, to drink the beer that reached the parts which sissies didn't even possess. Or . . . was he a secret sissy, too?

He made a right turn with an astonishing lack of care, and was followed by a blare of horns as he sped away into more traffic. A hot flush washed over him. Was this the male menopause? He blushed again at the very thought. He'd avoided a pile-up, then, by inches. He shouldn't drive when he was in this state. Women shouldn't be allowed to insult men: to cast aspersions upon their holiest and most sacred abilities. It was bound to lead to bad motoring. Michael sighed deeply. He was haunted by the feeling that he was driving back to prison after what should have been a moment of escape, but had instead turned into a different form of torture of its own.

He wasn't sure what exactly he'd been hoping for, from Izzy. Perhaps just a break from the shape and smell of his own house, which the tiny Empress had claimed as her kingdom the moment she'd arrived. Perhaps just an amusing half-hour with a woman who still looked her best (although she had put on a little weight in San Francisco, Michael didn't mind). Perhaps a tender reminiscence about times past, with all the consciousness that the world had moved on since then and things could never be the same again.— Or *could they*?

Michael's silly old heart gave a feeble skip. Since Izzy had been away in San Francisco, he'd given in more and more to day-dreams about their naughty past, ignoring the more recent falling out of love and the remarkable tripartite friendship which had succeeded it. Izzy may have felt she'd grown up and away from all that, but

Michael could still slump into nostalgia about the early days. Mature friendship may have been sensible and right and inspiring, but it wasn't exactly the stuff that dreams are made of. The more Michael thought wistfully about the excitements of his affair with Izzy, the more his heart rekindled and yearned. He'd begun to feel that love can spring into leaf again, no matter how gnarled and woody the heart.

What's more, he was living through an era not very encouraging to philanderers. Michael had grown up in the sexy sixties and seduced his way steadily through the sensual seventies, but things had changed now. Every morning he looked at his tongue in the mirror with renewed anxiety. He often grabbed a take-away these days, and when he got an attack of post-curry diarrhoea, he became unduly alarmed. Was it just the usual, or something sinister? He coughed, even now, an unusually painful cough. What was this? He never coughed. Stopped in some traffic, Michael coughed again. Was it some odd bits of bile, with which his system had been flooded during the worst of Izzy's hurtful remarks? Or was it the beginning of the end?

Michael thought once more of all the women with whom he had been entangled. St Augustine would have approved of the regret with which Michael surveyed his past. But the regret was mingled with most un-Christian terror, panic and the desire for self-preservation. What about Victoria? Hadn't she been about a bit? How *could* she? Michael shuddered. The fact that he had been about a bit himself was neither here nor there. And Theresa. Michael had been introduced to one of her ex-boyfriends once, and been secretly appalled, even at the time, to learn that he was bisexual. It was no use telling Michael, as Theresa had tried, that Shakespeare was probably bisexual, and Leonardo da Vinci, and Oscar Wilde.

Michael was a simple creature when it came to the mating game. He repressed certain memories of his public-school past as only natural, only a passing phase.

The world was composed of two forces, male and female: they fused to form a whole. Anything outside this rather uncompromising view of human passion, was incomprehensible to him. People had often told him that his inability to face up to such things was evidence of his suppressed fear of his own homosexuality. He had guffawed particularly heartily at such times, even though normally his laugh was more of a titter and his manner could be the highest of camp. Perhaps Michael did not want to face up to the possibility of his homosexuality because, given the large number of desirable women in the world, he felt he was rather pushed as it was.

Not that he was pursuing any desirable women at the moment. Since the Izzy business he had been a model husband. Now, a mixture of paternal fatigue and hypochondria kept him to the straight and narrow. Hence his increasing fantasies about Izzy. Apart from anything else, she was one of the few women in his past who hadn't mixed with high-risk groups. Although her year in San Francisco brought with it a frisson of fear. However, Michael reassured himself, there were reports – he'd read them in the reputable newspapers – that in San Francisco the reporting of new cases of Aids had dwindled to almost nothing. The safe-sex campaign had had results. All the same, Michael hoped that Izzy hadn't been indulging in any sex out there, however safe. Because – he now realized with a jolt – he had plans for her.

Better the devil you know, nowadays. Old flames were being re-kindled all over Europe, and Michael was more than happy to join in. As he drove through St John's Wood he began to feel more cheerful. St John's Wood can have this effect, though, alas, it has little to do with St John. Michael's bile seemed to have dispersed – he had probably coughed it up – and he reproached himself for his panic and rage. He must become civilized again. She had been lying. She'd said it just to upset him. She'd never complained in the past; indeed, she had complimented him on his amorous exertions. It had all been a storm in a tea-cup. Yes. Michael had regained his benevolence. His humanity. His dignity. He began to lay plans to seduce a married woman, one of his wife's best friends: his own very dear old flame.

This marriage to Dick was, in some respects, a good thing. If Izzy had married someone marvellous, how much worse things would have been. Imagine her simpering on the arm of an Ian Botham or a Daley Thompson, a Tom Stoppard or a Bob Geldorf. Then indeed Michael would have been suffused with a sense of his own inadequacies. Izzy would not have had to cast slurs upon his manhood. His ego would have been well and truly scrambled. His hand would have gone limp within her husband's mighty clasp. His knees would have buckled. His brain would have withered. He would not have dared even to recall the merest wink that had passed between him and the wife of one of these gods.

But Dick! – Why, it was almost a duty to cuckold him. He was one of Nature's cuckolds. You could tell that just by looking at him. Yes, it was Nature's plan. Michael was not executing any private desires in this case: he was merely the disengaged channel of universal energy. Nature's secret agent. It was a preposterous marriage: everyone could see that. Even Dick must recognize it. Why, he was probably longing to be cuckolded, so that he could once again make sense within Nature's plan. Michael was filled with sympathetic concern for poor Dick. Dick must not be cast against type like this. He could not be expected to play the Duke. Dick was, irrevocably, the Dupe.

Where would they meet? Izzy's old bachelor flat had certainly been convenient. Izzy's new abode had the added irritant of Aunt Vinny, who seemed to have taken such an unreasonable shine to Dick. Michael and Izzy might manage to get together there, at a moment when Dick was away on a course. Michael wondered if Dick was quite aware of how much his life would be enhanced by a few courses in Newcastle-upon-Tyne. But wouldn't Aunt

Vinny pounce and invite them both to more tea – endless cups of tea, all immaculately chaperoned, stretching from here to eternity?

Michael's mind fled to a hot, summer railway station. Somewhere in Kent or Hampshire where the wheat grows tall and the apple orchards dapple the long grass. Here they would frolic in their stolen hours, and then return separately to the metropolis, like secret agents with complicated alibis and that curious little spiral of excitement within that accompanies the inevitable deceit of adultery. They might even rent a cottage, a thatched cottage deep in the lanes, a cottage flooded by golden light and with nightingales singing in the eaves, to which, from time to time, they would repair to knit themselves more closely into their erotic tapestry.

Michael parked the car outside his house, switched off the engine, and sighed. He dawdled up the path, savouring the last shreds of fantasy. He would send Izzy flowers, to make amends for his bad behaviour. To heal the wounds caused by the row. But wait! – What would Dick say to that? Sending flowers to Dick's wife? He'd send them anonymously. She'd know who they were from. And then, after a few days' wait, Michael would go and see her. Just drop in casually. Just happen-to-be-passing. That's when it would all begin. In the eyes.

Michael turned the key in his front door and was faced with an extraordinary tableau: Louise had washed her hair, and it framed her face with a kind of amber glow. She was wearing one of her floaty dresses, and smiling in a touchingly hopeful way into his face. She carried Rose, and as Michael bent down to greet the little creature, Rose suddenly beamed up at him with all the seductive power in her tiny gums. Michael caught mother and daughter in a fierce embrace, and hid his shame in their warmth.

That night Michael slept in the matrimonial bed: it was Saturday tomorrow. No work. Rose snored in her Moses basket beside the bed. Louise fell asleep suddenly on her back, like someone dying. With a shock Michael realized that his wife would die, indeed, one day. Perhaps just like this, without any warning, lying beside him. He felt a wave of panic. He had never treated Louise as she deserved to be treated. He'd been semiconsciously postponing it for later on, when he'd have more time. When he'd slowed down generally. Then he had been intending to lavish his love and attention upon her: to get to know her, to rejoice in her, to make up for years of deceit.

His lies had put up a barrier between them all these years. It was as if Louise existed beside him, but somehow in another dimension: breathing other air. He saw her dimly through a window. As she lay now beautifully serene, the clear bones of her face exposed as the flesh fell away sideways towards the earth, he saw with panic that he didn't have forever. She had never been more tired, or needed him more. And even now, although he wasn't actually deceiving her, he had been planning to. That very day, driving home, he'd wallowed in the most depraved scenarios. Michael's self-disgust at this moment was too deep for groans. The gentle breaths of his wife, and the snortlings of his child, reproached him, guiltily awake. They were like figures on a tomb. Michael gazed at them in horror, perceiving them all at once as perfect, at peace with themselves. Whilst he, awake, wrestled with serpents.

He lay on his back and stared at the ceiling. Now was the moment. He had felt guilt and disgust at himself before: had reformed, temporarily, for a few months, but then – Michael sighed. He had taken refuge in an idea of himself as impossibly romantic, hot-headed, impulsive. *The guy can't help it.* Terribly flattering, really, that kind of weakness. So dynamic, so human, so interesting to be at the mercy of one's emotions. To be defenceless before the overwhelming power of Eros. What codswallop. Izzy had got it about right, today, when she was telling Aunt Vinny about her 'previous lover'. What had she called him? 'Unspeakably vile'? No, that was not it. 'An utter swine'! Exactly.

'Oh, Juno,' prayed Michael, lying on his back and gazing at the ceiling. 'You're the Goddess of marriage, aren't you? For God's sake give me a hand. I've never addressed you before, as you very well know, but even an utter swine can see the light in the end.'

Juno appeared upon the ceiling. She was wearing an awful hat and was clearly on the way to a Women's Institute jam and cakes stall. Michael winced. But this was where his duty lay.

'Dear Madam,' he murmured, 'I've had a lot of trouble up to now with a couple of colleagues of yours. Venus and Cupid. Eros and Aphrodite. Call them what you will, but they've more or less ruined my life and undermined my marriage.' Juno looked extremely disapproving. 'I just thought it was worth asking,' Michael went on, with a curious feeling that he was somehow addressing the Prime Minister, 'if you could do anything to blunt his arrows – to help me to resist. I'm determined, you see, to commit myself to my marriage from now on. To worship this fine woman who lies asleep at my side. The mother of my children. But years of utter swinehood have coarsened my moral sensibility, dear lady. Give me the strength to stick to the straight and narrow, for Christ's sake.'

It was crude, but it was heartfelt. And at least it was ecumenical.

A LOVER'S EYES

'Right, Dick,' whispered Izzy. She still wasn't entirely convinced that she could speak normally in her flat without being overheard by Aunt Vinny on the floor above. Even now, though Aunt Vinny was having a bath on the floor above that, Izzy had put some Glenn Miller on to cover the sound of her urgent instructions to Dick. Who knows, perhaps the place was bugged. Perhaps Aunt Vinny was some kind of voyeur. Perhaps even now they were on closed-circuit TV, their every nuance effortlessly relayed to the great lady as she luxuriated in the steaming foam of horse-chestnut oil. That's how Izzy felt, anyway. Watched.

'It's all very simple, really. There's this lovely flat. Well, it is wonderful, isn't it?'

'Oh – ah – er, yes. Smashing.'

'Well, it just sort of – fell into my lap, Dick.'

'Crikey!'

'Yes. You see, Aunt Vinny – the lady upstairs – is Louise's aunt. Louise and Michael put me on to her, and she just, well, just sort of seemed to like me.'

'Well,' faltered Dick, tempted towards a compliment but lacking quite enough nerve, 'well, of course, Izzy. I mean, you know.'

'The trouble is, though, she wanted a married couple to live here.'

'Ah.'

'So I . . . well, I hope you don't think it's – you see, I pretended we were married, sort of thing. I hope you don't mind, Dick.'

'Er – no, of course I don't, Izzy. It's a – a pleasure.'

Izzy panicked and pounced. She had to make it absolutely clear that it wasn't going to be that much of a pleasure.

'Well, after all, we were flatmates in San Francisco, Dick. I think we know each other pretty well.'

'Oh yes. Definitely.'

'Well, then – if you don't mind sleeping on the sofa – I think we'll be very comfortable here.' Dick looked round doubtfully.

'Isn't it a bit – expensive, though?' he asked.

'Ah! Yes. Well. I was coming to that. It won't be all that expensive, split between the two of us. And anyway, it's only temporary, isn't it, Dick? Just to give ourselves plenty of time to look for somewhere better. Cheaper, that is. Only it's so awful, trying to find somewhere to live in London. You know. So I thought you might like a kind of – well, launching pad, sort of thing.'

Dick did not dare to ask again how much it cost. If Izzy couldn't bring herself to mention it, it must be astronomical. All the same, Dick was a frugal soul and could easily live on stale bread and the occasional tin of baked beans. And really, the flat was so pretty and comfortable, and the situation appealed so much to his imagination, that even if it ruined him financially, it would be worth it just for a while. To be Izzy's husband! Introduced as such. Known to be. It made him swell with pride.

'Aye, well, I think it's great,' he concluded. 'So all I have to do is pretend to be your husband, like?'

'Yes, Dick. That's all. Think you can do it?'

'I don't rightly know. I've not had much experience. What's it like, being married?'

'Search me, Dick. I haven't been either, you know.'

'Oh. That's right. Well, I suppose – you won't mind if I – well, I suppose I'll have to – put me arm round you now and then, in public?'

Izzy was alarmed. Dick had a look in his eye. 'Well, maybe you should. Only make it – well, everso casual, you know. Automatic, sort of thing.'

Dick wondered if he would ever be able to put his arm round Izzy in a casual, automatic sort of way. Would she mind if he had some practice? Right now, for a start? His arm twitched in an ecstasy of anticipation.

'Mind you,' he went on, propelled by an increasing enthusiasm for the project, 'you did say that we'd only just been married, didn't you? Whilst we were in the States, you know.'

'Yes, Dick. What are you driving at?'

Izzy knew very well what Dick was driving at. He could be really irritating at times. Especially when he had ideas and tried to initiate things. Especially this sort of thing. Izzy did not like his tone. She required of him that he live with her as her husband, enacting all the duties of a husband but experiencing none of the pleasures. Actually, that's what a lot of real wives expect, too, come to think of it.

'Well, if we've only just got married, like,' persisted Dick, 'maybe we should – well, hold hands when we go out. Just as far as the corner, you know. And maybe I should kiss you goodbye.'

Maybe you jolly well should, thought Izzy, trying to keep a bright smile going. 'Of course, Dick. Now and then. Not too often. Mustn't act suspiciously.'

'But aren't we supposed to be on our – well, honeymoon, if you know what I mean?'

'No we are not! Don't be silly, Dick.'

'Sorry.'

'We probably got married – oh, months ago. We had our honeymoon in the hills. You remember.'

'Which hills?'

'Oh, I don't know. There are plenty of hills in California, for goodness sake.'

'We'd better have our story worked out well in advance, though,' Dick was really getting into the swing of things. He'd got the bit between his teeth. He was in a real-life ripping yarn, just like those in the *Boys' Own Paper*. Only with marital overtones. 'If we start contradicting each other it'll be a bit, well, suspicious, won't it?'

'Just don't say anything, Dick.'

'But I have to sometimes. When she asks me, for instance. Like about my mother being psychic and all that. I mean, Izzy,' he fixed her with a stern eye. By his standards, anyway. 'You might have warned me.'

'How could I warn you, you fool? You were in sodding Worksop!'

'Well, that wasn't my fault. You could have rung me.'

'I couldn't! You never gave me your number!'

'I did! I gave it to you in San Francisco!'

'You didn't, Dick!'

'I did, Izzy! Honestly, I did! It's not my fault if you lost it!'

'I did not lose it! And stop saying it isn't your fault!'

'Well, it isn't, Izzy. Honestly! Be reasonable!'

Glenn Miller stopped. There was a sudden silence. The silence extended vertically: the pipes had stopped growling and Aunt Vinny, seated in her tranquil bath, must have heard their raised voices.

'Hey!' Izzy whispered, with a giggle. 'We've just had our first matrimonial row, Dick! Isn't it funny!'

'I suppose – that's right,' faltered Dick. He didn't much relish this aspect of matrimony, preferring the hand-holding and the kiss goodbye. But he could see that the odd row would give them a little extra credibility.

'What else did you say about my family?' he ventured.

'Oh, I can't remember. I said you had lots of brothers and sisters. And two of your brothers work in a coffee mill.'

'A coffee mill?' Dick looked perplexed. 'I thought that was, like a kitchen gadget, sort of thing. To grind coffee beans.'

Izzy gasped. 'Crumbs, that's right! So it is! I thought she looked at me a bit strangely. Still, she seemed to swallow it. To tell you the truth, Dick, I think she's led such a sheltered life, you could tell her anything, and she'd believe it.'

'Do you really think so? I thought she was rather – well, rather frightening, myself.'

Izzy knew that this was true. Deep in her subconscious, she had a fear of upsetting or offending Aunt Vinny – a terror of her disapproval. And not only deep in her subconscious. Fairly high in her conscious, too.

Aunt Vinny's doorbell rang. Izzy thought she'd better go, since Aunt Vinny was probably still in the bath.

'Remember, Dick – you're my husband,' she hissed, pausing at the door. 'So jolly well act like one!'

Dick looked terrified. Izzy ran upstairs in a fit of irritation. She was beginning to wonder if this was such a good idea. She opened the front door, and there stood Charles Armstrong.

God, he was handsome. She hadn't had a chance to get a really good look at him last time, having had to flee to the bathroom to hide her nakedness. So she had a good look now. His hair was fair and smoothed back immaculately as in pre-war films. His eyes were the misty grey of English skies after rain. They had little speckles in them, like the markings of a bird's egg. And so did his tweed suit: a brownish-green, effortlessly authentic ensemble. And his smile! It seemed to light up the whole street. Behind him, the trees of Worcester Road shimmered in the sunlight. Izzy blinked at all this beauty. Even his glasses were attractive. They were horn-rimmed and made him look like an intellectual of the 1930s.

'Good morning!' he beamed. 'How very delightful to see you again. And I really must apologize for my intrusion the other day.'

Izzy blushed. 'Oh, no, not at all,' she stammered. 'It was my fault, really. I shouldn't have – well, er, you know. Oh dear. How embarrassing.'

'Forgive me! Very thoughtless of me to allude to it. I do beg your pardon.'

'Oh, no, it's all right,' Izzy somehow felt more naked than the first time. 'Anyway, do come in. Aunt Vinny is in the bath.'

'It's all right. I'll wait.'

'Oh no, do come down to – to our flat. Have a cup of tea or coffee or something.'

'Love to!'

Izzy led him downstairs, pleasure and embarrassment at war within her. She ushered him into the living room, where Dick was sitting at the table, paralyzed by awkwardness and trying to look as married as possible.

'This,' she said with a sense of desperate inconvenience, 'is my – my husband, Dick. Dick Barnes.'

'Delighted!' Charles advanced on Dick with his hand extended. Dick wasn't sure what husbands did in such circumstances, but he recognized an air of social superiority when he saw it and scrambled to his feet They shook hands. *At least Dick's hands are all right*, thought Izzy desperately.

'Pleased to meet you,' said Dick, and even as he said it, Izzy remembered reading somewhere that *pleased to meet you* was common. She was furious with Dick. But Charles seemed genuinely at ease, and charmed.

'Very good to meet you at last,' he smiled. 'May I sit down?'

'Oh – er, yes, please! Do,' concluded Dick, aware that the husband must take initiatives. 'Would you like a – something to drink?'

'How kind. That would be lovely. Anything you like. What you're having.'

'Tea?' asked Izzy. 'Earl Grey?'

She was aware that it sounded a bit like a form of address.

'Splendid,' said Charles.

Izzy hesitated. The men both looked at her as if they expected her to go away and put the kettle on. Now, if she'd been alone, Charles might have followed her into the kitchen and started a promising little *tête à tête*. As it was, he was bound to stay put for man-talk with Dick. Izzy was beginning to find her marriage something of a millstone. She went to put the kettle on, though. She thought it might upset Charles if she told Dick to do it. He seemed so terribly, well, old-fashioned, somehow.

'I hope you're comfortable?' she heard Charles ask Dick, in a semi-proprietary, landlordly sort of way.

'C-comfortable?' gasped Dick. He did have some dim theoretical understanding of the word. 'Oh, yes. Very. It's – it's very nice, the flat.'

Nice, thought Izzy. *I'm sure that's another of those vulgar words.* Nothing Dick could say would please her, today. He was irrevocably wrong.

'You've just got back from America, I believe?'

'Well, Worksop, actually. Well, America before that. San Francisco, in fact. When we got back – back to England, that is – I went up to see my folks, in, well, in Worksop, whilst my – my wife—' Dick hesitated at his own temerity. It sounded loud and preposterously wrong. *Did* husbands refer to their wives as *my wife*? Surely not. '— she stayed in London.'

Charles seemed fascinated by this piece of rather undistinguished information.

'Never been to the West Coast myself,' he confessed. 'What's it like?'

Ah, thought Izzy, waiting for the kettle to boil, *we're on safe ground here. Dick surely must be able to waffle on about the States without putting his foot in it.*

'Ah. San Francisco. Well, it's – it's not easy to generalize.' It wasn't easy to particularize either, as far as Dick was concerned. 'It's – you know, very prosperous, like.'

Izzy was mortified at the mention of money.

'A bit materialistic?'

'Aye. Right. Big cars and that. More money than sense.'

Oh no, he's fallen back on his proverbs now. Whatever next? Where there's muck there's brass?

'And, well, you know – where there's brass, there's muck.' Dick was quite pleased with this. Even Izzy was rather surprised.

'A lot of crime, and so forth? Corruption, I expect.'

'Oh, yes,' said Dick. 'Terrific corruption out there. And

drugs. Not that we saw much of that,' he added hastily. 'We're a bit old-fashioned, you see.'

Speak for yourself, Dick, you nit-wit, thought Izzy, carrying in the tea tray with what she hoped was a discreetly ravishing smile. Charles's air of old-fashioned charm was one thing: Dick's distinctly shop-soiled second-hand manners were quite another. *We're a bit old-fashioned*, indeed! It was an unpleasant novelty to hear him characterizing her like that. As if they were a sort of team. Two of a kind. She supposed that kind of thing happened all the time when you were married. It was terrible. Why did anybody stay married for more than a week? She set down the tray, and straightening up, caught Charles's eyes looking directly into hers.

'How splendid. Thanks so much,' he said quickly. But she was unnerved. What did wives say and do? How did they converse with strangers? What happened when they . . . caught someone's eye?

'What were you doing in California, actually?' Charles saved her with more conversation. He had an elegant enquiry for every awkward pause, it seemed.

'We're teachers,' she explained, falling into the *two of a kind* trap herself. 'We were on an exchange. A year's exchange, from our school. We teach in Islington. At a comprehensive.'

'Do you really? Good Lord, how admirable! Isn't it a bit wearing?'

'Oh yes, it's wearing,' conceded Izzy. 'But, well, you've got to earn a living somehow.' She began to wonder what Charles did. Perhaps he didn't have to do anything. Perhaps he had a private income.

'And you both teach at the same school?'

'Yes. We do.'

'That must be jolly convenient. And pleasant.'

'Sometimes it's awful,' Izzy blurted out, on the wings of a rogue impulse. 'We get sick of the sight of each other, don't we, Dick?' Dick looked startled. But before he had time to disagree, she swept on.

'I think it's much better for husbands and wives to work

in separate places. Otherwise you're on top of each other all the time. I see Dick in the morning, Dick all day and Dick all night. Dick, Dick, Dick. Nothing but Dick.'

Dick went pale.

'I hadn't thought of it that way, I admit,' said Charles. 'Perhaps one of you should change jobs.'

'Yes. Dick's wasted in the classroom,' Izzy gabbled in a surge of guilt. 'He's an absolute wizard with his hands,' she confided to Charles, hoping it did not sound too filthy. 'He can put up shelves like anything. And make things, you know.'

'Lucky fellow!' smiled Charles. 'I'm completely cack-handed, myself. Luckily I'm not married, so I haven't had to disappoint anyone over the shelf problem, yet.'

Luckily not married. The words went through Izzy like a spear. Was he gay? She doubted it, though his charm might hide a world of unexpected inclinations. Not married. Izzy's mind was correctly indifferent to this information, but her body was determined to be excited. It seethed and throbbed. Izzy told it to go and lie in its basket. But it was not well trained, and ignored her.

'What do you do, Charles?' she asked. Being married gave you a peculiar freedom, in a way. You could be bold where otherwise you would feel awkward and coy. Casual where normally you would be all agog. Actually, Izzy was terrifically agog, at this moment. But being married gave her the manner to hide it.

'I'm in architectural salvage,' he said.

'Crikey!' said Dick. 'You mean – like, raise *The Titanic*?' The *pillock*.

'Don't be silly, Dick!' snapped Izzy, although she wasn't entirely sure, herself, what architectural whoss-name involved. 'It sounds fascinating!'

'Well, I'm more or less obsessed by it,' grinned Charles charmingly. 'Have been ever since I was a kid. Never happier than when I'm poking about on demolition sites. Grabbing old Georgian fireplaces from the rubble, you know.'

'How marvellous, to be able to immerse yourself in the past like that,' Izzy glowed at him. 'To – well, actually save it physically with your bare hands!'

Charles gave her a particularly caressing look – the sort of glance which he normally reserved for elm floorboards.

'I have to admit I'm an absolute sucker for the past.'

'Oh so am I!' Izzy was glad that her recent smiles had not been too unequivocally modern. She was grateful, now, for Dick's having introduced them as old-fashioned. But what effect would all this nostalgia have on Charles's morals? Would he prove to be an embodiment of Victorian family values? What palpitations were permitted beneath that very distinguished tweed?

'Mind you,' Charles went on, addressing himself to the husband now, aware that he needed to remind himself of the husband's existence. 'I don't believe in ivory towers.'

'Oh no,' Dick concurred, not quite sure what an ivory tower was. Perhaps it was something which Charles salvaged. Although Dick had a vague memory that it was something to do with Oxford and Cambridge.

'We've got the whole business on computer. It makes sense.'

'Course it does,' agreed Dick stoutly. 'Computers. Aye. These days.'

'I have to admit I have a weakness for computers,' smiled Charles wryly, with a confessional glance at Izzy. She smiled encouragingly. Charles's weaknesses were a good sign. 'I play with mine for hours. Little boys' toys, I suppose.'

'Aye,' said Dick eagerly. 'I'd like to get my hands on one of them Amstrads.'

'You must come over to my place sometime and play with mine,' smiled Charles, including Izzy in the invitation. Dick asked Charles something about disc drives, and Charles began to rhapsodize about compatibilities. Izzy was getting a bit tired of all this man-talk. She was still frightened of word processors. And food processors. The whole idea of processing something was alien to her soul.

A process suggested organization: imposing your will on recalcitrant material. Izzy's way of getting through life relied on improvisation and bluff. She hoped Charles did not prove too terribly committed to due processes.

'But I'm afraid all these technicalities are terribly boring,' concluded Charles, with a sympathetic smile. 'And my job's not nearly so worthwhile as teaching. I mean, I just collect objects. But teachers have got the future of the world in their hands.'

'Izzy teaches drama,' said Dick proudly, as if there was something especially glamorous about it. Charles gazed at her admiringly. If only Dick would go away.

There he sat, gazing matrimonially at her. He was developing an air of real proprietorship already. It made her sick. How dare he? Charles Armstrong – and this was extraordinary – actually *thought they were man and wife*. He'd accepted it totally. Swallowed it whole. Izzy shuddered. How dare Dick be uxorious all over her? She felt attacked by little pin-pricks of rage. But she had to keep smiling sweetly.

'Drama? Really?' Charles was fascinated. 'I wish I'd had drama at school.'

'Well, the kids always run towards the drama lesson,' Izzy admitted, letting drama take the credit. Charles settled into a steady gaze that entered at her eyes and trickled all down inside, like rain getting in at the window.

'Izzy's a bit of a favourite, you know,' boasted Dick. The ass! Why didn't he push off and put up some shelves or something? Izzy withered silently and stared at Charles's shoes. Even his shoes were remarkable. They were what she believed were called Oxford brogues. Brown, shiny and utterly self-confident. She sneaked a look at Dick's shoes. Ugh! Cheap basketball boots! Izzy had never before worried about Dick's choice of shoes. Now even these modest accessories seemed deliberately designed to infuriate her.

Charles said he was sure that Izzy was a favourite. Izzy didn't dare to look at him. She just smiled absently at the tabletop. She had never felt so totally ill at ease with a man before. She'd presented an execrable impression, she was sure: a sardonic nag. Married to a man who wore basketball boots and said *pleased to meet you*. Izzy's whole being groaned silently. She'd thought it was going to be fun, pretending to be married to Dick. This was the worst fun she'd ever had.

'Coo-ee!' Aunt Vinny's voice floated down the stairs. 'Have you got my favourite nephew down there?'

'Coming, Aunt Vinny!' called Charles, getting up with effortless elegance. 'Thanks so much for the tea. Lovely to meet you.'

It sounded so formal, so final. He must hate them. Izzy almost wept.

'Do drop in again,' she faltered. 'Any time.'

Charles tried to catch her eye for one last time, but she looked aside. He gave Dick a brief handshake and was gone up the stairs. Dick got up and carried the cups into the kitchen. Izzy sat marooned in misery, her chin in her hand.

'Well,' said Dick, coming back in with the dustpan and brush, for he had noticed some crumbs and was anxious to make his contribution to domestic harmony, 'he was a nice enough bloke, wasn't he?'

STREWING HER WAY WITH FLOWERS

Days passed. Gradually Izzy and Dick worked out a routine. Dick, who'd slept on the sofa, would get up early to avoid being caught neglecting his marital duties by Aunt Vinny, who continued to pop down at the most inconvenient moments. Izzy started using the side entrance, which was at basement level and led directly into the flat. This avoided the necessity of trespassing through Aunt Vinny's hall – although Aunt Vinny gave every indication of wishing to be disturbed. After taking Izzy her morning cup of tea, and having his own modest breakfast of All-Bran with condensed milk, Dick would tidy up the flat and go out. Nominally he was flat-hunting. But really he was just being considerate: letting Izzy have the place to herself for her morning getting-up rituals, which evolved slowly and gradually from 9 a.m.

Izzy got up later and later these days. She wasn't sleeping too well, as a matter of fact. She had developed a slight inner ache. Though she had planned to put on her dancing shoes and skip out upon London's seductive summer pavements, when it came to it she felt rather half-hearted about the whole thing. She found herself resting her brow against windows rather often: sighing more than she was wont to do, and when she switched on the radio and there was a sudden surge of Mozart, she burst into tears. She hadn't been like this in San Francisco. There, she'd been heart-whole. Now, somehow, she'd lost a bit of it.

One day, resting her brow moodily against the French windows, she noticed Aunt Vinny out in the garden, kneeling and weeding. Izzy's interest in gardening was fairly minimal, but something made her open the windows and walk through.

'Can I give you a hand, Aunt Vinny?' she enquired, kneeling beside her.

'Thank you dear. Rupert is so particular about this border. He planted it, you know. Look at this bindweed! Dreadful stuff. There's a sharp trowel. See if you can dig its roots out, at the foot of the wall there.'

Izzy took the trowel and dug. Endless strings of white fleshy root spiralled away, lacing itself tightly into the smallest cracks. Silence fell. Izzy hesitated to break it.

'I know she should, dear,' said Aunt Vinny suddenly out of the blue.

'Sorry?'

'Only Rupert, Izzy. He says you should have gloves.'

'Oh, don't worry about that! I love dabbling about in mud. I was a farmer's daughter, you know.'

'Of course. Delightful!'

Silence fell again. Izzy wondered how she could transform the silence into a stream of important information about Charles Armstrong.

'What did your father do, Aunt Vinny? You never said.'

Fathers, after all, lead to brothers and sisters, which result, sooner or later, in nephews.

'Oh, he spent most of his time doing watercolours,' said Aunt Vinny, leaning back and wiping a strand of hair out of her eyes. 'He was a bit of a dilettante, really. Look at that beetle! What an extraordinary colour.'

'Er, did you have lots of brothers and sisters? You seem to have plenty of nieces and – um, nephews,' Izzy blushed slightly at the bindweed.

'No, only one sister, dear. Louise's mother, of course.'

'But what about – your, er, other side?' Izzy hesitated. She hoped Vinny would not get absorbed in the Beyond, again.

'Ah. That's Rupert's lot. Terribly county.'

'So your nephew, er – Charles, is the son of Rupert's brother?'

'Sister. Daphne. She married this Cambridge research scientist and he went off and made a fortune in fertilizers.'

'So that's where Charles gets his brains. I mean, he must have brains to do his job. All that computer stuff.'

'Little boys' toys, dear,' smiled Aunt Vinny, savaging some ground elder. Izzy waited hopefully, but no further information about Charles was offered.

'Do you still see much of his parents?'

'Oh no. They're down in Norfolk. And to be quite honest, Izzy, I'm not sure I would care to. I'm afraid they are slightly *nouveau riche*, my dear.' Izzy felt mysteriously sick.

'He didn't seem *nouveau riche* to me.'

This was gallant of Izzy, especially as she wasn't exactly sure what the symptoms were.

'Oh, Charles is a darling. It's his mother, really. Wealth brought out the worst in her. Charles is a sweetheart. I live in constant fear that some dreadful little fortune-hunter will get her claws into him and the poor chap will be done for.'

'Oh, gosh, that would be awful,' said Izzy with feeling. 'I mean, he's—'

Dimly, within the house, a doorbell rang with a deep grunt. It was Izzy's. She heaved herself up. The only doorbell she was looking forward to answering at the moment was Vinny's. Her own filled her with fear. She dawdled to answer it. Michael might come back at any time, and she still felt sore from their last interview. And there was always the danger that Gwyn or Maria might get hold of her address. She peeped through the security spyhole, and beheld a delivery boy carrying a vast bouquet.

Izzy opened the door. The cellophane crackled brilliantly in the sunshine.

'Miss Izzy Comyn?'

'Yes. That's me.'

The bouquet was handed over, and Izzy carried it carefully into the house and down to her flat. Nobody had ever sent her flowers before, though Michael had often brought them, especially when he was at his most guilty. But getting them delivered was a new experience. Izzy tore open the little envelope and pulled out the card.

FROM AN ADMIRER WHO HAS AN
APOLOGY TO MAKE

Izzy's heart lurched madly. An *anonymous* bouquet! Could it be – wasn't it just the sort of gesture – that a charming young thing might make? A new acquaintance? Izzy hesitated about the apology part. True, he had apologized all over again about having intruded into her flat and caught her capering about in the nude. Maybe he was apologizing again for having mentioned it. Sending flowers is such a very charming thing to do. Not a bit *nouveau riche*. Izzy tore open the cellophane and paper and shook their stems free, her heart racing and her veins singing like telegraph wires. The quivering sighs of the last few days were gone. She was bursting with happiness.

Dick's key turned in the lock and he came in through the side door. Izzy felt guilty. She hid the card.

'Hello,' said Dick. 'Somebody sent you flowers?'

'No!' she lied. 'I just – just bought them myself.'

Dick sniffed them appreciatively.

'Hope they don't set my hay fever off,' he observed.

Izzy realized suddenly that it didn't matter if Dick did know that someone had sent them. After all, they weren't really married, dammit.

'Oh listen, Dick – don't tell anybody – it's a big sceret – but they were delivered just now. And guess what! They're from a secret admirer!'

Dick stared at the card. He did not exactly light up with shared pleasure. He was, alas, all too obviously filled with consternation.

'Who's that, then?'

'How do I know? Honestly, Dick! That's the whole point!'

'Seems a bit silly to me,' said Dick grumpily, turning

over the card with suspicion. 'I mean, what's the point? If you don't know who sent them, then you can't say thank you, sort of thing.'

'Oh Dick! Don't you have an ounce of romance in your soul?'

Dick cringed. He stared dismally at the floor. The reproach stung like a whip. This was the woman who above all saturated him with feelings of romance, burdened him with them until his arms and legs felt like lead. If only he'd sent her flowers anonymously! Then she would be all excited and glowing – about *him*. Till she found out who had sent them, that is. The hopelessness of his situation brought him almost to the verge of tears. Izzy perceived it, and squirmed.

'Come on, cheer up, Dick! I didn't mean it.'

'Yes you did. And it's true.'

'No it's not.'

'Now you're just being kind.'

'No I'm not!'

'You are. I can tell.'

Izzy felt a mixture of rising irritation and pity – two of the most uncomfortable emotions, and ones which seem often mysteriously drawn towards each other. Why couldn't Dick be her buddy? God knows, that was the way she treated him. Why did he have to droop and mope and be obstructive just at the very moment when she wanted most to soar and sing?

'Hand me that vase, Dick – I must get these in water.'

Dick obeyed. It was a vase he had made, and a particularly handsome one. But Izzy didn't notice. She was burying her face in the silky depths of *Lilium Regale*.

'Just smell these lilies – aren't they fabulous!'

Dick kept his distance from the lilies, regarding their sumptuous Southern trumpets with deep suspicion.

'I don't – don't much go for lilies, to be honest, Izzy. They – they remind me of funerals.'

'Honestly, Dick!' Izzy snapped. 'You're just so negative! Why can't you – oh, I don't know—' Rejoice with

102

me, I suppose, thought Izzy. Here I am, feeling exhilarated for the first time for over a year: at last something's actually happening in my life, and all he can do is frown and sulk and be obstructive. Why can't he—

'Why do you have to ruin everything?'

Dick looked appalled. If this was being married, it was frighteningly painful. Izzy rammed the flowers into the vase, resisting the temptation to hit Dick over the head with them.

'I didn't mean to—' faltered Dick. 'I only—'

'Oh shut up, Dick! Stop apologizing, for God's sake! Sometimes you make me want to scream!'

Aunt Vinny chose this inopportune moment to glance in through the window which was open and rather inconveniently gave onto the side-passage along which she happened to be strolling, pulling out a weed here and there.

'Dear me,' she shook her head. 'Not having a lovers' quarrel, are we?'

'No, no,' smiled Izzy. 'Dick – er – Dick likes me shouting at him. Don't you, Dick?'

'Er – yes. Well, I don't mind. Sometimes I – well, I ask for it, a bit.'

'My word! Has he just given you those fabulous flowers?'

Aunt Vinny drew in deep breaths of lily scent. Izzy faltered. Could Dick have just given her the flowers? Or would that make her shouting at him all the more unforgivable? Did married people give each other flowers? Were they behaving suspiciously? For a moment she was tempted to make a clean breast of it, confess her single status to Aunt Vinny and ask her, rather urgently, for her nephew's phone number. Then she caught Aunt Vinny's hawk-like eye and changed her mind.

'Yes. Wasn't it marvellous of him? Darling old Dick!' Izzy seized him roughly by the scalp and bestowed a smacking kiss on his blushing cheek. 'And so horrid of me to yell at him about something else. I am a nasty old nag,

103

Dick. I wouldn't be surprised if you ran off and left me.'

'Oh, I'd never leave you, Izzy,' promised Dick, daring to extend a trembling arm around her waist. Aunt Vinny smiled admiringly at this picture of domestic bliss, and went off to discuss the problem of snails on the front lawn with her spectral husband. Did snails have souls? Would they be grateful for a quick passage to the after-life, assisted by a few small blue pellets? Rupert would no doubt be able to advise.

'I'm sorry, Dick,' whispered Izzy, skipping away from his arm, which dangled briefly in mid-air. 'I just feel a bit . . . moody, today. You understand?'

'Oh yes, Izzy. No need to apologize.' Dick gathered the discarded wrappings of the bouquet, scrunched them up and thrust them into the rubbish bin. He was at ease performing these modest tasks. These helpful clearings-aways. He had often removed Izzy's apple-cores from strange roosting-places, not without a momentary aware-ness that her fine white teeth and beautifully pouty lips had been in direct contact with them.

Izzy ran off to look at herself in the bathroom mirror. There were bags under her eyes, it is true, but the sparkle cancelled them out. She smiled intimately at her reflec-tion. This was the face of a woman with a secret admirer. It was a different face from the one she'd frowned at for the last year. How excitement can transform everything. The very bathroom flooded with luminous sun. She ignored the phone, leaving it for Dick to answer in case it was Maria or Michael or Gwyn. Not that her troubled relationships with them really mattered any more. After all, she had a secret admirer. Even now, across London somewhere, there was a man thinking of her – and of her receiving his flowers.

'Hey, Izzy,' said Dick, tidying the sofa cushions as Izzy emerged from the bathroom. 'That was Charles Arm-strong. He asked us round tonight. I said we'd go. Is that all right?'

Izzy's heart bounded. She was pretty sure she'd better

keep her feelings hidden from Dick, though.

'Yeah, fine,' she sang, and hid her delighted face in a magazine.

'He said about eight. He lives in Spitalfields. I'm dying to have a go at his Amstrad.'

There was just one little problem, though. As far as Charles Armstrong was concerned, Izzy was happily married to Mr Dick Barnes. But even this reflection could not spoil Izzy's mood. She would just have to commit adultery again. Only this time, it wouldn't be *real* adultery. It would be secretly innocent. See? She was cleaning up her act. What a pity Maria wasn't in a position to admire this moral progress.

PEACE AND GENTLE VISITATION

I mustn't be horrid to Dick, thought Izzy desperately. Poor Dick. It's not his fault. But all the same – how can I get rid of him tonight? Izzy was soaking in a hot bath – one of her favourite occupations. Although her hair was already clean, she was washing it again. Her toenails, perched up by the taps, sparkled discreetly with freshly-applied varnish. A clay mask was caking nicely over her face. Izzy was at her devotions again. Sometimes she felt the only creative thing she ever did was to get ready for a date. Architectural salvage, she thought with a grin. Still, you couldn't really call it that, yet. There were still a few months left before she turned thirty.

As for forty, well, by then everything could be different. Must be different. By then (please, God!) she would be happily married, perhaps with a horde of children. Perhaps . . . the children would wear horn-rimmed glasses. No! Stop! Wait! Izzy was appalled at the speed with which her imagination galloped, today. But it was such a very long time since she'd been in this position: getting ready for a date. Secretly admired – and by someone who wasn't someone else's husband already.

They had exchanged glances. And now, she felt sure, they were heading for completion. Of course Izzy knew there was a lot more to life than falling in love. There was work, friends, reading, the theatre, travel, good causes. But she'd had her bellyfull of all that recently, thank you very much. What she wanted now was the dart in the heart. And she was sure she detected the far-away twinkle of possibility. The faintest glimmer of dawn.

Bathed, wrapped in her dressing gown and wearing a

towel turban round her head, she burst from the bathroom in a cloud of freesia-scented steam and was irritated to find Dick sitting on the sofa reading a magazine. What was he playing at? Did he have no inkling of his responsibilities? Why was he not out, getting run over? Nothing serious, of course. Just mildly concussed. A night in hospital, perhaps. She and Charles could go and see him. Take him flowers. They could joke about the flowers and secret admirers. They could exchange significant looks.

'Cor, Izzy! You don't half smell nice!' beamed Dick, infuriatingly. Nothing's more irritating, when you've made yourself smell nice for somebody in particular, to find that other people are vicariously enjoying it. Especially people you don't really want to smell nice for. People you'd rather associated you with smelly socks and mousey biscuits.

Izzy swept past into her bedroom, not daring to speak in case she said something too cruel. Once inside, she addressed herself to the mirror. She wondered what to do about her eyebrows, which were distinctly bushy. Would Charles go for the Dietrich look, plucked into slim arcs? He was old-fashioned, after all. Or would he prefer the voluptuousness of nature?

But the problem of eyebrows was as nothing before the problem of Dick. Izzy peeped through the open door. Dick was still sitting annoyingly upright on the sofa, without betraying a trace of the sudden fainting fit or attack of food poisoning which would have been the immediate resort of a more tactful companion. Still, there was no harm in trying.

'Are you sure you're feeling all right, Dick?'

'All . . . right, Izzy?'

'You look a bit pale.'

'Pale?'

'Yes. Are you sure you're all right?'

'Fine. I feel fine, Izzy, honestly.'

'But Dick – you're positively green! There's a bug going about, you know. You ought to be careful.'

'Well, I feel all right so far.' Damn. Dick was clinging rather unreasonably to rude health.

Maybe she should stage a collapse, herself. It wouldn't be the first time. She could send him out for some aspirins and when he came back, tell him she'd rung Charles to cancel their dinner? Then it would be the work of a moment to get rid of Dick to a movie.

'You must see it, Dick. I think you'd look quite like Gerard Depardieu, if you grew about eight inches and shaved your beard off and got contact lenses. And worked out a bit. And he's absolutely *yummy*.' That should do the trick.

Whilst Dick was out at the movies, she could creep off to Spitalfields by herself.

'I feel a bit faint, myself,' she murmured, lying down on the bed for verisimilitude.

'Your bath was probably too hot,' said Dick. 'I'll make you a cup of tea.' He put the kettle on, wondering in what other humble ways he could augment her happiness. Alas, it never occurred to him to go out and get run over.

Evening drew nigh, and it was a particularly divine one. As Izzy and Dick walked through the streets of Spitalfields, pink Western light streamed over the bricks like a universal blush. The streets were full of summery smells: hot kerbs, cucumber, garlic, pollen, and just a hint of carbon monoxide. Even the traffic hummed with the distant drone of satiated bees.

Dick felt immensely happy. He was going out with Izzy – after a fashion. And she was looking riotously pretty, in a new green and blue print dress that fluttered winsomely around her brown arms and legs. She had outlined her eyes with that black stuff that made the green of her pupils gleam almost dangerously. Dick was delighted with the prospect of a whole evening pretending to be the husband of such a vision. He almost groaned aloud with pleasure when she caught him by the arm.

'Dick! We must take a bottle of wine!'

'Crumbs! Yeah! Good thinking, Izzy.'

'Look, there's an off-licence. Will you nip in and get one? I'll wait here.' Dick set off obediently.

He rummaged around in the off-licence, and finally emerged, blinking, into the sunshine, with a bottle of Sancerre clutched in his hand. But – where was she? The street was suddenly, treacherously empty. Had she been – Oh Lord – abducted? Had dark-eyed men in a limousine sped off with her towards Hounslow? Dick looked desperately up and down the street. He even shouted *IZZY!* a couple of times, despite an acute preference for remaining silent in public places. There was no answer. He ran up the street and looked up and down the main road. No sign. Only an old Pakistani man with a look of austere disapproval.

'Have – have you seen a woman?' Dick addressed him in panic. The old man frowned, as if failing to recall what exactly a woman was.

'A young woman with – with a blue and green dress?' Dick went on. 'And sort of bushy hair and – um – lots of earrings?'

The old man shrugged and shuffled off.

Dick hesitated. What should he do? Inform the police? It was a bit early for that, he supposed. Although perhaps even now she was being chloroformed and thrust into a trunk. Sedated and crated. Poor Dick's heart beat almost to bursting. Should he go back to the flat? Walk the streets till he found her? Ring her mother? Eventually he emerged from this mental turmoil and noticed he was holding a bottle of wine. Then he realized what he must do: he must go to Charles Armstrong.

Apart from anything else, it was a necessary courtesy to inform Charles that their evening with him was out of the question, now Izzy had disappeared. Moreover, Armstrong would certainly know what to do. He was educated. Civilized. A man of the world. Dick was sure that Charles Armstrong knew his onions, *vis-à-vis* missing wives.

But where the hell did he live? Dick had scribbled his address on a scrap of paper but it was Izzy who'd pocketed it. Izzy who'd been navigating them through this maze of streets, before she'd disappeared. The scrap of paper had vanished with her. So had the *A-to-Z* street plan of London. Dick was comprehensively lost. He did remember something, though: the number 46. That was Charles Armstrong's number, he was sure. It couldn't be far away. And surely, when he saw the right street-name, it'd ring a bell.

Thus heroically did Dick set out to scour every street in Spitalfields. Already he had worked up a disastrous sweat, but of that he was unaware. All he knew, as he strode urgently past dusty terraces and dingy warehouses, was that Charles Armstrong would be his salvation. Charles would restore his lost wife to him, Dick was sure. He would comb the area till he found the magic number 46 – or until he had a better idea. In Dick's case, this could take some time. This was exactly what Izzy was banking on.

AND WHO IS YOUR DEER?

Izzy was running very fast in the other direction. She was barefoot. Her dear old Italian high heels were not up to this kind of Olympic sprint. A gay ballet-dancer who had ransacked her wardrobe once in San Francisco had saluted these shoes with delight. 'Hey!' he'd drooled. 'Ghad! You've got some peep-toe, sling-back, mock-croc, Joan Crawford Come-Fuck-Me-Pumps!' And if he hadn't been six foot three he'd have tried them on right away.

Izzy had soon learnt there was no point in wearing them in San Francisco. Apart from the lack of male interest in her good self, there had been the gradients. If you have to walk down a hill of 1-in-5 it's pretty close to madness to add an extra 1-in-5 by way of high heels. You could soon find yourself in a kerbstone-to-eyeball situation, wearing shoes like these in San Francisco.

In fact, these shoes had been in cold storage since the old Michael days. Even during her Chinese sandals and baggy cotton trousers period, though, she'd found herself unable to part with them. They had been secretly hoarded with other seduction paraphernalia, just in case. In case the tide turned. Izzy was, in some deep instinctive way, capable of turning with tides. But she told herself it was only when it came to cultural and fashion details that she could turn and turn again. When it came to moral absolutes – she was as constant as the Something Star.

She was running in the opposite direction from the one in which she'd been leading poor Dick. She'd worked it all out, fiendishly, on the Tube. She'd led Dick off in the wrong direction, ordered him into an off-licence, then made her escape. Kicked off her shoes and run. Since she had the scribbled address, the *A to Z*, and most of the braincells, she reckoned she ought to have at least an hour alone with Charles. That ought to be enough to find out if her interest in him was reciprocated.

At the end of his street, she donned her peep-toe pumps and teetered – some would say delectably, some absurdly – up his steps. His bell did not buzz electronically, but tolled authentically somewhere far within. Brisk footsteps came to the door. Izzy braced herself, tried to wipe some of the ridiculous eagerness off her face, and prepared for the fortunate Charles Armstrong her most dazzling smile.

A woman opened the door. She was younger than Izzy; slimmer, blonder, better dressed and infinitely more socially at ease. All this Izzy understood at a glance, desperately shoring up her smile which had flown apart into odd droplets of scattered shine, like a smashed thermometer.

'Izzy?' smiled the young woman, with that automatic grace and poise that comes from expensive schools, houseparties, fathers in Parliament and mothers who never had to do the washing-up themselves. 'Do come in. I'm Sooty.' That's what it sounded like, anyway. Izzy wasn't sure if it was a name, or an apology.

'Sooty?' she faltered, crossing Charles's threshold and wondering if it was Sooty's threshold too. Even now she could imagine them embracing under this rather tatty chandelier. The wallpaper was slime green and oddly patchy. Old paintings hung everywhere and Izzy heard the stately ticking of a large and ancient clock.

'Sooty. Short for Sara. Silly really. Goes back to the nursery.'

Were they engaged? Izzy wondered. Or – even worse somehow – in the first flush of love? She heard the sound of well-heeled heels drumming down the stairs – and there, suddenly, was Charles. She tried to look brisk and friendly.

'I say – Izzy!' he placed a gentle finger on each of her shoulders. 'What a simply marvellous frock. You look wonderful.'

This, of course, was the sort of salutation a married woman might receive from a Charles who was newly in love with somebody else. Izzy raised her eyes and was surprised by the dazzle that seemed to come streaming off his face. He must be very much in love with Sooty. Ah well. Izzy took pleasure in his charming face, and his compliments. After all, what more did she deserve?

'I say – where's Dick?'

'Oh dear. It's so silly. I lost him.'

Even sillier did it seem now, privately, to Izzy. To have gone to all that elaborate trouble to ditch poor Dick, only to find Sooty firmly in possession. She had gone off now and was clattering about in what was clearly her kitchen. How much more in possession could you get?

'You *lost* him?' frowned Charles.

'Yes. You see, he went into the off-licence and then I remembered I needed something from the newsagent's on the corner, and when I came out, he was gone.'

'How extraordinary. Perhaps he's done a bunk!'

'I don't think so. He's not the type.' If only, thought Izzy, he was. Dick bunked would be thought of with great tenderness.

'Ah, but beware, Izzy. One never knows, and so forth. He could be heading for a new life with a new wife in Australia.'

'I don't think so,' sighed Izzy. 'Dick's not a terribly dark horse. You can see right through him. I expect he'll turn up. I'm sorry we're so – untogether,' she concluded with a wry grin. Even apart, she and Dick were too together for her taste.

Although now she could see that Charles and Sooty were enjoying some kind of deeply-settled domestic scene, she felt a perverse little twinge of annoyance that Dick wasn't there. She would feel less of a gooseberry with him, and less lonely knowing that his absorbent shoulder was ready for the journey home.

'What a fabulous house,' Izzy endeavoured to move the conversation away from her marital problems. Fabulous was the wrong word, of course. Far too sixties. Nineteen-sixties. Eighteen-sixties would have been all right, perhaps.

'Ah! It's an obsession,' grinned Charles at his staircase. 'I put these banisters in last week.' Izzy stared. The banisters looked eternal, somehow. As if they'd always been there.

'Charles is mad!' called Sooty from the kitchen. 'I hope you've got nothing Georgian on you, Izzy, or he'll have it off you in a trice.' Then Sooty did something extraordinary. She came out of the kitchen, took off her apron, and put on her jacket.

'Well then, Fortinbras,' she addressed Charles, moving – Izzy noticed with sudden hope – *towards the door,* 'have a wonderful time. It's all ready and it'll keep hot for hours.'

'You're an angel,' said Charles, kissing her on the cheek and opening the door. Was Sooty off to her self-defence course? Would she return in time to warm his bed? Or was she beating a convenient retreat? What the hell was going on? Izzy went quite giddy and rapturous all of a sudden.

'*Ciao,* then, Izzy,' smiled Sooty. 'Bye Chas darling. See you next Tuesday.'

And she was gone. What a wonderful woman. Izzy had never liked anyone so much in all her life.

As for *see you next Tuesday,* it was music to Izzy's ears. Nobody who could say that could be so very much in love, surely.

'Isn't she – nice?' concluded Izzy lamely.

'Isn't she?' affirmed Charles, quietly. 'She's a fantastic cook, Sooty. Runs a catering firm. Always helps me out when I have people round. Knows how useless I am.'

'Is she an old flame?' demanded Izzy in a sudden hot rush of boldness.

'Not even a flutter,' Charles shook his head. 'Not remotely my type. Too thick between the ears and too thin elsewhere.'

His eyes rested appreciatively on Izzy's plump cheeks and her brown shoulders, rising from the oceanic swirls of her dress like two round dolphins' backs, gleaming with light.

Izzy panicked. Her meagre supply of words dwindled to absolutely nothing. His evident admiration, shining quite honestly and overpoweringly out of his curious speckled eyes, simply defeated her. She could only stand silent and still and glow in response.

'I don't mean to sound unchivalrous to poor Sooty,' he smiled, having removed his eyes briefly to a tall blue and white china umbrella stand, 'and God knows she doesn't need my admiration. She's engaged to the Marquis of Westonbirt.'

'Ah, well,' said Izzy, beaming. 'I hope she'll be very happy.'

'So do I.'

Silence fell again.

Charles fingered the banisters, looking at the floor, then courageously found her eyes again. No more pretences at small talk were necessary. They simply swam in a sea of mutual attraction. Izzy was astonished to feel tears of relief welling up inside her: after so many arid months of mere existence, here was the leap of life again. Rain flooding the desert, swilling around the parched roots. She felt her roots uncurl and drink.

'Dear me,' Charles murmured, rubbing his banisters with a feverish fingertip, 'you are so very beautiful.'

Izzy almost cried with joy. Nobody had ever said she was beautiful before. Well, except Michael, and he hadn't meant it and anyway, that had been in the bad old days. She felt every little nerve in her body quiver with excitement. Surely, at last, after years of nothing very special, this feeling flooding through her had a pretty good claim to be described as It.

WHAT, FIRST PRAISE ME,
AND AGAIN SAY NO?

Standing there under the chandelier, Izzy felt that the collapse into his arms was more or less due. She longed for the rough rasp of his tweedy shoulder on her skin. Izzy did not believe in prevaricating where mutual attraction reared its snaky head. But Charles ran nervous fingers through his pre-war hair. He blushed desperately, and then did something completely outside Izzy's experience. He *backed away*.

'Look, I'm sorry,' he murmured. 'I've – I've got to get used to all this. Er – come out into the garden and let's have a drink.'

Izzy was slightly puzzled. She was all for staying in. Out in the garden seemed to her a retrograde step: back into the semi-public world they had just banished with the delightful Sooty. Here they were in this magical, submarine hall with its green depths and vaguely phosphorescent chandelier. This hall seemed perfect. Izzy would gladly have lingered for five minutes; nay, for five hours. But Charles was moving off, and she could only follow.

His garden was a small leafy enclosure with high brick walls. A dusty white geranium spilled out of an urn. At the bottom of the garden was a balustrade and a statue of a Greek youth. Leaves dipped and danced on all sides in the evening light. The only flowers were white. Izzy sat down on a white wrought-iron chair. The chaste good taste of the place, and the faint whiff of evergreens, reminded her briefly of a cemetery, but she suppressed the image hastily.

'Can I get you a drink, Izzy? What would you like?'

'Oh dear – we brought some wine – but Dick's got it. I'm sorry!'

'Don't worry. Muscadet be all right?'

Izzy nodded. Charles disappeared into the kitchen. Izzy felt odd. The storming excitement inside her had curdled slightly. She now had to sit down and drink a glass of wine, and talk in a way which might safely be overheard – for anyone might lurk behind these high walls. All the same, she was bathing in happiness. He had said she was beautiful. He had been, quite evidently, paralyzed with desire. Izzy heaved a tremulous sigh. It was all too wonderful. Happiness at last. What days, months, years of bliss might lie ahead. It made sense to hold back, to postpone each delicious droplet of joy.

He handed her the glass with a shaking hand. Her hand shook too. They both laughed. Charles sat down – too far away for physical contact, Izzy couldn't help noticing. But how civilized. When she and Michael – but she would not think of Michael now. That was the rotten old past. Today was the beginning of the rest of her life. And what a beginning! She held on tight to the stem of her wine glass, conscious that her head was reeling already.

'It's – it's extraordinary!' he burst out at last, turning to her. 'I've never . . . been in a situation like this before, you see.'

Suddenly he launched himself up off his chair, but not in her direction. He walked off down the garden. Admittedly it was a small garden, and it wasn't far. All the same, he walked away, and did not turn to face her until he was standing by the statue of the Greek youth. Then, he did permit his eyes to burn into her again. He shrugged.

'I simply don't know what to do.'

In a flash Izzy realized what was wrong. She was *married*. Of course! That was it. That was why he faltered and frowned and gazed at the ground. Here she was staring open-heartedly into his eyes, and forgetting quite that all the time she was a married woman. Poor Charles!

Poor, *decent* Charles! How different from, and superior to, Michael, who had grabbed her eagerly without the slightest scruple despite the fact that he himself was locked deep in matrimony.

Izzy's tongue leapt to reassure him. But wait! He was Aunt Vinny's nephew. Izzy bit her tongue. If she told him she wasn't married really, then she'd have to confess what it was all in aid of: deceiving his aunt. He might be appalled. It would certainly place him in a most uncomfortable position. Once he knew that she and Dick weren't married, he'd be *de facto* a party to the deception. Lying to his aunt. Why, she might disinherit him or something. Although from the hints that Aunt Vinny had dropped, it was clear that Charles wasn't exactly a needy dependant.

Izzy got up and teetered cautiously down the garden path. The Italian shoes made physical progress difficult: the dilemma wound her mind in coils. A rose bush caught at her as she went past. The thorn pierced her flesh.

'Look,' she said, not advancing any further, sensing his timidity, 'it's not the way you think. You mustn't worry. It's . . . all right.'

'Is it?' Charles frowned.

'The fact is,' Izzy faltered on, 'I'm not – it's not, well, you know – as bad as it looks.'

'Why not?'

'Well, the fact is,' Izzy spotted a lie and swam urgently towards it, 'Dick and I have a – a companionate marriage.'

Charles's eyes widened. 'Really? Good Lord. I can't imagine – do you mind explaining – what on earth *for*?'

Izzy cast about wildly.

'Ah. Well. You see, it's a long story.'

'We've got all evening. Do explain. I mean, I don't mean to pry, but I simply can't grasp – why on earth could anyone wish to have a companionate marriage – with you?'

Izzy blushed. This was another compliment. At last. She'd had to wait several minutes.

'It was Dick's nervous breakdown!' she blurted out.

'A nervous breakdown? When?'

118

'Oh, in the States. He got so terribly low. I couldn't work out what I could do to help. So I – well, I married him.'

'You married him – as therapy?'

'Well, yes. I mean, no. That is, well, in San Francisco, there's a big move to break the mould, you know.'

'What mould?'

'Oh, marriage, the family, that sort of thing. The nuclear family, you know.'

'How ghastly.'

'Well, of course, yes. Really ghastly. I mean—' Izzy sensed the earth growing more and more slippery underfoot. 'I mean, I'm all for the family. I want one of my own one day.'

'And does Dick?'

This was a trap.

'Oh no. He's not – well, to be honest, he's not fit.'

'You mean physically fit? Or mentally?'

'Both!' cried Izzy, glimpsing a double infirmity which looked as if it might suit Dick down to the ground. 'Poor Dick. I shouldn't be telling you this, really. He doesn't like people to know. About the breakdown and everything. And the trouble is, you see, he's always had, well, trouble.'

'Trouble? What sort?'

'Well, er – um, impotence.'

'Impotence? Did you think being married to you would cure his impotence?'

'Goodness, no! I mean—' Izzy hesitated. She wanted above all to make one thing clear. 'The thing is, I've never remotely fancied Dick. And that's how I persuaded him that this marriage would be a good idea. I mean, since he was impotent, he could appear to be married to me all the time, and hold his head up in the world, sort of thing, without anyone ever suspecting.'

'But what on earth was in it for you?'

'For me. Ah. Well. I was in quite a state, too. I'd been involved with this married man. He'd been really beastly to me. Messed me about. Chucked me in the end. After promising marriage and all that. I was – well, I was a bit shaky. I quite liked the idea of a nice safe brotherly marriage to Dick.'

'Goodness me,' Charles tore his hair briefly. 'I'm quite out of my depth, I'm afraid.'

'Oh no, I'm sure you're not. I mean, Dick and I, well, we've got this brother and sister relationship, you know – sort of spiritual harmony. A bit like the Wordsworths.'

'But they *were* brother and sister.'

'Well, that's what we are, really. That's what our so-called marriage is. Yes! Brother and sister.'

Charles seemed to have cheered up slightly. His frown had gone, and he loosened up and sighed. What sort of sigh was it? Izzy trembled in case it was an *I've had enough of this insane woman I wish she'd go home* sort of sigh. But then he smiled.

'Come here,' he whispered. 'But slowly.'

Izzy would be slow. By God, she would crawl. She would ruthlessly repress her impulse to bound. His eyes were fixed on her again now, and slowly he reeled her in, like a fixated fisherman with a fat gleaming trout. Their breaths were close enough to mingle when – the doorbell rang.

'Oh no!' groaned Izzy, 'I bet that's Dick! The stupid idiot! Damn him!'

STILL AND CONTEMPLATIVE
IN LIVING ART

'Izzy!' cried Dick in relief. 'Where did you get to?'

'Where did you get to, you mean?' snarled Izzy, rather venomously, perhaps, for a man with whom she shared a sacred spiritual harmony.

'I came out of the off-licence and you'd vanished!'

'No I hadn't, stupid! I just nipped into the newsagent's for a minute and when I came out, you'd gone! Honestly, Dick! You might have waited!'

Dick looked crestfallen. Hadn't he waited? He supposed not. Was that what he should have done? He supposed so.

'Sorry,' he mumbled.

'Never mind!' cried Charles, who felt guilty towards Dick and wanted to enforce a welcome. 'You found us! That's the main thing!' Was that *us* a bit of a Freudian slip, too? Just who was the couple round here?

'Yes,' conceded Izzy, recovering. 'Well done, Dick. And I had the *A to Z* and the instructions. However did you manage?'

'I rang Aunt Vinny,' explained Dick.

Izzy had underestimated Dick again. It was easily done. Still, at least she'd had twenty minutes alone with Charles, and things could not be more satisfyingly clear. Izzy was in such good spirits that she didn't even wish, as she sometimes did, that Dick had resisted the temptation to move down to London two years ago and had gone to Kalamazoo instead.

'Come on, Dick,' she smiled, 'look what a marvellous house Charles has got!'

Dick looked around, surprised at Izzy's enthusiasm. The hall seemed pretty dingy and damp to him. Those green walls could do with a nice coat of white emulsion, for a start.

'Would you like to look round?' asked Charles eagerly.

'Oh yes please!'

Charles led them upstairs. The house was large: he occupied the bottom two floors, and the proportions of the rooms were lofty and airy with high ceilings.

'This is the bathroom,' said Charles, revealing an austere chamber adorned with marble and mahogany. The bath itself stood quaintly upon antique clawed feet. The towels were all sage green and folded neatly. How very different, thought Izzy, from the shrieking multicoloured heaps on the floor whenever I have a bath. Dick wondered if Charles would like him to panel the bath nicely for him, but he said nothing.

'Oh look at that lovely marble!' cried Izzy, running her hand along the top of a washstand, conscious of gathering a little dust en route.

'Brocatello,' said Charles helpfully.

'What?'

'It's called Brocatello. It's Spanish. Pretty, isn't it?'

'Gosh!' exclaimed Izzy. 'I didn't know marble had names!' Then, suddenly, she wished she hadn't said anything.

'Yeah,' added Dick, 'Brocatello – sounds a bit like pasta.' And he laughed – rather oafishly, Izzy thought.

'Oh yes,' said Charles. 'There are lots of different sorts of marble. There's a rather good bit of Belgian Black in my bedroom.'

Charles's bed was immense: canopied, with vast carved portals.

'Crikey!' gasped Dick. 'It's like something out of a stately home!' Izzy cringed.

'I think it's wonderful!' she sighed, and would fain have flung herself upon it there and then, but that would have been a little too fast, she supposed – with her husband right there in the room, after all. Izzy had a shrewd instinct that Charles did not like his women fast and loose but slow and cool.

'It's got knobs on,' observed Dick irritatingly. 'What are those curtains for?'

Charles just laughed. 'They're for fun,' he explained. But Dick couldn't quite see the joke. 'There's the Belgian Black,' Charles went on, gesturing towards the fireplace. It had a black marble chimneypiece and reminded Izzy slightly of a tomb she had seen somewhere, on a school trip, long ago.

'Lovely!' she murmured, with a shiver.

The spare bedroom was extremely spare. It contained an iron bedstead which stood on bare boards. The boards had an odd look: they appeared to have been whitewashed with what Dick supposed was extremely cheap paint. Fancy a bloke like Charles not being able to afford a carpet. You'd think his Aunt Vinny would've slipped him a bob or two. Dick was sure Charles could've got a nice cheap polypropethylene carpet for under £5 a square yard. And yet there was something so determinedly austere about the room that Dick hesitated to offer his advice. He sensed he was in the grip of a perverse but authoritative taste.

'How – how – cool!' Izzy faltered. It looked monastic but she thought perhaps Charles wouldn't like her to say so. The only colour in the room was a large jug on the small bedside table. 'What a pretty jug!'

'Pink lustre,' commented Charles. 'Naïve but yes, rather pretty.'

The words attracted Izzy. It was reassuring to know that Charles cherished the Naïve.

They clattered downstairs again. There was no carpet here, either, Dick worried. What about the draughts? He had noticed that there were no comforting little snakes of shiny white draught excluder round any of the windows, or doors. No double-glazing either. Only big sash windows that rattled loosely whenever a plane went over.

What would it be like in a midwinter gale? Dick shivered to think.

'Must cost a bomb to heat this place,' he observed. 'High ceilings and that.'

'I quite like things cool,' said Charles. 'Open fires, you know. Mottled knees and a freezing back . . . This is the drawing-room.'

The ground floor had been knocked-through into one long room. At each end was a large window. And the curtains! My God, they were like theatre curtains! Draped and folded in great swags, the whole ensemble presided over by a carved pelmet and a huge gilt crown.

'Crikey!' observed Dick.

'Your curtains!' added Izzy.

'Ah yes. Terribly lucky. Found them on a market stall. Edwardian floral and turn-of-the-century silk damask.'

Izzy had never given a serious moment's thought to curtains before. She was silenced.

'I'm a bit of a curtains buff,' Charles went on. 'Gesso mouldings, finials and rings – unpolished brass rosettes, you know!' Izzy nodded, hoping that was the right thing to do. 'I just salivate!' Charles confessed, gazing passionately at the huge gilt crown.

Dick just gawped. He felt even more out of his depth than usual. Why, there was a *statue* in the fireplace! A great white marble head. It looked a bit like Everton's goalkeeper, but Dick did not dare to say so.

'Who's that?' he asked instead.

'Bernini,' said Charles. 'Or so I like to think.'

Dick nodded emptily. Bernini, Gesso, Brocatello: he was lost. He had, over the past two years, got to grips with Frascati, but now he was groping in a blizzard of incomprehension. Luckily Charles seemed a nice friendly chap who hardly noticed the havoc he was causing.

A supremely elegant sofa dominated the room. It was very long, with a lavishly curved and curled back, and deep red upholstery.

'Oh,' breathed Izzy, 'the *sofa*!'

'Yes,' beamed Charles. 'It's my favourite place to be on a winter's evening.'

Izzy couldn't wait for winter, so she could curl up with him there.

'Is it old?' enquired the dreadful Dick.

'George III,' Charles purred. This wasn't much help to Dick, in fact. 'Camelback!'

Camelback? Dick hesitated. Was this – an insult? A form of upper-class contempt for those base forms of life who didn't know when George III had been? *Camelback?* Dick straightened up.

'Oh yes!' cried Izzy. 'I can see its humps! Look, Dick!' Dick blinked. Ah, it was the sofa they were insulting.

'And what a lovely colour. I love that deep red.'

'Rough silk,' said Charles caressingly. Izzy almost fainted with pleasure. Rough silk! What a delicious juxtaposition of ideas. A Charlesian kiss, she was sure, would be composed of just these elements. Soon she would learn to use the word *Carolean*. She had a lot of learning to do. But Izzy loved learning. It was sheer pleasure to her to discover the new. This was the reason she was such a good teacher, of course. And now, obviously, the new world she was to discover was The Past. It could not have suited her mood better.

She had arrived back at Heathrow bursting with longing for some idea of an England that would be solid and yet luminous: real and rooted. San Francisco had seemed terribly recent, and fragile, too, with the warnings in the phone directories about what to do in case of an earthquake. She had arrived home with a hunger for history. And here it was, embodied in this quaintly authentic young man, with his horn-rims and tweeds and Gesso mouldings.

Izzy gazed at him as a cat contemplates a saucer of cream. She was sure she'd have this Bernini business under her belt in no time. Meanwhile, she was reassured that, amongst the delighted gazes he bestowed upon his beloved house, he still shot the odd glance of feverish attraction in her direction.

Dinner – or *supper* as he called it (Dick had more or less learned by now not to call it tea) was an odd affair. Sooty had concocted a chicken-in-almond-and-sherry sauce, which they carried into the garden. Neither Izzy nor Charles could eat much, sickened by their secret desire. Dick was hungry, luckily – all that Italian had given him an appetite. He devoured almost the whole dish without noticing the strange languor of his companions. Charles kept up a pretence at conversation whilst Izzy sat abstracted, paralyzed with happiness. Eventually Charles took Dick indoors to worship the Amstrad (housed, ingeniously, within a Very Fine Empire Roll Top Secre taire, circa 1810.)

Izzy stayed out in the garden to quiver slightly and watch the moon rise. She wandered down between the shrubs, and admired a white rose with strangely ruffled petals and a green eye in the heart of the flower. As she bent to sniff it, an overpowering whiff of Tandoori drifted over the fence from the nearby take-away and mingled – satisfyingly, Izzy thought – with the rose's light scent.

As the last glimmers of daylight lingered on the statue at the bottom of the garden, Izzy suddenly realized with a jolt that there was something strange about it. The Greek youth – so elegantly turned on one hip, so carelessly displaying his chaste white charms to the enchanted observer – wasn't a real statue – he was a mere picture: painted onto the flat wall.

'My God!' exclaimed Izzy softly, craning her neck forward, the better to examine the artifice. 'I really must get my eyes tested. Why, he isn't real at all!'

SAINT CUPID, THEN, & SOLDIERS,
TO THE FIELD!

Days passed. Charles rang Izzy up early in the mornings, when he knew Dick was out, to arrange assignations in Covent Garden. They sat on Piazzas and sipped coffees Izzy would never have dared afford on her own. His brogues nestled up against her Joan Crawford peep-toes, which she found agonizingly charming. They didn't hold hands – they held feet. Mind you, Izzy's feet were fairly agonizing, too. They were held together with bits of sticking plaster. She couldn't take much more of this high-heeled teetering.

Charles leaned forward on one such occasion and placed a chivalrous hand on her arm.

'Izzy,' he ventured, 'forgive me, but why do you wear such awful shoes?'

Izzy blushed. Her heart pounded. She felt like a stupid fifth-former called out and humiliated before the whole school. 'Oh – er, don't you like them?'

'Well, to be honest – I go for something a little lighter. A little bit more like an Empire pump.'

An Empire pump? What was that? Some archaic piece of agricultural machinery?

'What do they look like?' asked Izzy eagerly. She would gladly have crammed her little feet into sardine cans to please her new love.

'You know, like dance shoes. Ballet shoes. That girl over there's wearing some.'

Izzy followed his gaze and identified a much younger girl, wearing a short skirt and stripey tights. Her very long legs terminated in tiny flat shoes which evidently Charles much admired.

'Oh those! Of course. What did you call them? Empire pumps?'

'Well, they're of the period, you know. The early nineteenth century.'

'Ah yes!' Izzy had learnt to greet the early nineteenth century with a broad smile. 'They are pretty little shoes. Much more to my taste, really. These were – were—' She hesitated. Whom could she blame them on? 'Dick's choice, I'm afraid. He thought they might help his – his problem. I'm only wearing them at the moment because I thought it would – would be a good idea to wear them out, you know. And to tell you the truth, I'm so hard up I can't afford new ones.'

'Dear little Izzy,' whispered Charles intensely, 'I cannot have you in this state. Come!' And he paid the bill, and led her off to a nearby shoe shop.

Izzy wasn't really ready for shoe buying. If she'd known she was going to take her shoes off in public she'd have washed her feet before she left home, and renewed the sticking plaster. As it was, she found herself in one of the most elegant and disdainful shoe shops in Covent Garden: the sort of place where shoes are hardly displayed at all, but concealed behind artful antique urns and modish arrangements of giant pebbles.

Izzy kicked off her shameful Joan Crawford peep-toe jobs and whipped off the bits of dirty plaster clinging to her heels and toes. She asked the salesgirl for a stocking, and waited for it with her feet tucked up under her, to shield Charles from the overwhelming odour of hot-footedness which she felt was spreading inexorably through the whole shop. But Charles didn't need protecting. He was off among the Empire pumps, sniffing and wagging his tail like a dog at the fair. He emerged with two tiny, soft cringing shoes: one pale green, one faintest face-powder pink.

'Try these on, Izzy,' he beamed, and slipped them tenderly onto her feet. 'The eau de nil is stunning, I find,' he concluded. Izzy thought it would at least match his hall wallpaper. She herself inclined to the pink. But so did he. 'Blush pink . . .' he pondered. 'It really is flesh pink, isn't it? A bit like Madame Jules Thibaud.'

'Who?' asked Izzy, wondering if he was savouring the memory of some previous affair with a married French woman. Just the sort of previous affair Charles might have had, too.

'She's a rose,' laughed Charles, caressing the little flesh-pink slipper. 'An old-fashioned rose, you know, Izzy.'

'Oh yes. How lovely!'

'I think we'll take both pairs, shall we?' he said. 'You look splendid in them, Izzy. And these are on me. An un-birthday present, if you like.'

'Oh Charles! Thank you!'

Izzy was a bit worried about the dear little slippers, though. What was she supposed to wear for stomping round the muddy cobbles and desperately hard granite setts of the filthiest capital city in the Western World? Her little shoes seemed too frail even for the silky-smooth floor of this terribly up-market shoe shop. Still, she smiled gratefully at her benefactor. It was a new experience, being treated like this. Most of her previous boyfriends had been even poorer than her. It was touching of Charles to want her to have nice things.

'I'll wear the eau – the green ones now,' she said, executing a little twirl in them.

'Yes,' beamed Charles. 'We'll take a taxi home.'

Home? A taxi home? Izzy's heart skipped a beat. So far, though Charles and she had enjoyed several coffees and teas, he had not offered her hospitality at his house – with all that that implied. They had sat and chatted in the sunshine, and he had gazed deep deep into her peerless eyes, but he certainly didn't seem in much of a hurry to get on to the next bit.

Izzy, on the other hand, was dying for it. She was more or less out of her depth in discussions about different sorts of marbles or the exact pink of certain old roses – things Charles seemed to spend much of his time exploring – but

129

when it came to the cuddling business, she did feel she was on home ground. Once she could get to grips with his skin – on a really large scale – she was sure she'd be able to contribute a little more to what was, so far, in some ways rather a one-sided relationship. She ached to fold him comprehensively in her arms, but dared not initiate such a thing. So they hailed a taxi, hand-in-hand, with a breathless sense of things to come.

In the taxi, he lifted her foot onto his lap, and caressed the frail kidskin of the slippers with touching tenderness.

'You know,' he whispered, 'when I first met you, I was struck immediately by a resemblance.'

Oh no, thought Izzy. *I look like some girl out of his past. She jilted him and now he's trying to turn me into a model of her or something*. . . . But he was not thinking of his own past.

'Who?' enquired Izzy.

'Emma Hamilton.'

Izzy had vaguely heard the name before, but wasn't sure who Emma Hamilton was. Was she perhaps one of the old roses about which he so often raved?

'I can't remember who she was!' laughed Izzy.

'You know – Nelson's mistress.'

For a moment Izzy thought foolishly of Nelson Gabriel. But he meant *the* Nelson.

'Yes. I've got a picture of her at home. I'll show you. She was a great beauty.' He let his eyes run boldly over her. They came to rest on her eyes. 'As indeed you are, my dear Izzy.'

Izzy thought for a moment he might kiss her, then. Really kiss her for the first time. In a taxi. How romantic. But he didn't. He turned instead to her feet again.

'When we get home,' he whispered, apparently addressing her toes, 'we will throw your ugly old tormentors away.'

Izzy wondered what on earth he meant.

They got home, paid the cabbie, and then Charles gently relieved her of the paper bag containing her old

Italian peep-toe Joan Crawford C-F-M pumps.

'Goodbye to all that,' he whispered, perhaps a bit portentously, and dropped them into a rubbish bin.

Izzy felt a twinge of hurt. She had had a good time in those shoes, in the past. Why, Michael had – but she would not think of Michael. As this dear delightful eccentric fellow who undoubtedly loved her had indeed insisted, Goodbye to all that. She took Charles's arm and as they walked up his steps and across his threshold; through the skin-thin Empire pumps Izzy felt the cold hardness of the flagstones in his hall.

She hesitated at the foot of the stairs. Were they, she wondered, in an upstairs-situation now? Dare she hope for a closer acquaintance with Charles's freckly person? Or were more chair-rituals necessary, first? Or perhaps the camelback sofa was destined to witness their first embraces. Yes, probably that was it. Charles disappeared into the drawing-room. (Izzy had already learned not to call it sitting-room. She was making good progress.) Izzy followed. He stood at the far end of the room, with a small picture in his hand. He turned to her.

'Here's your *doppelgänger*,' he remarked. 'Emma Hamilton.'

A very pretty face looked out at Izzy: a face with large grey eyes and framed by pretty black curls. Emma Hamilton was a lot handsomer than Izzy would ever be. So of course she was immensely flattered by the comparison.

'I do wonder,' mused Charles, putting down the picture and lifting Izzy's hair up off her neck, 'whether you've ever thought of a chignon.'

'Oh, you mean, put my hair up, sort of thing?'

Having Charles so close to her, and in an utterly private place at last, made her heart beat so fast that she could hardly speak coherently. But Charles seemed unaffected. He stood back from her slightly, and examined the effect of her hair up.

'Yes,' he concluded. 'Yes, it does look good. Having it all bushy around your face like that—' he let it drop into

131

its normal wild tangles ' – is such a waste. It looks a bit like a Brillo pad, you know.'

Izzy was mortified. Had her hair really irritated him so much? She hardly ever thought of it. And when she did, she was glad it curled so wildly, because that way it didn't really matter when she forgot to brush it or went out in the wind. A Brillo pad! She felt slightly sick.

'With it up,' concluded Charles, 'you look simply magnificent. Like a Goya or a Gainsborough.'

Izzy felt humbled. It was as if she had never really understood what she could be. But here was her saviour. He would salvage her and set her up shining on some remote throne. She could feel it. She could feel the conviction of happy-ever-after humming in every vein. She lifted up her face to him again and there was nothing but delight in it. In such circumstances, and standing so close to her, Charles could not in all conscience avoid the ultimate kiss.

They stood under the chandelier for some minutes, Izzy's heart racing and rattling like a rickety old train going out of control down a precipitous slope. When the first kiss turned into a panting hug, she was relieved to hear his breath roaring in her ears and to feel his surging excitement.

'I'm going to take you upstairs,' he whispered. 'I can't resist you any longer. Come.'

They went upstairs. Into the Master Bedroom, with its awesome canopied bed and its handsome black marble chimneypiece. Charles's silver-backed hairbrushes gleamed from a mahogany chest. Izzy saw herself reflected in an oval mirror, as she came into the room: and her face looked open and frightened, but with a glint of excitement, like a child's playing hide and seek. She sat gravely on the bed, repressing her urge to hurl herself on it, and waited for his instructions. She wanted so desperately not to jar on his refined nerves: not to be vulgar and wrong.

'Why don't you undress here,' said Charles decorously. 'I shall undress in the bathroom.' And he bent down and brushed a kiss on the top of her hair. Izzy was astonished. Getting undressed, first! It was extraordinary. In her experience, the tearing off of clothes was all part of the fun. Once the train had started to run downhill you let it carry you helter-skelter and bumpity-bump until you arrived breathless and bruised at the bottom. These gracious pools of inactivity puzzled her. These pauses, of course, only intensify desire, she thought, tearing off her dress. I am really such a very crude primitive creature, compared to him.

Naked, she stole into bed. The sheets did not smell of male body, at all. They were clean on today, obviously: they crackled slightly. Had he planned it for today, then? She lay back on the pillows, tucking her hair away under her head in order to look more like Emma Hamilton and less like a hawthorn hedge in a gale. These were the civilized rhythms of a new order, she told herself. These pauses, these gradual modulations, these discreet arrangements, they were the way to live. Her hopeless history of scrambles and scrapes must give way to real grown-up life, at last.

Izzy sighed and stared at the canopy above her. She was filled with portentous feelings. This was It. Here she was at last. In a moment the bedroom door would open and he would be revealed. Somehow she hoped he wouldn't be entirely naked. But of course he wouldn't. He'd have a dressing-gown on. Probably a Chinese silk one with dragons embroidered on it. He'd sit on the edge of the bed, then lean down and kiss her brow. This was how it would all begin. Restrained. Careful. And scintillating with erotic energy. Izzy tried hard to relax every limb, but they were all fizzing with excitement. She knotted and un-knotted her toes in an ecstasy of anticipation.

Five minutes later, she began to worry. Where the hell had he got to? Had he had a stroke in the bathroom and was even now slumped upon the floor, among the sage-green towels? Had he cut his throat with his silent movie type cut-throat razor? Was he lying in a pool of blood, turning the sage green red? Had he – the thought was even worse, somehow – done a bunk? Decided she was too smelly, too vulgar, too Brillo Padesque? Was he even now shinning down the drainpipe from his bathroom window? Flitting away through the streets of Spitalfields, never to be seen again? Izzy's heart palpitated now with terror. It was getting a lot of exercise these days. Should she get up, venture to the door, open it and peep out? Knock, everso gently on the door of the bathroom? But what if he was – on the lavatory? Nothing could be more disastrous than to be importuned by an anxious woman when you have only taken a few moments off to attend to the demands of nature.

Izzy tossed and turned uneasily. The canopy shifted slightly above her head. Outside, a lorry went past. Somehow its cheerful rumble was immensely reassuring for a moment. Izzy felt a twinge of regret as it faded away in the distance and was replaced by the stillness of the house. Then she heard a dim sound in the bathroom. The sound of running water. He couldn't be completely dead, then. Or utterly fled. Perhaps he was still contemplating a visit to her violently empty arms. But still he did not come.

Izzy curled up in the foetal position. It must be at least ten minutes since he'd gone. More, maybe. What was he doing? What should she do? Suddenly she wished she wasn't naked. She felt, not triumphantly naked, but awkwardly so. Was he her Lord and Master? If so, what the hell was keeping him? She pulled the covers over her head and closed her eyes tight. Izzy had a useful faculty of being able to fall asleep in self-defence. When most of us would be bound to wakefulness by the intolerable coil of nerves, she somehow managed to wrench herself away from the world and slide gratefully into sleep.

She was with some children on a hillside. They were perhaps on a school trip. She was definitely responsible for them – and they were venturing far too close to the edge.

'Come back!' she called, knowing there was a precipice

there. But on they ran: and disappeared into the cloud. 'Come *back*!' screamed Izzy, and tried to run after them. But her legs were too heavy to move. With a supreme effort she dragged herself to the edge of the beetling cliff: she looked down, her head swam, the edge of the cliff crumbled under her foot, and she plunged towards the abyss. With a scream and a great convulsion of limbs, she awoke to find Charles beaming down at her.

For a moment she did not recognize him without his glasses. He looked like Trevor Howard. Had she awoken in some other life, some 1940s film? He was sitting on the edge of the bed, as she had foretold, but his dressing-gown was not Chinese silk with dragons. It was simple traditional camel wool with brown and cream braid piping. She realized as she admired its austere integrity, how vulgar her idea of Chinese dragons had been. Luckily she had not confided it to Charles. She blushed at her secret lapse of taste.

'You were asleep!' he seemed amused and slightly pleased. 'So the prospect of going to bed with me is so exciting that you can't even stay awake?' She reached up and pulled him down. She'd had enough of higher forms of communication. It was time for skin to talk unto skin.

Twenty minutes later, Izzy was staring at the canopy again. So there. They'd done it. They had become lovers. Part of her celebrated, exulted. This very superior man had proved himself in love with her. She hoped so, anyway. He hadn't said so in so many words, yet, of course, but Charles wasn't the sort of man for casual sex. She wasn't the sort of woman, either. Not now. She was becoming more refined by the moment. She tucked her hair under her head again, wanting to give the illusion of a chignon. But Charles stirred beside her, and pulled her hair out again, and spread it over the pillow.

'Now,' he patiently instructed her, 'it's best like this.'

Izzy smiled. Let him do what he wanted with her hair. She knew men had funny little ways. And Charles being so definitively a man of taste was bound to have more funny

135

little ways than most. She snuggled in to his curiously white chest. A few fair hairs nestled modestly there, and a tasteful light scattering of freckles. Her own arm looked as brown as an Indian's, thrown across his flesh. Mahogany and marble. This was, Izzy concluded, the most satisfying moment of her life. Even if – but never mind about that. There was plenty of time for that.

Not all men are such practised seducers as Michael Tristram, she reflected. Charles had probably not had many girlfriends. He had spoken of two – not a terribly impressive score for a man of thirty. He had lived a celibate life for the past few months, and there had been long periods in the past when he'd also been solitary. Nothing wrong with that. It showed a man of prudence and with a sense of dignity. Charles was not a bed-hopper. So compared to Michael's feverish repertoire of erotic technique, Charles's simple English bull-at-a-gate approach was not surprising.

Izzy was surprised that the bull-at-a-gate image had crept naughtily into her consciousness. She smiled secretly into Charles's armpit. There was something touching about his simplicity. She would teach him, gradually, new refinements. After all, they had the rest of their lives together. She hoped. And anyway, it was only the first time. The first time is always a little rushed, a little fumbled. Next time she would initiate things. How long would it be till the next time? she wondered. There was a clock on the wall – a ship's clock, possibly, gleaming with brass and mahogany – but it did not appear to be working. Izzy wondered if he'd like her to go down and get a cup of tea whilst he recovered his strength.

'Shall I nip down and get us a cup of tea?' she ventured.

'No thanks,' said Charles, sighing. 'I'm afraid I have to see a man in half-an-hour. Better get up.' He kissed her temple and swung himself out of bed, pausing only to dive into the camel dressing-gown. So Izzy was cheated of a brief glimpse of his male beauty. He went out into the bathroom and she heard the sound of rushing water again.

He was evidently having a shower.

Izzy lay in a stupor. She was disappointed that this delicious afternoon was not going to be prolonged. That there would be no opportunity for her to demonstrate the peculiar charms of Michael's breathing-on-the-pulse-points technique. It was interesting that Charles seemed to be all for delay in the endless social rituals leading up to bed, but once in, he couldn't wait to get it over. Izzy smiled indulgently. She was glad to have an area of expertise to offer her lover in exchange for the universe of taste and judgement in which she was his apprentice.

Still she wondered about what his hopes and expectations were. Was she just a brief fling, for him? Or was there any future in it? Then, with a spasm of discomfort, she remembered her wretched 'marriage' to Dick. She longed to tell Charles the truth: that she was free, single, independent and piping hot. Ready to have slipped a diamond ring onto the appropriate finger any time he liked. Were diamonds vulgar, though? She thought they probably were. Never mind the actual ring. She'd let Charles choose that. But he simply had to be told that the business with Dick was an elaborate – but harmless – lie. He had to be told.

He came into the bedroom again, dressed and fresh-faced. He sat on the bed. For a moment Izzy was tempted to hurl herself at him with renewed vigour. Michael had always responded very well to such provocations. But she resisted the temptation. She knew she had to box clever with Charles. In the absence of actual cleverness on her part, the next best thing was to lie doggo and say nothing. Let him make the running. Or in his case – the crawling.

'Still in bed, eh?' he mussed her hair up a little. 'You look like a little weasel with your slanty eyes. A weasel in its nest.'

Izzy smiled. It was the first time she'd been called a weasel. But it was quite a lovable image.

'Look, Izzy, this Dick thing is bothering me,' Charles went on. 'I mean, you are so – so wonderful. But what can

137

we do until this business is sorted out?'

'I know,' said Izzy, on the verge of confession, but failing at the last moment. 'I'll – I'll get a divorce.'

'That's right,' said Charles. 'And be quick about it, darling. Because do you know what? I want you to be around for a long, long time.' He bent down and gave her quite a promising kiss – a kiss which uncurled and grew and almost sucked him down into more afternoon madness. But Charles was a man of business and dragged himself away.

'I must go and see a man about some mouldings,' he grinned, leaping up. 'Stay as long as you like. Help yourself to anything you want.'

'When will you be back?' called Izzy.

But he was already thundering down the stairs and did not hear. *Just as well*, thought Izzy, getting up and pulling her clothes on. *I must not be here when he gets back. I must be mysterious. I must not hang about boringly. I will be cool and elusive.* She slipped her dear little Empire shoes on, twinkled down the stairs, resisted the temptation to leave a loving note, and opened the door to a great welcoming whelm of sunshine. On the way home, she felt every cruel stone through her skin-thin slippers, but she did not care a bit. Sunshine and the chance at last of real happiness were flooding through her and singing in every vein.

HE'LL NEVER HIT THE CLOUT

Izzy filled with a great urge to see Michael and Louise. They knew Charles, of course. So they might have all sorts of exciting information to impart. Izzy had not mentioned Charles to Aunt Vinny, since the falling-in-love had got under way. She wasn't confident about her ability to stop her eyes from shining or her voice from trembling when talking about him. Every morning when she woke up, she felt a great kick of happiness when she remembered that he was in love with her. She'd even started writing poems. She simply had to share this overpowering excitement with somebody.

Louise would be the person. And Michael of course. She'd wanted so much to introduce a really impressive man to Michael, to be able to say, 'This is my husband.' Or even better, fiancé. Better because more *exciting*, newer, with the bloom of love still shining upon the whole thing. And now here she was, near as dammit, with the very thing on her arm. Except that they never did go arm-in-arm – or hold hands, except in taxis – because of her supposed married state. She would reveal her treasure to Louise and Michael. This would get Michael out of her system for good. She still had surprising dreams about him. She'd had one only a night or two ago. Odd. It took the subconscious so long to catch up.

But first she must have a word with Dick. The first grains of truth must be shaken in poor Dick's direction. She'd hardly seen or noticed him, now, for days. He lurked about the flat, still brought in her morning tea before disappearing tactfully onto the streets. But since Izzy now spent so much time with Charles, she was very seldom home. She wondered vaguely what Dick had been up to, if indeed Dick could be said ever to be up to anything. He would rejoice with her, she knew. He was her comrade, her mate. They had been through a year in San Francisco together. He was a good sort. A brick. Izzy decided to tell him all about Charles this very morning. She stretched herself out voluptuously in her empty double bed and waited for her tea.

Punctually at eight-thirty, Dick knocked softly on her door. He loomed up with a steaming cup, and Izzy pretended to waken, smiling sleepily at him, since actually lying waiting for one's tea did seem rather, well – over the top.

'Morning, Izzy,' he said. 'The weather's broken. It's raining.'

'Oh, is it really? I bet it'll smell lovely! Just open the window, would you, Dick? Let's smell the wet garden!'

Dick fumbled with the latch. The sash window looked out onto the garden: the bench under the rosebush, all Aunt Vinny's precious shrubs: everything was glittering with droplets of water. And the smell was heavenly. Wet earth. Wet leaves. Izzy inhaled deeply. Wet dust.

'Oh Dick! Isn't it marvellous!'

'Yeah. Great.' Dick hesitated. This was usually the moment at which he withdrew. But Izzy seemed open, this morning: welcoming, almost. He shuffled towards the door, nonetheless.

'Wait! Sit down, Dick.'

Dick looked round awkwardly.

'On the bed! It's all right. I won't bite you!'

More's the pity, thought Dick.

'We haven't had a good talk for ages. How are you, Dick? How's tricks? What have you been up to?'

Dick flinched. To be honest, he'd been spending more time than was absolutely desirable in Soho. He didn't know what was the matter with him at the moment. Perhaps it was the school holidays. In a school term he'd be too tired for wicked thoughts, but at the moment he was absolutely rampant. He was beginning to wonder if he'd better pack his walking boots and depart for a really gruelling hike through the Lake District. With thirty miles' worth of blisters, and dense Cumberland rain sluicing down the back of his neck, perhaps his mind would at last falter and abandon its persistent images of feverish ravishment. Even then, though, he had his doubts.

Especially this morning. Mornings were always the worst, in any case. The body was rested and fed and raring to go. And there was this tip-toe ritual into the holy of holies, to give Izzy her tea. Often she was lying half out of bed. Dick felt like a priest maddened by the proximity of a tormenting goddess. He placed her libation on the bedside table and was glad enough, most days, to flee. But today she detained him. She made tender enquiries about what he was doing with his time. How could he tell her?

'Well, I haven't got very far with the househunting yet, I'm afraid. I have seen some places in Hackney which – well, the thing is, Izzy, I don't suppose you'd consider sharing with me again?' There. It was out. Blurted out. Well, it might as well be out in the open. Dick cringed, confident of rejection.

'Oh Dick – I'd love to.'

'Would you really, Izzy? I mean—'

'I'd love to – in normal circumstances. But something very very extraordinary has happened.'

'What?'

Dick couldn't decide whether it was bad news or good. Izzy was beaming at him. Maybe she'd inherited some money, and they could stay here. Dick had worked out that they could realistically afford to stay in this flat for another three days, so the need for an inheritance had become urgent.

'Oh Dick – I'm in love.'

The ceiling, and the three floors of Victorian brickwork above it, fell in on Dick's head. Despite the pressure of several tons of masonry on his shattered skull he nevertheless managed to smile – sort of.

141

'Wow, Izzy! Congratulations!' Dust filled his ears. He could not hear what she was saying. Perhaps he was already dead.

'I'm so glad you're glad. Oh Dick! Give me a hug!'

Dick flung his arms around Izzy with superhuman strength, and hugged her with all the despair of his thirty-two years. But Izzy only felt his comradely delight. He was taking it very well. He really *was* a brick. Nay, a brick, merely? He was a brickworks.

'Well,' said Dick, leaving her arms with a tragic sense that this was the last time he'd ever be admitted into them, even for congratulatory reasons. 'Well, Izzy, I am surprised. I mean, I never guessed – who is it?'

'Charles!'

'Who?'

'Charles, Dick! You know, Charles Armstrong. Aunt Vinny's nephew.'

Dick was crestfallen. For a moment he couldn't work out why. Then he realized that Charles was one of the few people who thought that he, Dick, was Izzy's husband. He felt in a way betrayed. Why, he and Izzy had gone and had dinner round there only a week or two ago! As husband and wife! What the hell was this Charles geezer playing at? Dick was mortified. If this was what it was like, being a husband, then he didn't want any part of it, thank you very much.

'Charles. Crikey!'

'Why Crikey?'

'Well, you know – he's – well, I wouldn't have thought he was your type, Izzy.'

'Not my type?' Izzy panicked, and yet was filled with sudden unreasoning fury. 'Why not? What the hell do you know about it, Dick?'

'Oh, nothing,' Dick shrank back into his shell instantly. 'Just – well, I just thought – well, I don't know what I did think, to tell you the truth.'

'Oh yes you do, Dick! You thought something! I know you did. What was it? Come on. Tell me!'

142

'No, no, it was nothing. It was silly.'

'You must tell me, Dick. Honestly. It's your duty. It's terribly important to me. Come on.'

Dick couldn't tell her the real reason – that he had wanted to preserve the illusion of his marriage to Izzy in one tiny corner of credulous humanity.

'No it is silly – I just thought, I mean – I thought he thought we were married.'

'Oh, he does.'

He does? This was horrible. Charles had seemed such a nice bloke. And here he was – stealing Dick's wife! Dick could have murdered him – although he wasn't quite sure, upon reflection, whether he shouldn't murder Izzy too.

'I told him it was a companionate marriage,' said Izzy. 'I'm sorry. I mean, well, I'm not sure what I do mean. But it seemed the best idea at the time.'

'Companionate? What's that?'

'I think it means, well, sort of Platonic. You know. No Sex Please We're British, sort of thing.'

Dick boggled. 'But what's the point of that?' he floundered. 'I mean, why would we be married at all, then?'

'Why are you making such a fuss, Dick, for heaven's sake? I mean, we weren't really married anyway. So what's the difference? I mean, why should you care?' Izzy was conscious of getting into rather hotter water than she'd bargained for. She'd wanted to share her wildly wonderful in-love-ness with a friend. With Dick. She'd wanted him to smile indulgently and say, *Fantastic* as more details of her luck emerged. To support her in her moment of triumph. And here was Dick being all obstructive as usual. She might have known.

'Well, I told him you'd had a nervous breakdown,' she admitted. 'And that I rescued you on Golden Gate Bridge.'

'You – rescued me?'

'You were trying to throw yourself over. To commit suicide, you see, Dick.'

'Blinking Heck! Honestly, Izzy!'

143

'So I married you to – well, sort of cheer you up.'

'But that still doesn't explain why we would have had a what's it called – companionate marriage.'

'Ah, well, there was one other thing.' Izzy blushed and hesitated.

'What?'

'Well, I told him you were – were impotent.'

'Impotent! Bloody hellfire, Izzy!'

'I'm sorry, Dick. I hope you don't mind.'

'Don't mind! Don't mind! Bloody hell!'

Dick got up off the bed and walked around the room, looking for some innocent piece of furniture upon which to vent his wrath. Some small table to swallow whole. It was all so monstrously unjust. Izzy watched him anxiously. This wasn't exactly the friendly *tête à tête* she'd wanted. She'd never seen Dick so angry. What might he not do? He might even strangle her, or something. You never knew with these quiet types. These loners.

'Look, Dick, I thought you wouldn't mind, because you and I know that it's very very far from the truth.'

'You can bloody well say that again!'

Indeed, Dick had for the past few days felt he was cursed with potence. It was the inappropriateness of it all which infuriated him. God knows, he offered enough inadequacies to the malicious observer. His acne-scars. His mangy beard. His dandruff. His smelly feet. His gushing armpits. His unfortunate habit of going to the lavatory. But impotence! Of all accusations, the most shaming.

'But what'll he think of me?'

'Oh, I'll tell him the truth – today, I expect. I couldn't face it at first, you know, because he's Aunt Vinny's nephew.'

'I see,' said Dick, though he didn't, really.

Izzy was encouraged by these modest monosyllables. They didn't sound like the words of a strangler; she drew the covers up to her chin, and smiled encouragingly.

'There's no need to be upset, Dick. If you want to

know, you're the least impotent man I've ever met.'

Dick frowned. He didn't want to look too pleased. All the same, he wanted to hear more.

'Am I? Really? Surely not.'

'Oh yes. It's the sort of thing that you don't usually say, but, well, you are. Believe me.'

'Hasn't done me much good, though, has it?' he remarked bitterly.

Izzy sighed. Men were so silly about this sort of thing. As if it mattered.

'Your time will come, Dick. Honestly. It's just that you haven't met the right person yet. Someone who'll really get you going.'

Dick was silent. He could not tell her that such a person was at this moment engaged in spreading lies about his virility.

'Come on, Dick. Don't look so hang-dog. Maybe you should get out more. Go to the movies. There's a fantastic French film on at the Curzon. With Gerard Depardieu. Did anyone ever tell you you look just like him?'

'No,' said Dick, getting up. 'I think I'd best be going.'

'Oh no, Dick, I mean, don't be like that!'

But Dick went. What a relief!

Izzy abandoned herself to dreams about Mr Right. Soon she must come clean about this absurd marriage business and then – why then it would be trips to see his parents, trips to meet her Mum, and who knows – his wonderful house was quite large enough for two. She sipped her tea. It was colder than one would have hoped.

Izzy went to Muswell Hill. She needed Louise. She needed a friend's receptive ear. She needed to spread her glorious new state about a bit. It would be good to tell Michael, too, although she was a little more anxious about him. He was capable of cruelties towards her and goodness knows how he might react when he heard that she was not, after all, married to a man he despised, but in love with a man he probably admired and looked up to. So off she went to Muswell Hill and in no time at all found herself sitting at the dear old kitchen table where she had learned so many truths about life.

Louise was alone. The nanny had taken Rose shopping, and Michael had taken Jack to the cricket. In fact, Louise had been deeply asleep for a delicious forty minutes – the prologue, she hoped, to at least another hour – when Izzy had rung the doorbell. Louise was contemplating murder as she bore down on the front door. But, of course, Izzy had the power to turn aside wrath. To a certain extent, anyway. Louise was still distinctly frowsy and bad-tempered as they sat down. A return of consciousness wasn't particularly welcome to her, these days.

'How are you?' asked Izzy, aware she must not blurt out her happiness without due acknowledgement of the trials of others. Louise looked ghastly, and Izzy was filled with a brief uneasiness. It seemed odd that some people could be in love whilst others were barely able to drag themselves from one day to the next. 'You look tired, Louise. What you need is a day out. I'll take you somewhere.'

'What I need,' snapped Louise, not too rudely, she hoped, 'is a decent sleep. A couple of hours' undisturbed would do. Four hours, even better.'

'Poor thing,' soothed Izzy. 'Still, this stage will soon pass. I expect. I mean, of course I don't know anything about it. I'm talking through my hat. But it is a stage that'll pass, isn't it?'

'We shall see,' said Louise grimly, resting her head on the tea cosy.

'But it's only tiredness, isn't it?' persisted Izzy. 'I mean, you're not ill or anything, are you? I mean, you haven't got post-natal depression or anything nasty like that, have you?'

'Oh no,' said Louise, laughing hollowly. 'Nothing like that.'

'And I'm sure Michael is doing his best.'

'He is – and that's what's so infuriating!'

'What?'

'This bloody nanny is practically climbing up him and installing herself in his breast pocket, Izzy.'

'Oh don't be silly, Louise, I'm sure she isn't.'

'She bloody is, I tell you! You haven't seen her! Honestly, Izzy, do at least give me the benefit of being able to assess the attractiveness of other women even if I have lost all my own.'

'You haven't lost all your own.'

'Don't be so patronizing! Of course I have! We've got mirrors in this house, dammit, Izzy! I still have eyes behind these bags, you know!'

'Well if you do look a bit worn out, I'm sure it's only temporary. While you're so tired. As soon as you have time to yourself and get a bit of strength back, you'll realize – well – it's just not true.'

'Don't tell me what's true or not true! I live here, Izzy – I live it, day to day. That woman is brooding over me like a bird of prey. She's wheeling about waiting for me to give up the ghost. Then she'll step in and walk off with the lot.'

'Surely there must be some fat old nannies you could have instead? Like in "Christopher Robin"?'

'Not any more, Izzy. They're all glamorous now. And I

147

can't face all the hassle of trying to recruit one, anyway. It's extremely difficult to get anybody at all in London. Oh yes. Everybody tells me how lucky I am to have Melanie.' Louise ground her teeth rather alarmingly.

'Wouldn't you like a biscuit?' suggested Izzy. Those teeth must be given some useful occupation before they buried themselves in harmless human flesh.

'There aren't any bloody biscuits. And Michael will have forgotten to buy some more.'

'Look, Louise – you need a holiday. Really.'

'A holiday? Oh, spare me all that, Izzy. Have you any idea what a nanny costs? What with Melanie and the mortgage I'm surprised we can even afford to go out into the garden, let alone on holiday.'

'But don't you know anybody you could go and stay with? Just for a few days?'

'But she'd have to come with us, don't you see?'

'Why?'

'To help with Rose. Otherwise we'd just both be totally exhausted all the time.'

'Well, why not go away on your own? You could go and stay with my Mum in Yorkshire. I'll come, too.'

'Oh dear, Izzy, you are being kind. I do appreciate it. But I couldn't possibly go away and leave my baby here.'

Izzy sighed. There seemed no way out of this maze. Izzy had been looking forward to having babies of her own in due course: thinking increasingly about it, recently. But she was beginning to have cold feet.

'At least it's only a stage,' she murmured, aware of her own total inexperience.

'But while it lasts, Izzy, I'm stuck with it. Oh God. I'm sorry to be such an awful bore. How are things with you? I heard you were married. Oh dear, I'm sorry – I should've congratulated you long ago.'

'Oh, it's not—' began Izzy, but stopped at the sound of the front door opening. Michael and Jack came in, and were followed by a blonde girl carrying the baby. Louise stared. Michael intercepted the stare.

'We saw Melanie and Rose in Muswell Hill,' he said quickly. 'So we gave them a lift home. Hi, Izzy! This is Melanie. Melanie, this is our newly-married friend, Izzy. How's married life?'

'Look,' said Izzy suddenly, 'the thing is, it's all a big mistake.'

'You can say that again,' smiled Michael, slumping down on the nearest chair.

'You see, I'm not married to Dick – not really.'

Michael boggled. He wasn't sure whether to exult or despair. He had been looking forward to cuckolding Dick in due course. Quite soon, in fact. And having Izzy safely married off to Dick meant that she wasn't in any danger of marrying anyone too wonderful. Michael wanted always to be able to patronize Izzy's husband. On the other hand, if she wasn't married, that would mean she had a place of her own – or could have – to which, in theory, he could from time-to-time bend his straying footsteps. The nanny tactfully withdrew upstairs, to change Rose's nappy. Jack went out to converse with his toad in the shed. The coast was clear for some grown-up talk.

'Not married? Why ever did you say you were, then?'

'It's terribly silly, really. Only your Aunt Vinny's flat was so nice, and I was so utterly shattered the day I went there – and she said she wanted a married couple for the flat, so I told her I was married.'

'You are completely mad, Izzy,' Louise shook her head in disbelief.

'I know. I realized that the next day. But it was worth it for the sleep. I had the most delicious sleep. It went on for hours and hours. Like a princess in a fairy tale. I think I might even have lost a whole day. It was jet-lag, you know.'

'And you awoke to find you were married to a toad.'

'Michael! Stop it! But Izzy – do you really mean that you and Dick have been living in Aunt Vinny's basement, pretending to be married?'

'Yes. Dick's been sleeping on the sofa. It's silly, really,

but I was so desperate. Do you think she'll mind when she finds out?'

'Of course she won't, silly. You really must tell her, Izzy. I mean, what if she found out by accident?'

'I know. Isn't it awful?' Izzy shivered. 'I'm a bit afraid of her to tell you the truth.'

'Who isn't?' agreed Michael, placing glasses of alcohol upon the table, although he wasn't sure there was all that much to celebrate, at the moment. He discovered that he'd been quite attached to the idea of Izzy being married to Dick. 'The old bat scares the living daylights out of me, I can tell you. All that about her spectral spouse hovering uxoriously behind the sofa. Not a place to loiter on a dark December evening, quite frankly, Izzy. The sooner you get out of there and into somewhere sane, the better.'

The problem of visiting Izzy at Aunt Vinny's had been tormenting him for some days. The idea of her living there alone was even worse. So tantalizing.

'Don't say such awful things, Michael! She is my aunt and she's a dear old thing. And she thinks the world of you, Izzy. She rang me up only a couple of days ago to say what a perfect couple you were.'

'But will she still think the world of me when she knows we're not a perfect couple?'

'Oh, I'm sure she will.'

'But I lied to her.'

'Yes, well, there is that. But if you come clean and spell it all out about Dick being a dear old friend and sleeping on the sofa, I'm sure she'll find it all a great adventure. *Such fun!* Can't you just hear her saying it?'

'So all that about Dick being such a great lover was all hogwash, Izzy?' Michael's mind was working fast.

Izzy hesitated warily. Though she and Dick were now, thank God, merely good friends, there had been one occasion, over a year ago, when she'd recklessly taken him home. Out of pity, mostly. But this was a trick question with many hidden trip-wires. Did she want Michael to suffer, at the moment, or not? Not, probably. She was delighted to discover that her instinct to hurt him had entirely evaporated. Being in love with Charles had wiped out the last shreds of bitterness.

'Honestly, Michael!' she managed a playful giggle. 'How should I know what Dick's like in bed?'

'Quite, my dear. He is rather a Knight of the Bargepole, isn't he?'

'I thought he was rather nice,' said Louise wistfully. 'Quite sweet, really. Shy.'

'Yes, well, let us not dwell on the doubtful virtues of Dick. May he find true happiness in the arms of an honest wench.'

'Dear Dick,' smiled Izzy. 'I really am very fond of him.'

They sipped the wine. The sun came out, and the whole room glowed briefly. Louise took off her headscarf and shook out her hair. Michael reached across and tousled it affectionately.

'So you reckon I should tell Aunt Vinny and it'll be all right?'

'Oh, yes. You must, Izzy. She's so pleased with you. She says you're the perfect tenant.'

'Ah, well . . .' Izzy smiled her secret smile. 'The trouble is, I might not be able to stay there very much longer.'

'Oh no! Really? Why ever not?'

'Well, the rent, for one thing. And there's something, well, you see. . . .' Izzy's happiness was bursting out of her at the edges: it simply could not be contained. Michael felt a cold hand squeeze his heart. He held on tight to the bottle of wine and tried to crank up a grin.

'What's cooking, Izzy? Don't tell me you've fallen for one of the ghastly layabouts that litter Westbourne Grove. Who is he? Let me guess – the Pakistani youth in the delicatessen. The one who thinks he's Imran Khan. In my view he more closely resembles Ghenghis.'

'Be quiet, Michael. Is there somebody, Izzy? Is something going on?'

'Of course something's going on. Look at her face. *The*

lineaments of gratified desire as old William Blake put it. And may I say you look very well on it, my dear.' Thus did Michael whistle in the dark. He was drinking very fast, but Louise did not notice.

'Who is it, Izzy? Go on – tell us.'

'It's Charles.'

'Who?'

'Charles Armstrong. You know, Aunt Vinny's nephew.'

'Oh no – not Charles!' cried Louise with a sensational hiss. Izzy was not sure what was coming. She trembled, dreading what they might say.

'Why not Charles?' she faltered. 'What's wrong with him?'

'Absolutely nothing as far as I can see,' said Louise. 'I've only met him a couple of times, though. A bit of a cold fish, I thought, but I'm sure I'm wrong.'

'What's he like in bed, dear heart?' sneered Michael, trying to fend off despair. Izzy married to Dick was a convenient arrangement: Izzy in love with Charles Armstrong was a disaster. 'Do drop a hint. I must say, from my brief conversation with him last October I had taken him for a poofter.'

'Michael! Don't use that word!'

'I'm sorry, Louise. A lamentable lapse. But all the same, Izzy – even my dear wife had perceived a whiff of cold fishery about him. Can two people of such maturity and objective judgement be wrong?'

'You certainly are wrong,' cried Izzy. 'He's quite passionate enough for me, thank you very much.'

She was aware, here, of a slightly heroic quality in her answer, a slight papering over of certain tiny hairline cracks that had spread across her sky of cornflower blue, but she dismissed it ruthlessly. She had already promised herself that she would be able to do something about that, given time. Besides, it was sweet and touching. When one was being worked upon, in a seductional scenario, by a man like Michael or Gwyn, one was all too aware of a long and varied history leading to a skilful technique. With

Charles, all she felt was his feelings. Under all his sophistication and knowledge he was still almost a little boy. She liked that, very much.

'Well, well, Izzy. How extraordinary.' Louise gave her a strange look. In fact, it was the look of one wrecked by fatigue, trying to remember what it was like to fall in love. But it was a look which froze Izzy's spine. She waited, desperately, for congratulations, for sympathetic exultation, for delight, but she got none. Michael looked quizzical and tormenting: Louise looked appalled. Izzy suddenly felt in danger of tears. What were friends for? For scaring the living daylights out of you?

'I have to go, though,' she said, getting to her feet. 'You must come to dinner. He lives in Spitalfields. Maybe you'll like him more when you get to know him.'

'I must get on with my script,' blustered Michael, taking his wine glass upstairs. 'Toodle-oo! And don't get engaged without asking our permission first. We are *in loco parentis* don't forget.' And he slammed the door and went upstairs to his den.

'He's gone up after her!' hissed Louise, instantly oblivious to all thoughts of Charles Armstrong. Her face had gone quite twisted and livid. Izzy felt frightened. She made her goodbyes and left. Louise, sunk in misery and getting drunk, was hardly aware of her going.

But Michael was. Leaning against the window upstairs, he watched her little figure go scurrying off down the hill. She was wearing an odd pair of flat slippers, he noticed. They enabled her to disappear far too quickly into the distance. The thought of her running with open arms towards Charles Armstrong, of them embracing and whispering, filled Michael with the deepest regret and the sourest pangs. It wasn't so much mere jealousy of Izzy's lover, though that was the sharpest sting: it was a sense of loss. His life, which had once been resonant with many different keys and cadences of love, seemed now no more than a bleak forced march.

A soft hand plucked at his shoulder. Melanie was

looking up at him with those large pleading eyes, carrying his child – though only in the literal sense, thank God.

'Is anything wrong, Michael?' she enquired, in her softest and most syrupy tongue. Michael groaned inwardly.

'No,' he said brusquely. 'I must work.'

But once in the safety of his study, he wandered to the window again. The road was an empty vista. Izzy was gone.

MELANCHOLY, SAD AND HEAVY

It was a dark day in Cambridge. One of the darkest places on such days of awful summer gloom, was New Court, Trinity College. Bill Bailey's van plunged up a deep green avenue of lime trees and then wheeled round into the sombre court of dark red brick, dominated by a huge tree which did its bit to overshadow the windows that opened hopefully onto the court. Under this tree on the north side, Bill Bailey parked his van. A porter who happened to be passing stopped and inspected it curiously. Bill jumped out.

'Ah,' said the porter. 'Good afternoon, Sir.'

'It won't be here long, Sid,' said Bill. 'Just unloading some stuff.'

''Course, Sir. Need any help?'

'No, thanks. It's okay. There isn't much.'

The porter nodded and went on his way, through Neville Court and towards the Lodge. He shook his head privately once in the Renaissance privacy of Neville Court, his footsteps echoing curiously over the flagstones that were beaten almost hollow with age. The college seemed empty during the Long Vacation, though some undergrads were up for the Long Vac term and they'd also had a conference or two. He met Ruby Miller by the screens outside the Hall.

'Just seen Dr Bailey moving his stuff in,' he commented quietly. Ruby was a special friend of his and she was Bill Bailey's cleaner.

'Oh dear,' she sighed. 'Poor love. I can't understand it. Can you, Sid?'

'Women,' shrugged Sid, as if Ruby were an honorary man. 'Who knows? She's shacked up with that Baumgarten. Zoology, you know.'

'What, that American fella?'

'Jewish,' confirmed Sid with distaste. 'I don't know!' And with heavy sigh and heavy tread he was off through the large echoing spaces of Great Court.

Bill Bailey unpacked his van. A few suitcases containing clothes and sheets and towels: these he deposited in the stark little bedroom. There were several cardboard boxes containing files and books. These were extremely heavy, but Bill, though thin, was strong. He'd been on a lot of solitary bike rides recently, out on the fen, bent double on his racing bike under a great boom of wind that seemed to blow down on him straight from Russia. The wind was trying to press him into the earth, but his legs and arms clung to movement. It was like climbing up the wind. Wiped clean with effort, his brain was burnished into a blank mirror like the sky. Thus did he strengthen his body whilst his soul reeled fainting down far-away precipices of harm.

Five cardboard cartons were soon stacked by the window of his first-floor room: by now he was panting, and he sat down on them to rest for a moment. He could see right down the avenue from here. Far away in the distance he sensed the heavy traffic passing along the Backs. Here it was quiet. He might find it difficult to sleep here, at first, after the relative rumble of Eltisley Avenue. During the day there had been the din from the garage next door. And most of all the prattling and shrieks of Susannah. He dropped his head into his hands, and pulled his hair until the roots screamed against his scalp.

At length, he looked up, and stared down the avenue, driving his eyes out of focus: beyond the traffic, beyond the Fellows' Garden on the other side: beyond Bedfordshire: beyond the Rocky Mountains on the other side of the earth. He had never felt so tired. Perhaps he would manage to sleep a bit here despite the silence. Despite not being woken up by a deep croaky little voice calling 'Dada!' in the night: wanting her pee or a drink of water. Despite the terrible stillness and solitude, perhaps he would be able to sleep at last.

He almost fell asleep in his chair. Then he shook

himself, reached down and opened one of the briefcases. A few seconds' scrabbling and he had found what he wanted: a handful of framed photographs. He selected one immediately: it was of himself, looking rather Rupert Brooke-ish with a long strand of hair falling down the side of his face, holding Susannah. She clung to his head with her mighty little arms and her black curls danced eternally in the wind. Behind their heads was blue sky. She didn't look much like him, at all: the black curls and the snub nose were Marianne's. But perhaps there was something there in the genes, something that would emerge sooner or later. Something invisible of his that would nevertheless link her to him, across the years and the miles. His smile, perhaps. His voice. His inner music.

Who had taken that photograph? Ah yes, Charles. Bill put the photo away and sighed. He arranged the ones of Susannah on his mantelpiece, but left Marianne's image to smile at itself in the shadowy depth of the briefcase. One day he would feel able to take it out again. Not now. He wanted to remember the irritable, faithless woman she had become, not the Goddess of the brambles gleaming three years ago. He clung to his hate. He felt it could give him the strength to get through the next little bit of life. Susannah was now grinning at him from among the curls and whorls of his fossil collection. Something barely three-years-old peeping from forms which had lived millions of years ago. Before mantelpieces. Before man.

Ah well. He must go and take the van back. He locked his rooms and drove back towards the van-hire place. He passed crowds of French adolescents milling about outside the language schools. The place was thick with tourists. He passed the house in Bateman Street he'd shared with Charles before he'd met Marianne. That seemed such a very long time ago – but it was only about eight years. He wondered how Charles was. Of course he'd have to write to him. He'd have to write to all his friends, and tell them that he and Marianne had split up. Otherwise they'd all experience a series of embarrassing meetings, phone calls, impromptu explanations, blushings, awkwardness. Marianne would

157

never think of writing to everybody. And of course, with Susannah on her hands all day, she'd have a lot less time.

He returned the van and paid the charge. There was a TV set flickering in a corner with the Test Match on it.

'What's the score?' he asked the man.

'They bowled us out for 121,' he grumbled. 'Bloody selectors want their heads examining.'

Bill grinned as he wrote his cheque. It was funny how you could still grin.

Walking home – or rather, back to Trinity – he heard a child sing, and thought of Susannah.

I'll teach you a song about me, he'd said to her once . . . *It goes like this:* WON'T YOU COME HOME, BILL BAILEY, WON'T YOU COME HOME. . . . She had laughed delightedly and it had become one of her favourites. She called it the Dada-song. Was she singing it now? Was she saying to Marianne, 'Where's Dada gone? When's Dada coming home?' He bloody well hoped so. He wondered if he could drop in this evening. Marianne had asked him to phone first. He supposed that was reasonable, but he found it monstrous. Telephoning to make an appointment to see his daughter! She who had always been on his knee, rolling on the floor with him, or at the very furthest, roaring out music hall songs in the next room.

King's Parade seemed artificial in the gloom. It seemed spectral, cut out of grey paper. He had been in Cambridge too long. But how could he apply for jobs elsewhere, whilst Susannah was in the same town? It was likely that one day Baumgarten would take Marianne and Susannah back off to the States. At the thought, his guts knotted themselves into a fierce ball of anguish which could only be relieved by vomiting or tears. He strode down Senate House Passage and arrived eventually at New Court.

As he leapt up the stairs and fumbled for his keys, he thought how fortunate it was that he had had these rooms in college, with all his work things already installed. He had never spent much time here apart from teaching. Well, now he had to live here. At least it was central. Very convenient if you're caught short in town and need to rush back and howl or puke. He locked himself in and threw himself on the bed in the tiny dark cell of a bedroom. He drew the pillow over his head and let the tears flood out. Then the phone rang.

He leapt up. He'd always been the one to leap up to answer the phone, door or baby. Marianne was a bloody idle cow. He liked that thought, as he ran into the other room. It was distinctly helpful. Bloody idle cow.

'Bill Bailey.' He sniffed slightly.

'Hello Bill! Got your hay fever again? This is Charles.'

'Charles! How are you?'

'Well, not bad at all, as it happens. Better than for a long time, in fact.'

'Really? Good!'

'Yes. The business is really taking off. The house is nearly done now. And I've – well, I've met somebody.'

'Ah. I see. Who is she?'

'Oh, just a schoolmistress. But she's quite something, Bill.'

'She must be. Yes. I'm sure she is.'

'There are a few problems to be sorted out – she's married to somebody else, in a way. But it's more or less over as far as I can make out.'

Bill felt a sick spasm. Everywhere it seemed to be the same. He wondered about this woman's husband. Where was he, whilst Charles courted his wife? How was he? Bill felt a great urge to have a drink with him. For a moment he could not speak to Charles. For a stupid moment Charles was the enemy.

'Hey – Bill – are you still there?'

'Yes. Yes, I am.'

'Well, listen, there's this ball in a couple of weeks – you know – the Conservation Ball.'

'Oh yes.' Bill was vaguely aware of it. He had seen the posters. He realized that he wouldn't get much sleep that night with the endless thump of bands and the shrieks of revellers. Never mind. He would work. He had to finish his book by the end of the summer.

159

'Well, I was thinking of bringing her up to it. So we could see you.'

'That would be – yes, very nice.'

'I say, we couldn't possibly stay the night with you, could we? I mean, say no if it's inconvenient.'

'Look, Charles, things are a bit difficult at the moment.'

'Oh well then, never mind.'

'You see, it's just that – Marianne's kicked me out.'

'What? Good God! Surely not! I rang her just now and she didn't say anything. She just said you were in college.'

'Well, she has kicked me out. I've just been moving my things in here. I'll have to live in my rooms for a while.'

'Oh God. How awful for you.'

'It's been rather hard. Yes. But I'll be all right.'

'You probably feel better now you're out of it.'

'Well, in a way. Yes. But there's Susannah, you see.'

'Of course!' Charles had forgotten the child. Typical. He hadn't got a clue. Bill smiled to himself.

'And it's hard to feel that home isn't home any more and you have to make an appointment to go there.'

'Jesus! How ghastly.'

'Yes. But, anyway. There's nothing I can do about it.'

'Was it – er – was it mutual?'

'No. It wasn't. She got involved with someone else. A zoologist.'

'Oh dear,' Charles sounded guilty and embarrassed. 'Life is a mess, isn't it?'

'Well, it's all coming right for you, by the sound of things,' Bill reminded him. 'I'm glad. Yes.'

'Well, look here, Bill, I hope we'll be able to see you, at least.'

'Oh yes. Of course. It'll be – lovely.'

'We'll stay at a hotel then.'

'I'll book you in somewhere, if you like.'

'Oh, would you really? It's the night of the fifteenth. Well, it'll be the following day really, I suppose. I don't know if I can last the course, to be honest.'

'We're all getting old, aren't we? Unloading the van just now I nearly had a coronary.'

160

'Bollocks.' (Charles allowed himself the occasional judicious oath – he felt it gave his male discourse a necessary touch of sinew.) 'You're always frighteningly fit.'

'Not at the moment. Bit down.'

'You need a holiday, old man. I'll see if I can fix something.'

'Well, you know, I've got that book to finish this summer.'

'Don't worry. You'll get it done. You were even scribbling away at something that time we were walking in Umbria.'

'Oh yes. The Darwin book.'

'Christ! Wasn't it hot? Now look! You're a genius, Bill. Don't let this Marianne business get you down. Someone else will come along. Even I got lucky in the end.'

'Yes. Congratulations.'

'Got a bit of sorting-out to do first. Then I think it'll be a trip to meet the Aged Ps.'

'Really? It's as serious as that, then?'

'Deadly, old man. Wait till you see her.'

'I'm looking forward to it.'

'I'll ring you soon then – about the hotel.'

'Yes. Goodbye.' Bill was looking forward to seeing Charles with a woman. It had been a fairly rare sight over the last ten years. Those that had appeared had not distinguished themselves by their vivacity. Mind you, he was used to Marianne. Charles's taste was a little more muted. Bill wondered idly about this new woman of Charles's. A married schoolteacher. She sounded a bit more interesting than the usual Sloaney types. Perhaps she'd settle down with Charles and make him a bit more human.

Bill was looking forward to seeing them. It was something to have a tiny sliver of life to look forward to. He would go out now and have something hot to eat. He felt hungry. Life was not letting go. And after his meal he would have his hair cut very short. He was fed up of looking like Rupert Brooke.

O MOST PROFANE COXCOMB

Izzy was vacuuming in a frenzy. She was expecting Charles. Today was the day. Today she would make a clean breast of it, privately and quietly to him, and then he would no doubt work out the best way of telling Aunt Vinny. Izzy dreaded Aunt Vinny's displeasure – although even if Aunt Vinny was hurt enough by the deception to ask her to leave, that would be all right, too. Izzy knew she could go and stay at Charles's place. The thought of living with him was frightening and exciting and wonderful, all at once. Izzy hadn't really properly co-habited with anybody before. She'd always kept her own place to escape to if things got a bit difficult. But now she felt sure she was ready. She longed to be part of Charles's elegant establishment: to adorn the camelback sofa with her hair up, looking like Emma Hamilton. She felt as if she would then be grown up, at last.

Right now, she had to get rid of these crumbs. And there were the last of the flowers to throw away. She felt a twinge of sentimental regret as she plunged them into the rubbish bin. They marked the first day of her being in love with Charles, and they had lasted for over two weeks. Now, though, they had withered and gone smelly. She gasped with nausea as the foul water cascaded out of the vase and down the sink. Strange that something that began with such beauty could end so horribly. She sluiced plenty of hot water down and scrubbed the sink urgently with bleach. Dear Charles! She had never thanked him properly for those flowers.

The doorbell! She charged upstairs, struggling with her rubber gloves as she went. It was a shame she smelt of bleach rather than Diorissimo, but he was a bit early. She flung the door open eagerly, and there, to confound her tender expectations, stood Gwyn. Head on one side, leaning against the pillar, with a strange lopsided smile on his face. Panic leaped in Izzy's throat.

''Ulloa, my dear little darlin'!' he boomed. Not a very helpful salutation for Aunt Vinny to overhear.

'Gwyn! How are you? I haven't seen you for ages!'

She did not ask him in, but he came anyway.

'My, my, you got a stupendous bloody place here, girl. How much does it set you back, like?'

'This bit isn't mine,' flustered Izzy, shooing him urgently downstairs. 'We live in the basement. And do you mind keeping your voice down a bit? I don't want to disturb the landlady.'

'Well, well,' grinned Gwyn, taking in the comfortable furnishings with an expansive sweep of the eye, 'you certainly fell on your feet again, Izzy Comyn. I'll 'and this to yew, girl, you certainly know 'ow to feather your nest.' And he collapsed onto the sofa with an unnerving finality.

'Actually, I can't possibly afford it,' whispered Izzy. 'I'm going to have to move out soon. Just as soon as I find somewhere. Or – I mean, it's just a temporary sort of place, you know. She's Louise's aunt.'

'I knoa. I found out all about you from Louise, see? Rang 'er a few days agoa. Now what's all this about yew bein' married to that Dick bastard, sweetheart?'

'Oh, that's all a mistake,' said Izzy, hurriedly.

'Tellin' me it's a mistake, girl. You're not goin' to be allowed to throa yourself away on some 'alfwit ceramics artiste, Isabelle – even if he has got impeccable proletarian origins.'

'Well, I haven't. We just—' she dropped her voice to a whisper. 'We just had to pretend we were married, to get this flat. She wanted a married couple, you see.'

'Aye aye. Soa – Dick's a lucky bloake, like, for a coupla months, is it? Did yew couch up to 'im in San Francisco then, girl? Case 'o the babes in the wood, was it?'

'No, no, Gwyn. There's nothing between us. Dick sleeps on the sofa.'

'Well, I'm very very glad to hear it, girl. I came over here, see, to apologize, like, for my unspeakable conduct last time we met.'

'Ah. Yes.' Izzy blushed.

'Read your signals wrong, like. Mind you, you should be more careful, darlin'. Flashin' them sparklin' little eyes o'yours around!'

'Hush, Gwyn! Let's say no more about it. Look – I'm expecting somebody just now. Would you mind going? Maybe we could all get together for a meal sometime. I haven't seen Maria for ages either.'

'Aye. Aye. We noticed, sweetheart. That's why I came round to apologize, see? I doan't want to get in the way o' my wife's best friend comin' round and cheerin' her up.'

'Oh dear. Is Maria depressed? I'll ring her this afternoon. Only would you awfully mind – just, well, sort of going, Gwyn? It really is a bit inconvenient, at the moment.'

'Ah. Well, as to goin' – I'd be only too happy to oblige you, darlin', only I got certain procedural obstacles to negotiate.'

'What?'

'I've over-indulged in alcohol this lunch time, girl.'

Izzy tugged urgently at his sleeve. 'Look, please go, Gwyn! I'm expecting somebody, any minute.'

'You ashamed o'me, then? Ashamed o'your old Uncle Gwyn?'

'Of course not!' Izzy blushed desperately. He seemed to have taken root in the sofa.

'Trouble is, darlin', I can't walk. I'm immovable, sweetheart. Sorry.'

He keeled over slightly sideways and looked up at her through weird glazed eyes. Izzy grabbed his arm and pulled.

'Come on! Please, Gwyn! Listen – you can sleep it off in the bedroom if you like. As long as you lie still and say absolutely nothing.'

He grunted, and got up and lurched into the bedroom quite easily after all. He fell onto the bed.

'Take my shoes off, will you, sweetheart?' he mumbled. 'It's about a hundred miles to me feet from where I'm standin'.'

'You aren't standing!' scolded Izzy, taking off his shoes. She had an acute feeling of *déjà vu*. What must it be like to be married to Gwyn? For a moment she felt a shock of guilt about Maria. She had totally neglected her. Ignored her. She would ring her and go and see her – as soon as this business with Charles and Aunt Vinny was over.

Gwyn snored peacefully into the pillow. Izzy tip-toed out and shut the door firmly. She was sorely tempted to lock it, too, but thought, upon reflection, it might lead to worse trouble. Then she performed a few last tidyings, thinking about Maria. She hadn't just neglected her because of that awful scene they'd had, although she cringed whenever she thought of it. There had also been an instinct, once Charles was on the scene, to stay away from Maria. Izzy dreaded Maria's verdict on Charles, somehow. But at the same time, she did miss her dreadfully. She had occasionally felt very lonely in the past couple of weeks and she knew she needed her friends. Louise hadn't been much use. She felt a great urge to ring Maria right now. But the doorbell interposed.

'Darling!' whispered Charles, embracing her with his eyes. Izzy just beamed at him. For a moment they stood together on the threshold, admiring each other – but also listening, for the house was full of possible spies and eavesdroppers. In fact, it was even fuller than Charles suspected.

'Come down!' whispered Izzy, and they crept into the relative privacy of the flat.

'Is Dick out?' asked Charles.

'Yes!' whispered Izzy, launching herself into Charles's arms. They surrendered to a sixty-megaton kiss, and experienced that loss of confidence in the legs which leads inevitably to the joys of the horizontal. Charles sought the sofa, and drew her down towards him. For a moment Izzy collaborated, then she froze. What if Gwyn woke up? What if he came floundering out? And what if Dick came home? Or Aunt Vinny called down, *Coo-eee! Are you decent?* – and they weren't?

'Oh dear, this is no good,' she whispered, escaping. 'This place really isn't safe. But things will soon be better—' She paused and took a deep breath. Now was the moment to tell him everything. That she wasn't married to Dick. That she was perfectly free to give all of herself to him, if that was what he wanted. And she fervently hoped that it was. 'You see, Charles, I'm not really—'

She was interrupted by a deep, earth-shaking snore from the bedroom. Charles nearly jumped out of his skin.

'What in the world was that?'

Another snore arrived, even more emphatic than the last.

'It's – it's Dick!' gasped Izzy.

'But I thought you said he was out!'

'I thought he was! But he must have been in, after all!'

SNOOOOOORE!

'How desperately inconvenient. But I thought you said Dick slept on the sofa?'

'Oh yes, he does. Usually. But in the daytime, sometimes, when I'm out, he has a little snooze, you see.' Izzy was nearly fainting with the effort of preserving her world. 'Because he can't sleep very well on the sofa. He often has bad nights. So then he just catches up a bit in the daytime.'

Charles looked cross. And worse, he looked suspicious. Izzy leapt up.

'Let's go out into the garden,' she urged. 'It's so lovely out there. The roses smell fabu – exquisite.'

Charles obeyed. So out they went. Izzy felt physically sick. One moment she had been within seconds of clearing the air and coming clean with Charles – and the next, she was sunk in even deeper swamps of deceit. Why was her life like this? What malicious fairy was casting a blight on

166

her best attempts to be good? That was the most awful thing of all. It seemed to be so very hard to be good. It seemed as if the universe was warped.

Izzy sat on the bench and Charles joined her – decorously apart, for the garden was communal and overlooked by all Aunt Vinny's windows as well as Izzy's bedroom. Thank God there were net curtains in there, thought Izzy. And thank God she hadn't locked Gwyn in. If he had any tact he would rise from his slumber and quietly depart. Alas, she was fairly sure that tact wasn't one of Gwyn's conspicuous virtues. At this moment she wasn't confident that he could even make any claim to consciousness.

'Coo-eee!'

Before they could so much as exchange a single word, they were hailed from Aunt Vinny's windows, above.

'Charles darling! How lovely! I'll come down and bring some Pimm's!'

'This really is an impossible situation,' remarked Charles very quietly.

'I know, I know, I'm sorry,' said Izzy.

'Well, it's not your fault, Izzy.'

'Isn't it? Oh, crumbs, I suppose it isn't.'

Izzy was sure it was, though. In fact, she was losing her grip on what exactly the situation was. And whatever it was, it couldn't possibly get worse. Could it?

It could. The French windows swung open and Dick, of all people, walked towards them with a strangely purposeful air. Dick! He had an absolute gift for being in the wrong place at the wrong time.

'Dick!' choked Izzy. 'You've woken up!'

Dick was surprised. He'd been awake for six hours. But he was not going to let himself be distracted from what, to him, was a deeply important mission.

'Have a good sleep?' enquired Charles amiably.

Dick ignored all these tiresome references to sleep. He was a man with a message.

'Look here, Charles,' he said, purposefully – he had

three pints of Newcastle Brown inside him, and was determined to restore his dignity. 'I want you to know that I am not, repeat not, impotent.'

'Good heavens, old chap!' gasped Charles. 'Anything you say.' Aunt Vinny took this opportunity of bursting forth from the house, carrying a tray.

'Hello, everybody! What's going on? Anything exciting?'

Izzy cringed. It was all far too exciting. But on the other hand, they couldn't go on talking about impotence with Aunt Vinny there. So perhaps her arrival had been a blessing. Perhaps Izzy's good angel had sent Aunt Vinny out. The drinks were certainly welcome. Izzy seized hers and emptied it almost immediately.

Aunt Vinny settled herself comfortably on the bench – Dick was crouching on the grass at her feet, like a faithful hound. Izzy needed a subject of conversation that was reliably fascinating. The men seemed silenced by thoughts of impotence. Even Charles was unable to utter the slightest syllable of small talk. Izzy knew what he was thinking. He was thinking – if Dick *isn't* impotent, then what? What the hell is Izzy Comyn up to?

'How's Rupert these days?' Izzy snatched at the only straw that offered itself.

'Ah! My dear, how strange that you should ask. Today's Rupert's birthday! And all day I have had the most curious feeling. . . .' They all sat very still. An aeroplane crawled in the sky overhead. The garden took on an unearthly calm. 'I've been feeling, well, almost as if he might put in an appearance!'

Goosepimples fled across Izzy's skin. She would never have believed that she could feel so spooked in broad daylight. But the intensity of Aunt Vinny's conviction was infectious. Izzy drank another glass of Pimm's, as if it was lemonade. Her head began to swim. The leaves all glimmered eerily, now: the back of the house cracked in the heat.

'In fact . . .' Aunt Vinny put down her glass, and

stared. 'In fact, even at this very moment, I feel he is very very close to us. Yes! Rupert darling, we are ready. Do, please, send us a sign. Come, Rupert! Come!'

'Crikey!' said Dick suddenly, 'there's smoke coming from the bedroom window!'

'No, wait! Be still!' commanded Aunt Vinny. 'It is not smoke! It is – ectoplasm!'

They all stared at the window, Smoke was billowing through the net curtains, inside. Izzy was frozen with horror. Then the window was thrown open.

'I saw his hand!' shrieked Aunt Vinny. 'Oh Rupert! Is it you?'

A TV set, smouldering and sparking, was hurled out onto the grass. Aunt Vinny fell to her knees before it as if supplicating some primitive icon. 'Dear Rupert! Is this a sign?'

'The bloody TV exploded!' boomed a voice within.

'Oh *Rupert!*' screamed Aunt Vinny, 'Please, darling! Reveal yourself!' There was a moment of complete silence. The TV crackled faintly but not portentously. The only danger was that Izzy might die of embarrassment. The net curtains were thrust aside by a majestic hand. Gwyn appeared at the window. He was obviously naked apart from red underpants of a skimpy design. He leaned on the windowsill and surveyed his audience.

''Ulloa, everybody,' he grinned. 'Luckily I was able to draw on my superhuman strength, like, and chuck the bugger out.'

'Who *is* that person?' enquired Aunt Vinny.

Dick leapt to his feet. Now Charles knew he was not impotent, he was Izzy's knight at arms again.

'It's just a friend of mine—' he mumbled. 'A bit the worse for wear. He's been celebrating. I'll deal with him.' And he ran indoors.

By now Izzy felt she was no more than a small carrier bag full of old clothes which has been set aside for the jumble sale. Gwyn was still grinning from the window. Izzy dared not look at Charles. Was this the end of everything?

'I feel as if I'm on TV, like,' confided Gwyn. 'Sir Alistair Burnett. *And now, cricket. Glamorgan beat the West Indies today by an innings and six hundred runs.*' Gwyn was seized from behind and disappeared in a froth of whirling net. *Please God,* begged Izzy, *give strength to the arm of thy servant Dick Barnes as he struggles with the forces of Dionysus.* The window slammed shut. She needn't have worried. Dick was eager to prove how potent he was and folding up and getting rid of Gwyn was the perfect scenario. There were sounds of a scuffle from within, but there was a sense of diminuendo about them which was reassuring.

Izzy felt it was up to her to speak. Her credibility was in ruins – must be, by now. She was too dizzy and too drunk to work out exactly how bad it looked, but she was sure it looked pretty bad. She had to grasp the truth now, before she was hurled to Outer Darkness and Destruction.

'Look!' she cried, so urgently that Charles and Aunt Vinny both turned their faces with some alarm towards her, 'the thing is, I must tell you. Both. I'm not married to Dick. Never have been. There's never been anything between us. We're just good friends. He sleeps on the sofa.' And, to her astonishment, she burst into tears.

WHO IS HE COMES HERE?

Charles was driving north. From time to time his left hand strayed from the wheel, found Izzy's hot little paw, and squeezed it. Charles was feeling better. At first, mind you, the revelations had rather numbed his mind. The fact that Izzy had never been married to Dick was almost disappointing. After all, Emma Hamilton had been married to old Hamilton. And they had had a very civilized little understanding with Nelson. Very early Georgian, that ménage. Still, it was with some relief that he realized that Izzy was his for the asking – if that was what he wanted. He wasn't quite sure if it was. He thought so, probably. But this trip north would help. Meeting Izzy's mother would be quite informative. They say women come to resemble their mothers.

'Oh dear,' shuddered Izzy, quite pleasantly, now they were travelling comfortably away from London and from the recent past, 'wasn't it awful when Gwyn looked out of that window? I nearly died!'

'Frankly, darling, it was no more than mystifying, to me. And it had the very salutary effect of jolting Aunt Vinny out of her religious ecstasy.'

'I suppose so. Didn't she take it well? About Dick and me not being married, I mean.'

'Well, she is an old sport, of course. And the truth was so very innocent – or was it, my darling?' This, playfully. For Charles.

'Of course it was! How many times do I have to tell you? I've never had any kind of scene with Dick. Or Gwyn. They are both just friends. And always have been.'

'Well, look here, Izzy – I hope you never feel the need to

tell lies to me. About anything. OK? I hate deceit and I'm a very straightforward old buffer. You don't need to be ashamed or embarrassed about anything any more. I can take it! Is that clear?'

'Oh yes, Charles! Thank you! You are – lovely!'

Izzy relaxed and contented herself with a series of sly glances at his profile. Driving really brought out the best in him. He was wonderfully sensible and phlegmatic at the wheel. Not like Michael, who lurched and juddered according to the beatings of his heart. Or Maria, whose driving was Kamikaze in its aggression. Maria! Oh help! Izzy still hadn't got in touch with her. A wave of guilt flooded over her. The Dénouement in the Garden – Aunt Vinny's – had blotted out all Izzy's other obligations.

She wondered, with some anxiety, what her mother would think of Charles, and vice versa. At least, she worried about her mother's reactions. She knew Charles would adore her mum. Everybody else had, so far. Although with Charles you could never tell. But what would her mum think of him? Of this? Of Izzy's impossible-to-conceal in-loveness that twinkled wantonly from her eyes? She must try and be a bit sensible at home and play the cool and poised creature that Charles would probably have preferred anyway. She must not blurt, or bound, or snatch. She must be careful.

'I like Yorkshire,' observed Charles as they encountered it. Huge airy vistas unfolded on each side: small square fields looked across at them from hillsides: sheep were everywhere, and streams, and little humpbacked bridges, and stone walls. 'I had a friend at Cambridge who came from Ripon. Lovely little town.'

'Are you still in touch with him?' asked Izzy.

'Her.'

This odd little monosyllable caused a twinge of panic in poor Izzy's heart. She was rapidly reaching the stage of insane jealousy of all Charles's previous girlfriends.

'An ex-girlfriend?' she asked, with, she hoped, a gossamer lightness hiding her inner dread.

'Yes,' replied Charles. 'Not for long, though. She was a manic-depressive.'

Silence fell. Izzy did not want to hear more about the manic-depressive from Ripon. There must be happier topics which could enliven their last half hour in the car.

'Look,' she said, playfully, 'I hope you realized that my mum will have put you in the spare room.'

'Well, of course,' smiled Charles.

Izzy felt rather foolish. 'She's a bit – you know – old fashioned, you see.'

'Naturally. She sounds quite splendid.'

'And after all, we haven't known each other very long.'

'Quite. I can assure you, my dear, that the spare room will be extremely acceptable.' Izzy felt oddly disappointed. He might at least have said how much he'd miss her cuddly little person in the night. 'Though I shall, of course, miss your furry little body in the night, my weasel.' Ah. There it was. You see? It was all right, after all. She quite liked being called Little Weasel. It was, in an odd way, an endearment.

'What time does your ma have dinner?' enquired Charles presently.

Izzy felt a qualm of unease. 'She doesn't have dinner,' she faltered. 'She has tea. You know. High tea.'

'Ah, yes, of course,' smiled Charles. 'Yorkshire.'

That made it all right, somehow. Izzy was left with a feeling that it was lucky that she had grown up in Yorkshire. It enabled her to get away with things that might otherwise be a Bit Off.

They arrived at the farm house in a spell of windy sunshine. Izzy's mother appeared on the doorstep, flanked by the two cats. She held her hand up to her eyes to shade them from the strong sunlight. Izzy hadn't seen her for a few months, since her mother had braved the Atlantic and visited her in San Francisco. As she bent to kiss her mother's cheek, Izzy noticed that she looked smaller, thinner and more fragile than before. Her heart lurched with fear. Was something wrong? Was she ill? Or just beginning, suddenly, to get old?

'This is Charles, Mum,' she said, putting her arm round her mother's small shoulders. 'Charles, this is my mum.'

Charles was delighted – and delightful. The farmhouse was a gem, the situation wonderful, with the sort of wild views he admired. Indoors, he was ravished by the two oak settles, gleaming in the firelight. He was dazzled by the rows of sparkling plates on the dresser.

'Why it's absolutely superb!' he cried, more moved than Izzy had ever seen him. 'Simply marvellous! What a wonderful place for you to come home to, Izzy.'

It was, in fact, an almost intact Georgian farm kitchen Charles's head swam in sheer pleasure. He sat down, as invited, upon one of the settles, admiring its upright hardness.

Mrs Comyn was setting before them a Yorkshire tea, and at the same time keeping a shrewd eye on this young man. She quite liked his looks, though she was puzzled by the sense that he belonged somehow not to Izzy's generation, but to her own. Didn't Izzy's contemporaries wear bomber jackets and jeans? The Young Fogey phenomenon had not yet reached this corner of Yorkshire. The young fogey in question looked out of the window and up the moor.

'One can almost imagine the Brontës striding around up here,' he observed.

'But they *did*!' cried Izzy, eager to ingratiate her native landscape in her metropolitan lover's heart. 'They lived just down the road in Haworth, you know. And if we walk up there after tea, I can show you the site of the original Wuthering Heights.'

'Top Withens,' added Izzy's mum, somewhat cryptically.

'That's what it's called,' Izzy explained. 'It's only a ruin now, but everybody goes up there and tries to imagine what it might have been like, then.'

'No end of them Japanese, every summer,' commented Mrs Comyn.

174

Dear me, thought Charles. Izzy's mother was very much a countrywoman, even unto her syntax. But all the same, she showed a correct aversion to the Japanese tourist. Charles also preferred a Mrs Comyn who was absolutely genuine, of the people, than some middling middle-class parvenue who said pardon and put the milk in first.

'Milk and sugar in your tea, Charles?' enquired Mrs Comyn, putting the milk in first. Oh well. You can't have everything. Charles accepted milk and sugar as if they were the first delicacies he had experienced in his thirty-odd years on the planet.

Mrs Comyn sat down and stirred her tea. Izzy's heart fluttered anxiously. She feared this look in her mother's eye. Even so had she looked at ewes that were bad mothers, or lambs not likely to survive.

'It's a long time since Izzy brought a friend home,' commented Mrs Comyn. Everybody knew she didn't mean just friend, either. It was a warning of her deep puritanism.

'Well, I'm very glad she was kind enough to invite me,' beamed Charles. 'Such a lovely spot! I'm surprised you can stay away so long, Izzy.'

'Aye,' commented Mrs Comyn. 'I'm surprised, too, sometimes.'

'Oh Mum!' cried Izzy in dismay. 'I know I haven't been for a year, but I have been on the other side of the world.'

'I believe you visited Izzy in San Francisco, Mrs Comyn?' asked Charles, obliging his hostess by tucking into a buttered scone.

'Aye, I did that,' Mrs Comyn sipped her tea with Sibylline poise and silence.

'What did you think of it?'

'Steep.'

'Ah! How interesting. In what sense, exactly?'

'In every sense.'

'Mum found it all terribly expensive,' added Izzy, hoping to get off the subject of money soon – a subject, alas, all too fascinating in Yorkshire.

'I'm sure it was! And there must be a lot of wealth over there.'

'More money than sense.'

'Quite. Absolutely.'

'And how do you earn your bread, Charles?'

'I've got an architectural salvage business.'

'Run your own business, do you? You must have your head screwed on.'

Charles modestly inclined his head – to demonstrate, perhaps, the extent of its reliable embeddedness upon his trunk.

'Oh yes!' enthused Izzy, 'Charles is a real businessman, Mum.'

'I hope so,' commented Mrs Comyn. ''Cos this one's half-daft.' She nodded curtly at her daughter, who blushed and cringed.

Charles was caught in a delicate paradox. Should he defend his fair one's mental capacities? Or would that be offensive to the mother? Did the mother, in fact, know best? *Was* Izzy perhaps half-daft? Charles threw her a brief glance and yes, he had to admit it, there was the faintest suggestion of daftness hanging over her. But he found it rather lovable. She who thought Carolingian had something to do with Christmas carols. She had so much to learn. Dear Weasel!

'The thing is,' he explained, 'I've always been fascinated by old buildings. So running the business is more of an enthusiasm than anything else.'

'If you like old buildings,' observed Mrs Comyn, 'you'll find plenty to your taste in Yorkshire.'

'Oh yes! It's absolutely wonderful up here.'

'Another cup of tea, Mum?' Izzy hovered with the tea pot, anxious to be of service.

'No thank you, duck,' Mrs Comyn pressed a napkin to her lips. 'The second cup's always a disappointment.' She cast a critical eye over Charles's plate. 'Not eating much, are you, Charles? You'll waste away, lad.'

'My dear Mrs Comyn! I am attempting to do justice to

your magnificent spread. That chocolate cake looks particularly tempting.'

He was given a piece which, in other circumstances, might easily have delayed the progress of a lorry down a hill, and bit into it gallantly. When his mouth was full of cake, Mrs Comyn smiled slightly more expansively than she had hitherto. *She's melting,* he thought. *I just have to eat myself sick, and I'm home and dry.* Izzy smiled encouragingly. She was resisting the chocolate cake so far. She was much too excited to eat.

'Well,' observed Mrs Comyn at length. 'I was surprised to hear Izzy was bringing you home, Charles. I hadn't heard anything about you before, you know.'

'I know,' gasped Charles, almost choking to death on a crumb. Mrs Comyn's timing was lethal. 'Of course. I hope it wasn't too much of a shock.'

'How long have you two known each other?'

'Oh, not long,' admitted Izzy. 'But we got to know each other quite fast, didn't we, Charles?'

Charles hesitated. The conversation was skirting dangerously close to certain deep pools.

'I know our Izzy, lad,' said her mother. 'She jumps into things with both feet and her eyes closed.'

'Oh Mum! I don't!'

'I think perhaps your mother has a point, Izzy.'

'She's like a cat, though, is our Izzy. She always seems to land on her feet.'

'I'm sure she does.'

'Where do your parents live, Charles?'

'Norfolk.'

'Oh, Norfolk.'

Mrs Comyn nodded. Charles had the feeling that he'd just managed to escape some unspeakably dissolute county. Surrey, perhaps. But Norfolk had backbone and history: they both knew it. And while it was not Yorkshire, it was at least austere and empty.

'Have you taken Izzy home to meet your parents yet?'

'Not yet. We wanted to come here first. I so much wanted to meet you.'

Mrs Comyn gave a pleased little nod. Charles felt he was winning. But he knew he must not pile the compliments on too thickly.

'And what line of business is your father in? Farming?'

'In a way,' Charles faltered here. He realized that farming would have been the best answer. And in a sense his father did dabble in sheep. But honesty compelled him to acknowledge that there was more to the picture. What's more, he wanted to reassure Mrs Comyn that her daughter would be financially comfortable. 'He has a business too, so the farming is really more of a hobby.' Mrs Comyn arched her brows to hear of farming so described. 'He's got a fertilizer company,' Charles went on. 'He did research at Cambridge and then went into the agrochemicals business. FARMSTRONG. His name's Frederick Armstrong, you see.'

'Oh, Charles! How clever!'

'I know Farmstrong,' acknowledged Mrs Comyn. There was no need to say any more. Charles was evidently a man of some wealth as well as good manners. What lay within would only emerge with time. 'Come upstairs,' commanded Mrs Comyn, rising.

Charles leapt to his feet. What was this? A matriarchal rite? The *Droit de la Mère*? Was she going to give him the once-over in the high old feather bed in which his little Izzy had, in all probability, been born? He cast a quick glance at Izzy, but she was looking equally puzzled. Mrs Comyn brushed the crumbs off her lap and looked Charles up and down.

'I think you're the right size,' she pronounced. The right size – for what? And was she going to ask him to strip off, upstairs, whilst she made absolutely sure with the yellowing old Yorkshire tape measure in which every inch was equal to two standard ones? 'Come up.'

They trooped upstairs, Izzy as mystified as her consort. Mrs Comyn led them into the ancestral bedroom, where

178

indeed Izzy had started life. Its beams and fine mullioned windows caught Charles's eye, but it was the wardrobe the little old woman was making for. There, next to her own clothes, hung three suits that had belonged to Izzy's dad. Mrs Comyn took one out. It was brown tweed, evidently of fine cloth. She stroked it tenderly.

'My late husband's,' she said softly. 'I think you're about his size. Now would this be of any interest to you?'

Izzy gasped. The thought of Charles wearing her dad's clothes was odd. But she felt a rush of love for her mother, who had been so formal and careful in this interview so far. 'If it's of any interest to you,' said Mrs Comyn, 'tek it into the next room and try it on, love.'

Charles obeyed. Izzy fizzed with love for her dear old mum. She had called him *love*. Izzy flung her arms round her mum's shoulders and hugged her passionately.

'Oh Mum,' she whispered, 'you are lovely!'

'Nay, nay,' protested her mother, returning the hug, however, 'thou'rt daft as a brush.'

The hug persisted. Izzy kissed her mother on both russet cheeks. 'It's lovely to see you again, Mum,' she smiled. 'But you've got a bit thin.'

'I only want you to be happy, Izzy, love.'

They sat down on the bed to wait for Charles to emerge. When he did, he saw two pretty little women, one brown, one grey, with their arms round each other. A more charming sight he had seldom seen. They could have been a Hogarth, what with the modesty of the setting and the simplicity of their dress, and the sparkling light in their eyes. Mrs Comyn regarded him benevolently, and then broke out in one of her most appley smiles.

'To the life!' she pronounced.

'To the life!' breathed Izzy. It sounded like a dedication.

REASON AGAINST READING

'Well, your ma is an absolute poppet, darling,' observed Charles as they drove south. Two days of hill-walking, eating huge teas and sleeping in a hard single bed with the deep silence of the hills ringing in his ears, had impressed him with the integrity of Izzy's origins.

'Oh, I'm so glad you like her, Charles! And she was completely bowled over by you, honestly.'

Well, not quite honestly. But pretty nearly. Mrs Comyn had seen much to approve of and was sensible enough to leave the rest to time. She had kissed Izzy goodbye with her very best Hard Look, as if to impress upon her daughter the awful need to avoid daftness if at all possible, but she had said nothing to jar the pleasantness of the moment and had waved them goodbye with a blessing. It was time Izzy was properly married, she reckoned. And of course his money would help. Her fingers itched to start knitting. But till then she would polish the brass.

Izzy and Charles drove south in a trance of pleasure. Izzy had a sense of history in the making. She would remember this always, she was sure, this drive south into the sun. Every glance sideways confirmed her view that Charles had the straightest nose she had ever seen. And three days' abstinence had sharpened her appetite for his caresses. Charles had not been game for a romp on the moors, pointing out the absence of cover and the likelihood of their being spotted by a gaggle of Japanese photographers. *I'm not much of a Heathcliff, darling*, he had confessed, and Izzy contented herself with the thought that most other men weren't, either.

He may not have been a Heathcliff, but Charles was capable of surprises. At a certain stage he turned off the motorway and plunged into East Anglia. Izzy was dozing at his side. So much the better. He was in the grip now of a fantasy he'd had for ten years. He had, he was convinced, the right woman at last. All he needed was the setting. He drove fast – but not recklessly – towards Cambridge.

Izzy awoke to find him parking in a tree-lined road. She yawned and stretched with delicious abandon.

'Where are we?' she asked. 'Somewhere in Notting Hill?'

'Not even close. Guess.'

Izzy peered out of the window. She saw quite a lot of people on bicycles, an endless vista of trees beyond trees; much shade, and she sensed large important buildings secreted away amongst the leaves.

'It doesn't feel like London,' she admitted. 'It's not – somewhere in Norfolk, is it?' She hoped not. She wanted the assistance of a different wardrobe when she confronted Charles's parents. She was not ready for that, yet. Charles laughed and tickled her nose.

'Silly weasel,' he said. 'No sense of geography! It's Cambridge!'

·Cambridge! Izzy was delighted. She knew that Charles had been to Cambridge, and all she had heard about Cambridge over the years had conspired to give it a fairytale quality in her imagination. She squealed with delight.

'How lovely! Show me everything!'

'Steady on, darling! First I want to take you to a very special place. And it's going to be even more special, today, than it's ever been.'

Charles led her briskly down an avenue and onto a bridge. The bridge was a gentle upward curve, and its balustrade was ornamented with large balls.

'What enormous balls!' said Izzy, and immediately wished she hadn't. Charles ignored this unfortunate outburst, and leaned on the parapet with the air of a man who has reached his journey's end. Izzy settled beside him, admiring the view down the river, where punts threaded their way among willows.

'Isn't this lovely?' she ventured.

'Absolute heaven!' he replied. Then he threw his arm around her shoulders and drew her close to his side. Izzy reciprocated. She was feeling violently squeezy today. 'Listen, my darling little weasel,' said Charles, in a strangely serious tone. 'I always said that it would be on Clare Bridge that I would say what I am going to say.'

Izzy panicked. He had already lost her in mazes of sayings. But she held on tight to his tweedy side – to her father's coat, in fact.

'You see, my darling, I have got to the stage of having to say something very important to you, and I want it to be here.'

Izzy's heart bounded. What had she done wrong?

'I want it to be here, with us both looking down this lovely river.' The river rippled playfully away from them. Izzy waited with bated breath. 'You see, Izzy, I have reached the point where I simply have to ask if you will marry me.'

Izzy gasped, choked, and coughed violently. 'Oh yes, Charles!' she croaked. 'Yes please!'

A puntload of young people passed beneath them.

'Toby, you are an utter prat!' screamed somebody with an expensive voice. Charles was annoyed that this intervention had jarred his sacred moment. But Izzy didn't mind. The upper-class yowling from the punt drowned her coughs. *I mustn't choke to death, at this of all moments*, she thought desperately. *After all, this is the happiest moment of my life*. Eventually her breathing cleared again, and the punters drifted off, haphazardly, their intoxicated insults softening with distance and becoming almost picturesque. Charles retrieved the shattered bits of his fantasy, glued them together, and varnished them. Soon it was as good as new. Yes. He had proposed on Clare Bridge. And he had been accepted.

Now she had stopped coughing, Izzy couldn't help feeling it was time to slip into an endless kiss, or at the very least, gaze into his eyes for ages. She turned to him, face uplifted, but he merely gave her an affectionate hug and started off walking again.

'I don't know about you,' he said, 'but I'm absolutely starving.' They went to a wine bar in a cellar, where they ate smoked mackerel and salad. Izzy managed to slip a few morsels between her lips, but again she felt too excited to eat much.

'Look here,' said Charles, and she saw a swathe of coleslaw turn a somersault in his mouth as he spoke, 'you must eat, darling. Don't want you fading away. No need to slim, you know.'

'You did say, a few days ago, that I was within two millimetres of being too fat,' Izzy reminded him.

'Only within. Being on the verge of being too fat is just about right, you see,' Charles began to expostulate about the joys of pink female flesh as exhibited in the paintings of Titian. Izzy did not really listen. She was much too happy. All the women in the wine bar were, she was sure, casting admiring glances at Charles. And he was hers. Hers! Her husband-to-be.

Outside again on the pavement, Charles pointed out King's College Chapel. Izzy thought it was rather large for a college chapel but after her remark about enormous balls she thought she had better remain silent.

'D.H. Lawrence said it looked like a sow lying on her back,' Charles informed her. Izzy could see what he meant. She liked D.H. Lawrence. He was always rude where other people were reverent. She wondered what he would have made of Charles, but abandoned the exercise hastily. He would have despised him automatically, for the wrong reasons. For Lawrence was wrong as well as rude. This only endeared him to her more, of course.

'I love Lawrence,' she said, on home ground for a moment. 'Don't you?'

'Haven't really read much of his stuff,' admired

Charles. 'Only the sexy bits at school, of course. Think I prefer Hardy, on the whole.'

This information made Izzy feel rather sad, but she could not quite work out why.

'And Jane Austen, of course,' added Charles, running his eyes along familiar porticoes. 'Good old Jane. Nobody like her. What a wonderful woman! I wish I'd met her. I'd have been at her feet.'

Izzy endured a pang of jealousy directed at Jane Austen, whom she had never altogether admired. Jane Austen made Izzy feel more than usually untidy. Untidy all over. It was a feeling she did not like. Whereas D.H. Lawrence made her feel that her untidiness was only part of an earthy, tangled mass of life-energy. Or something. She was just about to try and express this, when Charles turned the conversation abruptly away from literature.

'We're going to meet my friend Bill Bailey, now,' he said. 'This way.'

'What a funny name!' said Izzy. 'Like the song. What's he like?'

'Desperately clever,' said Charles. 'Got a Double Starred First.' Izzy knew what this meant, having got a single benighted Third herself at a much less glittering university.

'Gosh. What subject?'

'History, of course.'

Of course. As far as Charles was concerned, there was no other subject.

'He's had a rough time recently, though, poor chap.'

'Oh dear. How?'

'His wife – dreadful woman, never liked her – left him. Or rather, even worse: kicked him out.'

'How sad. Is he very upset?'

'Couldn't really tell on the phone. Bound to be, I suppose. The poor fellow was absolutely bats about her. And they had a little girl.'

'Oh no! How old?'

'Not sure. Two, maybe. Or three. I can never tell. But of course poor Bill misses her like mad.'

'It's so sad. Oh Charles — we must never break up,' concluded Izzy with a desperate squeeze of her father's sleeve.

'Quite right, darling,' affirmed Charles. 'None of that nonsense for us. Bad for John.'

'John who?'

'John Ruskin Armstrong.'

'Who's he?' Izzy was puzzled.

'Our son and heir, idiot weasel. Our firstborn. Get it?'

Izzy collapsed into grins and giggles and Charles, carried away by the thought of posterity, almost kissed her in the street.

'Wait a minute, though!' she objected playfully. 'What if she's a girl?'

'Come come, darling!' said Charles masterfully, sweeping her through some tall gates, 'First things first.' Izzy smiled. He had such an eccentric sense of humour: she never quite knew when he meant things seriously.

'This,' said Charles, as they walked into a rather dark courtyard with a large tree in the middle, 'is New Court. *Why did they bother?* you may well ask. But though it is not a distinguished building, it does house the great Bailey.' Izzy looked around for the Bailey. She remembered it dimly from Norman architecture.

'This is his staircase,' announced Charles, and leapt up the stairs three at a time. Ah! Bill Bailey. Of course. His name was painted in white letters on a black background, along with several others, at the foot of the staircase. *Dr W.J. Bailey.* Charles hammered on a door on the first landing, with his own special knock: da da da DUM! The motif from Beethoven's Fifth. The door opened and a rather frail-looking man stood there. He had very short fair hair and a thin face that broke into a radiant grin at the sight of Charles. They exchanged a manly bear hug.

'You've cut all your bloody hair off,' observed Charles. 'You look like Machiavelli. Never mind. Bill, I want to introduce you. This is my fiancée, Miss Isabelle Comyn.'

His hand was warm.

IS THE FOOL SICK?

Bill Bailey's room was dark, and full of half-unpacked cardboard boxes. On the mantelpiece were several photographs of a very pretty little girl. Izzy made straight for these and examined them whilst Charles and Bill were exchanging the usual when-did-we-last-meet talk. Bill's voice was light, non-committal. You couldn't tell where he came from. Charles's voice rolled out with baritone emphasis, by comparison. Their voices knitted together in the confident way of old friends. Izzy felt at home here. The little girl looked out of the photographs with an enchanting sense of mischief. When she smiled, her nose wrinkled. She did not look anything like Bill Bailey. Her mother must be dark and gypsyish.

'Is this your little girl? She's absolutely lovely!' said Izzy. 'You must miss her terribly. Bill told me about it. I'm so sorry for you.'

Bill Bailey looked directly at her for a moment, then nodded.

'Thanks,' he said. 'Yes. I miss Susannah.'

'Bad show, old man,' added Charles. 'Must cheer you up somehow. I know! A picnic!'

Bill hesitated.

'I think Bill was in the middle of some work,' said Izzy. 'Perhaps we've disturbed you. We should have rung. I'm sorry.'

'No – no, not at all,' Bill's manner was, for such a clever man, curiously hesitant. He seemed to pick his way between words as between nettles or sharp stones, aware of the hurt they might cause. 'In fact – just about ready for a distraction. Just about ready for a – yes, a picnic.'

'Right,' said Charles. 'Good man. A picnic it is. I have the car. So name your choice of rural haven and we shall whisk you thither.'

'Oh, I don't mind,' said Bill. 'Anywhere would be nice. Out in the wind and the sun.'

'That's what you need, old chap. Wind and sun. You look damned pale, I'm sorry to say.'

'It's just the light in here,' said Bill Bailey. 'Or rather, the dark.'

'Never mind. I shall go and buy a picnic,' said Charles decisively. Izzy was relieved. She knew that if she went, she might be in danger of buying the wrong food. It was odd, that certain food should be wrong, when all you really had to do with it was put it in your mouth to keep you alive, but there it was. Izzy was happiest with bread and cheese.

The minute the door banged behind Charles, Izzy started to feel hungry. Her stomach gave the most deafening rumble.

'Oh dear! I'm sorry!' she laughed. 'I'm starving. We did go to a wine bar for lunch but I didn't feel hungry then.'

'I've got a packet of crisps,' said Bill. He produced a battered packet and Izzy tore it open.

'Oh, they're scrumptious!' she laughed, revelling in the salty explosion upon her tongue. 'I expect you keep them for your little girl, don't you.?'

'Got it in one!' laughed Bill Bailey. 'You understand greedy little girls, don't you?'

'I was a greedy little girl myself, once,' confessed Izzy. 'To be honest, I still am. Have one! Before I gobble up the lot!'

Bill Bailey accepted a crisp and they crunched companionably.

'Crisps are so nice! What is it about them?' asked Izzy, smacking her lips. 'Like fish and chips.'

'Fish and chips are the best thing there is,' agreed Bill.

'But what is it? What is it that makes it so wonderful?'

'I think it's the salt,' said Bill.

'That's right! I know it's bad for you, but I can't help it! I even stick my finger down into the last corner of the bag, if nobody's looking.'

'Go ahead,' laughed Bill. 'I'm nobody.'

'Oh good,' said Izzy, excavating the last crumbs. 'I hate somebodies.'

The crisps had come to an end. This was felt to be a sad thing.

'I need salt,' said Bill. 'I don't care what the doctors say. Sometimes when I'm at the seaside I have to run down and lick the sea.'

'You lick the sea!' laughed Izzy. 'You must have an enormous tongue!'

'I have – look. I can touch my nose.' Bill Bailey did so. Izzy laughed coarsely.

'How disgusting! – Got anything else naughty to eat, Bill?'

'Well,' said Bill, opening a drawer, 'I have got a tube of Smarties somewhere in here.'

'Smarties! Smashing!' Izzy's yelp of delight could be heard all round New Court. Not that anyone was listening.

'When I was a little girl I used to lick the red ones and then smear the red all over my lips,' Izzy demonstrated the process. Bill watched her with delight.

'Look,' he said suddenly, in a tone of voice that pulled her up sharp, 'are you really engaged to Charles?'

'Yes, of course,' said Izzy, deadly serious, licking the carnival off her lips. 'We got engaged today.'

'Today! Well! Congratulations, is all I can say.'

'Thank you.' Izzy inclined her head with mock politesse.

'I have to admit I'm . . . surprised,' said Bill carefully.

'Surprised? Why?'

Izzy was afraid. How could Charles's friends be surprised at his choice, unless she was lacking in some vital quality? All the mischief drained out of her face and she looked up like a frightened child.

'Don't look so tragic,' grinned Bill. 'I was just wondering how Charles managed to corner someone so . . . well, like you.'

'What am I like?' demanded Izzy urgently.

'I don't know, really. Sort of, well – alive if you like.'

'That's not saying much!' Izzy laughed nervously.

'It's saying a great deal,' Bill corrected her.

'But it's not what you'd expect, from Charles?'

Bill hesitated. He started unpacking one of his cardboard boxes, placing a row of fossils on his desk. Izzy watched, fascinated.

'I'm delighted – for you both,' he concluded, and Izzy was overjoyed. Charles's friend liked her! Approved of her! And she hadn't even been trying.

'Have you been up to Thraxton yet?'

'Where?'

'Thraxton. Where his parents live.'

'Oh, in Norfolk? No, not yet. We're just on our way back from meeting my mum.'

'What did she think of him?'

'Crumbs! I don't know, really. But I think she must have liked him because she gave him one of my dad's suits.'

'What did your dad think of that?'

'My dad's dead.'

'Oh dear! I'm sorry. So is my mum. She died last year.'

'My dad died six years ago. I remember thinking how odd it was that our two cats were still alive, and he wasn't.'

'Do you get the dreams?'

'Oh yes! Aren't they terrible! Or at least the waking up is. I dream that dad's in a hospital somewhere, and I search and search for him and then suddenly I find him, and he looks awfully pale and ill, but he says, *Cheer up, lass. 'Twas all a mistake. I'm not dead after all. And the doctors say I can come home tomorrow.* And then you wake up and he really is dead.'

There was a brief silence.

'He calls you lass,' observed Bill. 'I like that.'

Izzy felt glad he had used the present tense. He *calls* you. As if he still did.

189

'He does,' she said, 'in my dreams, at least.'

'Yes,' said Bill Bailey. 'Waking up can be a horrible moment.'

'It must be for you, now.'

'Yes.'

'Do you see Susannah often?'

'What's often? I used to see her every day. Long days. Starting at six a.m. I don't think Marianne's enjoying that bit very much,' he added grimly.

'Is she upset? Susannah, I mean. No, of course, she must be upset. Silly of me.'

'No, it's all right. I'm grateful that you want to talk about it. Nobody here does. They're all afraid that I'll get upset.'

'But you are upset.'

'Yes,' said Bill Bailey, gratefully. 'Yes, I am.'

'It's ridiculous expecting you not to be! It was the same when Dad died. Lots of my friends didn't speak to me at all. They were afraid I would embarrass them.'

'By feeling. Yes. The English hate feelings.'

'Are you – do you – can you – speak to your wife – I mean, your ex-wife – without, you know, too much—?'

'I feel consumed with hatred of her at the moment, I'm afraid.'

'Oh dear.'

'Yes. It's awful, isn't it? And I can't bear to think about what things used to be like a couple of years ago. I've had to hide all the photos.'

'You poor thing! Did she – was there someone else?'

'Yes. I'd suspected it for some time. He always seemed to be hanging round our place. Then one day I'd taken Susannah to the park and we came home early because she'd got a tummy ache, and I found them – together.'

'How – how terrible.'

'I remember thinking, the bloody cow's even got me organized to do her babysitting for her whilst she does her fornicating!' Bill's face turned white. His hair appeared to stand on end and quiver with intense heat. His eyes were dark and full. 'I'm sorry, Izzy, I am a bit over the top, I know.'

'No, no, don't apologize! I don't mind feelings. Say what you like.'

'The thing that was worst was that there was poor little Susannah in my arms, with a tummy ache, and being brave.' His face buckled. Izzy stood up and swept him into a powerful hug.

'You poor, poor thing,' she whispered. 'Have a good cry. You deserve it.'

He was halfway through his good cry when the door burst open and Charles came in.

'Bill is having a good cry,' said Izzy. 'I think he needs one.'

'Oh,' said Charles. 'Right. Well. Good. Here's the picnic, anyway.' He dumped the shopping down on the table. There was a pause during which Bill did a lot of sniffing and shuddering and Charles stood around awkwardly.

'I got his favourite pâté,' he said eventually, as if Bill was not there, or temporarily deaf or feeble-minded. 'And some smoked salmon. And lychees.'

Bill looked up and blew his nose. 'Well, for God's sake let's go and eat it, then,' he said.

They had a good picnic somewhere down by the river, in a meadow full of long grass and buttercups. Bill pronounced himself immensely improved by his cry.

'Izzy should be available on the National Health Service,' he said.

'That reminds me, darling,' said Charles, 'have you got medical insurance?'

'No,' said Izzy. 'It's all right. I'm never ill.'

'I'll fix that up for you, then, if you've no objection,' said Charles. 'Can't be too careful, *et cetera.*'

'If you like,' agreed Izzy. It seemed a lot of fuss about nothing, to her. Up till now she had never felt ill or that she was likely to be ill. But Charles was quite right. She really was irresponsible.

'I suppose I might be ill, one day,' she reflected.

'Oh no you won't,' grinned Bill Bailey, who was lying on his back. He looked up at her through delicate seed-heads of quivering grass, 'You'll be fighting fit till the day you die. And probably even after that.'

'Seriously, though,' persisted Charles. 'Childbirth can be no joke, and so on.'

'You two thinking of starting a family, then?'

'Oh yes – in due course. Whenever Izzy feels ready.'

'I am nearly thirty,' said Izzy seriously.

For some reason, Bill Bailey laughed. 'I hope they take after Izzy rather than you, Chas.'

'So do I,' said Charles gallantly. Though for a split second he did rather hope that any son of his would not inherit Izzy's short legs.

Thus did the afternoon slip away into a golden flood. Izzy didn't like the pâté much, but Bill slipped her Smarties while Charles wasn't looking.

'Excuse me, good people,' said Charles at length. 'Must go and look upon the hedge.'

He wandered off along the riverbank until he was lost from view. Izzy and Bill sat in silence. Izzy was admiring the fine grids of pink cloud that stretched away and away in the sky, towards the sea, she supposed.

'Is the sea somewhere over there?' she asked.

'Yes. Fifty miles away, though, I'm afraid.'

'What a shame,' said Izzy. 'I wish we were by the sea, now.'

'So do I,' smiled Bill.

'If we were, would you lick it?'

'Definitely. And we could go to a fish and chip shop.'

'Oh, yummy!'

They were silent for a while.

'Do you know,' said Bill Bailey, 'I haven't thought about sad things for a whole three hours. You are a tonic, Izzy – what's your surname again? I don't even know your surname.'

'Comyn,' said Izzy.

'Thanks very much,' grinned Bill. 'I think I will. Sorry, I suppose everybody says that.'

'Like everybody saying *Won't you come home Bill Bailey*.'

'Yes.'

Another silence fell. They were almost as enjoyable as the conversation. Izzy sat stock-still, soaking up the last warmth of the sun and the smell of the grass.

'Do you know,' said Bill, 'I can see all the buttercups in the world reflected under your chin.'

Izzy hesitated, somehow wishing Charles would come back immediately, and somehow also wishing that he would not.

'I do like butter,' she admitted. 'Very much, I'm afraid.'

She looked away, over Bill Bailey's head, to where frogs leapt among the bulrushes, with strange little plopping sounds. She knew how important it was to keep looking at those bulrushes.

On the way back down the M11 to London, Charles surveyed the day with satisfaction. He had gained a fiancée, and gained her upon Clare Bridge, as he had long ago made plans to do: he had won, he was sure, the approval of her mother, and the gratitude of his friend. They had cheered up poor old Bill quite comprehensively.

'Dear old Bill,' he said. 'You were very good to him, darling.'

'He is a lovely man,' said Izzy quietly. 'Lovely.'

'He certainly is,' affirmed Charles. 'Salt of the earth.'

WHY LOOK YOU PALE?

Charles and Izzy kissed goodbye through the car window, and then Charles zoomed off eastwards towards Spitalfields. He had to catch up with his work, which he had been neglecting shamefully, for the past week or two. Although his yard functioned perfectly well without him. It was run by two stout fellows called Trev and Roy. Trev had the physique of a Michelangelo, and a squeaky little Scots voice as if a Gorbals gnat was sitting on his shoulder and speaking for him. Roy looked like a Rubens satyr, came from Camberwell, and knew even more about architectural salvage than did Charles himself. He had made Charles a lot of money over the years.

'I'm sure that 'orse is a Watts,' he'd said, peering closely at a battered bronze they'd found in a ruined garden in Hertfordshire. And on another occasion he had been poking about in a heap of twisted metal in a junkyard and gave a great cry.

''ere, Chas, come 'ere! Some geezer's thrown away an armillary sphere. Look at that! Early nineteenf century or I'm a Dutchman. Lovely bit of wrought iron. Shove it up your jumper, Trev.'

'Aye. Mind your backs!' squeaked Trev, who was capable of carrying stone statues home over his shoulder like a fireman rescuing distressed maidens from a blaze.

Going off with Roy on scouting expeditions was a bit like taking a pig to sniff out truffles. To tell the truth, Charles had rather missed his work recently, and now his courtship was successfully concluded, he was looking forward to salvaging with renewed vigour. He had waved Izzy goodbye with a lighter heart than he could ever remember having.

194

Tonight he would ring the Aged Ps and break the news to them. The Old Man would like Izzy, he knew. Her combination of sex appeal, childlike artlessness and genuine Yorkshire origins would be just the ticket. Such women were so much more comfortable and warm-hearted than the vapid Sloanes he had hitherto associated with. The way she had comforted poor old Bill, for example. Motherliness. Charles smiled at a taxi-driver: a sign of very unusual grace.

Izzy was greeted by the sight of Dick working in the garden.

'Dick!' she cried from the French windows, 'I'm home!' Then she remembered Aunt Vinny, and waited until Dick was close enough to whisper. She wasn't sure if Charles wanted to tell Aunt Vinny about the engagement himself. Aunt Vinny had been told that Izzy and Charles were indulging in dalliance, and had professed to find it all terribly exciting. But Izzy felt uneasily that this engagement might seem a little too rushed, as far as Aunt Vinny was concerned. A little too mad. All the same, she must tell *somebody*. Dick took off his muddy boots and stepped inside.

'Shall I get you a cup of tea, Izzy?' he enquired.

'Oh yes! I'll get it! You sit down. I've got some fantastic news, Dick. Guess what?'

Dick hesitated in misery. He did not like Izzy's fantastic news. The more fantastic her news, the more redundant did he seem. Hitherto he had been her husband: several pieces of good news later, he was reduced to a mere friend again. Any more news and he was sure he'd be left behind in her delicious slipstream, for ever.

'Er – you've won the Pools,' he suggested fatuously.

'Don't be stupid, Dick. I don't do the Pools! I could never remember to get the coupon in on time. No. It's much more exciting than that. I'm engaged!'

'Engaged!' Dick boggled. Even for Izzy, this was fast going. 'You mean – to Charles?'

'Of course, idiot!' laughed Izzy, amiably. 'He proposed in Cambridge. On a bridge with enormous balls. It was so romantic.' Dick's imagination attempted to re-create the scene, and failed. 'And my mum thought he was the bee's knees.'

'Well, he is, isn't he. I suppose,' Dick was trying hard to enter into the spirit of the thing. 'I hope you'll be very happy, Izzy. Yes. Congratulations.'

'Oh thank you, Dick! You are a darling!'

Izzy flung her arms around him and embraced him mightily. Dick quite liked all these surplus hugs he was getting. Perhaps it was all right being a mere friend, after all. When he'd been her husband he'd got nothing but the sharp end of her tongue.

'I've got some news for you, too,' he began.

'Found somewhere to live, yet?' asked Izzy. She assumed that her removal from this flat was only weeks away. 'Of course, you could stay on here after I've gone. But it's so expensive.'

'Aunt Vinny's given me a room upstairs.'

'What? A room upstairs? Hey, Dick! What's going on? Does she fancy you?'

'Oh no,' said Dick. 'Nothing like that. She was just being hospitable, like. I expect.'

Actually, he did have certain qualms in that direction, but he did not wish to rehearse them now. He had sense enough to keep his darkest thoughts and most perverse inklings strictly to himself. That way they seemed less real.

'Well, that's awfully nice for you, Dick. A proper room! You can stop sleeping on the sofa. Will you stay on here for next year?'

'Oh no. I'm looking for a place in Hackney now. But the prices are pretty high there, too. The Yuppies have moved in.'

'Blast them!' cried Izzy. 'Where are we poor teachers to live if everywhere is taken over by these horrible whizz-kids with their obscene money?'

'Will you be – carrying on teaching, then, Izzy?'

Izzy was caught out by this. 'I – I'm not sure.' Izzy had very recently fantasized with Dick about giving up teaching. But she hesitated. From this delicious vantage point in the middle of a long summer holiday, teaching seemed not so bad after all. She felt she wanted to hang on for a while, at least.

'Well, I'll have to do another term, anyway,' she concluded. 'To work out my notice, you know. And maybe – to tell you the truth, Dick, I hadn't really thought about it very much.'

'Spitalfields wouldn't be too inconvenient for school,' observed Dick helpfully. 'You ought to get Charles to put some draught excluders into that house, though – before the winter. I'll give him a hand if you like.'

'Er – thanks.' Izzy realized that Dick was imagining her living in Charles's house. The thought excited her. All the same, this little flat was beginning to feel like home, and it was with a twinge of regret that she looked around and began to see herself leaving it.

'I still haven't told you the news, though,' Dick broke in upon her reverie. 'Maria's pregnant.'

'What! Really?'

'Yes. She rang up. Said she'd really like to see you.'

'But Dick – that's marvellous!'

'Yes. She was a bit low, though. I don't think she's feeling very well.'

'I'll go round and see her tomorrow.'

Izzy fled to the phone, and rang Maria's number. Nobody answered.

'She must be out. At her ante-natals or whatever they're called. Isn't it exciting, Dick? I wish I could knit.'

Izzy yawned. Maria pregnant. This summer was getting more and more like a case of happy-ever-after. A great contented tiredness spread over her limbs. It was time for sleep. In the morning she would go and see Maria and celebrate with her. The pregnancy took away all the awkwardness she'd been feeling about Maria. She longed to see her.

Lying in bed that night, Izzy's mind was full of images of home. Her imagination lingered especially on one stone: the huge stone that acted as a step up to the barn door. It was worn smooth and slightly cupped by the feet of centuries. Bits of corn and straw usually lay around it. It had been her favourite place to sit when she was a child. The exact feel of its warmed smoothness against her bare legs was vivid in her senses. She had sat there and played five-stones with her friends, and played school with her dolls and teddies.

Would she ever find a home of her own, that felt so much like home? This flat was beginning to relax around her and welcome her back, but it would never be as friendly as her old Earl's Court flat, up under the eaves of Nevern Square, with crumbling brickwork outside the windows and damp-stains in the bathroom and pigeons cooing on the parapets outside. That had indeed been home – for a while. But taking Charles to meet her mother had filled her with an aching sense that the Yorkshire farm was still much more of a home than any of her temporary London addresses had been.

Her mother was getting thin. Izzy trembled. Surely she would go on strongly for another twenty years? She'd been a bit too plump, before: the losing weight could be a good thing. Izzy had been too nervous to ask her mother about it. To ask if there was anything wrong, if she had seen a doctor, or just been on a diet. Suddenly she realized that she wanted her home up there to stay the same for ever, with her mother always there, always welcoming, so that one day Izzy could go back and be a little girl there, all over again. Enter that world again, of carefree games among the sun-warmed stones, of parents always there, opening their big arms, cuddling you on their warm laps, and nothing to be frightened of beyond the dark.

The only way she'd ever get beyond this strange buried longing to go home was if she managed to make a home of her own one day, with her own little girl in it. Well, she was nearer to achieving this now than ever before. She might get her own little girl quite soon, though she must remember to provide Charles with his John Ruskin Armstrong first. She smiled at this thought. Then she tried to imagine herself and two children living in Charles's house. It was hard to imagine children in that house, at all. Perhaps they would have to move to somewhere larger. Izzy was frightened of the idea of a large house. She'd always felt most comfortable in the smallest of flats: nests, in fact. As she went to sleep, she thought vaguely that it was a shame Charles had quite so much money.

Next day she was on Maria's doorstep by 10 a.m., bearing a huge bouquet. Maria opened the door, looking pale.

'Maria! Congratulations! It's marvellous! I'm so happy for you!' Izzy buried her beneath a vast embrace, and showered flowers on her. Maria did not feel right in Izzy's arms, though. She stood immobile. It was like hugging a thing.

They went upstairs at a snail's pace. Izzy was puzzled. What was this? She associated pregnancy with riotous good health and radiant good looks: the advertising image, of course. Why didn't Maria get a move on?

'Sorry it's taking me so long,' said Maria. 'My legs feel like lead. It's extraordinary.'

When they finally got upstairs, Maria immediately lay down on the sofa. Izzy put the flowers in water and placed them on a small table by Maria's head.

'Thanks,' said Maria. 'They're lovely. It was very nice of you, Izzy.'

'Nice?' cried Izzy. 'Rubbish! It's the least I could do! You deserve a whole lorryload! How do you feel? A bit better?'

'Sick,' said Maria. 'And tired. So tired. I can hardly speak.'

'Oh yes, but this stage won't last long, will it?' Izzy did not know much about the timescale of pregnancy but she was reluctant to give up her optimism.

'It could last for months,' said Maria. 'Nobody knows. But it usually gets a bit better after the first three months, they say. God knows it can't get any worse.'

'When will that be?'

'End of September. However am I going to teach, Izzy?'

'You'll probably feel all right by then. Have a grape!'

Izzy had one herself. She'd brought grapes, too. She

199

wasn't sure if it was appropriate. Was pregnancy an illness? They must be good for the expectant mum. And the baby. Izzy took another.

'They weren't South African,' she promised. 'They were from Chile. I made sure.'

'The regime in Chile is nothing to write home about either,' remarked Maria. 'Not that I care much about regimes at the moment.'

'Do have one,' urged Izzy. 'I'm sure they'd be good for the baby.'

'I'm sorry, Izzy. The only thing I can eat at the moment is cream crackers.'

'Oh. How weird.'

'It's the constant nausea, you see.'

'Well, is there anything I can do? Would you like a cream cracker now?'

'Yes, I would. Would you mind? Only it seems such a long way to the kitchen.' Izzy looked towards the kitchen. It was no more than three yards. 'Odd, isn't it?' Maria went on. 'The tiredness is really unbelievable. I've never felt anything like it. I'm too tired even to be cross.'

Izzy marvelled. Maria's tone did indeed seem almost transparent. There had been no sardonic remarks, no playful attacks, no aggressive questions. She just lay on the sofa and looked pale. It was odd that the starting-off of new life should so closely resemble death. Perhaps it was the death of Maria's old self. Izzy went to the kitchen and fetched a packet of cream crackers and a glass of water. A strange, penitential meal. Maria just looked at it for a while.

'I might manage a sip of water in a minute,' she sighed. 'I don't think I can really face a cream cracker, though. Not yet.'

Encouraged by Maria's stillness, Izzy forged boldly on towards her news.

'Maria,' she began, 'something extraordinary's happened.'

'What?'

'I'm engaged.'

'Look, what's all this Dick business? Louise told me you were married to Dick. That can't be right.'

'Oh, no. The Dick business was just a smokescreen. A joke. I'm engaged to a man called Charles Armstrong.'

'Oh,' said Maria blankly. 'Congratulations, then.'

'Yes. Thanks,' said Izzy. It was really odd, this absence of attack. It was almost disappointing. What had happened to Maria? Was this really Maria, at all?

'What's he like?'

'Well,' said Izzy, determined to be cool and civilized. Not to gush and rush. 'He's about my age. He's got an architectural salvage business.'

'Oh yes. Panelling and fireplaces and things?'

'That's right.'

'Thank God he's not a teacher.'

'Yes, I suppose so.'

'When's the big day, then?'

'I don't know, really. We haven't discussed it. Quite soon, I think.'

'Have you known him for long?'

Izzy hesitated. She was sorely tempted to lie. It did seem such a very short time since she had met Charles. For a split second she thought she would say she'd known him for years, vaguely – but Maria would never let things stay vague. And anyway, Izzy wasn't telling lies any more. This was the new life of simple truth.

'Not – er, not long. It's all been a bit of a whirlwind romance, really.' She cringed, waiting for Maria to jump down her throat. But Maria just sighed.

'It seems so impossibly remote to me, Izzy. The idea of whirlwind romances and engagements and things.'

'Well, of course it is, to you. You're onto the next stage.'

'It feels like the next stage but six.'

'I'm ever so envious of you, Maria. I think I'll have a baby as soon as possible. Just think! We could share babysitters and things. Do you want a boy or a girl?'

'I just want to stop feeling sick. I can't believe in it all, Izzy. It just doesn't seem real. If it wasn't for the fact that I feel iller than I've ever been, I just wouldn't believe the evidence.'

'You must be incredibly happy, though,' suggested Izzy,

very tentatively, for Maria looked as if she could not even remember what happiness was. But under the pallor and the sickness and the fatigue, she must be happy, surely. After all, she'd been trying to have a baby for years, she'd said.

'I know I ought to be happy, Izzy,' she mused, staring at the ceiling. 'And I suppose in some far-away other life, I am. But all I can feel is scared.'

'Scared? Oh, of the birth, you mean.'

'Of the whole thing. Honestly. When I begin to think of what it means, of how my life's changed, I just want to run away and hide. I want someone else to take over.'

'I'll help you, Maria! It'll be all right.'

'You'll be busy with your own life, Izzy.'

'No I won't! I'll always have time to help you if you need me. Would you like me to do something for you now? Tidy up? Vacuum? Go shopping?'

'Oh Izzy,' Maria crumpled slightly, on the verge of tears. 'Would you? Thanks so much! Everywhere's such a mess, and it's as much as I can do to get up off my back, these days!'

'Why don't you have a sleep?' suggested Izzy, rolling up her sleeves and making for the pile of washing-up.

'I'd rather lie here and watch, if you don't mind. It gives me the illusion that I still belong to the human race.'

'By the way, Maria, where's Gwyn?' asked Izzy, as the plates began to steam and gleam in the rack.

'Gwyn!' Maria almost spat. 'Where do you bloody think? Rock-climbing in Miller's Dale!'

'Oh,' said Izzy, surprised. 'I hope he's having a good time.'

'I don't. I hope he breaks his bloody neck.'

Izzy found this reassuring, somehow.

SEE WHERE IT COMES!

Dick and Aunt Vinny were talking upstairs. Aunt Vinny had got into the habit of dropping into Dick's room for a chat. At first she leaned against the doorpost: then by degrees, gently, she seemed to invade further and further until now she was perched upon the bed. Dick had beat a corresponding retreat. He was now seated on the window-sill, and glanced down occasionally into the garden like a cat which is keeping its options open.

'Isn't it absolutely wonderful about Charles and Izzy!' Aunt Vinny seethed with delight.

'Aye – it's, well, great.'

Dick's enthusiasm for the project was still fairly limited.

'It seems so strange talking to you about Izzy's engagement. I mean, it hardly seems any time at all since you were married. Or at least, I thought you were married.'

'Yes, er, sorry about that.'

'Oh no, don't apologize! It was a wonderful wheeze! And it's turned out so well, too. Much nicer to have you up here.'

'Nice to be up here,' affirmed Dick, his throat drying inexplicably.

'And you know, Dick, although I thought you were married, there was always something about it that didn't quite ring true.'

'Was there?'

'Oh yes! Couldn't say what, exactly, at the time. But a little something. When I look at it in retrospect, I can see that Izzy isn't at all your type.'

'Isn't she? No, I suppose she isn't.'

'Oh no! You're both such – well, such innocents, in a way. Don't misunderstand me, Dick. Innocence is a very very precious quality. I wish more people had it.'

Dick could not comment. If he was innocent, he didn't exactly recommend it. He did not find it at all comfortable. What he yearned for was a nice hard shell of experience to shelter under.

'Izzy and Charles make a splendid couple!' continued Aunt Vinny, leaning rather alarmingly on one elbow. 'He has such taste. You can just see him, can't you – guiding her, sharing his enthusiasms with her.'

Dick could indeed see it all, and wished there was a good excuse for the feelings of envy and nausea which resulted.

'He's – very knowledgeable,' he agreed.

'He is a sensitive boy,' sighed Aunt Vinny. 'I have been worried about him, you know. He's going to inherit an absolute fortune. And that can encourage the wrong sort of people to hang about and lead one astray.'

'I don't think Izzy even knows about that,' said Dick. 'She's never said anything to me about his – his fortune.'

'Well, of course, dear Izzy will never even notice it,' said Aunt Vinny. 'It'll just come naturally to her, I expect. She seems to have a curious ability to adapt herself to her surroundings and get on with life whatever happens.'

'Aye. She does.'

Dick had often envied Izzy's elasticity. He never felt at ease whatever his surroundings.

'Whereas you, dear Dick—' *Dear*? Oh dear. '—you have something altogether different.'

Well, that much was true enough. Dick waited in silence for Aunt Vinny to anatomize him: mercilessly expose his tender areas.

'You have integrity, Dick. True grit. You have absolute honesty.'

'Do I? Crumbs.'

'You must certainly do. Do you know who you remind me of?'

'Who?'

'Adam Bede.'

'Who?'

'Adam Bede. A hero in one of George Eliot's novels.'

'Ah. No. I haven't read many of – George Eliot's novels.'

'Adam Bede was an artisan. That's what I like about you, Dick, and you have physical strength. I like that in a man. Rupert was wiry, despite his asthma. But he never had real physical strength.'

'Nor do I, really,' said Dick hurriedly. 'I'm pretty much of a wimp, you know.'

'Oh no, Dick! Let me see your muscles!' Aunt Vinny sprang alarmingly from the bed and approached the windowsill. Dick tensed, wondering what his chances would be if he bounded down onto the peonies. Aunt Vinny stood before him, an expression of monstrous playfulness on her face. 'Come on, Dick! Let's feel your biceps! Be a sport!'

Dick obligingly flexed his arm. Aunt Vinny's fingers massaged the erect muscle with undisguised relish.

'There, you see!' she breathed. 'Wonderful! Dear Dick, I've been meaning to ask you something for ages – only whilst you were married to Izzy, I didn't like to.'

Dick looked down into her face. She was quite appealing, really. Her mysterious grey eyes were heavily hooded – a bit like Marlene Dietrich. Her legs weren't bad, either – Dick had noticed. Now she was so close, he couldn't be sure how old she was. She might not be so very old after all. And whatever her age, her fingers were warm and soft. Dick breathed in her scent, It rose, spicy and extravagant, up his hairy nostrils, and befuddled his brain.

Who was he to resist the appeal of a lonely and defenceless woman? It would be chivalrous to incline to her, to give her a few moments of happiness. Bloody hell, she thought he was strong and had integrity. Grit. Dick took a deep breath.

'Ask me anything,' he said, abandoning plans to jump

out of the window. 'I'd do anything for you, Aunt Vinny.'

'Well, could you start by putting up a few shelves in the utility room? And one other thing – please don't call me *Aunt* any more. I'd rather be just plain Vinny to you, Dick.'

'OK, Vinny,' said Dick, sliding down off his perch. 'Lead me to your toolbox.'

Downstairs, Izzy and Charles were making love. Now that Dick had been banished from the flat, and now that they were officially engaged (a fine old ruby on Izzy's finger witnessing the fact), they felt safer down here. Izzy had managed to lure Charles into the bedroom, helped by a deep vein of Mitsouko down her generous cleavage. Charles buried his head in it.

'You smell wonderful,' he breathed. 'Of old French chateaux, somehow. Pot-pourris. Tapestries on walls.'

Ah well, thought Izzy, whatever turns you on. Once he was well and truly asphyxiated with the smell of history, he reeled upwards towards her face. Izzy licked her lips slowly. He lay beside her, transfixed.

'Do that again,' he whispered. 'Only more slowly.'

Izzy lolled her fat little tongue languorously across her gleaming lips. Charles gasped. Then, very slowly, she leaned forward and did the same to him. Reluctantly he abandoned himself to mere sensation. Izzy's tongue was like a sea-creature, coming out of the shell of her skull to do mischief on the ocean floor. She eased him onto his back. He closed his eyes. It must feel like this for Hostas, Charles thought, being nibbled to death by nubile young snails. He heard Izzy undoing the buttons of her shirt, and her great scented breasts dropped onto his face. Now he was suffocated by softness. He must escape, he must assert himself, he must—

'Oh damn,' said Charles. 'Damn. I am sorry.'

'It doesn't matter,' smiled Izzy, 'it happens all the time. To everybody.'

'I'm so sorry, Izzy. I'm a useless lover.'

'You are nothing of the sort,' she snorted. 'And besides, if you're such a useless lover, why am I marrying you?'

'Ah well,' sighed Charles. 'As long as you are.'

'I most certainly am.'

'Be patient with me, Izzy. I'm out of practice.'

'I like that.'

'Things will improve.'

'Of course they will. We've got all the time in the world.'

'You are a darling, little weasel.'

'So are you.'

Izzy enjoyed his sexual gaucherie. It was the only time when she was with Charles, that she felt in control. Except that even then he had a way of – well, slipping away, sometimes, and leaving her stranded on an empty beach with the tide going out. Once they were married, and could settle down to a proper rhythm of life together, everything will be all right, Izzy told herself. And it was all right, anyway, really. He could do the necessary. And she was sure that given world enough and time, she could teach him how to do the unnecessary, too.

'By the way, darling, I rang the Aged Ps last night.'

'What did they say?'

'I spoke to the old man. He was delighted. Insisted on throwing a bit of a party. Nothing too gross, just the families and a few friends. We thought, the next weekend but one. Would that suit you?'

'Oh, yes!' Izzy was pleased. She loved parties. And if there were a few other people there she wouldn't feel so conspicuous.

'Do you think we could get your ma to come down?'

Izzy hesitated.

'Well, I managed to get her over to San Francisco, so I should think so. I'm sure she'll be very keen to meet your parents.'

'And they're dying to meet her! Has she got a long dress, by the way? We thought it might be rather nice if it was black tie.'

'Crumbs!' said Izzy. 'I don't know. Oh, I'm sure she has. If not, we can have fun shopping for one.'

'Well, quite. Trotting round the West End, eh? And maybe you could go to a hairdresser whilst you're at it.'

'Oh – is there something wrong with my hair?'

'Couldn't be better. But wouldn't it be nice if it was thinned and shaped a little, around your face?'

'Do you mean, a bit like Emma Hamilton?'

'Yes. I could come with you, if you like.'

'Oh no,' said Izzy hastily. She didn't want Charles hanging around and fussing over her and all the other clients staring and wondering what on earth was going on. 'I must get a long dress, too.'

'As to that, my love – I absolutely insist on its being my gift to you.'

'But Charles—'

'Don't argue. We'll go out to South Molton Street one day next week, and have a whale of a time.'

Izzy was silent. Having money spent on her was a strange sensation: half-delicious, half-alarming. Since she always bought clothes on impulse and was inevitably disappointed with them afterwards, and distressed at the way they fell to pieces, she was quite looking forward to having Charles choose something for her. She wanted, above all, to evoke that curious light shining in his eyes that told her that she was ravishing.

'Now, which of your friends would you like to come? I suppose we'll have to have old Dick.'

That was oddly put, thought Izzy. If only he'd said, *We must have old Dick*. Never mind. She knew what he meant. Dick's presence didn't exactly add panache to a social occasion. All the same, if impatience towards Dick was to be expressed, she wanted to be the one to express it.

'Oh yes. And I'd like to have Maria and Gwyn – and Louise and Michael.'

'Louise and Michael, fine. Haven't seen him for over a year. And Gwyn – that's that chap who was here the other day, isn't it?'

'Er – yes,' admitted Izzy. 'But he's not always like that. He'd had a bit too much, you know.'

'Well, I certainly hope he won't have too much at our party. Can't he be relied upon to behave?'

Charles sounded quite irritated. Izzy considered the question. There was only one possible answer: no. Gwyn could only be relied upon to misbehave. Perhaps it wasn't such a very good idea to ask Gwyn and Maria, after all. Izzy dreaded Gwyn making a scene, but the thought of celebrating without them made her feel sad.

'Maria will keep him in order,' she promised.

'Well, darling – if you say so. It's Mother, you see. She's rather – well, she can be difficult.'

A cold wave broke inside Izzy.

'How, exactly?'

'Oh, not in any – just a bit, well, she's a bit shy really,' he concluded, unconvincingly. 'People think she's a bit standoffish but it's only, well, reserve.'

Izzy was silent. She had a distinct impression of approaching choppy waters. But Charles did not want to talk about his mother.

'We'll have Sooty of course – and maybe she can get old Westonbirt to come along too. That would be jolly.'

A Marquis! Izzy quailed.

'And Bill, of course. He needs cheering up. You were good for him the other day. I could tell.'

'He was so nice,' said Izzy. 'I do like your friends, Charles.'

'Good,' said Charles. 'That's very important, isn't it?'

Then he got up and dressed, glasses first, which gave him an odd look: like an unfinished creature. The image disturbed Izzy for some time afterwards.

''Bye, darling,' he kissed her nose. 'Be good. I must go and see a man about a torso.'

Izzy lounged about in bed for a while afterwards, feeling rather lonely and wishing Dick would come down and watch the new TV with her. It was odd, thought Izzy, that one could not go on being ecstatically happy for ever. In the end one's appetite came back and hours became hours again. She hauled herself out of bed and made for the fridge. As she opened it, the phone rang.

'Hello?'

'Is that my dear little weasel?' He was ringing from a call-box. How romantic. He'd wanted to pour a few more endearments into her enchanted ears.

'Hello, Charles!'

'Listen, darling. Forgot one thing. Brain like wool. Will your ma bung it in *The Times*, or shall we?'

'Bung what—?'

'The engagement thing. Announcement, you know. It's all right, we'll do the necessary. Don't worry your ma about it. Leave it to us.' And he rang off, leaving her wondering.

A LADY WALL'D ABOUT WITH DIAMONDS

Izzy plunged enthusiastically into the West End, with Charles clinging to her elbow like a lost soul in Dante, whirling through deepening circles of the damned. Izzy made straight for Top Shop. Down, down the snakes' backs of escalators, into the den of Narcissus. Mirrors on every wall offered them reflections of their oddly vulnerable, almost middle-aged faces: hers, flushed and eager; his, worried and remote. Music blasted across the sea of clothes and the scrum of intent shoppers: mostly young girls dressed in the current fiercely Amazonian style: campaign boots, medieval archer's tights, Roman centurion's skirts, and jackets of Cromwellian black leather, studded with metal badges, chains and other sharp instruments of pain. Their earrings, of which there were many on each ear, bristled and glittered like glass fragments on top of a wall. Brave indeed would be the man who thought of nibbling those ears.

Charles's thoughts were very far away from teenage ears. He was wondering how quickly they could find a charming Empire-style dress in here which would transform his gauche nymph into an Empress Josephine. It had been Izzy's idea to come to this Babylonian hell, into which he had never before ventured, but where she apparently had habitually found the odd assortment of rag-bag gypsy and lumberjack clothes in which she never, in his view, quite attained real elegance. Charles had acquiesced in this voyage to the bowels of the garment industry, because he was sensitive enough not to insist on his own inclinations for a ramble through the more expensive boutiques, where the air was milder, cooler and altogether more fragrant, and into which these hordes of hoydens never dared venture.

Izzy was almost oblivious of him. She had her head down and was sniffing through a rack of dresses like a dog at a fair. Well, she was not altogether oblivious of him. She was looking for the sort of dress which might appeal to him – in vain. There were plenty that appealed to her, though.

'Oh, look, Charles. Do you like this snakeskin sheath? Only mock snakeskin, of course.'

'My dear,' observed Charles mildly, 'you must be joking.'

Izzy laughed unconvincingly. 'I thought you might like me to look like a Hollywood vamp!'

'Come on, my dear. Be serious! I don't want to spend all day here. I shall go deaf, blind and mad.'

Izzy returned to the racks with urgency. 'Nothing here,' she reported. 'Let's have a look at EGO.'

'Where's that?' asked Charles, making for the escalator in his desperate urge to escape.

'No, no,' instructed Izzy, 'it's just over here – another part of Top Shop.'

There were some really nice things at EGO, Izzy thought, but everything she pulled out was greeted with pursed lips and an expression of slight toothache on Charles's part.

'There really isn't the right calibre of dress, here, my little bear,' he sighed. 'I mean, beautiful long dresses of the type that you will still be wearing twenty years hence. Shall we go to South Molton Street?'

'All right,' agreed Izzy, reluctantly abandoning a dark blue slippery dress that lapped eagerly around her knees, 'If you're sure. But I don't want you to go mad and spend too much.'

'Leave that to me,' insisted Charles, and taking her by the elbow, steered her masterfully towards the escalators. They would soon be out of this hall of hoydens. Two particularly grisly specimens were approaching: their hair teased up into tormented pineapples of orange and green fluff, their potentially supple young limbs trapped and strapped into what appeared to be plastic armour. Charles shuddered as they approached. He did not like to think of his Izzy choosing her frocks in such company. Then a terrible thing happened. One of the hoydens grabbed Izzy by the arm.

''Ere – Miss Comyn!' she cried.

'Why, Sharon!' cried Izzy, in delight, it seemed. 'And Lorraine! How lovely to see you! How are you?'

'Great thanks, Miss. How are you?'

'I'm fine!'

Izzy turned to Charles, who had gone rather pale. She had been on the point of introducing him joyfully as the man she was going to marry, but something made her draw back.

'This is – this is Charles Armstrong. Charles, these are two of my old pupils – Lorraine and Sharon.'

'How do you do?' enquired Charles, with a slight nod.

Lorraine and Sharon giggled obscenely for a moment or two, then Sharon recovered.

'Ay Miss 'ow was San Francisco – didyer find yer millionaire then ay?'

Izzy cringed, and turned to Charles.

'We had this joke that a millionaire – a movie director was going to discover me in Hollywood!'

Charles did not appear to see the joke. 'I see,' he observed. 'And did he?'

'Of course not!' Izzy was still managing to grin, but it was very hard work. For all she knew, Charles might be a millionaire. It wasn't such a lot of money, these days. She didn't want him to think she was one of the dreaded fortune-hunters. 'How is everybody? Has anybody managed to get a job?'

'Oh yes, Miss, yes. Andy's got a job in a garage, Miss, down Hackney.'

'What about Roger and Jonathan?'

'Well Razors, Miss, he's dealin' drugs, Miss, down the West End. In clubs and that.'

'No he ent, Lorraine, he's working in this pub, Miss, down the Docks.'

'Oh yeah wiv all them Yuppies, Miss. That's his like proper work, right?'

'I sincerely hope he's not being silly enough to have anything to do with drugs,' said Izzy, uneasily. 'He's perfectly capable of making a success of his life without any of that. What about Jonathan?'

'Jonathan's inside, Miss. He got mixed up in this stabbing, Miss, outside Arsenal.'

'Oh, no!' Izzy was horrified. Still, she had always known that Jonathan was depraved as well as handsome. He worshipped strip-cartoon macho warriors whose muscles bulged obscenely from leather holsters and whose chief occupation seemed to be impaling enemy women on various spikes. All the same, she had prayed that he would somehow magically transform himself into a decent plumber or gas fitter.

'He's a real hard nut ent he Lraine?'

'Yeah,' Lraine's restlessly moving jaws were endlessly pounding a small bright pink pellet of gum. It had apparently reached some significant moment of readiness, for she suddenly flicked it across her tongue and blew a large bubble, which burst into sticky threads all over her chin. 'Gary's on the dole, Miss. And Mark.'

'Darren's got a job in MacDonald's, Miss.'

'Oh well. That's something, anyway. What about you two?'

'I'm unemployed, Miss,' said Lraine with a sly grin.

'I do a bit of dancing, Miss, in the pubs, like,' said Sharon.

'Dancing? In pubs? What sort of dancing?' asked Izzy, instantly knowing that this was a very silly question.

'Topless, you know,' admitted Sharon, blushing slightly beneath her orange hair. 'Go-go dancing. At least it's a job, Miss, ennit ay?'

'Well, I suppose so,' admitted Izzy. 'Couldn't you get a job making use of your artistic talents, though? You were always so good at drawing.'

'It is artistic, my Mum says,' argued Sharon.

Izzy sighed. Who was she to argue? Topless dancing was, in some ways, an inevitable resort for poor Sharon in this darkening land, placing a value on her as so much poundage of flesh. Izzy had noticed long ago that Sharon's bust was visible even from behind. Ah well. It seemed time to go.

'It's back to school for me again in September,' said Izzy. 'I shall miss you all. Tell everybody to drop in and see me if they're anywhere near the school. I'd really love to see them again.'

'Right Miss, yeah, we'll tell them.'

'And you want to come and see Sharon's act, Miss, down The George weekends,' added Lraine mischievously.

'Shrup, Lraine, leave off! Don't come, will you, Miss, I'd go all you know.'

'Don't worry, Sharon,' Izzy reassured her. 'I don't really think that's my sort of thing. But good luck! And see you again soon, I hope!'

They parted: the girls moved off towards the display of cruel shoes, and Izzy and Charles glided upwards into a refined grey drizzle. Charles took her arm again and guided her West, towards Mayfair, without a word. Izzy was rather nervous about his silence. She had to say something.

'Poor girls,' she began. 'They lead such awful, hopeless lives.'

'My admiration for you increases by leaps and bounds, my dear,' was all he said. Izzy relaxed slightly. It must have been all right, then, after all.

Charles soon found emporia more to his taste: places where he could sit on a comfortable chair and glance at *The Times* whilst Izzy was closeted with a hand-maiden who zipped and hooked her into a succession of ravishing gowns. Each time Izzy emerged flushed and a bit damp round the edges. She did not like the woman helping her like this. It made her feel sweaty and fat. She felt nostalgic for the anonymous scrum of Top Shop's communal changing rooms, where one's own smell was lost in a general zoo-like miasma.

She had to admit the dresses were sumptuous, though. Every time she came out, Charles gazed up and down, ordered her to turn, even got up and fiddled with straps and details. She became more and more passive. He was paying. Let him choose it. It could have been quite relaxing, really – if only this woman with her insistent *Madam is so very tiny* would kindly leave the stage. Izzy knew she wasn't tiny: anyone with eyes could tell, from one glance in the mirror, that Madam was, in fact, nicely covered to put it mildly. Ah well. Izzy surrendered herself to the torment of real service.

The next dress was a winner. She knew the moment she slipped it on. It was a long, straight tube of cream satin: Empire style and high-waisted, effortlessly elegant. Izzy's brown shoulders looked even browner and beautifully round against the shimmering cloth: Izzy's rather generous bosom became properly majestic and pivotal: the dress was at the same time sexy and sober, classic and erotic. Izzy groaned with pleasure at the sight, and when she emerged and presented herself to Charles, it was, for the first time, with a smile.

'Ah,' said Charles. 'That's it.'

He paid, without even a tremor, a sum approximating to three weeks of Izzy's salary, and they went off for a cup of coffee in a quiet and obscure little coffee-house hidden away down an alley.

'You know such nice places, Charles,' she sighed, enjoying her hot chocolate with whipped cream. It was pleasant to have got her appetite back without sacrificing anything but the most painful edge of falling-in-love. 'And the dress is wonderful.'

'It's the first time I've really seen you looking as outstandingly beautiful as I know you can be,' said

Charles, smiling benevolently at her. 'It is hard to find the right clothes, these days. Fashion is for the most part unspeakably awful, and it's impossible to concentrate anyway in places like that bear-garden.'

Izzy felt very happy, sitting here and holding hands very tight. She still melted within when gazing into his eyes. And it seemed that whenever slight problems arose, they could surmount them. Last night, for example, they had enjoyed quite a successful hour of physical love. Well, it was an hour if you counted the bit at the table first, and then the bit on the sofa. Indeed these were nearly always the best bits. Izzy was sure everything was going to be all right.

'Will you go on teaching after we're married, little weasel?'

The question took her by surprise.

'I'm not really sure,' she mused. 'I think so, for a bit. But if we're going to start a family fairly soon, I suppose that would be an end of it.'

'It certainly would,' said Charles. 'And a good thing too.'

'I'd miss them, though,' Izzy thought of her old 4C with tenderness: she'd miss the robust humour, the crises, the communication, the sense of them all being humans caught up in the same universal dramas. She'd miss, above all, the laughs.

'Miss them? Really?'

'Oh yes!' she smiled at him. 'They're lovely really, when you get to know them.'

Charles leaned back and wiped his lips. 'I'll take your word for it,' he shrugged, and called for the bill.

That night Izzy rang her mother. She had written her a long letter, explaining all about the engagement, and urging her to come down to the party, and saying how much Charles's parents were looking forward to meeting her. She had tried hard not to be too enthusiastic in the letter: to avoid any suspicion of daftness. But she still felt nervous as she dialled home.

'Hello?'

'Hello, Mum! Did you get my letter?'

'Aye, I did.'

'Well, can you come? Oh, please do! Please, Mum! I so much want you to!' This was, she knew, a daft outburst. It was succeeded by a silence punctuated by distant crackles.

'Mum! Are you still there?'

'I'm here, Izzy. I've given this some thought, my love, and I'm sorry to say that I don't think I will be able to.'

'Oh, Mum! Why not?'

'Plenty of reasons. No need to go into them now. If you reflect on it all a bit, I think you'll come to the same conclusions.'

'What reasons? What are they?'

'I don't think I should be comfortable, my duck.' Izzy felt sick. And yet instantly she knew her mum was right. 'And I don't think you would be comfortable, having me there.'

'Oh, Mum! I should! I'd love it!' Izzy heard the hollowness of her own reassurances.

'No, I'm sorry, love, but I really don't think I can.' She knew it was useless to argue once her mother adopted this tone.

'But what am I going to tell them?'

'You can tell them that I've been ill, and I'm not fit to travel.'

'Oh Mum – you haven't, have you? I thought you looked a bit thin when we were up, the other day.'

'It's nothing. Just a bit o' stomach trouble.'

'Have you been to the doctor? What did he say?'

'He says I shouldn't eat anything too rich. Not that I ever do.'

Mrs Comyn's idea of rich food did not include the glistening cakes and cloud-like scones which regularly billowed forth from her oven.

'What else did he say?'

'Nothing to worry about, love. Now you enjoy your

party. Don't worry, I'll send them a proper letter.'

'It's a shame,' said Izzy. 'I'll miss you.'

'I'll come to the wedding,' promised her mother. 'I don't suppose you're planning to get wed up here?'

'I hadn't really thought. But, well, no, I don't suppose we would. It would mean so many people having to travel and things.'

'Quite right, love. I couldn't be doing with it.'

'No, of course. I expect it'll be in London. But nothing's been fixed yet. We're not in any hurry.' Izzy was quite pleased at the sensible sound of this last bit. Nothing daft there.

'Well, I must say goodbye, Izzy. I've got a cake in the oven.'

'Right, Mum. I'll ring again in a few days.'

'Take care, my duck. I hope you know what you're doing.'

Izzy cringed slightly at this last remark. But she assured her mum that she did indeed have her hands firmly on the steering wheel.

That was another thing. She must learn to drive. Charles had been aghast to discover that she did not have a licence. This whole business was certainly proving to be a long-overdue growing-up. Izzy sat still and listened to the house tick. There were no sounds from upstairs. Aunt Vinny and Dick had, unknown to Izzy, gone to a Gerard Depardieu film together. Dick was even now blushing furiously in the dark and breaking out into a panic-stricken sweat, for the film had turned out to be outrageously filthy. How was he ever going to look Aunt Vinny in the eye again, when the lights came up? He needn't have worried. Aunt Vinny was having the time of her life.

So Izzy had the house to herself. It seemed a lot of house when it was empty. She thought perhaps Charles's house might feel like that as well. She wondered, rather timidly, if there was any chance that they could buy a place together to start their married life. Somewhere new to both of them. She wondered if she would have the courage, at some future date, to mention this possibility. Then her thoughts turned to the party at Thraxton, and meeting Charles's mother. At least her mum would not be there. Izzy was mystified to discover that she felt relieved.

Izzy's instinct was to shy away from mysteries. She hesitated to rip aside veils, in case what they revealed was best left concealed. So she distracted herself with a bit of housework. This was the cleanest, tidiest flat she'd ever occupied. What was happening to her? Was this the effect of true love? Her mind suspended in some dark ante-chamber, unfocussed, Izzy automatically polished surfaces which were already clean, until they acquired a dazzling shine. There was something curiously comforting about it.

YOUR DARK MEANING

Izzy appeared on Maria's doorstep at her usual morning hour. More housework, this time of an altruistic sort, was due.

'Mornin' missus,' she squawked in her best drama-teacher's Cockney. ''Ow you doin' today, then, lovey?'

'Good morning, Mrs Mop,' drawled Maria. 'My husband's coffee spoon was covered with dried old egg this morning.'

'Ah, well,' said Izzy, bounding upstairs, 'the real gentry has them horn spoons, you know. When I came and did for Lord and Lady Flapdoodle, they had a set of horn spoons for egg, off of one of them deers what his Lordship had shot.'

The long haul upstairs wiped the smile off Maria's face. She went green and sat down on the sofa.

'What is it?' asked Izzy. 'The fainting, the sick, or the terminal tiredness?'

'All three at once,' whispered Maria, lying back. Izzy plumped cushions up under Maria's head, ran to get her a glass of water, a cup of raspberry-leaf tea, a plate of cream crackers, and a bowl. Then she set to work on the kitchen.

'You know, Maria, I really enjoy these sessions here!'

Maria merely groaned. 'I don't know what it is. Maybe I'm one of nature's chars. I hate cleaning my own place but I love cleaning yours.'

'Ah, but it's in your genes. Think of your mum. She turns housework into an art-form.'

Izzy admired the reflection of the window in the shining

221

top of the fridge, and then devoted herself to the washing-up.

'Have you had your hair cut, Izzy? It's nice. Let me have another look!'

Izzy peeped round the kitchen door. Her hair was cut in a pretty frame of feathery curls that framed her face and made her eyes look bigger.

'It's really successful, Izzy. I approve.'

'It was Charles's idea.'

'Well, good for him. He's obviously a man of taste. I'm looking forward to meeting him – Hey! We had the invitation today.'

'I'm quite nervous about meeting his folks,' admitted Izzy. 'But it'll be so much better, having you there.'

'If I make it.'

'Of course you'll make it! I expect they've got lots of sofas and things. You might as well lie on one of theirs as yours.'

'I wouldn't miss it for the world. Nor would Gwyn.'

'I say, Maria, Gwyn won't . . . well, get drunk or anything, will he?'

'Don't worry, Izzy. Impending fatherhood's had a sobering effect. I think he's quite curious to see the Armstrong estates.'

'Well, I hope he won't get all political, and be rude, or something. I mean, I think Charles is a bit worried.'

'It's all right, Izzy. If Gwyn steps out of line I shall marshall what's left of my puny strength and give him one hell of a smack across the snout.'

'And Maria – will you talk to them about antiques and things? I mean, I feel such a fool because I don't know anything about anything. I don't want Charles to be ashamed of me.'

'Good God, Izzy, don't talk like that! How could he possibly be ashamed of you? He'll be bursting with pride, you'll see. What are you going to wear?'

'He's bought me a special dress. It's sort of Empire style, in cream satin. He says it makes me look like The

Marquise von O. Who's she, Maria? I didn't dare ask.'

'It was a film,' explained Maria. 'One of Rohmer's, I think. Set in the Napoleonic era. The Marquise von O was a young widow who got pregnant in mysterious circumstances. And I must say, she looked stunning. Empire style suits pregnant women. Maybe I should get myself something like that.'

'Oh yes, do! What are you planning to wear?'

'Only my old black. It's comfortable and loose. And I couldn't possibly face going shopping at the moment. Gwyn's gone off to Safeway's, by the way. He says he's shopping for two and drinking for three.'

'I thought he always drank as if he was drinking for three.'

Izzy attacked the carpet with the vacuum cleaner.

'Oh dear,' said Maria, 'I don't like the way it swoops and drones. I'm going to be sick.'

She disdained the awful bowl and ran off to the bathroom. Izzy continued vacuuming. She knew Maria well enough to respect her need for privacy at such times. Once the vacuuming was done, Maria was back on the sofa, looking perhaps a little paler, but still dignified.

'I can't think of anything worse,' she said, 'than being sick in public.'

'Oh, I don't mind at all,' said Izzy, who had been sick dozens of times on school trips.

The door burst open and a vast brown box of groceries entered, followed by Gwyn.

'Izzy, darlin'! Hulloa! And may I take this opportunity of thankin' yew for all the sterlin' work you're doin' for my incapacitated wife.'

'It's all right, Gwyn. It's quite fun, in fact.'

'Housework still has novelty value for Izzy, apparently.'

'Well, it's at times like this that yew find out who yewer trew friends are, see? Just wait till I'm on the Council – you'll be declared a Heroine of the Socialist Republic of Islington, girl. What can we do to shoa our appreciation?'

'Listen, Gwyn, I've got to have a serious word with you.

You've been invited to our engagement party on the strict understanding that you behave, right? No drunken brawls, no politics and no shouting.'

'I stand rebuked, girl. An' speakin' of your elevation to the ranks o' the predatory capitalists, guess what I've just realized.'

'What?'

'Have yew got the slightest idea how your fiancé's father earns his grub?'

'Er – some kind of farming thing. A business.'

'Aye, aye, but what sort, exactly? Doan't yew knoa? Haven't yew any idea at all?'

'I don't think I've ever really asked. What's so important about it?'

'Get this, Maria – it dawned on me this mornin', as I was lingerin' in the booze department at Safeways – where I get moast o'my stroakes o'genius, by the way – *Farmstrong*. Ring a bell?'

'*Farmstrong?*' cried Maria, and sat bolt upright.

'That's it,' said Izzy. 'Yes. I'd forgotten. That's the name of his father's business. He's called Frederick Armstrong, you see. Clever, isn't it? And it sounds all agricultural. Fertilizers and things.'

'Listen, Izzy, darlin'. Try and wrap your infatuated little brain cells around this, like. *Farmstrong* produce fertilizers, right? And these fertilizers are full of phosphates and nitrates. Now, farmers have been throwin' so much of this stuff around that it's got into the drinking water.'

'Is it dangerous, then?'

'You bet it's dangerous, darlin'. It can cause blue babies by buggering about with the haemoglobin, so the poor little mites can't get enough oxygen.'

'God! How awful!' Izzy felt weak.

'*Farmstrong*'s been one o'the worst outfits. And one o'the most successful, o'course. It's all led to the death of the small farmer, the dreaded monoculture, greater susceptibility of the crops to pests, and of course the increasin' use of pesticides. Which your father-in-law's outfit also provides, o'course, at a vast profit.'

'Are you sure?'

'Sure I'm sure. I been readin' it all up, girl. In fact soa many pesticides have been used against sheep scab that British lamb is saturated with it, see? This stuff called lindane. Causes cancer, right? The French won't even buy British lamb because of it.'

Izzy sat down. She was assailed once more with the feeling that knowledge brought only despair. How happy she'd been, only a few moments ago, cleaning Maria's flat for her and looking forward to the party. And now all this.

'Is this all true, Maria?' she appealed.

'Absolutely. Gwyn's right, Izzy. I'm sorry.'

'Oh hell. Well, look – don't, for God's sake, say anything about it at the party, will you? Promise!'

'Doan't rock the boat, is it, eh?' grinned Gwyn. 'Want me to sit there and lick the bastard's arse?'

Izzy flinched. A deep feeling of depression was seeping through her. She was losing her appetite again, but not with joy.

'I know it's silly of me, and pathetic, and all that. I just want to have a quiet little party and celebrate with my friends. Just for once, Gwyn, bite your tongue. Please! For me! You could always write to his dad afterwards and tell him what you think of his business.'

'I'd rather wring his neck right there on his own hearthrug, darlin', if it's all the same to you.'

'Don't worry, Izzy,' promised Maria. 'We won't ruin your party. Gwyn's only teasing. There's a time and a place for everything.'

Izzy was glad Maria had been softened by pregnancy. She squeezed her hand.

'Thanks, Maria,' she said. 'It's not Charles's fault, what his dad does, after all.'

Gwyn took the shopping away to unpack it in the kitchen. Izzy stared sadly at the rug. Even its extreme cleanness could not cheer her at the moment.

'Chin up, Izzy,' whispered Maria. 'Think of it! You've found Mr Right at last.'

'If I've found Mr Right,' asked Izzy miserably, 'why does everything still keep going wrong?'

'Oh things never stop going wrong!' said Maria with a certain grim gaiety. 'And if you have found Mr Right, that only gives more scope for things to go wrong. Wait till he starts running around with other women.'

Izzy tried to imagine Charles running around with other women, and failed.

'I don't think that's going to be my problem,' she grinned ruefully.

'Is he undersexed, then?' asked Maria. 'Thank your lucky stars.'

'Oh not, not *under*,' mused Izzy. 'About average, I should think. Just a bit shy.'

'Well, you do come on a bit strong, sometimes, Izzy.'

'Do I?'

'You bet. You probably scare the living daylights out of the poor chap.'

'I don't think so. He's pretty even-tempered.'

'He sounds rather boring. Mr Average, eh? Are you going to have 2.5 children?'

'You must be feeling better, Maria. It's ages since you had a go at me.'

'Missing the aggro, Izzy? Odd, isn't it? And when I've got a child to nag, that'll really let you off the hook.'

Izzy felt slightly more cheerful – just enough to contemplate more housework, and seized the dustpan and brush. The great thing about dirt was, if you swept and mopped and scrubbed, it did utterly disappear for a while. If only the rest of life would be as tractable.

That night, Charles rang from the yard. He'd promised to come round and take Izzy out to supper.

'But I'm afraid it's out of the question, darling. We've got a big job on in Ipswich. Driving up tonight and probably home by the day after tomorrow: but I'll ring you.'

'Oh. All right.'

'Did you have a good day, little weasel?'

'I went round to Maria's and helped her out with the housework a bit.'

'Can't she get a girl in to do that?'

'Oh, I don't mind. They couldn't afford to pay somebody. And it's quite fun, really, for a change.'

'Dear Izzy! You are extraordinary!'

'They're both looking forward to the party. Oh, and I rang Michael and Louise and they'd very much like to come too – but they'll have to bring the kids.'

'What kids?'

'You know – Jack and the baby.'

'I'd forgotten they had kids. Oh well, I suppose – if they can't get a babysitter.'

'It's not just that, Charles. Louise is still feeding Rose.'

'What, herself? Is she really? How old is the baby, then?'

'Oh, about three or four months, I think.'

'Well, I suppose we can provide a special room for nursing mothers. I just hope the kids don't make a row in the middle of the recital.'

'Is there gong to be a recital? How nice!'

'Yes. I've persuaded Bill to play for us. He's a pianist, you know. And a violinist.'

'Really? How wonderful!'

'Yes. It's a pity none of your friends are musical, isn't it? We could have had a good old musical evening.'

'Never mind. They're very good at telling jokes.'

'Nothing blue, I hope. Mother is a bit old-fashioned.'

'Don't worry, Charles! Everyone's going to be as good as gold!'

Reassured, he rang off. But Izzy was haunted by the wish to go to sleep and wake up to find the whole wretched business was over.

I NEVER KNEW A MAN HOLD VILE STUFF
SO DEAR

Izzy cried aloud at her first view of Thraxton. It unfurled its
pink brick façade, with its rows of windows, across a vast
park. An avenue led straight up to the front door, and as
Charles turned into it, the sun came out and all the windows
flashed in unison.

'There you are, my darling,' he whispered. 'Even dear old
Apollo is welcoming you.'

Izzy was mesmerized. The avenue seemed to aim them at
their destination like an arrow: as they got nearer the house
grew bigger and bigger, until it almost reared up, ready to
fall on her.

Three dogs stirred on the porch and bounded to the car as
it turned and stopped in the gravel. They lifted up their
heads and bayed a welcome. Charles leapt out and greeted
them enthusiastically, seizing their heads playfully and
shaking them from side to side. Izzy watched nervously from
the car. She had been bitten by an Alsatian, once, and hadn't
been terribly fond of large dogs ever since.

'Come on, darling,' urged Charles jovially. 'Can't sit there
all day!'

'I'm – a bit frightened of dogs,' explained Izzy through the
open car window. 'An Alsatian bit me on the bum once. I
was working for the Post Office – you know, at Christmas.
My bum was sore for a fortnight.'

Then she noticed a tall figure standing in the shadow of
the door. Izzy's voice died away, but the unwelcome word
bum still somehow hung, echoing, on the air. This was,
without a doubt, Charles's mother – a conviction confirmed
by Charles's striding up the steps and delivering a filial kiss
on the cheek.

Izzy fumbled with the door handle. She must get out. She must greet his mum. The handle jammed. She wrestled with it. The door flew open. Izzy struggled out. Her handbag, which had been on her knee, turned a neat somersault and spilled its entire contents – including some of an intimate nature – onto the gravel. Izzy swooped to pick it all up, and her sunglasses fell off. She stooped for her sunglasses, and all her loose change, which had been in the breast pocket of her sensible meeting-his-mum shirtwaister, cascaded out upon the debris from her handbag. At this point, one of the large dogs, unable to resist the invitation of Izzy's upended bottom, gave her a friendly head-butt on the rear and she fell nose-first onto the drive.

'Ah,' said a level voice, 'you must be Isabelle.'

'I say, Izzy,' Charles's voice sounded not a little irritated, 'what are you playing at?'

'I'm sorry,' mumbled Izzy. 'I got in a tangle.'

'Help her up, Charles,' instructed his mother. 'Jason! Franco! Pericles! Go to the barn! Go!'

The dogs slunk off, and Izzy, brushing bits of gravel from her knees, longed, despite her fear of dogs, to go too. Charles's mother drifted elegantly down the steps, and extended her hand.

'Er – my hand's got dirt on it, I'm afraid,' faltered Izzy, looking up into the rather formidable face of Mrs Armstrong. The great lady ignored this and indicated that her hand should be grasped, if only briefly. Charles was piling Izzy's belongings back into her bag. Izzy was sure he was not pleased. What could she say to please him, and to convince his mother she was not a complete idiot?

'I'm so pleased to meet you,' she spluttered.

Oh no! *Pleased to meet you!* How the hell had that slipped out? Izzy almost fainted with annoyance at herself.

Charles's mother had faded fair hair, greying at the edges, and a very long nose. Her pale blue eyes took in Izzy's face and hair without softening or smiling, but her voice was calm and not hostile.

'Charles has told us so much about you.'

Izzy wondered if this was true, and if so, what he had said.

She must, she must, say something not altogether naff, to save the situation.

'Isn't it absolutely lovely,' she stammered, indicating the house, and hoping that Mrs Armstrong would not find this enthusiasm out of place.

'The Alstroemerias are out to welcome you,' remarked Mrs Armstrong. Izzy looked round with alarm. What on earth were Alstro – whatsits? An exotic kind of dog? Izzy felt that it would be the last straw to be bitten on her arrival by an Alstroemeria.

'Mother is a passionate gardener,' explained Charles, kindly indicating a mass of orangey-pink flowers growing at the foot of a sunny wall. Izzy found it hard to imagine Mrs Armstrong being a passionate anything. 'I find Alstroemerias rather vulgar, myself,' Charles grinned at his mother – rather bravely, Izzy thought.

'I like them,' said Izzy. She was immensely cheered by their gaudy orangey-pink.

'Are you interested in gardening?' asked Mrs Armstrong, with a quick, hawk-like plunge of the nose. Izzy flinched. She sensed a direct route to her future mother-in-law's goodwill. Could she possibly bluff her way, horticulturally, for a whole weekend? She decided, reluctantly, to be sensible and honest.

'I'm afraid I'm terribly ignorant about it all,' she said, 'but I do adore gardens.'

'I'm so glad!' Mrs Armstrong almost smiled. 'Perhaps you'd care to have a look round after tea?'

'Oh, yes, I'd love to,' said Izzy. She liked the idea of being outdoors. Social gaffes, outdoors, seemed less overwhelming somehow. And there was so much more space to run away into.

They went indoors. Thraxton House rejoiced in a vast, light hall which could have contained an entire council house. It was full of flowers. Izzy hesitated. Should she admire it, or would that be vulgar? Oh dear. She felt paralyzed by ignorance and fear.

'How beautiful,' she whispered, looking at the flowers. If she whispered, then Mrs Armstrong could choose to ignore any comments which were too unbearably vulgar.

'Yes, we've had fairly decent lilies this year.' Mrs Armstrong fixed the flowers with a stare of fishy approval. Would she, in due course, acknowledge that her future daughter-in-law was also fairly decent? Izzy fervently hoped so.

'What are these lovely pale lacey things?' asked Izzy, fingering – but not too damply, she hoped, a strange old-fashioned-looking flower.

'Oh, don't you know the Astrantias?' It sounded as if she was referring to an ancient family. The Astrantias of Axfordshire. 'They're a wonderful family,' confided Mrs Armstrong, clearly wishing her son had had the sense to marry into them. 'Frightfully good value. Keep going till October.'

Izzy felt depressed. She was fairly sure she wouldn't manage to keep going till six o'clock.

'Show Isabelle to her room, Charles,' commanded his mother. 'I've put her in the Blue Room.'

'Thank you,' said Izzy. Surely *thank you* couldn't be wrong? Mrs Armstrong ignored it, anyway, and glided off through double doors.

'Tea in the Drawing Room!' she called, as they went upstairs, and her voice echoed flutily in the stairwell.

'Here we are, then, darling,' Charles sounded decidedly more friendly as he showed her into a pretty, light room about the size of a netball pitch. 'The bathroom's through there!'

'Oh, Charles, it's all lovely!' whispered Izzy, peeping into what was clearly her very own bathroom, blue to the last detail: blue soap, blue towels, a small jar of cornflowers on the windowsill.

'Just powder your nose and come down to tea!' said Charles, and was gone, further up the stairs, to some remote filial antechamber.

Tea in the Drawing Room was not such an ordeal after all. Charles was very animated and amusing, no doubt to protect Izzy from the danger of uttering anything ludicrous. Izzy enjoyed the cucumber sandwiches and cake and ate far too much, seeing too late that Charles and his mother had taken almost nothing. Was this delicious tea just a symbolic object, then? To be contemplated, not ingested? Oh, well. Too late. Izzy complimented Mrs Armstrong on the cake.

'Daisy is very good,' was the enigmatic answer. Was this an attempt to turn the conversation to horticulture again? Or did the cake perhaps *contain* daisies? Charles leapt to the rescue again.

'Daisy has been with us for twenty years,' he explained. 'You'll taste her haddock mousse tonight, I bet. Right, mother?'

'Gravlax tonight,' remarked Mrs Armstrong, rising. Izzy wondered if she would ever understand anything this woman said. She got up, too, since that might seem polite, and to escape the sense, when Charles's mother was standing and she was sitting, that the great lady was so very, very tall: a kind of totem pole before which Izzy's best bet was to prostrate herself, without waiting for the dogs to do it for her.

'Dinner is at eight,' said Mrs Armstrong, and swept out. Charles turned to Izzy and smiled his very best smile.

'You're doing wonderfully, darling!'

But Izzy was not convinced. 'I keep saying the wrong thing.'

'Nonsense. And you look marvellous. Why don't you go for a wander before dinner? I'm just popping off to the works to see the Old Man. He's got some sort of new computer there. I don't suppose you'd like to come?'

'Oh no,' said Izzy. 'I'll walk in the – the garden.'

Izzy crept out into the garden. *Was* it still called a garden, when it was this big, she wondered, hoping that Mrs Armstrong would not materialize from behind a bush and insist on introducing her to any more Astrantias or Alstroemerias. Izzy skirted a number of formal beds and balustrades and urns and headed for the wildest and most park-like fringes of the place. Soon she was out of sight of the house, wading in long grass amidst orchards.

The sun strengthened, though it was late enough in the day now to be merely soothing. Izzy felt encouraged. The more she walked, the better she felt. The smell of the grass was sweet and the grasshoppers seethed amongst apple trees, giving a sort of electric hum to the world. Izzy saw baby apples peeping from the branches. She felt stronger, now, and relaxed, for the first time today. She still had to meet his dad – but Charles had said that he would be all right. And even though there was the family dinner to get through tonight, before the other guests arrived tomorrow, Izzy had at least met his mother and had tea with her, however unsuccessfully. The die was cast.

A little further along a path between high hedges, in which birds chirped, Izzy came to a gate. It was a tiny, secret gate, and Izzy hesitated at it – it had a private quality that felt unusual, here, where even the bedrooms had the look of places where one might receive and entertain hordes of mere acquaintances. The path swerved just beyond the gate, so Izzy could not see what lay beyond. There was a thick hedge with roses scattered on it, and behind that, who knows? All the same, she longed to go through, and gingerly lifted the latch.

One turn of the path, and the most enchanting sight met her eyes. A dear little pink-washed cottage perched on the edge of a stream, with a riotous jungle of cottage garden all around. Bees buzzed companionably amongst the flowers, and the sweet scent of herbs and roses all mixed up with sweet peas and lavender and box hedge and warm earth swirled round her on the rising heat.

'Ah, you must be Charles' fiancée,' said a friendly voice behind her. Izzy turned to see an upright old woman, with a brown weatherbeaten face and rather crooked glasses. 'I'm Daisy. Come in and have a radish, my dear. I just picked these for young what's his name.'

Izzy was ushered up the garden path, past pots spilling out little blue star-like daisies, and under the low doorway into the dark kitchen. For a moment she was dazzled, after the bright garden, by the shadow indoors. But she could make out somebody sitting at the kitchen table.

'Ah. There you are,' said the somebody. Izzy's head cleared. It was Bill Bailey.

233

'Sit you down, my dear, and have some bread and butter and radishes,' Daisy insisted. Izzy sat.

'I like to dip them in salt, of course,' said Bill.

'How are you?' asked Izzy.

'Not so bad, since you and Charles came up. I managed to do – well, quite a bit of my book.'

'What you need's a holiday,' commented Daisy, sluicing the radishes in her old enamel sink.

'Ah yes. Well – later maybe.' Bill Bailey looked out of the low kitchen window and across a rushing brook. 'I saw a kingfisher here, once.'

'Do you – come here often?' asked Izzy with a grin.

'Only in the mating season. How's your – betrothal coming along? You must have met Charles's mother by now.'

'Yes,' sighed Izzy. 'I'm afraid she realized straight away what a fool I am.'

'That's just her way my dear,' explained Daisy. 'Don't you pay no heed to that, now.'

She placed a plate of radishes on the table. Bill pounced.

'Have one, Izzy,' he urged. 'They'll set your mouth on fire.'

'Thing is, dear – will you have a cup of tea?'

'Oh – no, thanks, I've just had one.'

'Thing is, Mrs Armstrong's got her funny little ways. If truth were known she's a bit shy. She's had a lot of disappointments in life, look. Lost two babies – well, it's bound to make a difference.'

'Have you been with her for long?'

'Me and Bert came here in '57. From Somerset, you

know. Bert was a gardener, see. They'd just taken over this place.'

'Oh, I thought it had always been in the family.'

'Bless you, no. Mr Armstrong had started his business up after the university. That must have been about 1950. Well, it did surprisin' well, and what with one thing and another, I think he came into some money too, when this place come on the market, he snapped it up. Mind you, it was in a dreadful state, dear – he's done wonders with it, really and truly.'

'Was Charles born just after you came, then?'

'That's right, dear. Bert did the garden and I helped Mrs Armstrong out in the house.'

'So you were Charles's nanny?'

'Well, they did have a nursery nurse, but she didn't last long. Flighty thing, she were. Went to America. Well!'

'What was Charles like as a baby?'

'Good as gold, bless him. Placid little thing. Never a bit of trouble. Not like my David.'

'How many children did you have?'

'Three, dear. Jenny and David and Susan. Jenny's in Wolverhampton, David's in London, but Susan lives nearby.'

'That's nice for you.'

''Tis indeed. Specially since my Bert's gone now.'

'Oh dear! I am sorry!'

'Yes, dear. Went this spring. He sowed the beans, first, and put in the onions and potatoes. And the early peas o'course. Then one evening, we were just watching the Nine O'Clock News, he just says, *Daisy*, he says, *I'm feeling a bit faint*. And then he just sort of fell sideways onto my shoulder.'

'Goodness! How awful!'

'Oh no, I don't think so, dear. Not altogether. Very peaceful 'twas. Mind you, it was a shock for me. I shook for a fortnight. Then I went out and saw that his beans and peas were coming up, and so were the weeds – my! – I was ashamed to see them. So I set about it, dear, and after I'd been weedin' for a couple of hours I started to feel a bit better, you know how 'tis. There's a divinity that shapes our end rough hew them how we will, dear.'

'I'm sure you're right. But what will happen now? Did they get a new gardener?'

'Boy from the village comes in. Darren Shaw. Nice lad, and he's willin' enough but there isn't the knowledge, dear.'

'No. Of course.'

'That's the thing, you see. Years of experience. You can't replace that.' At this point Daisy darted abruptly out.

'Oh dear,' said Izzy. 'I hope I haven't upset her.'

'No, don't worry. She's like that. Can't bear to be out of her garden for more than a minute or two.'

'Isn't it – lovely here?'

'Paradise.'

'How long have you known her?'

'Ten years. Since Charles and I were undergraduates. I always stay with Daisy when I come here, now.'

'What – you don't stay with the Armstrongs? Don't they mind?'

'They take it as my – eccentricity.'

'Do you really come here often? I mean, really?'

'I do, now. Quite a bit. And I did before I was married. I like cycling round Norfolk. Churches. Birds. Samphire growing on the coast. It's quiet. Sometimes I come and stay with Daisy without the Armstrongs even knowing. Well, if they knew, I'd only have to – go and see them.'

'Don't you like them?'

'Charles is one of my best friends. Yes. Really good man. But – well, let me tell you something, before Daisy comes back. She won't want to talk about it, but a few weeks ago Armstrong told her that he'd got to expand. Business is doing so well, and so on. The best possible site for the expansion is – guess where?'

Izzy shrugged.

'Right across here. This cottage, this garden. Her home for thirty years.'

'I don't believe it!' Izzy was horrified. 'You mean — they're going to knock the cottage down? And build on her garden? But they can't!'

'But they can. Economics, you see. It's perfectly situated for his purposes.'

'But what — what about Daisy?'

'Well, they've offered her a room in the house. Or there's a little flat in the yard, that used to be the old dairy. They usually let it out in the summer. Holidaymakers, you know. But they're prepared to let her have that if necessary.'

'What do you think she'll do?'

'I think she should get out. I wish all my money wasn't tied up in that wretched house in Cambridge. I'd buy a little house out in a village somewhere, and she could live there. I could go at weekends. But there's no use fretting about it. There's nothing I can do.'

'We could talk to Charles about it. I mean, this cottage might be a — what do you call it — a Listed Building or something.'

'I don't think it's a very good idea to talk to Charles. No. He's a bit strange about this kind of thing. A bit — yes, sensitive.'

'But it's criminal!'

'Don't be sad,' he whispered. 'This is your big weekend.'

'I don't want a big weekend,' sighed Izzy. 'I've never wanted anything big.'

Bill Bailey watched her with his head cocked on one side, like a bird's.

'Is your mother coming?' he asked.

'No. She said — she said she wouldn't be comfortable.'

'Sensible woman. Yes. Thraxton—' he shook his head, 'is not a comfortable place.'

Daisy came in again, carrying a bunch of chives. She bustled around the kitchen for a minute.

'There's a pizza for your supper, Bill,' she said. 'I'll have to go now, and get cracking with this dinner at the house.'

'Aren't you coming to the dinner, then, Bill?'

'Not on your life!' grinned Bill. 'Family only, tonight. Secret pizzas in Daisy's kitchen, for me. Don't tell anyone I'm here.'

'I won't.'

Izzy got up. Daisy had already rushed off. They heard her foosteps echoing down the path.

'I ought to go, too, I suppose,' said Izzy, hesitating. It was hard to leave. 'I like it here. I'd much rather stay.'

'Well,' said Bill. 'You've got to go and be the model daughter-in-law, so hard luck.'

Izzy did not like his tone. 'But I'm not the model daughter-in-law.'

'Never mind. You've completely transformed Charles.'

'Have I?' Izzy was astonished.

'Oh yes. He's happy, now. You've made a good man happy. Think of that. All your own work.'

Izzy could not believe it, somehow. But it was encouraging to think that she had had some effect on Charles. She must go back to the house and try not to trip over his father.

'Goodbye, then. I'm looking forward to your piano thing tomorrow night. Shall I – shall I see you before then?'

'You'll be sick of the sight of me by then,' promised Bill, grinning. Izzy went back through the little gate, feeling a little puzzled and pained, at life in general and life in particular.

She ran after Daisy's straight back, and caught her up in the orchard.

'Bill's just told me a dreadful thing,' she blurted out. 'He said I shouldn't mention it, but I can't help it. He says you're going to lose your house and garden. Is that true?'

'Yes, dear.' Daisy's pace did not slacken.

'But that's terrible! After all you've done, and – it shouldn't be allowed to happen.'

'Oh no, dear. 'Tis all for the best. I'll have central heating in the house, look, and 'twas all getting too much for me, to be honest.'

'But it's your home!'

'They can't take away my memories, dear.' Daisy tapped her skull and winked. 'That's the real treasure, see? Safe and sound.'

Izzy could only fall silent in the face of such fortitude.

The Family Dinner began badly. Charles's father, a tall, bald and genial man, had kissed Izzy's hand when they met. Mrs Armstrong had watched with icy hauteur.

'Charles had warned us that you were pretty, my dear, but he was putting it mildly,' said the great man, twinkling at her with slightly more than necessary chivalry. He had insisted on her having a drink before dinner – a dry sherry that puckered up her mouth but warmed so many of her cockles that she even began to think kindly of Mrs Armstrong, and feel very sorry about the two lost babies. It would have been so nice if Charles had had a brother or sister to dilute the company.

'Such a shame your mama couldn't come,' drawled Mr Armstrong.

'Yes!' agreed Izzy. 'She was very disappointed. But I hope she'll meet you soon – no thank you!'

Mr Armstrong failed in his attempt to top up her sherry. Izzy knew she must not get disastrously drunk. And yet it was so very nice to feel warm within, so warm that a few smiles insisted on squeezing out in Mrs Armstrong's direction. *Am I grinning at her in an uncontrollably pissed way?* wondered Izzy. Soon it was time to go in to dinner, and Izzy's legs still worked more or less normally. So far, so good. She would ask for some water with her wine. That would do the trick.

'Could I have some wine with my water, please?' she enquired. Mrs Armstrong raised her eyebrows and looked curious. 'Oh crumbs!' exclaimed Izzy, 'I mean water with my wine.'

'Not actually in the same glass, surely, old thing?' frowned Charles. 'One is not a French toddler, is one – thank God!'

The men brayed a bit. Izzy was given two glasses – one of water, one of wine. It all seemed a bit Biblical.

Daisy came in, wearing a black skirt and white blouse. She placed a silver dish on the table, and withdrew.

'And what is this, my dear?' enquired Mr Armstrong.

'Gravlax,' explained his wife. 'Marinaded salmon.'

'This is new,' observed the lord of the manor to Izzy. 'This is one of Ma's experiments. Some kind of Scandinavian recipe.'

'I'm sure it'll be delicious,' said Izzy.

She was wrong. Izzy's tastes were simple. But this gravlax had a strange, rubbery texture. The idea of slugs came into Izzy's mind, and unfortunately stayed. Izzy's first mouthful went round and round and round. All her teeth in turn had a jolly good go at it, and still it remained, bouncy, slimy, and cheekily intact. A surge of nausea rose in Izzy's stomach. She ruthlessly swept it aside. She must not feel sick.

A swig of wine might do the trick – wash it down. Alas, the slug seemed stubbornly attached to life upstairs, and refused to accompany the wine down the red lane. Izzy was afraid to swallow it unchewed in case she choked to death. That, surely, would be the biggest social gaffe of all.

'Hhh-eeeeeecch!'

She would slump face-down on the table, turn blue and expire. Izzy had a horror of dying in public, and dying at the Armstrongs' dinner table would somehow be worst of all. His mother would never forgive her.

Izzy panicked. What was she to do? Then an idea came. She fished for her handbag, and whipped out a handkerchief. It was rather a dirty one, but never mind. Charles was busy discussing the latest additions to his father's wine cellar. There was plenty of robust baritone noise about Beaune and Chateauneuf du Pape. Izzy pretended to blow her nose, and swiftly spat out the offending morsel into her hankie. She bundled the disgusting little parcel back into her bag, not daring to look at Mrs Armstrong, whom she was sure had observed the whole charade.

But there remained a problem: the rest of her portion, virtually untouched on her plate. Izzy drank some more wine, and stared at the gravlax. She had helped herself quite generously, partly because she wished to ingratiate herself with Mrs Armstrong and partly because she liked salmon. Usually. But this salmon hadn't even been cooked! Not cooked! Whatever would her mother have said? Thank God she wasn't here. Izzy cut a tiny sliver off the horrid thing and prodded it with her fork. She couldn't. Another wave of nausea swept through her. Her very tongue shuddered. It was impossible.

'I'm terribly sorry,' she said, putting down her knife and fork.

'What is it, old thing?' enquired Charles.

'I really am most terribly sorry, but I can't eat this.'

'Quite right!' cried Charles's father. 'It's no good, Charlotte. Like eating bloody squash balls. Take it away.'

Mrs Armstrong did not betray any emotion, but swiftly removed Izzy's plate.

'I think it's delicious,' protested Charles, gulping ingratiatingly at his mother.

Izzy stared at the shining mahogany of the table in deep embarrassment. This was the end of her relationship with his mother, she was sure. But thank God the awful plateful of slug had gone.

'I like a woman who's not afraid to speak her own mind – hey, Isabelle?'

She gave Charles's father a grateful little glance. 'Would you mind – calling me Izzy?' she asked, shyly, hoping to divert the conversation away from the drawbacks of gravlax. 'Isabelle sounds a bit – well, formal, to me.'

'And what are you going to call us, I wonder? Charles calls us Old Man and Ma. That's not really on, is it? Call us Fred and Charlotte, my dear, that's the best solution.

Can't have this *Mr Armstrong* business for the rest of our lives, can we?'

Mr Armstrong was irritated by his Mr. He had hoped, by now, that it would have been replaced by something more musical.

'All right, then,' faltered Izzy. 'Fred. And – and Charlotte.'

Mrs Armstrong graciously inclined her head towards her, and showed her slightly yellow teeth.

'What's next, Charlotte? Get this fish out of my sight.'

'One of Daisy's stews,' murmured Charlotte.

'Ah, that's the ticket,' bawled the great Fred, or as Izzy was coming to think of him, Frederick the Great. 'Daisy! Bring us your stew, for God's sake!'

Daisy came, bearing a tureen whose ambrosial scent promised Izzy that the worst moment in the evening was over. As she set it on the table, she gave Izzy a secret wink. It helped, a lot.

ALL HID, ALL HID

Breakfast next morning was much easier. Mrs Armstrong breakfasted apart, in her boudoir. Mr Armstrong was ensconced behind *The Times*, eating what appeared to be a whole series of boiled eggs. He greeted Izzy with a dazzling smile, complimented her on her looks, and continued to talk about cricket with Charles, who, thank God, was already there when Izzy arrived.

'Bloody TCCB!' roared Fred the Great, gesturing violently towards the sports page, 'Should be shot, the whole pack of them.'

Daisy placed a generous rack of toast conveniently close to Izzy's plate, and promised her the tea of her dreams: British workmen's tea, brick-red and steaming. The sun shone. Izzy was getting used to the size and shine of the table, and beyond it, the endless windows of the dining room, all open to the terrace, so that the sound of bees and the scent of roses drifted in. She ate a lot of breakfast, happy to be ignored.

Then the door opened, and Bill Bailey appeared, dressed all in white: white T-shirt and rather crumpled cotton trousers.

'My dear fellow, how are you?' enquired Charles's father, pumping Bill's hand but not getting up. 'Have some breakfast.'

'No, thanks, I've already had some. Well, perhaps just a cup of coffee, please, Daisy.'

'You drink too much coffee,' scolded Daisy quietly.

'Did you sleep well, Izzy? No bad dreams?' enquired Bill.

'No! Lovely dreams, in fact.'

'You've cut all your hair off, Bill. You look like Machiavelli,' the senior Armstrong observed.

Izzy wondered if the Armstrongs knew about Bill's marriage breaking up. They must do, surely. But it was not mentioned.

'You should approve of that, Old Man. I thought Machiavelli was one of your heroes.'

'You bet. Cunning old devil. Not sure I approve of his haircut, though.'

'Ah,' said Bill, stroking the top of his head, which looked like a cornfield after the combine harvester, 'it's penitential, you see.'

'Don't approve of penitence either. Never apologize.' Frederick the Great got up, folded his copy of *The Times* and threw it at his son. 'Ready in ten minutes if you're coming to see this house, Chas.' He strode out.

'What house?' asked Bill.

'Oh, a nice little Georgian job in Beccles. It's the Old Man's hobby, buying old houses and restoring them,' Charles explained to Izzy. 'It looks as if he's going to need my help with this one. It's got a little niche in the wall and I may be able to find a garden gnome of some sort to fit into it.'

'I think I'd better take Izzy to see Blythburgh, then,' suggested Bill. 'Keep her out of trouble till tonight, shall I?'

'Good man!' beamed Charles. 'You'll love the angels, darling. You can borrow my car, Bill.'

He threw Bill the keys, kissed Izzy on the head, and was gone.

'I suppose you'll want sandwiches, then,' said Daisy, clearing the table. Bill thought they probably would.

'You don't object to a picnic, I suppose?' he smiled. 'Not against your principles or anything?'

Izzy felt a rising rush of pleasure. This weekend, which she had been dreading so much, was turning out to be a delight.

'And by the time we get back,' he promised, 'your friends will be arriving.'

Izzy had a feeling of increasing sunshine.

'The only thing is,' faltered Izzy as they drove off down the avenue, 'I didn't even see Mrs Armstrong to say good morning to her or anything. I mean, since I've come here to meet them, it might seem a bit rude to go off like this.'

'Want to go back, then?' Bill stopped the car and grinned.

'No! No! Go on! Go on!'

'Don't worry about Charles's mum. She very rarely sees anyone in the mornings, ever. She says she never feels sociable, then.'

'Crumbs,' mused Izzy, 'that's a frightening thought.' The car turned out of the avenue and roared off southwards.

'Over the border, down Blythburgh way!' sang Izzy. 'What does Blythburgh mean?'

'It must mean Happy Town.'

Soon they crossed the border. The idea of Suffolk felt warmer than Norfolk, somehow. The landscape was lush: the countryside rolled, the clouds sailed in great galleons of cumuli, across a sky of sailor-boy blue. The fields of corn and barley blazed on either side, the hedgerows reared up and waved at them as they passed: joyous green flags and tendrils, white flower-heads, feathery whirls of grass; the trees cast deep pools of shade through which they plunged in moments of delicious freshness.

'Oh it's so beautiful, so beautiful!' cried Izzy. This was the England she had come home to seek.

They did not talk much. When they arrived at Blythburgh, it seemed as if no time at all had passed, or a century. Bill switched off the car engine and opened his door. There was the sound of the ticking engine, someone mowing a lawn in the distance, and up above, a lark. They sat perfectly still, listening to it for a while, staring ahead at the church they had come to see. Izzy became uneasy about looking at him again. But there was no need.

'M.R. James!' he said suddenly, and produced a thick,

battered old book. Izzy got out of the car. She wanted to plunge her head into the air.

'It's so incredibly peaceful!' she breathed.

'Ah, but there were terribly bloody battles here. In the seventh century. Between the Christians and the Pagans. Which side would you have been on, Izzy?'

'I don't know. Which would you?'

'Here – page 12. "The next king of the East Angles was also a saint and martyr, Anna, nephew of Redwald and father of at least five sainted persons." There! How would you like to be the mother of five sainted persons, Izzy?'

'I'd hate it,' grinned Izzy. 'I'd feel so inadequate.'

'Be nice on Parents' Evenings, though, wouldn't it?'

'Did you say this was a *bloke* called Anna?'

'That's nothing. Listen to this: "Anna fell in battle fighting against the old heathen Panda in 654."'

'What? *Panda?* I don't believe it!' Izzy snatched the book. 'You see? It's someone called Penda. "The heathen Penda." '

'All the same, imagine them hacking each other's heads off,' pondered Bill. 'In that field over there, perhaps.'

The lark dropped like a stone to its nest in the grass. Izzy gazed out across the shimmering countryside and marvelled.

'Tell me something else.'

'No. Come and see the church.'

On the church door was a notice: PLEASE SHUT THE DOOR, it read, OTHERWISE BIRDS FLY IN.

'Can you blame them?' smiled Bill as they stepped inside the beautiful space. The floor was paved with red and sandy-coloured stones: light flickered down from the windows and danced under their feet and across their cheeks. Everywhere Izzy looked she saw extraordinary carved figures: the bench ends were adorned with small people whose faces were blurred and flattened with age.

'Look!' cried Izzy. 'Here's someone sitting up in bed! What does that mean?'

'M.R. James reckons it's one of the Works of Mercy.

You know, caring for the Sick, and so on.'

'He doesn't look very sick.'

'Well, perhaps it's Sloth, then. Would that suit you better?'

'Oh yes! That's one of my absolute best favourite sins.'

'What about the others?'

'Oh – just gluttony,' said Izzy, blushing.

'Here it is.'

The figure was holding its stomach.

'Oh dear!' laughed Izzy. 'I've often felt like that. What are your favourite sins, Bill?'

'I've got a bit bored with sins recently,' he smiled. 'I'm going for austerity and abstinence now.'

Izzy wondered if this was a joke. She hoped so.

'Look up,' he said suddenly.

Above their heads, all along the roof, were carved angels staring down on them, their wings spread wide, their faces astonished and slightly blank.

'That's what you'll start to look like,' whispered Izzy, 'if you get too keen on this austerity lark. Aren't they beautiful? No wonder the birds want to fly in. If I was a bird, I would.'

'You are a bit of a bird, actually.'

'What do you mean?'

'Nothing. Never mind.'

'No, tell me what you mean.'

'You mustn't always ask me what I mean,' Bill frowned.

'Why not?'

He did not answer, but walked back slowly to the door. There he paused, and waited for her to catch up. 'There are things I can't mean,' he said quietly, and they went out into the light.

Izzy felt sobered, but exalted. Thinned, refined, dazzled, lifted up. As if she was rising up on the air and hovering above these scattered tombs.

'They bless the animals here sometimes,' said Bill. 'Everybody brings their pets – budgies and cats and everything, and they are blessed.'

Izzy burst into tears. 'Oh dear,' she sniffed. 'I can't explain—'

'No need to explain,' said Bill, handing her a handkerchief. Izzy blew her nose.

'Why don't people ever blow their noses when they cry on the movies?'

'It would make them look too real.'

'Bill . . .' handing the handkerchief back, 'do you – er, believe in, well, God, sort of thing? I mean, those angels and everything, looking down. I mean, I do have a feeling, sometimes, that someone is up there in the sky, watching me. Don't you?'

'Especially in East Anglia,' acknowledged Bill. 'But, really, it's all a mystery to me. I want it to stay a mystery.'

'But do you think death is the end?'

They stood among the tombs. A hot wind stirred the grass. Bill kicked a stone into the shade.

'Who knows?' he shrugged. Izzy was silent. In the silence her stomach suddenly rumbled loudly.

'So much for the sky,' laughed Bill. 'Back to earth. I must feed you. Time for the picnic.' He started the car. 'Now all we need is the sea. It's only a couple of miles.'

They drove south, skirting tracts of heather and clumps of woodland, and eventually arrived at the wide glitter where the land ended. Bill led her onto the beach.

'This is Dunwich,' he swept an arm across the waves. 'It's fallen into the sea. It was a city once. Had fifty-two churches.'

'*Fifty-two?*'

'Yes. The sea ate it up.'

'So there are – churches and houses and things – all out there under the waves.?'

'Yes. Can you hear the bells? Want to picnic here, or is it too spooky?'

'No. No, I like it.'

The beach was almost deserted: a middle-aged couple with a dog strolled along the shore: some children shouted in the distance. Daisy's sandwiches were very good. Izzy felt perfect peace steal over her heart. It was as if she had somehow got back into that childhood world again. Hard-boiled eggs, and salt, and bread and butter, all tasted newly delicious with the sound of the sea in your ears and its smell in your nose. Izzy thought of all the bones silting up out there under the sea's glitter: young women's bones and young men's bones, who had picnicked once, perhaps, under the drifting clouds.

'The great thing is,' she said, sipping tea from a plastic cup, 'it's our turn now.'

'You're a healthy old thing,' observed Bill.

'Well, it's our turn now and we ought to make the best of it. Their world's gone but it's still here for us.'

'Only just, though. The sea won that battle, but if man goes on the way he is, we may kill the sea.'

'Oh shut up, Bill, I was enjoying a perfect moment. And anyway, how could anyone kill the sea?'

'Man's a dirty devil,' Bill lay back, having finished his lunch. 'He's doing his best to foul his own nest.' He closed his eyes. Izzy was glad of the chance to look at him without being observed. He looked like the statue of a Crusader on a tomb.

'Sit up,' she said. 'You look dead.'

'I must have my forty winks,' he insisted. 'All this driving makes me sleepy. Go and have a paddle.'

Izzy took her shoes off and walked in the edge of the sea, where two worlds meet. The water washed grainily around her feet. Weed, fragments of wood, shells, tiny bits of plastic, frail shreds of bone and fin, all thrashed around her ankles with each collapsing wave. And who knows what else, in this ancient soup: medieval hair, Elizabethan threads and Georgian fingernails might have whirled and swirled along this beach. Men snatched each other's homes, wives, kingdoms, but the sea and the earth received them all impartially in the end. Izzy waded in a sea of mortality.

She tucked her skirt up into her knickers, like a child, and felt the cold currents move around her knees. The sunlight on the water dazzled her. She looked up, wondering if any austere eyes were fixed on Dunwich Beach from up there behind the wind: eyes, like the stars, invisible by daylight. If the stars were there, why not the eyes? But there was no sense of being watched from above, today. Only from the beach. Bill was sitting up and looking out at her. She waded ashore, but paused at the very edge of the sea, where thin sheets of water slide back off the land, and looked down at her feet. And there she felt that childhood sense that her fixed feet were actually rushing forward out of the sea, flying towards something like a goddess or a ghost.

'Come on,' said Bill Bailey. 'Time to go home.'

THE TRUMPETS SOUND: BE MASKED

Izzy arrived back at Thraxton to find Maria and Gwyn and Louise and Michael all having tea with Mrs Armstrong. Sooty was also there, and a blonde woman Izzy had never seen before. Izzy hesitated in the doorway, aware that her legs were still sandy and that a trip to the Blue Bathroom was decidedly overdue. On the other hand, she hadn't seen Mrs Armstrong all morning, and was desperate to ingratiate herself after the gravlax episode.

'Ah,' she stammered. 'Hello.'

'Come in, darling!' ordered Mrs Armstrong with an imperious wave. 'Did you have a lovely time?'

'Oh yes – thank you. Hi!' Izzy grinned at her friends. The blonde woman extended a hand.

'I'm Georgie Pope,' she said. 'How d'you do?'

'Hello,' said Izzy, shaking her hand. Then there was the problem of where to sit.

'Sit by me, Izzy,' ordered Maria, making room on the sofa.

Izzy sat down, tucking her legs as far as possible under the sofa – so far, indeed, that she was in danger of slithering onto her knees on the carpet. Surreptitiously she rubbed her calves against the sofa, to get rid of some of the sand. But even Izzy, who was reasonably agile, could not rub her shins on any of the furniture without drawing attention to herself.

'I hadn't realized you were a schoolmistress,' said Mrs Armstrong, handing Izzy a cup of extremely pale tea.

'Had – hadn't you? Really? I thought Charles would have told you that.'

'Oh, Charles never tells us anything. It must be

251

absolutely riveting, teaching in a comprehensive.'

'I like it,' said Izzy. 'The kids are great.' Immediately she felt that she had sounded simple-minded. She reached for a cucumber sandwich, food being always a comfort at moments of distress – though, of course, she would have preferred bread and jam. Bill Bailey had disappeared. Izzy felt paralyzed – desperate to talk to her friends, and afraid to say anything whilst Mrs Armstrong was there, in case it was wrong. There was a brief silence, in which Izzy became aware that she was the only one eating, and that it was impossible to chew quietly.

'Well, Charlotte,' remarked Gwyn, 'great 'ouse you got here.' Izzy cringed, but Mrs Armstrong seemed quite charmed with Gwyn. 'Got any ghosts, has it? I always had an ambition to be scared out o'my wits in the middle o'the night.'

'They do say that the Long Gallery is haunted,' smiled Mrs Armstrong. 'It's one of the Bride in a Box stories, you know.'

'Ah yes,' said Michael. 'Bride plays hide and seek at her wedding celebrations – or perhaps even her engagement party – hides in old chest, can't get out, guests search in increasing panic, do not hear her faint cries, skeleton in chest discovered two hundred years later.'

Izzy felt suffocated. She could almost sense the heavy lid pressing down on her, shutting out the air and forbidding escape. She wished she was not so pre-menstrual. The slightest thing made her feel depressed and tearful. It was very unfortunate timing, this party.

'Tell you what, Charlotte, I wouldn't mind a wander round outside, like. Cast an admirin' eye over the parterres an' what have you.'

'Oh, do,' said Mrs Armstrong, getting up. 'I have to go and see to things in any case.'

'Can I help, Charlotte?' Sooty bounded from her chair, and they disappeared kitchenwards.

'Comin' for a stroll, Maria, darlin'?' enquired her husband, hesitating by the French windows.

252

'Oh, no, Gwyn. I couldn't possibly. I'll just lie here for a bit longer.'

'I'll come, Gwyn. I have a curiosity to inspect the acres of which one day young Izzy will be mistress.'

'What?' Izzy's mouth dropped open. The only thing she had hitherto been mistress of was Michael.

'This rather pleasant house and its adjoining land, will one day, by the laws of nature, becomes yours, old thing.'

Michael smiled at Izzy's wild eyes and open mouth.

'Oh God! Michael! I hadn't even realized!'

Louise and the blonde woman, Georgie, laughed heartily.

'Oh, Izzy, you are an innocent!' cried Louise. 'Only you could have got this far without having had that thought.'

Izzy boggled. This house – hers? These acres, these orchards – well, of course. Now she came to think of it. Charles was the only child. Sole heir.

'Good God,' she said, and fell silent in awful contemplation of her destiny.

'Come on, old thing,' urged Michael, 'give us the works. Show us round.'

'Oh no, Michael, I couldn't! I'll stay here with Maria.'

'I'll come,' Georgie got up and tossed back her hair. 'You mustn't miss the gazebo.'

Louise looked alarmed at the prospect of the dazzling Georgie accompanying her husband to remote gazebos, and leapt up to join the party. This left Izzy and Maria on the sofa, which was just what they wanted.

'Oh Maria!' whispered Izzy as soon as they'd gone. 'It's so weird! I don't seem to be able to say a thing right!'

'Well, of course not,' sighed Maria. 'Your education hasn't prepared you for this kind of thing, at all.'

'I know. It's terribly hard work. I mean, if Charles's mum was, well – different – but, she doesn't seem a – a very easy person.'

'She's awful.'

'But I'm sure I'm awful, too – I mean, I keep saying the wrong things and falling down and getting sand on my legs. And last night I couldn't eat her fishy thing she'd made. It was sort of raw fish, Maria! Absolutely Yuk-a-hoola. Oh dear. I wish I had a bit more experience of the upper classes.'

'Don't let her intimidate you,' warned Maria. 'They're not real gentry, only terrible arrivistes. That's why she's trying to put you down, all the time. She's desperately socially insecure, herself.'

'Surely not? I mean, with this house and everything.'

'She may have this house, which, incidentally, they bought, not inherited, but she hasn't got everything. All her Hepplewhites are nineteenth-century fakes, for a start.'

'What? You mean – the furniture's not real – I mean, true?'

'I'm not sure about the philosophical position *vis-à-vis* real and true chairs, Izzy, but hers are not what they pretend to be.'

'Imagine chairs pretending to be anything! It's all so confusing.'

'And all those colour co-ordinated bathrooms! Terribly vulgar.'

'Really? Mine's, well, rather comfortable.'

'Oh yes. Aristocratic bathrooms are always fiendishly uncomfortable: cold and draughty, with old white loos with cracked seats. And hard loo-paper.'

'Charles's bathroom is like that. In his London house, I mean.'

'Ah, well, you see, Charles is a man of intelligence and taste. So he makes himself a bathroom which is impeccably aristocratic. But a real aristocrat would already have bathrooms like that. I mean, they would be there, already, in the house.'

'It's all terribly confusing,' complained Izzy. 'And boring and silly, I think.'

'You'll have to come to terms with it,' warned Maria, 'if you're going to marry this bloke. His mother will never like you, for a start. She'll always be trying to put you down.'

'Why? Because I'm vulgar?'

'Because she's a frightful snob and wishes he had married Sooty or Footsie or whatever that brainless Sloane is called. If she was a real aristocrat, she wouldn't be so insecure, and she'd be much more likely to be really nice and welcoming to you. And she wouldn't mind if you said *pardon* or *toilet*.'

'What's wrong with saying pardon?' Izzy panicked.

'Nothing. Look, Izzy, the best thing you can do is stay your sweet self. Don't worry about being acceptable to her, because you never will be. Just concentrate on being happy with Charles, and bugger the rest of it.'

'Maria – how do you know all about this?'

'A friend of mine at Oxford was a Duke's daughter.'

Izzy was grateful for her friend's experience. 'You've made me feel a lot better, Maria.'

'Well, now you can make me feel a lot better. Come upstairs and talk to me whilst I lie down. I'm not quite horizontal enough, here.'

The afternoon ran swiftly to its close. After an hour with Maria, Izzy emerged cheerful and encouraged, and met Charles on the landing.

'Hello, darling!' he cried, giving her an enthusiastic kiss. 'Good to see you looking so bright and furry. Having a good time?'

'Oh lovely, Charles! Blythburgh was beautiful!'

'Bill look after you all right?'

'Oh yes, he's wonderful. I do like your friends. Where is he now?'

'Practising upstairs.'

The faint sound of a piano being played drifted down from above.

'Oh yes! He is good, isn't he?'

'And how are you getting on with Mother?' Charles dropped his voice slightly. Izzy fidgeted.

'I find her a bit – well, frightening, really,' she admitted. 'And I keep saying the wrong thing.'

'Don't worry, little weasel.' He gave her a persuasive hug. 'You're doing fine. The Old Man is completely bowled over by you. Ma will come round in time. And remember, the main thing is, I love you.'

Izzy threw herself into his arms. Dear Charles! Everything would be all right. She would be herself, as Maria instructed, and trust to nature. She was, after all, Charles's little weasel. He embraced her briefly and then pointed her in the direction of her room.

'Baths for weasels,' he said. 'So they can emerge with shining fur and stun the assembled company.'

Izzy went.

The Blue Bath was, even if vulgar, sublimely comfortable. Izzy lay and steamed for too long, enjoying the solitude and surveying her day with some satisfaction. The worst was definitely over now. The mother was met, and her disapproval dispersed by the support of Izzy's friends. The day with Bill had been absolute heaven. Even now she could dimly hear him playing, up in the brains of the house. Charles's dad liked her. Charles seemed pleased with her. And she was going to look good tonight in her cream dress. Izzy washed her hair, and then heaved herself out.

As she stood up, a dizzy spell hit her between the eyes. She sat on the loo with her head between her knees for a while, and then felt better. That bath had been too hot. Silly of her, especially since she was pre-menstrual. Izzy's only concession to illness was an occasional bout of bad period pains. She hoped one was not on its way tonight. She dried herself and dressed, slowly and luxuriously. Soon she was ready. The Izzy in the glass looked extraordinary: poised and elegant. Perhaps, at long last, she had grown up.

Everyone was gathering in the drawing room. Charles saw her coming down and went out to meet her at the bottom of the stairs. He kissed her cheek, and looked at her with shining eyes.

'You look magnificent,' he said – a word he had hitherto only applied to Adam fireplaces. 'You look as if you'd been here all your life. You look as if you'd been born here.'

Izzy beamed gratefully at him, and followed him into the drawing room on her thin little slippers. As they went in, there was a cheer and Frederick the Great raised a glass.

'To Charles and Izzy!' he cried, and there was a corresponding roar of congratulation.

Izzy looked around: the room was full of the people she loved. Mrs Armstrong was seated conveniently at a distance with Sooty and Georgie: they raised their glasses to the happy couple and blew kisses. Maria, looking thin in her black dress, managed to smile, though her lip was trembling somewhat: Gwyn strode across the room and gave Izzy one of his rib-cracking hugs.

'Congratulations, darlin'!' he boomed, and then pumped Charles's hand. 'You're a very very lucky man, Charles – I hoape I make myself clear!'

Louise and Michael came up, too. Louise gave Izzy an emotional hug.

'Dear Izzy!' she whispered. 'Be happy!'

Michael bent and kissed Izzy's soft cheek. It was not the kiss he'd been planning for Izzy, this summer, but he couldn't help being moved by the ritual elements in the situation, and by the sight of his dear little mistress transformed into a swan. He rather liked the thought of weekends here in the future. It would also be handy to have access to this house in case he ever managed to claw his way out of Schools Television and got a chance to film *Mansfield Park*. If Izzy must marry, how convenient of her to marry a guy with at least two houses. It should be pretty easy to make sure that Charles was always at the other one. For a moment Michael rejoiced, if not exactly with them, then at least alongside them. His cough was better, too. It seemed as if he would not die this year, after all.

A pale fellow with very short fair hair slipped into the room behind Charles. Michael thought for a moment he might be the butler, but he was too scruffy. He was evidently a friend of Charles's, for he put his arms around

257

both Charles and Izzy and kissed each of them on the cheek. Izzy responded with enthusiasm. Michael did not much like the idea of Charles's friends. Still, there was always the rather gorgeous Georgie. Michael drifted away in her direction, leaving Izzy to bask in her moment of complete – well nearly complete – happiness before they went in to dinner.

PLAY, MUSIC, THEN

Dinner was a buffet, an excellent thing, since everyone was much more interested in having secret little snippets of conversation with one another than the ordeal of a public exchange across the mahogany. Daisy – with a little help from Mrs Armstrong and Sooty – had provided a marvellous array of dishes so that there was no danger of the gravlax situation repeating itself. And if by chance something not quite delicious managed to insinuate itself into one's mouth, it would be the work of a moment to wander out onto the terrace and spit it emphatically into one of the Versailles tubs full of verbena.

The terrace was adorned with a scatter of white chairs, and at this moment when the garden was drenched with the golden syrup of evening sunshine, nothing could spoil Izzy's delight. Charles was at her side, ever attentive, making sure her glass was refilled with the most delicious cold crisp white wine, his eyes always shining, his hand often brushing her arm or shoulder.

'It's like that last duet in *L'Incoronazione di Poppea*,' he whispered. Izzy did not spoil the moment by asking him to explain. She knew that if she was patient, things would gradually become clear: how to talk to his mother, how to walk, sit, eat – everything. One day she would even understand all about the Incoronwhatsit of Poppea. For the time being she would follow Maria's advice. After all, he had chosen her as she was. What could be wrong with that?

She noticed Bill Bailey was standing by himself on the terrace, looking withdrawn.

'Hey!' she whispered at his elbow. 'What's wrong?'

'I just rang Marianne,' he said. 'I don't know – I think I

was hoping . . . But there seems to be no prospect at all of a reconciliation. She wants a quick divorce. She's going to the States.'

'Oh dear,' Izzy felt sad that he above all others should be cast down at her feast. 'I am sorry, Bill. Have something to eat.'

'Don't feel like it yet. Later, maybe. Think I'll get a drink instead. I must have a word with Charles.'

He threaded his way off through the others. Izzy turned and found herself face to face with the blonde, the beautiful Georgie.

'Izzy!' she hissed, insisting on a bit of attention. Izzy tried to shake off the residue of Bill's sadness, and pay attention to this stranger, who was very striking tonight in a long shimmering pleated dress of turquoise.

'You look marvellous!' said Izzy. 'Like a Pharaoh. Did they have female Pharaohs?'

'Oh yes. And you look stunning in that cream satin.'

'Charles chose it.'

'Charles does have an eye for things. But you've no idea what a difference you've made to him.'

'Have I?'

'Oh yes. He was so solitary, before. Completely wrapped up in his work. There was the occasional girlfriend, but it never seemed to last. We were all getting quite worried.'

'Well, no need to worry any longer. I'll take care of him.'

'Well quite! And frankly, Izzy, I'm really surprised and delighted that he had the sense to choose somebody like you.'

Izzy was flattered, though she couldn't think what Georgie meant. And in any case, Georgie couldn't possibly know what she was like, anyway – they'd never met before today.

'Oh, I'm very ordinary.'

'Oh no, you're not! You're extraordinary, Izzy. I've been talking to your friends. And to Charles, of course. I think he's a very lucky man.'

'Well, I think I'm a very lucky woman,' purred Izzy, munching the last of her cold curried chicken. It was delicious. The praise was delicious. At this moment, everything was delicious.

'Tell me, are you thinking of carrying on with your work?'

'Oh yes. For a while, anyway.'

'I mean, long term.'

'Well, no. Not really. I don't think it's a good thing to go on teaching for years and years.'

'Well quite! Absolutely! One must get terribly stale.'

'And tired. You should see some of my colleagues lying around in the staffroom. Like dead donkeys.'

'Poor things! Well, Izzy, it did occur to me that you might feel like a change. And if you ever do, I might have something to interest you.'

'Oh yes?' asked Izzy. 'What do you do?'

'I'm in films,' Georgie set aside her plate and got out her handbag. 'We're an independent company, growing fast I'm pleased to say. Here's my card – in case we don't get a chance to fix anything up. Give me a ring when you're back in town and we'll have lunch. My assistant is going to have to leave me in December – she's having a baby. I just wondered if you might be interested?'

'Oh – yes, I would be!' Izzy's mind whirled. The film business! Izzy was a film addict. The thought of exchanging the smelly corridors of Stansgate Comprehensive School for the secret studios of Wardour Street made her feel physically faint with excitement. If she gave in her notice at the start of the autumn term, she could leave at Christmas. Izzy felt the whole seedy fabric of her previous life drop away in shreds. It was replaced by a glorious tapestry of comfort, style and opportunity.

'Right. We'll have lunch, then. That's marvellous!' Georgie was poached, at this interesting moment, by Sooty, leaving Izzy to discover Michael waiting by a balustrade.

'Congrats, you sly old puss!' he hissed. 'I must say, you're looking staggeringly attractive. I can't interest you in an assignation in the kitchen garden, can I? A chaos of passion among the cucumber frames?'

'Shut up, Michael!'

'Sorry, darling, but old habits die hard. I don't know whether to slap old Charles on the back or break his neck in a frenzy of jealous rage.'

'Don't be so silly. You've got Louise – and she's looking much better, isn't she?'

Louise's hair was springing up like flames again, and she was wearing a glittering green dress which hung in folds about her, kindly concealing the ravages of child-bearing. She was sitting a few yards away talking animatedly to Mrs Armstrong.

'My dear, I have to inform you that the improvement is only superficial. In fact things are going what can only be described as rapidly downhill.'

'What! Why?'

'She's got obsessed with this idea that I'm knocking off the nanny. Ludicrous idea. The girl makes my skin creep.'

'She's very beautiful, though.'

'Not to my eyes, Izzy. Bulging brunettes are more my style, as you know. And in any case, even I would not be such a cad as to seduce a woman who was actually living in my own house, dammit.'

'Oh wouldn't you? You could have fooled me.'

'The situation between us, dear heart, was entirely different, as you very well know. And what's more, the moment you moved in it was Goodbye Eros. Or had you forgotten?'

'No, that's right.'

'Now you've moved out again, however, I have to report a vague trembling in the loins at the sight of your rampant little corsage, but so what? I am an officer and a gentleman. I suffer in silence, even though the woman I love is whirled off before my eyes by a mere aesthete – what was I saying?'

'About Louise and the nanny.'

'Ah. Yes. Well, this weekend is a sea of peace in an ocean of ghastliness, Izzy. Because the wretched nanny has been left firmly behind in Muswell Hill in charge of the son and heir.'

'Have you brought Rose, then?'

'Yes. She is even at this moment snoozing in her carry cot in the Morning Room.'

'Doesn't she cry so much, now?'

'No. We must acknowledge the crumbs of comfort thrown us by an otherwise pitiless fate. Rose is improving. But Louise is going rapidly round the bend.'

'What do you mean?'

'Accusations. Things thrown at my innocent head. Threats to separate. To kill the nanny.'

'Surely not? Michael, you must be kidding.'

'I do not jest. I am in deadly earnest. The trouble is, the wretched nanny seems to have some kind of crush on me. Always fawning round. Warming my slippers *et cetera*. Meaningful glances. Brushes past on the stairs. Honestly, darling, I am performing an act of great heroism by resisting. But resisting I bloody well am.'

'Why not sack her?'

'Louise is in this Catch 22 situation. She wants to kill her, but she doesn't want to upset her.'

'Jesus!'

'The dilemma, my dear Izzy, of the liberal intelligentsia. Not a social class with which you are going to waste much more of your time, I fear.'

'What? What do you mean?'

But Gwyn had arrived.

'Now look yere, Michael, I'm not goin' to allow you to monopolize the blushin' bride-to-be. What she needs is the blessin' o' Dionysus.' Gwyn raised his glass and waved it in Izzy's face. 'Here's to you, darlin'!' he bawled. 'You've infiltrated the rulin' class and all I can say is, more power to your elboa!'

'Shush, Gwyn! You mustn't get drunk.'

'Too late, darlin'. It's a positive duty to expose one's self unstintin'ly to wine of this quality, which I'm never likely to experience again. Mind you, I'm tactfully drunk, like. I'm still capable of resistin' the temptation to punch the smug capitalist bastard on the nose.' Izzy thought this must be a reference to Charles's father. 'Noa, noa, darlin'.

This is your party, right? Nothin's goin' to spoil it, not even the class war.'

'I hope not,' said Izzy. 'If you misbehave, Gwyn, I'll never speak to you again.'

'Darlin'! Your hurtful words plunge daggers into my faithful old Welsh heart.'

'Well, all right. I hope you haven't brought any horrible drugs.'

'Ah!' A smile of revelation burst over Gwyn's face. 'I'm obliged to you for remindin' me, sweetheart. Michael, come with me to the Billiard Room, mon. I got a little something to lighten your heart.'

Michael shepherded him off, turning to Izzy as he went. 'I'll sort him out,' he promised, with a wink. 'Go and talk to Louise, Izzy. Please! Get her to see sense.'

Izzy helped herself to some more salad, as Louise was still talking to Mrs Armstrong. She was beginning to feel the first dreary old abdominal cramps. How inconsiderate of her reproductive system to go into its spasms now. Perhaps a few mouthfuls of potato salad would set things right. She was halfway through the first large mouthful when Mrs Armstrong appeared at her elbow.

'I've just been talking to Louise,' she said, fixing Izzy with her basilisk eye. 'Curious that I've never met her before, though we are obscurely related by marriage.'

'She's a very nithe perthon,' said Izzy through too much potato salad.

'Yes. She was talking about her children. She's very worried about her little boy.'

'Oh dear.'

'One does worry about one's little boy, I'm afraid. And the worrying doesn't stop when the little boy grows up.'

'No, I'm sure it doesn't,' agreed Izzy, trying to imagine Charles aged four, sitting on this woman's lap.

'I'm still very anxious about Charles,' announced Mrs Armstrong bluntly. 'He is so unpredictable.'

Izzy considered this for a moment. To her Charles seemed very far from unpredictable: a man of certain tastes and fixed habits. It dawned on Izzy that she was being cleverly insulted.

'Is the unpredictable always a bad thing?' she asked. 'I would have thought it was quite healthy, really. Better than being in a rut.'

'I often think that Charles doesn't have the faintest idea what he is doing. He exposes himself to all sorts of dangers.'

'Does he?' Izzy's courage was failing fast.

'I'm always afraid he's going to take some fatal step which will lead him off in entirely the wrong direction.'

Izzy set aside her potato salad. She felt sick. She stared at the floor, unable to speak a word. What more chilling and comprehensive rejection was there? But at this point Mrs Armstrong swooped.

'You must try and keep him to the straight and narrow, Izzy. Remember, darling – I depend on you!'

This last unconvincing flourish was, no doubt, a concession to the duties of a hostess: a pretence that she hadn't been saying what she had, without a doubt, been saying. Mrs Armstrong went off purposefully to initiate the pudding. Izzy found a chair and sat down. Mrs Armstrong's words echoed in her mind. *You must try and keep him to the straight and narrow.* This was entirely the opposite of what Izzy sensed she must do with Charles.

Maria suddenly appeared and sat beside her. She looked pale and tired.

'How do you feel, Maria?'

'Sick. How do you feel?'

'Faint. This party's a disaster, Maria. Bill's heart-broken—'

'Who's Bill?'

'That fair chap in the corner. His wife's left him. Louise is going round the bend, Michael says. Gwyn's drunk. And Mrs Armstrong hates me.'

'Is that all? Well then, we've got nothing to worry about.'

Charles approached bearing a plate. 'This,' he pronounced with the air of a conjuror, 'is Daisy's summer pudding. One taste and you'll be in heaven, darling – I promise. Can I get you some, Maria?'

'No, thanks. It looks lovely, but I don't think I can really face food tonight.'

'Maria's having a baby,' explained Izzy. 'You remember, Charles.'

'I do,' Charles bowed. 'Not yet, I hope. Not actually tonight? Awful business, this reproduction. You girls deserve medals. Can I get you anything else? A glass of juice? Water?'

'No. Nothing, thank you. I'm looking forward to the music,' said Maria. 'What's he going to play?'

'Not sure. Mozart, probably. Maybe some Schubert.'

'Lovely,' Maria leaned back in her chair. Izzy devoured the summer pudding. It was certainly the most delicious thing she had tasted in her life: strawberries and raspberries and blackberries and currants all heaped together with cream and sugar and sops of bread.

Charles wandered off to talk to some other guests who had arrived late, and Izzy sighed.

'It's a shame you can't eat this, Maria,' she said. 'Really. I'm sure it would do you good. Go on!'

'Oh, all right. I do love summer pudding. Would you mind getting me some? I'm too tired to get up.'

As they trooped upstairs to the Long Gallery for the music, Izzy thought well, at least Maria ate something. And I was offered a job. She was on the arm of Charles's father.

'We restored this gallery in 1962,' he was saying. 'It had been partitioned off into servants' bedrooms by the Victorians. Frightful mess.'

'Restoring things is very important, isn't it?' Izzy hoped she was managing to talk rationally despite a really bad bout of indigestion that had arrived with the cramps.

'Terribly. The past, you know, is a treasure-house left us by our ancestors.'

'Not just large houses, either, but little cottages too.'

'Quite right! England's cottages are absolute gems. Couldn't agree more.'

'Daisy's cottage, for instance,' Izzy felt emboldened by pain. It was as if the pain forced this out of her. 'It's particularly pretty, I thought.'

'Absolutely.'

'I'd heard—' Izzy hesitated, and sat down on one of the chairs set out in an informal group by the piano. 'I'm sorry if I've got it wrong, but I'd heard you were going to have to expand – I mean – get rid of Daisy's cottage, sort of thing. Is that right?'

He threw back his head and laughed.

'Who's afraid of the big bad wolf, eh? No, your spies have got it all wrong, my dear. We're expanding, certainly. But Daisy's cottage is going to be restored, not flattened. It will form the pivot of the new reception area.'

'What about her garden?'

'Most of that'll be kept too. Just as it is: the Cottage Garden. It's the perfect setting for our new range of products. Did Charles tell you about our new range?'

'No.'

'They're going to be called The Gentle Gardener. Nice soft-focus packaging. Little old white-haired lady in cottage garden. I'm thinking of using a photo of Daisy surrounded by flowers, as the logo.'

'But she hasn't got white hair.'

'Oh, that can be touched in. Then when the clients arrive, they find themselves in that very garden.'

'But what about Daisy?'

'She'll be much more comfortable here in the house. That stream's bad for her rheumatism. She's not getting any younger. And the cottage is frightfully damp. We're having to gut it and put in a damp-proof course. They didn't bother about that sort of thing in old Shakespeare's time.'

By now everyone was seated and Bill walked to the piano. His face wore a defended, public look. He did not seem to see anybody, but addressed the rafters.

'I thought I'd begin with a bit of Bach.'

'Capital!' said Charles's father.

Bill sat down and began.

Izzy's thoughts immediately began to swirl about. She could not concentrate on the music, but peeped instead at those of her friends who were visible: Maria, sitting in a deep armchair, with Louise beside her. Izzy looked for signs that Louise was in a desperate state, but her head was bowed, as if she was studying the sumptuous Turkey carpet under her feet. Charles and his mother sat on the other side: Charles was nodding his head slightly in time with the music: Mrs Armstrong sat as still as a picture in her glass-grey gown. Behind her, Izzy sensed Gwyn's stertorous breathing. She hoped Michael was at his side and would prevent any Welsh wildness.

The cramps were getting worse. Izzy massaged her tummy under the cream satin. What she really needed was a hot-water bottle, a couple of painkillers, and an early night. Ah well. It would all be over in an hour or two. She felt guilty, experiencing Bill's playing as a trial to be endured. She'd been looking forward to hearing him, for hours: and now she could not concentrate. Bach's relentless rhythms drove onward like the passing of time itself, the hammering of some remorseless clock that insisted on their journey onwards, onwards, with a competitive energy that pulled and punched at her attention. She wished he would stop, and when the end came she clapped heartily with relief.

'Capital!' cried Charles's father again. 'Capital!'

'Ah,' growled Gwyn behind her, 'I hear the rallyin' cry of the rulin' class, Michael.'

'Quite so, old man. Good bit of Bach, though, wasn't it?'

'Aye. Mind you, I prefer Dire Straits myself.'

Izzy hoped this exchange had escaped Mr Armstrong's ears, as he was talking to Sooty on his other side. Suddenly there was the sound of a baby wailing, and Daisy carried in little Rose. Louise received her, and instantly gave her the breast. Mrs Armstrong exchanged a look with her husband, eyebrows arched in pained disapproval.

'Fine sight,' remarked Mr Armstrong gruffly, mitigating his wife's rather obvious disdain.

Bill Bailey had stared at Rose as she was carried in. Now he addressed the roof again.

'I think it is time for Schubert,' he murmured, and sank onto his seat. There was a moment of absolute stillness, and then the slowest, quietest, saddest music Izzy had ever heard, crept over them. The heart of it was loss – bitter loss and heartbreak. Izzy left her own discomforts instantly and saw through the music the photograph of a little girl with curly black hair, smiling into the camera as if the sun would never go in.

Great waves of pain flooded through Izzy's heart, soul, and womb. She drew her knees up in an attempt to soothe her knotting and un-knotting muscles. The music pulled her down, down, into a black pool of sorrow. Bill Bailey had lost his wife and child, and tears fled down Izzy's cheeks. She was helpless before this song of pain, and when at last the piece ended, everyone sat in stunned silence for a moment. Then a door opened, beyond the piano, and there, incongruously, stood Dick, evidently very hot and steamy, his face bright red with exertion. He gaped at the assembled audience.

'Oh, crikey!' he gasped. 'I'm sorry I'm late. I – I missed the train. And then I had to hitch from the station. And then I ran from the main road. I'm sorry I didn't ring, but I couldn't find a phone. I hope I didn't – er – inconvenience – things.'

'Dick!' cried Louise in horror, 'I'm so terribly sorry! I promised we'd give you a lift and I clean forgot!'

The baby burst into an intense shrieking. Then Maria stood up, her face a ghastly green colour. She reached towards Izzy, faltered, and vomited onto the Turkey carpet.

'Jesus Christ, Maria! What the hell—?' boomed Gwyn's voice. Izzy leapt to her feet to help her friend, but she had got up too fast. A stab of pain seared through her abdomen, and her head sizzled. Everything went white, her ears roared, her throat fluttered, and she fell insensible at Mr Armstrong's feet.

They drove home in the rain. It was over. In a way, the awfulness of her fainting and Maria's being sick had thrown a kind of pall over the whole weekend. Izzy felt numbed. That extraordinary moment: Bill's music, the sense of terrible pain and paralysis, and then Dick's bursting in, hot, and forgotten, and then – oh, she mustn't think about it.

'I still shudder when I think about it,' she murmured, watching the windscreen wipers' mad dance.

'Don't worry, darling,' said Charles. 'It was just one of those things.'

'But it was so awful, though! So many things going wrong at once! If was as if – well it makes me feel as if, as if – our party was doomed, somehow.'

'Don't be silly, Izzy! In fact, there's nothing like an emergency to make everyone pull together.'

'I'm sure your mother must've been terribly angry, though.'

'Nonsense! She was worried about you, of course, until we understood what it was all about – poor little weasel!' he squeezed her hand. 'I mean, it was marvellously melodramatic of you to crumple up at the old man's feet like that. I thought you'd died. You know, darling, in a few weeks' time, when you think about it, you'll be able to laugh.'

Izzy couldn't ever imagine being able to laugh about it. She would always remember opening her eyes, as the roaring in her ears subsided, and seeing Mrs Armstrong's face staring down at her out of the sky, with light behind her getting all mixed up with her face, and for a moment

Izzy had wondered, am I indoors? – is that the sun? – what have I done? And Mrs Armstrong's voice, coming strangely garbled from what seemed like a long way up in the sky, said, 'What on earth is wrong with her?' in such a curious, cold way.

'Daisy was very nice, though.'

'She's a treasure, of course.'

'She tucked me up in bed and everything. And she took care of Maria, too. Oh dear! I felt so ill. What did everybody say about it? Weren't they all terribly angry with me?'

'But my dear, why should they be angry with you? They were all concerned and glad to hear it was nothing serious.'

'And poor Maria! She must have been mortified! She's got a phobia about being sick in public. And it must have ruined that lovely carpet.'

'Not a bit of it! The carpet was the colour of summer pudding, already, darling. Only adds to its value. Think of all the Ottoman emperors who must've been sick on it in the past.'

'How dreadful, though.'

'No, no. Not at all. Cheer up, now. I'll put a bit of dear old Scarlatti on.'

'A jubilant harpsichord sonata was soon galloping, through the car. Izzy leaned back and tried to relax. Gradually, a strange feeling began to dawn in her mind. A feeling that the dreadful débâcle last night had actually been a very useful thing. It being such a very spectacular tableau, such a very dazzling disaster, had the effect of blinding the participants to the possibility of other, more submarine disasters, more serious and lasting. There was less chance of people saying to each other, *Wasn't Izzy awful? Not Charles's type at all*. It blotted out the awkward business of everybody assessing how poor a wife she would make. Izzy hoped so, anyway.

'Now listen, weasel,' said Charles when they were safely cruising down the M11, 'what you need is lots of treats.'

'Treats?' asked Izzy faintly. Images of jars of honey and

bags of chocolate drops drifted through her mind.

'Yes, treats. For a start, I've got two tickets for the Conservation Ball at Cambridge next week.'

'What, like a May Ball?'

'Yes, sort of. Except this one's not in term time and it'll be mostly for old lags like us. It's to raise money for the restoration of some neglected old buildings. You'll enjoy yourself there, my weasel.'

'Oh yes! How marvellous!'

'And that's not all.'

'What else? What else?' Izzy was greedy when it came to treats.

'I think what we need is a break, don't you? Get away from London. It's so hot and foul and smelly at this time of year. Well, how would you like to go to the sea?'

'Oh, the sea!' cried Izzy, instantly thinking of Bill Bailey on Dunwich beach. 'Oh yes, I love the sea!'

'We've got a house on the beach at Harlech,' Charles went on, encouraged by Izzy's enthusiasm. She was such a resilient little thing. 'It's a wooden house, built in the dunes. Right away from the road. Perfect situation: the beach all around, and the mountains in the distance. Have you ever been to North Wales?'

'No, I haven't. I've been to Whitby, though,' she added inconsequentially, as if it was a mitigating plea.

'Oh, Whitby's tremendous, of course. That church up on the cliff! Superb pews!'

'But tell me more about Harlech.'

'Well, it's small, and steep, with a lovely café and a terrace looking right out to sea where you can get cream teas – and my weasel will be allowed to get as fat as she likes – and all around are mountains and lovely woods and things. And of course there's Portmeirion. I'm dying to show you Portmeirion.'

'I'm dying to see it!' cried Izzy.

She felt enormously better. A holiday, on the opposite side of the country from Norfolk. She thought of mountains and woods, friendly mountains and trees under which she could shelter from the eyes in the sky. She thought of somewhere called Portmeirion, of which she had dimly heard at some time in the past, but which she seemed to associate with a teapot. Izzy closed her eyes and tried to imagine Charles's house on the beach. In her mind's eye she saw glittering waves, and far away amongst the mountains, the outline of a stupendous teapot.

First of all, though, the Conservation Ball. Izzy wanted to go to Cambridge again, and of course there would be Bill. Izzy was disappointed to hear he wouldn't be at the Ball itself, but he'd said they could use his rooms in College as a base since the ball was being held in Trinity. Izzy loved dancing. She danced around her Westbourne Grove flat at the very thought of it: danced her way through the washing-up, and then danced over to Maria's place to do her usual two hours of housework.

Maria was severely depressed. The tiredness was worse than ever.

'I feel nailed to this sofa,' she groaned, as Izzy tidied up around her.

'Look, my bewties,' called Gwyn from the kitchen where he was embarking on a huge washing-up operation, 'we gotta work out a more user-friendly method of perpetuatin' the species, like. I mean, the preamble's orright, o'course. But havin' you girls completely knocked out like this, it's just not on.'

'Men should get pregnant instead,' suggested Maria. 'Like sea-horses.'

'Oh yes! Wasn't that marvellous! I saw it on TV! All those baby sea-horses sort of bursting out of him in great clouds!'

'Tell you what, Isabelle, girl,' beamed Gwyn. 'We'll annexe that palace of the agro-chemical industry where we all behaved so disgracefully last weekend, and turn it into an experimental centre for alternative fertilities.'

'What – you mean, Thraxton?'

'Right first time, sweetheart. I couldn't help thinkin', all the time I was there, of what a stupenous children's

273

hoame it would make. Or a field centre, like. It's an insult to the rest of humanity, havin' a couple of middle-aged arrivistes livin' on that kind of scale.'

'Shut up, Gwyn. Izzy doesn't want to hear all this.'

'Noa, noa, Maria – let me have my say. I behaved impeccably last weekend, in case you hadn't noticed. Despite the furnace of proletarian indignation that was boilin' in my breast, I refrained from settin' fire to the edifice or stranglin' either of the inhabitants. In fact, it was you that couldn't control your emissions, girl.'

'Oh don't! I go cold inside when I remember it. You know how I've always dreaded being sick in public. And to be sick there – on that carpet! Ruining Izzy's party! I shall never forgive myself.'

'It was my fault,' soothed Izzy. 'I insisted on stuffing all that summer pudding down you.'

'No, no!' wailed Maria. 'And the look on their faces! Oh, Christ! And that beautiful carpet!'

'Charles said it was perfectly all right.'

'Well, of course he did. He went to an expensive public school, didn't he? Where you learn to bite your lip and keep mum. Stoicism.'

'Doan't insult the workin' class by talkin' about the Stoicism of those privileged layabouts!' roared Gwyn. His washing-up was getting louder and louder. He hurled a handful of forks onto the draining board. 'The best thing you ever did in your life was to puke onto that carpet, darlin'! I was proud of you! It was a heroic act!'

'Oh shut up, Gwyn. It's not fair to Izzy to talk like this. The Armstrongs are virtually her in-laws.'

'I don't mind,' said Izzy, uneasily, polishing the coffee table with fixed concentration. 'I mean, I'd hate it if Gwyn stopped saying what he really thinks, and well, it's Charles I'm marrying, not them. If you really want to know, I wish Daisy was his mum, not Mrs Armstrong.'

'Daisy! Now there's a woman! Too bad she's poured the treasure of her loyalty on the heads of those ungrateful bastards. She should've been ministerin' to her class, see?

Not bein' a servant all her life, for Christ's sake.'

'What's going to happen to her, Izzy?'

'I don't know. They think she'll come round to the idea of living in the house. Or moving into the flat over the stables. But I know that Bill would like to settle her in her own little cottage somewhere.'

'Who's Bill? The fair bloake with the piano?'

'Yes. He's marvellous, isn't he?'

'Didn't have a chance to talk to him, darlin'. Me an' Michael were in the Billiard Room most of the evenin', lamentin' the passin' away of all we held dear in the Sixties.'

'Is Bill Daisy's son?'

'Oh no. He's a friend of Charles's from Cambridge. He's a – a history person, I think. But his wife has just kicked him out.'

'Why? Was he messing about with other women?'

'No. She was, with another man.'

'Oh God! It's all so unbearably depressing!'

'Yes. And they've got this little girl who's about three, and he's not allowed to see her any more without ringing up first, and the mother's going to go off to America and take the child with her and Bill can't do anything about it.'

'Jesus, darlin'! Sometimes the horrors of the class war pale into insignificance beside the atrocities of the sex war. To tell you the truth, I'm often at a loss as to where to throa the main thrust o' my dialectical energies.'

'You can throw them into cleaning the lavatory if you've finished the dishes,' observed Maria. 'Last time I was staring into it, it didn't look too impressive.'

'Aye, aye. Tho' it's not exactly the way I was lookin' forward to spendin' the summer.' Gwyn went off to the bathroom.

'The summer!' groaned Maria, closing her eyes. 'I'm hardly noticing it. It's all impossibly far away. And all the time it's going, going, gone!'

'You poor thing. You could really do with a holiday, Maria.'

'We'd got one booked – in Tunisia. But since I started to feel so ill, we cancelled it. I couldn't face all that heat.'

'Oh no! Did you get your money back?'

'We had to pay a whacking great cancellation fee. I don't like to think about it. Are you going anywhere?'

'Nowhere much,' Izzy felt guilty about her good fortune. 'We're just going off to the Welsh coast for a week. After the Ball next Saturday.'

'What Ball?'

'In Cambridge. It's in aid of old buildings.'

'Well, Izzy, your life has certainly got a lot more eventful.'

'I know. Aren't I lucky?'

Maria suddenly fixed Izzy with a penetrating stare. 'Are you happy, then, Izzy – really happy?'

Izzy squirmed a bit. 'I really am. Yes. Not – maybe I'm not happy in the way you might have expected I'd be happy, but yes, yes, I am.'

'There's no need to be defensive about it. I just asked.'

'Oh, well, yes, that's all right. Only Charles—' Izzy's voice trailed off. She was unable to complete the sentence.

'If you tell me Charles is the right man for you, I'll believe you,' sighed Maria. 'I haven't got the energy to be sceptical any more.'

'But – erm, if you had the energy, do you think you would be? About him?'

'You know me, Izzy. If I had the energy, I'd be sceptical about everybody.'

This was not the quiet, understated reassurance for which Izzy had been hoping. She started to bite her thumbnail as the telephone rang.

'Oh answer it,' pleaded Maria. 'And if it's my mother, say I'm asleep.'

Izzy picked up the phone, remembering that she must phone her own mother and tell her how it had all gone. She'd been putting it off, for some reason.

'Hello?'

'Is that you, Izzy?' Michael's unmistakable tones burst breathlessly into her ear.

'I thought you might be at Maria's. Listen, dear heart, a disaster of major proportions has burst upon my innocent head. Louise has gone apeshit and told the nanny to get out. I'm ringing from the study. I'm hiding under the desk. They're at it hammer and tongs down in the kitchen.'

'At it—? What, do you mean fighting?'

'Well, when I fled it was still only verbal. But who knows? There are those damned *Observer* special offer kitchen knives down there on the wall. I knew it was a mistake to send away for them. Whenever I look at them I break out in a cold sweat.'

'Well, get back downstairs at once! And stop them doing anything silly!'

'Dear heart, the problem is to get a word in edgeways at all. But of course. I just wanted to beg you to jump into a cab and come over right away. Your arbitrator's skills are urgently needed.'

'I'll be right over. Now get back downstairs!'

'Yes. Quite. You are an angel. 'Bye!'

'Maria stirred curiously on her sofa. 'That wasn't Charles, was it?'

'No. Michael.'

'Ah. I somehow couldn't imagine you talking to Charles like that.'

'Charles is too sensible to need talking to like that. They're in the midst of some crisis, Maria. I must go. Sorry to rush off, but if I don't, Louise will kill the nanny.'

'Ah,' smiled Maria. 'The shape of things to come.'

BUT SHALL WE DANCE?

When Izzy arrived the nanny had already gone. Louise was crying in the kitchen, Jack was crying in the cupboard under the stairs, Rose was crying in her basket and Michael was white-faced and whispery.

'How much was it to San Francisco?' he murmured. 'I could sell the car and get on a plane tonight.'

'Don't be silly,' scolded Izzy. 'This house of yours is ten times nicer than San Francisco. Even with everybody crying like this.' She looked round, wondering where to start. Louise was howling into her arms, head down on the table. Izzy approached tentatively and touched her on the shoulder.

'Louise!' she faltered. 'It's me. Izzy. It's all right, I'm here.'

'Oh, go away!' wailed Louise, not even bothering to raise her head. Izzy suddenly saw a baby-sling hanging over the back of a chair. She had seen Louise carrying the baby around in it.

'Is Rose hungry?' she asked.

'Can't be. She had a whole bellyful just before the storm broke.'

'Well, put her in this thing, then,' urged Izzy, climbing into the straps. Soon Rose was bawling on Izzy's breast. Izzy opened the cupboard under the stairs. Jack paused in his howling for a moment.

'Hello, Jack!' beamed Izzy. 'What's up?'

'She won't stop crying!' he sobbed. 'I hate it. I wish she would stop. And Mummy won't stop either. It's not fair!'

'Let's go for a walk! I tell you what – we'll find some Video games.'

'Really?' Jack sniffed. 'Do you promise?'

'I promise. It'll be our mission. We shall boldly go into Muswell Hill and fight with the Thargs from Planet M.'

'Oh, great!' Jack bounded out of his hiding place. Izzy seized his hand.

'You must hold on tight, all the way,' she insisted. 'Because I am the Princess Thalia from Silverfart Galaxy and I need protection.'

Jack giggled. 'You said fart!' he cried. 'Say it again.'

'I shall say it again,' promised Izzy. 'At the end of the road. And if you're really lucky – I'll blinking well *do* it as well.'

Jack's mad skirls of laughter were heard in the kitchen. Louise lifted her head and looked blearily out. Michael hovered by the dresser, like a useless bystander at a traffic accident.

'Talk to your wife!' hissed Izzy, going. 'Tell her you love her!'

Michael looked appalled at being left alone with the woman whom he loved best of all in the world, at the moment when she most needed him. But Izzy strode determinedly towards the door and was gone.

By the time they were twenty yards down the road, Rose had stopped crying. Twenty more yards and she had fallen asleep.

'You see?' said Izzy. 'She's stopped crying now. She only wanted to go for a walk.'

'But if she only wanted to go for a walk,' objected Jack, 'why did she fall asleep? She's missing it all. Silly!'

'Babies like sleeping through things,' explained Izzy. 'And I don't blame them.'

'Say *fart* again,' pleaded Jack. 'Please!'

'Keep right on to the end of the road,' exhorted Izzy.

Two hours later they returned. Louise was out in the garden. Michael was sitting at the kitchen table with a glass of gin in his hand.

'She's weeding,' he said.

'Is that a good sign?'

'I think so. Symbolic, dear heart. The nanny had to be rooted out and thrown on the compost heap.'

'Where's Melanie gone?' asked Jack. 'Why did she shout at Mummy?'

'They were both angry.'

'Why?'

'Because they were tired.'

'Well, where's she gone?'

'She's gone to be someone else's nanny.'

'Can we have a new one then? Can we have Izzy? She's brilliant!'

The doorbell rang. Michael froze. 'It's her,' he panted. 'She's come back – with a machine gun!'

'Don't be silly,' said Izzy. She opened the door whilst Michael hid behind the fridge. A sour-faced pasty young man stood there, carrying two empty flight bags.

'I've come for Melanie's things,' he announced. 'And a cheque for four weeks' wages in lieu of notice.'

'Of course,' said Izzy. 'If you'd like to go upstairs and get her things, I'll get Michael to write a cheque for you.'

She returned to the kitchen. Michael peeped out from behind the fridge.

'It's a friend of Melanie's, come for her things,' said Izzy. 'And he wants a cheque for a month's wages.'

'What? He must be mad.'

'Oh, don't argue, Michael. Just write the cheque.'

'Is he bigger than me?'

'A lot bigger. And very ruthless-looking. Now write the cheque and we can forget all about it.'

'I can't! I haven't got the money!'

'You must have. You were going to pay her, anyway.'

'But I was going to pay her in a month's time! After she'd done a month's worth of sodding work. Sacred Norah! The little cow is shameless!'

'Hush! Where's your chequebook?'

'My dear Izzy, you don't appear to understand. There

are limits to my overdraft facility, and I am already caught upon them like a helpless old sheep on barbed wire.'

Izzy rummaged in her own handbag, found her cheque-book, and produced her pen. 'How much is it?'

'My dear, I couldn't possibly allow you to do that.'

'It's all right. I'll borrow it from Charles.'

'But I couldn't possibly . . . five hundred quid.'

Melanie's things were removed, her friend was handed a cheque, and Izzy saw him off the premises.

'I could say a thing or two about this business,' observed the pasty young man.

'Oh, I know, it's awful, isn't it? But please don't. Least said, soonest mended, and so on.'

He went. For the next two days, Izzy stayed with Michael and Louise. She slept in her old room – which had been marginally blighted by Melanie's cigarettes, the smell of which hung in the curtains and rose from the rugs. There were also a couple of small burns on the edge of the pretty rosewood chest, where she had obviously left a cigarette for too long. Izzy hoped Louise wouldn't notice them for a while.

It seemed a pretty safe bet that Louise wouldn't notice anything for a while. She retired to bed and indulged in a series of long sleeps. Izzy carried Rose in to her when it was time for a feed. But Rose was also getting seriously into rubber. Once she had ground her little gums feverishly around a synthetic teat or two, there was no stopping her. Water, juice, formula, were equally welcome. And she still seemed to want to snuggle up to her Mama from time to time.

'Oh, Izzy, I'm so glad it's just us, now!' whispered Louise on the second afternoon.

'That's right. Now have some more sleep!' insisted Izzy, and tip-toed out carrying the wriggling baby.

Michael and Izzy went on expeditions, leaving Louise to rest and learn to breathe again. They went to the zoo. Jack was fatally attracted by a pair of copulating Orang-utans.

'Daddy! Daddy! What are they doing?'

Michael stared at the apes with remote incredulity. 'I can't remember,' he murmured.

'What you need, Michael, is a holiday. You all do.'

'Could you come, Izzy? And, more important, could you pay for it? Otherwise I fear the whole enterprise is doomed.'

'Oh dear,' admitted Izzy. 'I have to go to Wales with Charles. Oh crumbs! Charles! I should have rung him days ago!'

She ran to the nearest phone and dialled urgently.

'Fortinbras Salvage.'

'Can I speak to Charles, please?'

'Right, love. Just a tick.'

There was a pause during which Rose awoke in her sling and gazed critically up Izzy's right nostril. *Gank*, she remarked. *Sssssh*, urged Izzy. She had a feeling it was terribly important for Rose to keep quiet in the next few minutes. *Honk*, said Rose. *Heck! Heck!*

'Charles Armstrong.'

'Charles! This is Izzy.'

'Where the hell have you been for the last two days?'

'Oh dear, I'm sorry, Charles, but we've had a bit of a crisis on.'

'Who's *we*?'

'Oh, Louise and Michael. Their nanny left after an awful row, and they rang me up in desperation, and I've been helping out. You know, taking care of the kids and things.'

There was a terrifying silence from the other end.

'You know, Charles, Louise is totally exhausted. She's needed a lot of sleep. She's been – well, sleeping.'

'Well, bully for her. I wish I could say the same. I've been worried sick about you, Izzy.'

'I'm so sorry. I should have rung. It's been so hectic. With two children, you know. And anyway – couldn't you have asked Dick or Aunt Vinny? They both have Louise's phone number. And Maria's. Maria knew where I was.'

'My dear girl, the whole house in Worcester Road is deserted. No sign of Aunt Vinny. No sign of Dick. Nor of you.'

'Oh crumbs. They must both be away or something. You must've been really worried.'

'I've been out of my mind.'

'Oh crikey. Look, come round to dinner tonight. The kids'll be in bed by then.' Izzy gave him the address.

'All right. But how much longer is this going to go on? Can't they find another nanny? London's crawling with the bloody agencies.'

'Oh yes. They're trying,' lied Izzy. 'They're interviewing some girls tomorrow. But it all takes time. I'm just tiding them over, you know. For a day or two.'

Charles rang off, and Izzy, guiltily, fled to Michael's side.

'He was cross,' she cowered. 'I asked him to supper tonight.'

'Oh Christ!'

'Don't be mean, Michael. He's my fiancé. And he was worried sick about me. I hadn't rung, you see, and – oh never mind. Can't you cook something delicious? You're a wonderful cook.'

'Not any more, I'm not. You can't cook from a shattered life. You can only grab a bag of chips and run.'

'Well, I'll bloody well cook, then!' cried Izzy.

'Don't be angry!' begged Jack. 'I don't like it!'

'I'm not angry,' said Izzy. 'Come on. Let's go and see those elephants. If you're really lucky, one of them might even – you know what!'

Jack screamed with delight.

Michael and Louise didn't have much food left in the house, but Izzy did find a couple of cans of chick-peas at the back of the cupboard, and in one of Louise's vegetarian cookbooks she found a recipe for chick-pea patties. They sounded nice. Whilst Michael put Jack to bed and Louise fed Rose, Izzy concocted her chick-pea mixture. They had to be deep-fried. Izzy loved things that were deep-fried. For food to be surrounded by a crackly, crispy coating was Izzy's idea of the sign of a superior civilization. She often thought soberly that Shakespeare had had to manage without chips. What might he have achieved on chick-pea patties?

Charles arrived, delivered a kiss on her nose, and in the privacy of the hall, gave her a reproachful but loving little look. Then he turned to his hosts with perfect good manners and offered them a couple of bottles of something special.

'Chateau d'YQuem!' gasped Louise. 'Oh, Charles! I haven't had it for years!'

'Well, it sounded as if you wanted cheering up,' said Charles. Izzy loved him for it. Things were all right after all. Michael asked him how his business was going and Charles launched into the subject with gusto.

Izzy slipped off, meanwhile, to fry the chick-pea patties. Louise had a large deep fryer and it was soon ticking menacingly on the hob. Izzy dropped a small cube of bread in to test the temperature of the oil, just like it told you to do in the books. The cube danced and bubbled merrily. Izzy lowered the chick-pea patties into the chuckling depths. There was a submarine explosion, and a sense of things not being quite as they should be. Izzy peered within. The chick-pea patties had gone! Vanished! Disappeared! Great Scott!

Mesmerized into idiocy, Izzy dropped in the last few. They, too, disintegrated. All that was left of their supper was some very hot oil, freckled with tiny black dots. Izzy turned off the gas, and approached the table. Everyone looked at her eagerly. Charles smiled expectantly. He had yet to sample Izzy's cooking.

'And what delightful delicacy have you conjured up for us this evening, darling?' he enquired.

'It was chick-pea patties,' said Izzy, 'but I'm afraid they've evaporated.'

It was not a glorious début, as regards cuisine.

They were all drunk enough to find it very funny, however, and Michael leapt to the rescue, ran to the local corner shop for eggs, and created a superb omelette. Izzy recovered from her shame, and started to mix the salad dressing. If only there were chips with the omelette. Never mind. She seized a bottle of olive oil. It was slippery. It plummeted through her fingers and smashed on the kitchen floor. She made a stupid, belated attempt to catch it, slipped, her ankle turned under her and she crashed down, knocking a chair flying.

'Izzy!' cried Louise. 'Are you all right?'

The pain in Izzy's ankle was too much to bear. She screamed aloud.

'I say, Izzy,' Charles did not like loud noises.

Izzy could not help it – a whole stream of foul Yorkshire expletives came rolling out, together with a number she had picked up in school playgrounds. It hurt so much, she felt sick. Only swearing helped.

'It's all right it's all right it's my ankle. It goes like this sometimes. Leave me! Don't touch me! Let me stay down here.'

'I hope you haven't cut yourself on the glass,' Louise began to pick up the fragments of broken bottle, and mop up the spilt oil. Charles removed her shoe. It was the frail little pink one.

'Oh, what a shame,' he said. 'Look! You've got oil all over your dear little shoe.'

'Damn the shoe! Ow! It hurts so much, Charles!'

'Well, what shall we do? Call a doctor?'

'No, no, it's only a sort of sprain. It happens sometimes. It'll get better. I'll be better in a few minutes.'

Izzy was right. In ten minutes time she was brave enough to permit Louise to bandage it, and shortly afterwards they all addressed themselves to the omelette, which was cold by now.

'Oh God,' groaned Izzy. 'I've ruined the supper – *again*.'

'Not a bit of it, darling,' Charles had recovered his good

humour again. 'Cold omelette is very good. Especially in French bread.'

'Sorry about that,' murmured Michael. 'No French bread. We aren't usually so useless, Charles.'

'Michael's a brilliant cook, normally,' boasted Izzy urgently.

'It's delicious!' Charles insisted. 'Just right, a simple supper today. After all, we'll be at the Conservation Ball tomorrow night.'

Izzy gasped. 'Oh crumbs! I'm so sorry, Charles! I shan't even be able to walk properly for a couple of days, let alone dance.'

Charles's mouth fell open in dismay.

'Oh, I know, though!' cried Izzy. 'Let's give our tickets to Michael and Louise! They really need a night out together! And we'll babysit for you.'

Michael and Louise sat stock-still, dazzled by the opportunity and the need to decline it.

'Oh, we couldn't possibly,' began Michael.

'Oh please, Michael! Go on! Really! I shan't be able to dance or anything.'

'But maybe Charles would like to take someone else – I mean, an old friend or something.'

'Not at all,' said Charles. 'If I can't take Izzy, I won't go anyway.'

'Oh have our tickets, and let us babysit for you! Oh do!'

'Look here – I'm sorry, but we couldn't possibly afford it,' stammered Michael. 'You know what our financial situation is, Izzy.'

'Be my guests,' said Charles, with a gracious smile. 'Please. Let me do my bit to help you out of this rather bad patch. I insist. You must go to the ball as my guests.'

Michael and Louise were silenced by this largesse.

'And now,' said Charles, reaching for the corkscrew, 'I am sure Louise would like a little glass of Chateau d'YQuem.'

Izzy could've kissed him. But it seemed vulgar, somehow.

A MARVELLOUS GOOD NEIGHBOUR

'You seem to have a positive genius for falling down, my pretty little weasel,' smiled Charles down the phone, late next afternoon.

'Ah. Yes. Well, I've always been a bit clumsy, I'm afraid. It's – I think I'm so often in a panic, and—'

'But you mustn't be in a panic, any more, my darling. There's absolutely no need for it. Now is there?'

'No. No, you're right. Only I – I seem never to be able to – deal with things.'

'You deal with things admirably. Now look, for example, how you're dealing with Michael and Louise's problems.'

'Oh Charles! – I hope you don't mind that I offered them the tickets for the Ball. I mean – were they terribly expensive?'

'They weren't cheap. But don't worry your little head about that. It can't be helped.'

'Oh dear. Still, at least they'll have a night out together. I don't suppose they've been able to relax on their own for ages.'

'Quite so. Anyway, my dear, I'm just off to Cambridge—'

'You're still going to Cambridge? But I thought you were going to come over and help me babysit?'

'Oh, no, sorry, darling, but that's absolutely out of the question. I wasn't just going up for the Ball, you see. I've got to do a bit of research in the college library. They've got some Pugin manuscripts which sound rather exciting. I'm getting more and more interested in the idea of doing a book about him.'

'Oh,' said Izzy. Pugin, she had learned, was a nineteenth-century architect – one of Charles's enthusiasms. Unlike babysitting, it seemed. 'Well, then of course. Yes.'

'It'll be a blessing in disguise, your not coming,' Charles went on. 'I can sleep on Bill's floor, you see. Easier on my own.' Izzy felt a twinge of jealousy.

'Give him my love.'

'Of course! And I hope the children behave. Oh, how's your ankle, by the way?'

'I can hobble round today. It's quite all right. Oh yes. I can manage. It'll be completely better by Monday.'

'And on Monday, my darling, we shall be off. Westward Ho!'

'Oh yes. I can't wait!'

'I'll ring you from Cambridge. Get better soon. And keep up the good work!' Charles rang off.

'When's he coming?' asked Jack, hovering at her elbow. Charles had been promised as a person of great jigsaw skills, though Izzy wasn't entirely confident about his ability to Boldly Go to Other Galaxies and Zap the Villainous Arkzanas of Janxafart. Jack jumped up and down in an ecstasy of anticipation.

'Sorry, mate,' sighed Izzy. 'He can't come.'

'Why not? It's not fair! Why *not*?'

'He's been zapped. By a Zurgelquoit. And I think there are some more of them, climbing in through the sitting-room window. Just run off and zap them for me, will you?'

It wasn't all that easy to babysit for twenty-four hours. Even if Izzy's ankle had been all right, she would have found it a strain to take care of a small baby on her own, let alone live up to the image of terrific entertainer she had unwisely projected towards Jack. By the next afternoon – the time when Michael and Louise were due to return – she was feeling decidedly spent. Rose had woken her up three times in the night, and Jack once. ('The curtains came for me!') A definitive waking-up had occurred around six a.m., an hour Izzy had never observed before, except from the other end, after a night of razzle dazzle. Jack had climbed into her bed to hide from the Thargs, and that had been that.

By teatime, when at last the front door key was heard in

the lock, Izzy had reached the end of her rope. So this was what Louise had had to put up with, for months and months. No wonder she was shattered. At the precise moment when Louise came home, Rose was snoozing in her basket and Jack performing acts of inter-galactic carnage with all his plastic mannekins on the floor. Izzy was propped up at the kitchen table clutching her fifth cup of tea and holding her eyes open.

'Everything all right? Thanks so much, Izzy!' cried Louise, seizing Rose from her basket and clasping her to her bosom. 'I got a bit full. Haven't quite adjusted yet.'

'But did you have a good time?'

'Wonderful!' Michael looked like a different person from the cream-faced loon who had failed to get to grips with Melanie's departure. 'I had a look round Queens' again. And the Ball was extraordinary.'

'We met Charles in Bill Bailey's room,' said Louise. 'I was surprised. I thought he was going to help you babysit.'

'Oh, no,' explained Izzy quickly. 'He had some research to do. For his book on – Pugilist. No that's not right. What is it?'

'Pugin,' Michael informed her. 'But I like Pugilist better.'

The phone rang. 'It's your Lord and Master, Izzy,' said Michael. 'Do you want to take it in the study so you can whisper passionate words of separation and longing?'

Izzy went upstairs. 'Hello, Charles! How's it going?'

'Tremendous. The manuscripts are fascinating. I'm just ringing to say I won't be back till late, tonight. So I don't think I'll be able to see you till tomorrow. And then it's Harlech ahoy. Shall I pick you up in the morning? Will you be going back to Westbourne Grove, now?'

'Oh yes. To pack and everything. Michael and Louise have had a lovely time at the Ball, Charles. They've just got back.'

'Blasted Ball! Thumping away all night. I hardly got a wink of sleep. I'm getting a bit old for this sleeping on floors lark.'

'You poor thing! I had a rotten night, too. Rose woke me

up three times and Jack once. But hey – how was Bill?'

'Oh, Bill's fine. By the way, darling, we had a splendid idea. He's coming to Harlech, too. A day or so later. With his little girl.'

'Oh, how marvellous! I'd love to meet her. How nice that there's room for them, too. I had somehow imagined it to be very tiny. Like a sort of – beach hut.'

'It sleeps eight,' said Charles importantly. 'And it's got a little summerhouse down at the side, in a kind of dip in the dunes, where Bill usually sleeps. I don't know whether he will this time, though. Because of the child.'

'Well, anyway, that's wonderful.'

'You don't mind, darling? I mean, it won't be quite the same as being there on our own.'

'Oh no! I love your friends! Bill is great! It'll be even more fun! And we can always slip off on our own at times.'

'I shall woo you in the oak woods,' promised Charles. Izzy wasn't too confident about what exactly the wooing would include. But it all sounded utterly idyllic. She couldn't wait. They promised to talk on the phone tomorrow morning to make final arrangements, and then said their prolonged and tender goodbyes.

Izzy limped downstairs, her strength temporarily repaired. Michael and Louise looked much perkier, now. Much more able to cope. She did not feel too guilty about leaving them.

'I think I shall have to go, now,' said Izzy, putting on her jacket. 'I've got to sort out my things, you see. We leave for Harlech tomorrow.'

'Of course! Your holiday! I'd forgotten!' Louise looked crestfallen. 'Well, I hope you have a lovely time.'

'Is it by the sea?' asked Jack.

'Yes,' beamed Izzy. 'The house is actually built right on the beach. In the sand dunes.'

'Oh brilliant!' cried Jack. 'I want to come, too! Oh please! Please Mum, can we go too?'

'I'm sorry, love,' explained Louise, 'but we've already explained that we can't have a holiday this year.'

'Not enough money, old man,' added Michael.

'But I want to go with Izzy!'

'Izzy doesn't want us hanging about on her holiday,' hissed Louise. 'And anyway there wouldn't be room for all of us.'

'Cheer up, old chap,' coaxed Michael. 'I'll take you to Kenwood.'

'Oh bugger Kenwood!' cried Jack in a passion.

'Jack! Don't, please! I've told you not to say bugger.'

'Well, Daddy says it all the time.'

'You can say it when you're a Daddy. But not yet.'

Jack burst into noisy tears. 'I don't want to go to buggery Kenwood! I want to go to the sea!'

Izzy had been thinking on her feet. On the one hand, it seemed impossible. But on the other hand – why not? The house slept eight. Bill Bailey was coming – with his little girl. They could all lend a hand with the domestic chores. It would be so good for them. And lovely to be with them.

'Listen!' she cried, 'why not? I'm sure you can come! It's a great idea!'

'Hooray!!' roared Jack. 'We can come!!'

'No, no, Izzy, don't be absurd. Really. We couldn't possibly.'

'But there's plenty of room!' she cried. 'It sleeps eight.'

'Yes, but it'd spoil your romantic week together.'

'No hearthrug couplings if Louise and I are playing Scrabble in the background, dear heart,' added Michael.

'But it isn't a romantic week together!' explained Izzy. 'His friend Bill Bailey is coming too. With his little girl.'

'Is he really?' asked Louise. 'I do like that man.'

'Well, there you are, then!' said Izzy. 'The kids could play together and everything.'

Michael and Louise looked blank and doubtful. But on the other hand, there was a dangerous kindling light of excitement just behind their eyes.

'I'll fix it!' cried Izzy, running to the door. 'Cancel everything else for next week!'

'There isn't anything else for next week,' shrugged Louise.

'Then pack your bags! I'll ring to confirm it! Dig out your buckets and spades!' And Izzy was gone: slamming the front door too hard, as usual.

She went to Highgate Tube and started the journey to Spitalfields. Her mind was racing. She would leave him a note. He would find it that night, when he came home. It would have to be a very clever note – somehow, instinctively, she needed it to be a written, not a spoken, request. She was sure, if she was trying to propose the idea out loud, she'd get in the most fearful tangle. She would leave him a note, and he would see the logic and be generous.

She let herself into Charles's house. It felt cold and empty. She shivered slightly, and went into the drawing room where there was a desk with paper and pens. Then she hesitated. The house slept eight. Wasn't it a terrible waste for it not to be a bit fuller? She seized the phone.

'Maria!'

'Izzy!'

'Listen. Oh, wait – how are you? Any better?'

'About the same. No worse. Still dead.'

'Well, listen. How would you and Gwyn like a week in Harlech?'

'What – where you're going . . . ?'

'Charles says his house sleeps eight. Bill Bailey's coming as well. And Michael and Louise. All next week. What do you say?'

'Oh, Izzy, I – it would be marvellous!'

'Great! Terrific! I'm so glad! I'm sure it'll help.'

'But Izzy – won't Charles mind?'

'Of course not! It was his idea. I mean, he asked Bill, first. It's not supposed to be a honeymoon or anything.'

'Gwyn will be able to climb all those mountains.'

'And you can lie on the beach all day and I will bring you cold lemonade and cream crackers.'

'Dear Izzy! Thanks so much!' Maria sounded near tears, so Izzy quickly made arrangements for further communication, and rang off.

The telephone's final *ping* echoed in the empty house. Izzy endured a twinge of guilt. She felt a bit like a burglar, being here at all. Hurriedly she found pen and paper. And then she stalled. How to put it, exactly? It was an imposition, of course.

Dear Charles,

I dropped in to make sure everything was OK. And I wanted to ask you an enormous favour. Since Bill and Susannah are both coming, wouldn't it be wonderful if Michael and Louise and Maria and Gwyn could come too? I mean, you did say the house sleeps eight, and they're all going through bad times and none of them can afford to even think about holidays this year. Poor little Jack is dying to go to the seaside.

It just seemed a shame that there should be that lovely house of yours, three-quarters empty, with all my poor friends stuck in hot sweaty old London. Look, Charles, if it's not what you want, please do just say so. But it could be terrific. They'd all help with the shopping and the cooking and everything. I mean, it could be quite convenient as well as enjoyable.

Tell me if it's inconvenient. But I do hope it won't be. Ring me tomorrow. I'm longing to talk to you again – and see you. I love you very much. More than ever.

Your very own, Little Weasel.

Izzy placed the note on the hall table and tip-toed out. She was so tired when she got back to her flat that she went straight to bed, and drew the bedcovers up around her ears, to shut out the sound of the phone.

It woke her many hours later. Her bedside clock said eight-thirty. Sun was flooding in through the garden. Izzy bounded up to answer the phone. Halfway to it she remembered that it would be Charles. He would have got her note. Fear leaped inside her as she answered it.

'Hello?'

'Izzy. Good morning!' He sounded cross.

'Did you get my note?'

'I did. And frankly, darling, I was surprised.'

'Yes. I know. But after you'd told me about Bill coming, it set me thinking.'

'It certainly did.'

'Yes but, well, do you mind? I mean, do you mind if they come? Honestly, Charles, it would be so wonderful for them. They've been through a lot this summer. They need a break.'

'It'll be a bit of a houseful, though, won't it?'

'Oh no, I mean, we can split up and things. I mean, I wouldn't want to be with them all the time.'

'I hope not. I've got some plans for you, my little weasel. I want to show you Portmeirion, and all my favourite places.'

'Oh yes, Charles! I can't wait! And they wouldn't come till tomorrow, or even the day after.'

Charles sighed. The sound of the sigh made Izzy shudder. But she held on, like a little terrier with its teeth sunk into a delicious morsel.

'Oh well, I suppose if you've already invited them, we'll have to make the best of it.'

'Oh thank you, Charles! Thank you! You're a darling! I'm so grateful! I'll remember this always, Charles, your being so nice.'

'Well, get your things together then. I'll be round in an hour.'

He rang off. Izzy bounded round the room in a dance of exultation. Then there was a voice from the stairs.

'Er – Izzy?'

'Dick!'

Oh crumbs! Dick! Forgotten, again.

'Oh, Dick! – Come down.'

Izzy wriggled into her dressing-gown. Dick clattered down the stairs.

'Where have you been for the last few days, Izzy?'

'Oh never mind about that, Dick. Guess what! We're all going to Harlech!'

'Where?'

'North Wales. On the coast.'

'Oh yes. Lovely.'

'You must come too, Dick.'

'Oh no. Surely.'

'Yes, you must! I couldn't bear it without you, Dick!'

'No, really, Izzy, I—'

'Oh Dick, please! Don't let me down! Don't stay here all sad and alone.'

'I wouldn't be sad and alone, Izzy.'

'You would! You would! What were you going to do this summer? For a holiday, I mean?'

'Go camping, I suppose. I thought of going to the Lakes – you know. Walking, like.'

'Well, think of Snowdonia! All those mountains! And you can camp on the beach, Dick.'

Izzy was particularly pleased with the refinement of this idea. She wouldn't be actually imposing another guest on Charles. Not under his actual roof.

'Camp – on the beach? That sounds – all right.'

'You bet it'd be bloody all right! And if it rained, you could always come into the house – I mean, kip on the floor or something.'

'Oh no, Izzy. I wouldn't want to impose.'

'But you'll come?'

'When?'

'Now! Today! Or tomorrow! Everybody's coming! Michael and Louise and Maria and Gwyn. And Bill Bailey. And all the kids. Maria and Gwyn will give you a lift, Dick. I'll ring them, now.'

Dick submitted to his good luck. He was quite keen to get away from Westbourne Grove, actually. Aunt Vinny had – but that's another story.

295

THE SCOWL OF NIGHT

Izzy had never seen such an empty beach. It seemed to stretch away for miles, towards a band of blue mountains to the north. All this she glimpsed as they drove along the coast road, high above: she feasted her eyes on the miraculous sweep of gold and blue, and forgot to look for the house.

'Did you see Angorfa? Just down below us there?' asked Charles, whose eyes were prudently fixed on the wickedly snaking road.

'Oh – ah – er – no,' admitted Izzy. 'I was – it all flashed past so quickly. But it all looks marvellous. Absolutely marvellous.'

A few more twists of the road, and they were in Harlech town. There was shopping to do before they made for Angorfa. Charles explained that it was quite a trek from the house to the shops: the town was perched high up the cliffs, for the most part, whereas the house lurked far away across an endless panorama of dunes.

'Besides, I want you to have your first cream tea,' beamed Charles, still capable of cheerful and chivalrous impulses after several hours' driving. They parked by the castle, which seemed almost poised to fly off into the pearly air, so perilously did it hang above the glittering vista of beach. But Izzy was not allowed to explore it yet.

'The Plâs Café, first,' said Charles firmly, taking her hand and leading her off along a very modest High Street lined with granite buildings and thronged with holidaymakers. 'Ghastly crowd,' muttered Charles. 'I must remember never to come here in the school holidays again.'

'But I couldn't have come here at all, except in the school holidays,' Izzy pointed out.

'We'll soon have those shackles off you, my weasel,' promised Charles, and led her inside a dark doorway.

The darkness soon gave way to light as they walked through the building: great swathes of light came flooding in off the sea and sky, and washed to beautiful effect over the conservatory that ran the whole length of the café, at the back. Out beyond the conservatory was a grassy terrace with tables and chairs looking out to where the sea crawled, far below, and threw itself noiselessly on the beach. There was a free table, which they seized, and Charles ordered cream tea for two.

'The beach looks almost empty,' said Izzy, hypnotized by distance.

'It's a splendid beach,' Charles agreed. 'And what a day! I've never seen it so clear. That's Snowdon —' he pointed amongst the range of mountains. 'We'll go up that one day.'

'Oh yes!' said Izzy. 'Gwyn loves climbing and hill walking. And so does Dick.'

'I do hope,' Charles remarked at length, 'that you and I will be able to have a few little expeditions of our own.'

'Oh, of course, Charles! And they're not even coming until tomorrow night, are they?'

The tea arrived.

'Thank you,' Izzy beamed at the waitress, poured the tea, and negotiated the largest dollop of cream she had ever seen outside Yorkshire, without a trace of nausea. After tea she volunteered to do the shopping, leaving Charles peaceably reading *The Times*. After all, the poor lamb had driven all the way from London and he needed to relax.

Izzy was rather nervous about the shopping, even though the small supermarket clearly did not aspire to the sort of food that Charles would have chosen in West-bourne Grove. Would he have preferred Cheddar cheese, or Lancashire? She hesitated. Was there something secretly vulgar about digestive biscuits? She took several packets of cream crackers for Maria. Were they, in their cheerful and slightly brazen orange wrappers, irrevocably petit bourgeois? Was there such a thing as a bourgeois biscuit? If so, Izzy was sure she was doomed to choose it.

Charles greeted her arrival, bowed down with bursting carrier bags, with abstracted pleasure and carried the bags back to the car. Izzy cast a brief look at the castle. There was plenty of time to explore its shadowy ramparts. She would bring Jack here. It was time he suspended his feverish trips into the future and got a few thrills out of the past.

Angorfa lay at the end of a very long twisting track through the dunes. The car crawled thither, gliding expensively over ruts at 5 mph, with Scarlatti thrashing away on the harpsichord at something more like 70. At last the pyramid of wooden roof appeared, and slowly the house revealed itself: a simple building, of dark brown timber, with a verandah on the seaward side and a parking space on the landward. Charles riffled through his keys and let them in.

'Oh, no!' he groaned, as they walked into the sitting room, 'somebody's left it in a total shambles.'

Izzy was surprised. It looked clean and tidy, to her. She liked the place very much, immediately: it had a worn, summery, seaside look: the rugs were threadbare but had once been good: the chairs were wickerwork: the old sofa had a patchwork quilt thrown over it, and the very quilt itself was bleached and faded, as if it had lain in the sun for years and years.

'What do you mean?' asked Izzy. 'It looks clean and tidy to me.'

'I don't know why people have to move furniture round in the first place,' grumbled Charles. 'I mean, what do they gain by it? Why bother? Why waste a minute of your precious holiday humping sofas about? But when you've been given a plan of where every single item of furniture should be, and have been asked, specifically, by the owner, to make sure that that's the way you leave it, well, it just seems like simple good manners to co-operate. But oh, no. Joe Public knows better. He thinks he's evolved an arrangement of furniture that's better than ours. So he can't help leaving it all like that just to let us know.'

'Do you – rent out the house, then?'

'We wouldn't, if I had anything to do with it,' grumbled Charles. 'But the old man has this passion for making use of all available resources. It's got him where he is, I suppose. But all the same. I mean, letting friends use it is one thing, but we're often rung up out of the blue by people we don't know from Adam, and this is the result.'

'But it looks all right to me,' persisted Izzy.

'It's all wrong,' sighed Charles. 'And I'm too bloody tired to do anything about it, now. Christ! They've even moved the pictures.'

'Shall I – try and put it all right again while you rest?'

'No, no, little weasel. You have a look round, and enjoy yourself. Besides, if you're humping furniture about the constant bangs and bumps will keep me awake. No. Relax. Do what you like. Make yourself at home. Wake me up at eight if I haven't come down by then.' He disappeared upstairs.

Izzy went immediately to the sea. She was tired, too: from the long drive, the last-minute rush to pack, and by her babysitting exertions of the past few days. She lay flat on her back on the sand, and soaked up the sun just as she was, without fussing about bathing suits or sand in her hair. She had kicked off her shoes, and small sand-creatures crept daringly over her toes as she dozed. The sound of the waves came and went in her ears: it was as if she lay on the breast of some universal mother, whose huge sleeping breaths lulled her like a baby.

Then, after her sleep, she paddled at the sea's edge with her skirt tucked into her knickers. She paddled for what seemed like hours, remembering Bill Bailey at Dunwich. The difference between that eastern beach and this western one, was that the sun, now considerably declined, sent long arms of fire to her across the waves. It must be late. Reluctantly she left the foam, and walked first across wet sand, then firm sand, then dry powdery sand, to her shoes. Then up the dunes and onto the verandah.

As she entered, Charles was coming downstairs. He looked crumpled. There was a huge weal across one of his cheeks where he had lain on a folded arm.

'Do you realize it's half-past eight?' he asked.

'Is it really? Oh dear – my watch must have stopped. It was so heavenly out there, Charles.'

'I'm hungry.'

Charles stumped off to the kitchen, where the two carrier bags were still sitting, waiting to be unpacked.

'Oh God,' he grumbled. 'Where to begin?'

'It's all right,' said Izzy hurriedly. 'I'll unpack and cook some supper. You take it easy.'

'I can't take it easy,' he snapped, 'as long as everything's in the wrong place. Look where they've put the sauce-pans!'

'Well then, you put everything back in the right place whilst I cook something.'

'All right. And make sure it doesn't bloody evaporate, this time.'

Izzy hoped this was a joke. It was quite hard to tell. She quickly made a salad, one of the few dishes she could be relied upon not to burn. She sliced the cucumber with trembling fingers, whilst Charles lumbered and crashed around her, disoriented by his sleep, moving piles of plates about. One slipped from his fingers and shattered on the floor.

'Oh Christ!' he wailed. 'Everything's going wrong! What a way to start our holiday!'

'Look,' urged Izzy, 'Here's a bottle of wine. Go and sit down and have a drink. Don't get into a state about this. We can move everything in the morning.'

Charles took the bottle into the sitting room. But Izzy could still hear him bumping and banging around in there. When she finally carried in the supper-tray, the furniture was completely changed around. Charles was sitting on the sofa, clutching the wine bottle with grim satisfaction.

'There, you see—' he indicated the new arrangement.

'Oh yes. Much better!' beamed Izzy, keen to cheer him up. 'Now we can sit and eat and look out at the sea!'

'What's for supper, then, darling?' enquired Charles. 'I'm ravenous!'

'Er – sardines on toast and – and salad,' faltered Izzy.

'Sardines on toast? How amusing!'

Izzy wondered if amusing was a good thing for food to be. She was fond, herself, of being amused. But somehow – never mind. Charles ate his sardines with relish, took her hand across the table, and actually smiled.

'Well done, little weasel! A splendid feast!'

Izzy relaxed at last.

After supper, she would seduce him. That's what he needed. He needed to be stroked and petted and drawn away from all his fretting about the furniture. Fruit and cheese further improved his spirits, as did the staggering sunset which spread slowly across both sea and sky. Then Izzy made coffee – he had taught her how he liked it, and she was obedient and careful in these important rituals. He took his coffee on the sofa, and Izzy sat at his feet, planning in due course to swarm up him like an affectionate boa constrictor. He was a hell of a long time over his coffee, though, talking of previous summers spent here, when he was a schoolboy. At last he laid aside his cup, placed a hand on each of his knees, and looked down at Izzy with a benevolent twinkle in his eye.

'Dear little weasel,' he whispered. 'She will make it the best time ever. Yes, she will.' And he stroked her head absently, as if she was a favourite labrador.

Izzy judged this to be her moment. She knelt up between his legs, put her arms around his neck and kissed him frankly on the lips. *Thank God*, she thought as their tongues entwined, *at least I know what I'm doing, now*. Her only education was in the school of love. So much for the Arts Department at Birmingham University. But what was this? Charles's tongue seemed only half-involved. It withdrew like a snail into its shell. He took her head in his hands and smiled into her face.

'Not so fast, my dear,' he murmured. 'I have things to do first. And there is something slightly sardiney about us both, at the moment, that is rather distracting.'

Izzy ran away in shame and cleaned her teeth. She washed up, whilst Charles got to grips with the sorting-out of the house, again. She could hear him upstairs now, dragging beds about. Why couldn't he just relax and enjoy being here? She supposed that order was quite important to him, and grinned privately. When they had a house together, she would have to have a room entirely for her own use, and whenever Charles got an attack of order, she would run into her room and throw heaps of dirty old clothes around, and step on apple-cores and kick over cups of half-finished cold coffee.

There! The washing-up was done. Even in houses where the participants were not madly in love, it would be time to go to bed. And it was their only night alone here. Izzy imagined that the house would creak rather disastrously at every tentative grope. She grinned as she showered off the last traces of sardine. Sand washed off her legs and feet: a delicious feeling, the absolute essence of being on holiday: sand between the toes. So that every step you take has a slightly different quality from your everyday walking.

Charles came into the bathroom. By now Izzy was wrapped in her towel, a good thing. She did not want to appear too wantonly naked. Mustn't scare him off. He peered past her, at the shower.

'Oh damn. I forgot to ask you not to let sand get into the drains,' he grumbled, mopping it up with a sponge. 'There's a bucket for washing feet, under there – look. Would you mind washing your feet in that first, in future?'

'Oh no! Of course! I'm so sorry!'

'Poor Izzy,' said Charles, giving her a curious look for a moment: an almost objective look, as one observes a cluster of aphids upon a rose. 'You'll get used to our little ways, in time.'

'Oh yes,' Izzy dabbed herself with the towel. She wondered if vigorous rubbing was vulgar. She no longer wondered, on occasions like this, why he did not tear her towel off: why, instead, he was inspecting his own face, with some discontent, in the glass. It was just his way.

Izzy crept into the only double bed in the house. All the other bedrooms had twins and singles. She wondered how long it would be before Charles arrived, and tried to doze tactfully, not to appear too eagerly awake. He came quite soon, undressed by moonlight – a promising start, thought Izzy – and crept in beside her. He gave her a friendly hug, and then turned over, away from her.

'Cuddle up to my back,' he said. 'I'm absolutely shattered after humping all that damned furniture about. Goodnight, darling.'

'Goodnight.'

Izzy's answer was subdued. She clung to his back for a while, but eventually turned over and stared at the ceiling. The sound of the sea, coming in through the window, was soothing, but she could not sleep: unusually for Izzy. Bright moonlight flooded the dunes outside. She remembered childhood picnics by the sea at Whitby and Robin Hood's Bay: remembered her mum producing wonderful picnics which they ate on the clifftop, amidst wind-tossed grass, with her dad, afterwards, lighting his pipe. The intense smell of tobacco on the air. Her dad's stillness. None of the photographs she had of him had been able to capture the quality of that stillness. But at least she could remember it: remember when his dear eyes had been open and alert, above ground, in the wind and the sun.

'I say, darling,' murmured Charles suddenly, 'would you mind not breathing so loud?'

'Breathing?'

'Yes. Your breathing is keeping me awake.'

'I'm sorry, Charles. Are you sure it's not the sea?'

'No. It's you.'

303

Izzy lay still and held her breath for as long as she could. Then gently she let it out, gradually, trying to make no sound. She went on like this for a couple of minutes, until she was sure Charles must be asleep. Then she relaxed and breathed normally. She was tired by the effort of not breathing for him. She lay there in the moonlight like a fish in a flood of silver; carried forward by the currents of time.

'You're breathing again!' said Charles sharply.

Izzy got up. 'I'll go into one of the other rooms.'

'That might be best. Sorry, darling. It's just the silence, here, after London. I'll be used to it by tomorrow night.'

Izzy slipped away.

She went downstairs, glad to be free to go out to the moon and the waves. She slipped on a pair of shoes and her mac, and managed to open the door without a sound. The sea was black, now, the moon sailing above it and flecking its waves with light. The white beach glistened where the tide had slid away, and above her head was a canopy of chaste stars. She walked down the path to the beach, through the dunes. There, kissed by the lovely black wind, she suddenly flung off her mac and kicked her shoes aside, so that the wind could kiss her all over.

She ran to the sea and plunged into its dark embrace. Surges bore her up, foam crashed playfully over her head, slithery strands of weed wound themselves round her feet and slipped away again. She sensed millions of fellow-creatures swimming in the same delicious salty element: meeting, breeding and dying without ever tasting the air. She floated now on her back, out beyond the breakwater, and the moon poured her milky light onto Izzy's upturned face, breasts and knees. At length, it seemed time to go back to the earth, so Izzy swam ashore and waded out dripping and sparkling.

She was halfway back to her mac, when she froze. A figure was walking towards her. A man. She could not see his face in the dark. A great shivering seized her. Was she now, at this moment of perfect joy, to be murdered on this beach? Or was it Charles, come out of the house to seek her? It wasn't Charles.

'You forgot your towel. Here's mine,' called a light voice. It was Bill Bailey.

He showed no embarrassment at her nakedness, but simply draped the towel round her.

'Oh, thank you so much!' said Izzy. 'It was so silly of me to rush into the sea like that, on the spur of the moment.'

Wrapped in his enormous warm towel, she felt utterly safe.

'I was planning to swim,' said Bill. 'That's why I brought my towel out. And then somehow, I just sat and stared at the sea. And then you came out of the house and – well, I did wonder if you were doing a John Stonehouse. Planning to swim to Ireland and start another life with a different identity.'

'Oh, no!' laughed Izzy. 'I like my life as it is.'

'Yes,' agreed Bill. 'You're lucky, there. Mind you, you must take the credit for that.'

'For what?'

'Oh, never mind.'

'When did you arrive?' asked Izzy, drying herself. 'We didn't hear a thing.'

'About an hour ago. Parked in the dunes so we wouldn't disturb you. I wanted to drive at night so Susannah could sleep. It's horrible for kids, driving in the daylight. Hot cars, and so on.'

'Of course, Susannah's with you! Where is she! I must see her!'

'Asleep in the summer house,' said Bill. 'That's where we always stay.'

He led her through the dunes to a little wooden hut, no bigger than ten square feet. At one end was a portable travel cot. Izzy tip-toed to it and looked inside. Susannah was lying on her back, her long curved eyelashes brushing her cheek, her fat little mouth set in a pout, and slightly open. Her dark curls were damp and stuck to her head.

One hand lay by her lips, as if she had been sucking her thumb: the other clutched a worn teddy to her heart. Izzy knelt down and stared for a long time. Susannah's breath came up into her face, in waves, like a land-breeze promising spice islands to a parched old sailor who has been lost adrift for weeks.

Eventually Izzy got up. She looked down at Susannah again, and shook her head, unable to speak.

'Time I went to bed,' she whispered, reluctantly backing away from the shrine. Bill stood still where he was.

'Keep the towel,' he said. 'I've got lots.'

'Well then,' hesitated Izzy, 'goodnight.'

'Sleep well.'

She pushed her way up the rest of the path to the house. It was hard work, hauling herself up through so much soft sand. She slipped indoors. Charles would be asleep by now. She could easily creep in beside him. But Izzy thought the better of it, and went instead to another room and a friendly single bed.

YOUNG BLOOD

'What's your name?'

Izzy opened her eyes and saw a pretty young face six inches from her nose. Freckles, which had not been visible by moonlight, were scattered across Susannah's cheeks. Her expression was solemn.

'Izzy. What's yours?'

'Zoozanna. Is your mummy here?'

'No. My mummy's in Yorkshire.'

'Where's that?'

'A long way away.'

'My mummy's not here too. But my daddy's here. He woll take care of me.'

'Yes. And there are some more children coming today, for you to play with.'

'Who? What's their names?'

'There's a big boy called Jack. And a little baby girl called Rose.'

'How old is Dzak?'

'I think he's seven.'

'That's very very big. That's 'normous. I'm only three. How old are you?'

'I'm twenty-nine.'

'Is that old? Or just medium-sized.'

'I hope it's just medium-sized.'

'Have you got a baby in your tummy?'

'Not at the moment.'

'I've got seeds in my tummy,' Susannah confided, her brown eyes widening confidentially. 'AND. One day they will be my babies. But. Not yet. They're waiting to be my babies. First I have to grow up.' She sighed. 'I've brought my teddy, though. He's called Furze.'

'That's a very nice name.'

'That man with the glasses said there was a weasel in here.'

Susannah looked round the room in evident disappointment.

'You mean Charles?'

'Yes. Tsarles. He said there was a weasel in bed in here.'

'I think he meant me.'

'But you're not a weasel. Silly! You're a lady.'

'He pretends I'm a weasel, sometimes.'

Susannah gave her a sober stare. 'I wish there was a real one.' Abruptly, she toddled out.

That afternoon they sat on the verandah whilst Susannah played in a washing-up bowl of water.

'When's Dzak coming?' she enquired.

'Soon. Any minute,' said Izzy.

'Susannah will be glad to have other children to play with,' said Bill. Charles did not make any comment about the desirability of more children. Though he was looking forward in theory to having a son called John Ruskin Armstrong, it was as a pale serious youth of thirteen that he imagined his offspring, passing over the initial years of dirty nappies and nocturnal shrieking with averted gaze. Ideally he would have liked his son to spring immaculately from his head, much as Pallas Athene sprang from her father's. But he had reconciled himself to the necessity of going through the due processes. And the great thing about women was that they didn't seem to mind having the smelly little horrors on their knees and wiping their bottoms and clearing up their sick. Wonderful institution, women.

Especially his Izzy. His eyes lingered with pride on her brown motherly arms, exposed so fetchingly today by her blue sundress. Those were the arms which would carry away his bawling heir to some remote nursery quarters far away from the father's tender ears. Charles experienced a warm glow of anticipatory gratitude, and stroked Izzy's hair. Then he picked up *The Times*. 'And now, before the mob descends, I'll take advantage of the peace and quiet and catch up with news of fresh disasters!'

Bill and Izzy exchanged glances: the sea awaited them.

Bill swept up Susannah in his arms and they all whooped down to the beach. Charles watched them momentarily with an amused smile. Two of a kind, Bill and Izzy. Salt of the earth. Then he turned his eyes from the sparkling sea and the blue mountains to printed words about poisoned rain and mass murder. An hour later, they managed to persuade him to come for a long walk, looking for shells.

•

When they arrived back at Angorfa, Gwyn and Maria's car was parked by the house. Charles had left the key under a special stone so that they could make themselves at home. Gwyn walked round the side of the house and waved. Izzy was rather frightened to see that he was wearing pink shorts.

''Ulloa!' he called. 'Tremendous place yew got yere, Charles. I took the liberty of installin' my wife in the back bedroom. She's a little bit knackered by the drive, like.'

Gwyn continued down towards the beach. Charles seemed distracted. He was looking in the other direction, over the dunes.

'Who's that fellow putting up a tent?' he growled. 'Soon put a stop to that.'

'Oh!' cried Izzy, her heart in her mouth, 'it's – it's Dick! It's only Dick, Charles. He said he was thinking of camping in Snowdonia so I suggested he should come here and camp on the beach somewhere. Somewhere near us, you know. So he could, well, join in a bit. Dick's a very lonely person.'

'Anybody else you should tell me about?' Charles's sarcasm was somewhat undermined by his hat, a large

Mexican straw number which wobbled slightly ludicrously. 'Any single-parent families or one-legged lesbian poets due to arrive, my dear?'

'Don't be silly,' whispered Izzy. 'They're only my friends. What harm can Dick do?'

'What *good* can he do? Oh well, never mind. I don't suppose it makes much difference. Only I do wish you'd tell me beforehand. It rather drops me in it, otherwise, you see.'

'I know, I'm terribly sorry, Charles.' She was hating the hat more and more. If only he would take it off and throw it in the sea. It was almost as if it was the hat talking, and if he took it off, Charles would become sweet and light, again, not sour and heavy. 'Only, I was a bit – well, a bit scared of what you'd say.'

'Scared? Good God, woman. I'm your fiancé, not the big bad wolf.' Charles took off his hat and fanned himself with it. Izzy almost gasped in relief. But Dick was approaching, laboriously, through soft sand. At least he'd had the sense not to put on any shorts, yet.

'I – I hope it's all right,' he panted, 'Pitching the tent over there. I mean, I tried to keep out of sight of the house. Out of the view, you know. And I thought it might be quite convenient, over there, because it's not too far from the – from the toilet.'

'Yes. The outdoor lavatory,' confirmed Charles, correcting Dick's vocabulary. 'Glad you could come, Dick.'

See? It had been the hat talking, before.

'Maria's got a – um – migraine,' confided Dick. 'She was sick twice on the way here.' Charles put on his hat again. Dick was quite reassured by Maria's tendency to vomit. It kindly distracted attention from his own emanations. 'Seems such a shame she has to be – you know, lying down in a dark room. When there's all this—' he swept his arm across the bay.

'Yes!' cried Izzy. 'Isn't it marvellous of Charles to have a house here! But I must go and see if there's anything I can do for Maria.'

'There's nothing anybody can do for migraine, darling,' observed Charles. 'My mother's suffered from them for years.'

'I think I will go, all the same,' insisted Izzy gently. 'I mean, I might be able to get her a glass of water or something.'

Charles accompanied her towards the house. 'I suppose I must start to think about dinner,' he grumbled.

'Oh, I'll do that!' said Izzy. 'You relax or go and play football or something.'

Gwyn, Bill and Susannah were playing football on the beach. Charles stood and watched them for a moment.

'I've never been much of a chap for ball games,' he admitted.

There was the sound of a car's engine among the dunes, and Michael and Louise's old Volvo estate rode majestically into view. Jack was leaning out of the window at the back shouting *there it is there it is there they are!* Charles sighed.

'Dinner for eight adults and three juveniles,' he affirmed. 'I hope you did some sensible shopping yesterday.'

'Stop worrying, Charles. Please! I bought enough to feed the five thousand.'

'Just as well,' remarked Charles sardonically and went inside to seek refuge in his bedroom. Luckily he had brought the papers on Pugin, and only the sound of Maria retching in the next room disturbed his meditations until supper.

Outdoors, the car drew up and Jack burst from the back seat like a guided missile.

'Izzy Izzy Izzy!' he shrieked. 'The sea the sea the sea!' His little face was transfixed with excitement. He hurled himself into her arms and kicked her in a mad paroxysm of joy. Izzy felt an odd tear burst from her left eye and lose itself in his hair. He wriggled free; and ran away over the dunes to the football game.

Louise, very crumpled and tired, emerged from the car.

311

Michael was unstrapping Rose from her baby throne. Louise and Izzy embraced.

'You must be hungry,' said Izzy.

'Michael made three quiches before we came,' said Louise. 'And a potato salad and all sorts of things. They're all in the cold box in the back of the car.'

'Oh, how kind of you!' beamed Izzy.

'No, my dear,' Michael kissed her firmly on the cheek. 'This – all this – our exposure to this mind-boggling panorama, is all the result of your kindness. I just hope you don't live to regret it.'

'Michael! Get that food out of the car. I'll take Rose.' Izzy kissed Rose on her bald head. Little wisps of red hair were beginning to grow there. She beamed at Izzy.

'Clynt!' she said. 'Blech! Hwyllog! Goch! Coch! Heulog!'

'You see?' said Louise proudly. 'She speaks Welsh already.'

WOMEN'S EYES

Charles was mollified by the excellent supper; by the wine that Michael had brought, and by the gratitude and admiration that he, as host, excited. That night in bed he took Izzy in his arms and kissed her anxious brow.

'I'm sorry I was grumpy today, little weasel,' he whispered. 'Just unwinding after the journey, you know. We shall have fun. Oh yes we shall and we shall have treats.'

Izzy kissed him, and for once he let himself be led astray. After all, he had promised that she should have treats. Mind you, he did often wish that Izzy was more cold-blooded, or at least distant and mysterious: she was as eager as a little dog begging to be taken for a walk. How much more erotic would the whole thing be, for him, if she seemed indifferent! Looking away, out of the window. Her head turned elsewhere, her face hidden. These smiles, all this love, these kisses that she showered on him, were like too many sweets. Nevertheless, that night Izzy fell asleep without any tormenting thoughts or unfulfilled needs.

'Now,' said Charles next morning after breakfast. 'We're off to Plas Newydd.'

'Oh yes!' Izzy got up. 'I'll just pop up and see how Maria is, first.'

'I shouldn't bother, darlin',' Gwyn warned her, from the depths of yesterday's *Times*. 'It's even worse this mornin'. All you'll get is streams of sentimental free-association. She goes in for these deathbed scenes, like. Tells me 'ow much she loves me really, despite my appallin' record in the matrimonial stakes.'

'Well, I think I'll just nip up and see her anyway.'

'Give her our love, Izzy,' said Louise. 'And I hope the children aren't making too much noise. Actually they should be on the beach most of today.'

'Plas Newydd?' Michael asked Charles. 'Isn't that some kind of Gothic pile up on Anglesey?'

Izzy went upstairs and opened Maria's door very cautiously, hoping she would be asleep.

'Shut the door!' came a desperate croak.

'Oh, are you awake?' whispered Izzy, peering through the dark to where a tumbled shape lay on the bed furthest from the window. 'Is there anything – anything at all I can do?'

'Oh please, Izzy – just stay here and talk to me for a bit. You get to feel so lonely. So desperate. I was crying with self-pity a few minutes ago. Sickening.'

'Of course I'll stay.'

'I was thinking, all night,' said Maria. 'All about this business. Having the baby and everything. About my fear.'

'What about it?'

'I think I'm beginning to understand my whole life, Izzy. I mean, really understand it for the first time. It's amazing. I don't know whether I'm hallucinating or something, but it all fell into place, last night. At about four a.m.'

'How extraordinary! Tell me.'

'It's a long story.'

'Never mind. Go on.'

'Well, it all started because I was thinking about you.' Izzy felt nervous. 'All that business when you came back from San Francisco. When I said I was in love with you.'

'Oh – erm, yes.'

'It seems ages ago now. Even though it's only a few weeks, really. It seems to belong to another era.'

'Well, it does, really. I mean – you're pregnant now.'

Izzy hoped that the pregnancy had established itself as a priority that would put any feelings towards herself firmly in the shade.

'That's right. And being pregnant has changed everything. It's extraordinary. I remember how I felt, when I found out I was going to have a baby. I simply couldn't believe it. I nearly fainted with shock. I really felt it couldn't happen to me. I felt it almost biologically. I wasn't surprised that it took so long to get pregnant. In fact I was sure it would never happen. Do you know why? Because I've never really *believed I was a woman*.'

'What? What do you mean?'

'It goes way back. To when I was a little girl. Except my mother wasn't terribly pleased that I was a little girl, so she tried to minimise it.'

'What was wrong with your being a girl?'

'Well, my father had wanted a son. My mother didn't bring me up as a girl, at all. I had this short haircut. And I always wore trousers except to school. Mind you, the school I went to was a perfect imitation of a boys' public school. There we all were in shirts and collars and ties and blazers. Bizarre! And as for puberty – what a nightmare!'

'Oh, it wasn't so bad,' said Izzy, remembering secret talks and jokes with her mum.

'It was terrible! I didn't have a bra till I was fifteen.'

'Goodness, Maria! How awful for you!'

'As for boyfriends – forget it. There was no doubt about her feelings on that score. Once I started getting interested in boys, that was proof that I was a woman after all – and heading straight for the servile condition. I was shameless, I was the town-harlot, every single person in the street knew about me and my wicked ways, how on earth was I hoping to pass my sacred exams, if I spent all my time *hanging around men* as she put it.'

'How unfair. She must have been really screwed up herself.'

'She is. She told me I was betraying my intellect. That my father would never forgive me, *et cetera*.'

'But what about – when you and Gwyn got together?'

'Ah well, that was much later. By then I'd been living

away from home for five years. I think she'd reconciled herself to the fact that she couldn't control my life any longer. But Gwyn had the magic ingredient—'

'What was that?'

There was an urgent tap on the door.

'Oh, damn,' whispered Izzy, 'it's Charles. I won't be a tick.'

She slipped out. Charles looked peeved. Izzy quailed, than rallied.

'Are you coming, Izzy? I can't wait all day, you know.'

'Look, Charles, I can't. Not yet. This is very important, what Maria's telling me. It's probably the most important talk we'll ever have.'

'You women and your precious talks! What's so damned important about it?'

'Well, it's – very fundamental,' faltered Izzy. 'I can't explain. I'm sorry, Charles, but it might take quite a while longer.'

'I shall just have to go to Plas Newydd by myself, then.'

'Oh dear. I'm really sorry. But if you're so dead set on going now—'

'We're missing this perfect weather. It won't last. It never does, in Wales.'

'Oh, look, please, Charles, go. I mean, you must go and see these things that mean so much to you.'

'There's no need to be so dismissive.'

'Dismissive? I wasn't – I didn't mean—'

'Oh damn it!' cried Charles. 'I'm going. See you tonight – if you've finished your precious *tête-à-tête* by then.' And he thundered off downstairs.

'What was all that about?' croaked Maria.

'Only Charles being silly. Go on.'

'Where was I?'

'Gwyn had the magic ingredient.'

'Oh yes. He was working-class. My mother was an old-style Fabian Socialist, you see. Marrying a working-class man was the best thing I could do – if I insisted on marrying at all.'

316

'And Gwyn is a great character, too.'

'There is that,' admitted Maria. 'I've even begun to think that he'll make a good father.'

'Of course he will!'

There was a roar, outside the window, of a car leaping into life. Charles was taking it out on the starter motor.

'But the way this all relates to you, Izzy—'

'Ah, yes. How?'

'When I said I was in love with you, I don't think I meant it literally. Thinking about it now, it wasn't an erotic feeling. It was more that I wanted to be you. That I envied you.'

'But how could you envy me?' laughed Izzy incredulously.

'You're happy,' said Maria. 'You're happy being a woman. You know how to do it and be it. It's natural to you. You enjoy it, don't you?'

Izzy wrinkled up her nose. 'I suppose I do.'

'You like children. And you know what to do with them.'

'I just – well – I never think about it.'

'There you are, then. I'm dead scared of them. I don't know how to get to grips with this baby because I've always been tough Maria, sarcastic Maria, *afraid to be a woman* Maria.'

'Do you still feel like that?'

Maria lay still and thought for a moment. Then a strange half-smile began to hang about the corners of her lips. 'Do you know,' she pondered, 'I *do* feel different. I've begun to change into a woman. I mean, I'm so damned tired I can't be tough any more. And I keep crying. And somehow, it's a relief.'

'Of course it's a relief,' smiled Izzy, squeezing her hand. 'It's the best thing you can be, a woman. I feel really sorry for men.'

'How strange,' said Maria. 'I'd got you totally wrong. I thought you were man-mad.'

'I have had my mad moments,' admitted Izzy.

317

'And how's it with Charles?'

'Fine. How do you feel now?'

'Do you know, Izzy – I feel better. My head's not nearly so bad. I think I could even eat something.'

'Tea and toast?'

'Perfect! Oh thank you, Izzy. And bless you.'

Izzy ran downstairs.

Louise was sitting at the table staring out to sea. Izzy put on the kettle and joined her.

'Maria's feeling much better,' she said.

'Oh, good. Michael's gone to Plas Newydd with Charles. Jack's playing football with Gwyn and Dick, and Bill's taken Rose for a walk with Susannah. All this time to myself! I feel lost.'

'Is it nice?'

'Well, frankly – it's sheer heaven. Mind you, Izzy, I have been having rather a difficult time. I seem to be sort of haunted by my past. I'd like to have a really good talk to you, sometime.'

There was a frenzied whistling from the kitchen. The kettle needed her help, too, if it was not to scream itself into a white-hot burning death. Izzy ran to comfort it.

AFFECTION'S MEN-AT-ARMS

The men were at the pub. Dick had found it hard to tear himself away from Izzy, who had been kind and appreciative to him today. She had praised him for going shopping and for the Lancashire hotpot which he had offered to cook for supper. By gum, they'd all got that down their necks, quick enough. It was a shame Dick couldn't cook anything else. But there were so many of them staying together on this holiday, and only six days to go, so he reckoned he'd be safe back in London before his turn came round again. What a shame he'd been dragged out to the pub, though. He'd much rather have stayed with Izzy. She was wearing a particularly exciting blue sundress – one that was, quite frankly, a little bit too small. By going to the pub Dick was missing a whole two hours of the dress. She might not wear it tomorrow. Tomorrow it might even rain. Ah well. He couldn't very well have stayed with the women.

Although that Bill Bailey chap had chickened out. Mind you, he was a pianist. Probably couldn't afford to get too much drink down him in case he punched a few walls on the way home and couldn't practise properly for weeks. Dick had punched a fair number of walls in his time, but, he was proud to say, no people, yet. Of course, Bill Bailey had responsibilities: his little girl. Dick wondered if he would ever have a little girl of his own. He often tried to work out if his chances improved as he got older – within certain modest limits, of course. He thought not, probably. He tried to catch the eye of a Germanic-looking blonde woman at the other end of the bar. It was no good, though. The glances she cast in their direction were all directed towards Gwyn.

Gwyn grinned into his fifth pint. He had now established eye-contact with every woman in the pub. That had been a good walk, today, too. Dick wasn't a bad companion. Strong legs, and silent. A good listener. A bit too pure in heart to be absolutely ideal, – but who knows? Filthy furnaces must glow in Dick's secret heart as well. A girl walked in wearing a tight pair of denim breeches, knee-length, with long brown shanks beneath.

'Christ, Dick!' Gwyn nudged him. ' 'Ow'd she get into thoase, d'yew reckon? Vaseline an' a crowbar?'

Dick flinched. The hill walking had been a help, but he was still in a state of dangerous inflammability. Still, he must do his duty as one of the lads.

'Aye,' he observed. 'Circulation-stoppers.'

'Has an interestin' effect on my circulation, too, if you get my meanin'.'

Dick got his meaning. He wanted very badly to talk about something else. The Chancellor of the Exchequer was what he really needed to think about. Inflation, perhaps. No! Not Inflation. Nor Growth. Recession. Stagnation. Unemployment. A very old man farting quietly in a Dickensian solicitor's office. On a day of unusually severe frost.

'Tell me about your car,' said Dick desperately. His own van had collapsed quaintly in a shower of rust-flakes, about a year ago. He needed wheels. Then he could drive away fast from women in skin-tight pedal-pushers. What he needed was a car with no rear-view mirrors. Gwyn launched expansively into motor talk. Dick was safe.

Charles was enjoying Michael's company tremendously. He had found him an educated man, as they went round Plas Newydd together. He admired him for his wit, and a certain world-weary charm. His habitual irony was something Charles could relate to, but not emulate: and he had enjoyed the way Michael deferred to his own knowledge and judgement of, on this occasion, eighteenth-century Gothic.

'My dear fellow,' Michael was saying, now, as they sipped this rather delicious beer, 'I must congratulate you on the effect you've had on young Izzy.'

'Have I had an effect? I wonder, sometimes.'

'Good heavens, yes! She looks so much better for a start.'

'Of course – she's a friend of your wife's, isn't she?'

Michael smiled darkly at this. 'Of both of us. She was our lodger last year. But she's transformed, since she met you. Better clothes, better haircut, more confidence. Real elegance, old man, seems to have descended upon her at last. Congratulations!'

Charles shook his head and tried not to look too pleased as he smiled into his glass. He had enjoyed a very friendly reunion with his little Izzy, just before supper. She had looked up slightly apprehensively as he'd come into the room, but it was gratifying to see how easily her little face cleared when he poured upon it the blessing of one of his warmest smiles. His day at Plas Newydd, Izzy's welcoming kiss and Dick's unexpectedly delicious casserole, had put him in a rare good humour. He had even forgiven Dick for having had the temerity to think of camping uninvited on his dunes. Perhaps Dick was the salt of the earth, after all, rather than itching powder between the shoulder blades. And as for Gwyn – well, he was Welsh. So that couldn't be helped.

It seemed to Charles that Izzy had been right, after all: how very agreeable for him to be able to spend the evening in the pub with these really very decent chaps. How very pleasant for her to have female companionship back at the ranch. It made everything so easy. The domestic chores, shared between eight adults, virtually disappeared. Dear little Izzy! He would have to congratulate her, when they got back. He must remember to ask after the progress of Maria's migraine. He must tell Izzy that she, too, had splendid friends. More or less splendid, anyway. He was a bit alarmed at the rate at which very strong beer disappeared down

Gwyn's throat. But at least this was not Thraxton.

His own nerve ends were beginning to tingle and relax as the alcohol cheered its way through his system. He must be careful not to have too much and not be drawn into any awful macho competitive drinking. Dear Izzy! How beautiful she had looked, when she welcomed him home. In that dress she reminded him of a ship's figurehead. It wouldn't have done at Thraxton, of course:. rather too over-the-top. Literally. He supposed she would have to wear out her old clothes. Charles respected good husbandry and that included wearing things out. Mind you, maybe she could be persuaded to donate them to the Oxfam shop. That would be even better than wearing them out herself. She'd be helping the Third World and ploughing back resources. And then he could—

The Welshman was apparently addressing him, though the noise had increased so much that he couldn't hear a word. He leaned forward through the smoke and peered at Gwyn over his spectacles.

'What did you say?'

'Just congratulatin' you, like, Charles. I mean, I knoa I've congratulated you before, but anyway, here's more power to your elboa!'

The others raised their glasses to the happy bridegroom. He basked and purred in all this masculine acclaim. Especially since they were Izzy's friends.

'Well, you've all known Izzy for a lot longer than I have,' he smiled, 'and if you approve of me as a possible consort for her, well, that makes me very happy.'

' 'Course we approve!' roared Gwyn. 'What that girl needs is a man o'breedin' and sense. Mind you, she was nicely softened up, like, by Michael here.'

At these words, Dick stiffened. What they needed was to get back to car-talk, pronto. This was not the kind of revelation designed to animate the evening. Michael and Charles went white in unison. Charles gulped and tried hard to keep a steady hand on the tiller.

'Softened up? What do you mean?'

'Hey! D'you mean you didn't knoa about Michael an' Izzy's little escapade?'

'Escapade?' asked Charles faintly. Dick's knees felt weak in comradely horror. Would nothing silence this Welsh nitwit?

'Listen, Charles, there are certain things a bridegroom has a right to knoa. Mind you, I'm not advocatin' a wholesale acquaintance with his beloved's erotic history. But on that score, Izzy has participated in one of the truly heroic *ménages* of the century, in my view, like.'

'What do you mean?' Charles managed to sound casual. But Michael appeared to be choking on his beer.

'Didn't Izzy tell you? P'raps she's too modest, like. But this time last year she was firmly ensconced with Michael and Louise. In a *ménage à trois* as those filthy French bastards put it.'

Charles gaped at Michael. Michael shrugged.

'Is this true, Michael?'

Michael hesitated. In fact, the *ménage* had been one of the most blameless episodes in his entire life. The moment Izzy had stepped over his threshold, the erotic element in their hitherto steamy passion had evaporated. He hadn't minded Gwyn's playful references to it, before, but now – well, just how much could this Charles chap take?

'Oh, come on, Gwyn,' he protested, 'don't exaggerate. It wasn't a *ménage à trois*. That's your fantasy. Izzy was our lodger, that's all.'

The look of relief in Charles's eye was painful to see – because so doomed.

'Ah well, as to that, you do have this tendency to self-deprecation, Michael. One o'the more attractive habits of the rulin' class. But you surely won't deny that for several months before she moved in, young Izzy was enjoyin' a feverish passion with your good self.'

'Not feverish,' denied Michael hastily. 'Just a little flirtation.'

'That's not what she told me, like!' boomed Gwyn disastrously. 'If ever a girl had the hots for anybody, she had them for you. Doan't take refuge in false modesty, now, Michael. It's all ancient history in any case.'

'Well, quite,' said Michael. 'And best forgotten, in my view.'

'Did you have a – relationship with Izzy, then?' asked Charles cautiously.

'Oh, no, not a relationship. Nothing so substantial. Just a – you know, lunch now and then.'

'Out to lunch, like! As the sayin' goes!' Gwyn's laugh echoed unpleasantly among the tables. 'And Michael's not the only one to have got to grips with young Izzy's delectable little person. I once had the honour of spendin' a night in her company, tho' I have to admit that an excess of alcohol prevented me from risin' to the Herculean heights of passion demanded by the situation.'

Charles went red. He could not attack this person. These were not the revelations of a gentleman. But Gwyn would not claim to be one and was therefore beneath contempt. What's more, Charles's dexterity was limited to the manipulation of banisters. He disliked arguments and had never fought another fellow since the age of fourteen. And even then, he had lost. What's more, he was Gwyn's host. They had to spend the rest of the week together. What's more, it was indeed all ancient history. What exactly Izzy got up to before she met Charles was her business. He would rather not have known about it and it was his duty now to forget it. But the dreadful Celt could not be stopped.

'Dick!' he cried matily. 'I'm forgettin' your history of intimacy with Miss Comyn. It's nice and cosy, like, isn't it, if all us ex-lovers of hers can get together and raise our glasses to the man who swept the board?'

'Ex-lovers?' pounced Michael. 'Were you ever Izzy's lover, Dick?'

Charles waited with bated breath. This was a question about which he had often speculated. Dick was, he felt, a man dedicated to truth and forthrightness. Surely he didn't have the imagination necessary for a good liar.

Charles would hear the truth, now. He braced himself.

Dick paused. He perceived himself to be in a cleft stick. Here were all these blokes all reminiscing, sickeningly in his view, about their affairs with Izzy. In a way he longed to hit them. But in a way he longed to join in. To be one of the lads. For them to be able to say, well, Dick, you may smell pretty foul and your dandruff is appalling and you can't put two words together but by jingo you managed to slip her one, eh? And in fact, the night he had once spent with Izzy was the proudest moment of Dick's life, eclipsing all erotic experience that preceded it and consigning all subsequent episodes to dust and ashes. It would have been a moment of great glory to trump all this sexual boasting with a juicy little ace of his own. Then Dick thought of how Izzy would feel if she could hear them.

'Good God, no!' he blurted. 'What, me? Is it likely?'

'Izzy told me that you were her best friend,' said Charles, hopefully.

'That's – that's right. We're – we're like, you know, brothers. Sisters, I mean. I mean, brother and sister.'

'Yes,' said Charles gratefully. 'That's what she said.'

'That's not what she told me, like!' roared Gwyn. 'Unless I'm rememberin' it wrong, mon. I'm sure she told me once she'd had a night of steamin' passion with you, you sly old dog. C'mon, Dick, come clean. Admit it!'

'I didn't,' protested Dick. 'We didn't. You must be thinking of someone else.'

This was not, in Charles's view, all that reassuring. It was quite bad enough that every man around the table seemed to have some kind of amorous history with his fiancée without raising the spectre of a possibly somebody else. But he was saved from further embarrassment by Gwyn's perception that all their glasses were empty.

Gwyn lurched to the bar. Behind his back there was a moment of dreadful silence. Michael and Dick both looked helplessly at Charles. Only his consummate tact could release them from this malign spell.

'Well, all I can say is, thank goodness Izzy doesn't know any of my old flames!' said Charles with a heroic grin.

'Never trust a woman who hasn't any old flames,' affirmed Michael. 'Except Lady Di, of course – God bless her. By the way, Charles, isn't your princely namesake doing a splendid job? I have to admit there was a period in the early Seventies when I flirted with Republicanism, but not any more.'

Much to Charles's relief, the conversation now turned to the virtues of the heir apparent. At least he was one man who could be relied upon not to have indulged in amorous dalliance with young Miss Comyn.

But though there was no more talk of flames, Charles still burned within. He drank rather more than usual in an attempt to quench this unpleasant inner heat. And when at last they had returned to Angorfa, admired the moonlight on the sea and dispersed to their several beds, Charles watched Izzy undress with the troubling sensation that he was not the first man to do so. As long as these previous lovers of hers had remained decently anonymous, Charles was prepared to keep them out of his mind. But knowing that they were all tucked up cosily under his own roof – or upon his own dunes – was quite another matter. He felt them, as it were, breathing down his neck. He had drawn the curtains, tonight, for the first time since they'd arrived.

Izzy noticed his abstraction. She had been hoping for at least a cuddle tonight, but the look in his eye was not encouraging.

'Is anything wrong, Charles?' she asked, sitting fondly on the bed and taking his hand.

'I must say,' remarked Charles at length, 'I was a little surprised to discover that you'd brought all your ex-lovers here with you.'

'All my ex-lovers?' gasped Izzy, conscious simultaneously that many beans appeared to have been spilt in the last two hours, but that if Charles imagined that all her ex-lovers were assembled upon this beach, he was taking

326

rather an optimistic view of things. 'What do you mean, Charles?'

'That Welsh oaf got talkative, my dear. Very careless of you to invite people who know all your secrets.'

'Gwyn doesn't know any of my secrets! And he's not an ex-lover of mine, either.'

'That's not the impression I got.'

'Well, he must have been bloody well lying!' cried Izzy indignantly.

'He said he'd spent a night with you once.'

'Oh, that! Well, when he and Maria were separated, he did come round to my flat once – she was staying there – and demanded to see her. I steered him away into a little hotel down the road, and he was so drunk I had to sit with him all night to make sure he didn't do himself a mischief.'

Charles looked long and hard at her. Was she lying? He had unfortunately already had quite an extensive experience of her lies.

'I did ask you not to lie to me,' he said. 'I told you there was no need.'

'I'm not lying! I have never slept with Gwyn. Never! In fact, the last time he made one of his loathsome passes at me, I fought him off! I bet he didn't mention that, though.'

'As a matter of fact, he didn't.'

'No. Of course not. Far too humiliating.'

'What about Michael?'

'Well, I did have a brief affair with Michael, I admit. I told you about it.'

'You most certainly did not.'

'I did! I mean, I didn't tell you it was Michael, but I told you I'd been badly treated by a married man.'

'So that was Michael?'

'Yes. We're all friends now, though.'

'How bizarre. Still, he seems a very decent sort of bloke.'

'He's all right.'

'And what about Dick?'

Izzy sighed. 'Oh, that! It was only once, for goodness sake. Long ago. It didn't mean anything. I was sorry for him.'

'Ah, so you did sleep with Dick!' cried Charles in triumph.

'Well, yes. I thought you knew that anyway.'

'No. Dick vehemently denied it. He said you'd always only been good friends.'

'Oh dear. I expect – he was just trying to be tactful.'

'Lying bastard! I never liked him.'

'Don't be horrid, Charles. I'm very fond of Dick. He's been very good to me.'

'I can't help it, Izzy. I feel sick when I think of you with these other chaps.'

'But it's ridiculous! We're both thirty years old, Charles. We're bound to have, well, a history.'

'I hate your history. I don't want to know anything about your history.'

'But it's part of me.'

'I don't want it forced down my throat!'

'I didn't force it down your throat.'

'You invited them all here.'

'Not *all*, Charles – *both*. And I invited them here because they were both my friends.'

'Ex-lovers.'

'No, friends. Really. The thing with Dick was, well, nothing really. He's always been – just my friend. And Michael, well, he really is just a very good friend, now.'

'I find all this good friends business a bit hard to take. Once it's all over it should be all over, forever. That should be it. If we ever separate—' Suddenly it flashed through the room between them, like a dark crack in the world. 'I couldn't hang about being your mere friend, Izzy.'

'They're not mere. My friends are – well, just – almost as important to me as my love life.'

'Don't! I don't want to think about your love life. Or your friends. Every time I meet one of your damned friends now, I'll be wondering, was he one of them? I can't bear it.'

'You're just being silly. It's just what happened to me, before I met you.'

'A woman with a past!' hissed Charles with a shudder, and turned away to glare at the wall.

Izzy got up off the bed. It didn't seem that her cuddle was on the cards, this evening. It would seem like the greatest sort of invasion even to slide discreetly in on her side. She hesitated.

'Shall I go and sleep somewhere else?'

'Please yourself,' was the chilly reply.

Izzy left the room, tears welling up. She was tempted to go out and seek sanctuary with Bill Bailey and Susannah in the summerhouse, but it didn't seem quite right, somehow. Izzy wasn't sure any more about what was right and what was wrong. She made herself a little nest on the sofa, under the patchwork quilt. She would have to get up tomorrow before anyone else. It would seem like a betrayal to let the whole household know of their quarrel. The patchwork quilt was comforting. It absorbed her tears and spread a gentle warmth through her shivering body. Izzy wondered how many other tears it held, long-dried-up tears from previous years. It smelt of the past.

SHOT, BY HEAVEN

Izzy awoke, and instantly remembered her quarrel. She listened. Not a sound. It must still be early. She opened an eye. There, right in front of her, on the coffee table where she had put her earrings before going to sleep, was an exquisite little bunch of wild flowers in a mug. She reached out a sleepy arm and buried her face in them. They smelled of meadow and sunshine. Had Charles placed them there, as a peace-offering? She tiptoed upstairs and crept into their bedroom. He was fast asleep, with his face buried amongst pillows. He did not look like a man who had been up at the crack of dawn gathering wild flowers. Izzy dressed swiftly and slipped out again, glad that he had not woken up.

Charles was studiously polite and calm at breakfast: offering coffee and passing butter with perfect chivalry to men out of Izzy's past. Izzy had placed the little mug of wild flowers on the table and wondered if he would give her a secret smile when he saw them. But his eyes travelled across the table without registering them at all. So it couldn't have been him.

'What pretty flowers!' exclaimed Louise. 'It always cheers me up, having flowers in the house.'

'Yes!' agreed Izzy. 'Giving people flowers is one of the most – one of the best, you know, things you can do. Oh Charles! I never thanked you properly for that marvellous great bunch of flowers you sent me when we first met.'

Charles looked up in alarm. What was this? Some new devilish trick to disorient him? He set his knife down. 'I'm sorry, my dear, but I don't recall sending you any flowers, ever. Terrible to have to admit it, but nevertheless, there it is.' Izzy boggled. What was he playing at?

'But I was sure – they were from you. I mean, they were sent anonymously.'

Michael picked up a newspaper and hid behind it.

'Another of your many admirers, no doubt, darling,' Charles gave her a playful but painful smile. Izzy felt paralyzed. This had been intended as a gesture of reconciliation: demonstrating his chivalry to all her friends. It had gone horribly wrong.

'Were they really sent anonymously?' asked Louise. 'How marvellous! What did the card say?'

'Er – I think it was, *From an admirer* or something,' faltered Izzy. She did not want to mention the bit about the admirer having an apology to make. Her recent experience of rows with Charles had made her sensitive on the subject of apologies. They had started to play rather too important a role in her daily life.

'Well,' announced Charles, 'I'm off to Bodnant today. Would anyone like to come?' He smiled genially around the company, avoiding Izzy's eye.

'What's Bodnant?' asked Izzy timidly.

'Probably one of the finest gardens in the country. I'm particularly interested in the eighteenth-century garden house. It was moved from Gloucestershire, you know.'

'I'll come with you, old man,' said Michael, folding up *The Times*, and glad the conversation had escaped from the tiresome subject of secret admirers who sent flowers. Izzy hesitated. She had been very keen to go off with Charles today – to repair things, to be nice to him, to coax him back towards the happy harmony of the past. But with Michael? She shied away from the thought of such a day. Charles aware all the time that she and Michael had been lovers. Awkwardness between herself and Charles. No, she could not face such an expedition. She would stay here and help with the children. She avoided Charles's eye and said nothing.

'I think I might come, too,' said Maria unexpectedly. 'I feel so much better today. I'd like to sit in a shady garden somewhere.'

'I'm not much of a garden man, myself,' grinned Gwyn. 'Gettin' to grips with bare rock's more my style. In fact it has been said that this explains my marriage—' Maria threw a piece of toast at him. 'I can't explain the attraction of climbin'. All I can say is I have this overpowerin' urge to get further up.'

'It's your proletarian origins, old man,' said Michael. 'If you'd been to a public school you'd spend all your time trying hard to get down.'

'Please may I get down?' asked Jack.

'There you are, you see. Go and play, boy, play.' Jack ran out.

In the event, Gwyn and Dick went off to climb Cader Idris, and Charles set off for Bodnant with Michael and Maria. This left Izzy, Louise and Bill with the children. The day was bright, the waves were crashing down with gusto, and the beach lay virtually empty and welcoming before them. Izzy was preoccupied. As Bill built sandcastles and Louise lurked under a parasol (the penalty of being a redhead), Izzy worried that she had not had a chance for a few private words with Charles. He had not sought her out, before going. There had been endless opportunities for a quick kiss, a secret smile of reconciliation, but Charles had not seized his chances. A general wave to everyone had been Charles's goodbye. Izzy felt strangely heavy. She drew circles in the sand with her finger.

'Draw something! Draw something!' cried Susannah. Izzy drew a weasel.

'It's a mouse!' said the child.

'No,' said Izzy, 'it's a weasel.'

'Change it into a lady! I want a lady with long hair!'

Izzy drew a lady with long hair.

'Draw a monster now! I want a monster!'

Izzy drew a monster.

'You should really ask Louise to draw for you,' said Izzy, abandoning her monster. It looked too kind, really, for a monster: it was grinning in really a very engaging way. 'Louise is very good at drawing.'

'Proper drawing!' cried Susannah. 'On paper. Wiv felt-tip pens.'

'Later,' said Louise. 'First I have to stare at the sea a bit longer.'

'What you finkin' of?'

'I'm thinking about what it was like when I was a little girl like you.'

'When was that? Yesterday?'

'Years and years ago,' laughed Louise. 'Years and years and years.'

'Did you have long hair?' enquired Susannah urgently. 'Very very long right down your back?'

'Well, yes, actually, I did.'

'Did you?' Susannah turned to Izzy.

'No,' said Izzy. 'My hair was always very short.'

'My Mummy's got long hair,' confided the child. 'Long, long, very long hair. When's Mummy coming, Dada?'

Bill stood up, abandoning his sandcastle. 'Not this time,' he said. 'But we can ring her up if you like.'

'Yes. Yes! Ring her up! And I woll do the numbers and everything!'

'Gosh!' exclaimed Izzy. 'I must ring my mum, too. Later, maybe this afternoon.'

Bill picked up Susannah and carried her off towards the house.

'I'll bring some coffee out when I come back!' he called.

'Thanks!' bawled Izzy.

Silence fell. Louise stared at the sea. 'I do like that man,' she sighed.

'Oh yes,' said Izzy. 'So do I.'

'He's so unobtrusive and so – well, dignified.'

'And funny.'

'Is he funny, too? I hadn't noticed that.'

'Oh yes. And so easy to be with.'

'Yes,' agreed Louise. 'Not like the men we're used to, at all.'

Izzy was silent. The man she was used to had become an

enigma to her. But had she ever really got used to Charles, at all? The mere thought of his return, several hours later, filled her with alarm. How could she please him? It seemed so strangely difficult, somehow.

'I find myself . . . in a very strange situation, Izzy.'

'What! What? Sorry. I was miles away.'

'It's so silly, but – I'm quite, well, quite seriously attracted to that man.'

'To who? What, Bill?'

Panic flew through Izzy's every vein. Louise bit her lip. She seemed half in tears, half laughing.

'Yes. Bill. What a perfect name, isn't it? Bill. So simple. Like him. Simple and unusual.'

'But – but Louise—' spluttered Izzy. 'You can't! I mean, you mustn't!' Chaos howled in Izzy's insides. Strange seethings and violent flutterings shook her.

'Why shouldn't I? What do I owe Michael? Think of the times he's run off with other women.'

'Well, not actually – run off, Louise.'

'Sometimes I wish he bloody well had!'

'Oh no, Louise, don't. Please.'

'It's all this rest and relaxation. My libido's surfaced at last, Izzy.'

Izzy wished Louise's libido would sink again, and re-emerge, correctly aligned, on her return to Muswell Hill. Was Louise really falling in love with Bill? And was he – perhaps, who knows – also attracted to Louise? Izzy almost fainted with terror.

'Oh be careful, Louise. Please, please, be careful.'

'I can't help it. I like it.' Louise gave a strange, loud laugh, like a bird's cry. 'It's healthy.'

'Oh don't, though. I mean, what about Jack and Rose?' Rose was asleep in her little bouncing chair, a parasol nodding its shade across her face. Jack was a hundred yards away, chasing a dog through the spray and whooping like an Indian.

'It's nothing to do with them. Oh don't be such a spoilsport, Izzy. Can't I even have a little harmless crush on this man without you lecturing me?'

'I'm sorry,' said Izzy. 'But you know if you fell in love with Bill, you'd only fall out of it again in the end. It would all go wrong. So why bother? Why risk everything you've got?'

'I'm not risking everything I've got. Not for a minute. But Izzy, it's such a glorious feeling. I feel alive again. Are you going to deny me that?'

'No,' admitted Izzy. 'But, well – be careful.'

They sat in silence for a while.

'Here he comes with the coffee,' said Louise.

Rose woke up and was bounced. The coffee was drunk, but it curdled in Izzy's stomach. Was Bill looking at Louise in an unusual way? Louise stared modestly at her toes, and invited Susannah to count them. Susannah played with them: took Louise's sandals off and announced, 'You woll be the lady who wants new shoes and I woll be the lady in the shop.'

Bill watched them, smiling. Was he staring in a yearning kind of way at Louise's wonderfully handsome feet? Izzy tucked her own ugly paws under her. Such long toes Louise had! What man would not want to kiss them? To venerate them like a saint's feet.

'Come and see! Come and see! There's a big fish washed up on the beach!' cried Jack. Izzy was glad of the excuse to get up and walk away. She was leaving them alone, she realized. What glances might now be being exchanged, behind her back? What burning eyes and palpitating hearts? Izzy's feelings swarmed up her throat like a rope and almost throttled her. What business was it of hers? None.

'Look!' cried Jack. 'It's dead!'

A huge fish lay on the sand. Part of its belly had been torn away. It was beginning to smell.

'Come away, Jack,' said Izzy. 'It's going bad.'

'It's a porpoise,' said a voice close behind her. She jumped. It was Bill Bailey. He went forward and bent down to examine the fish. 'It was a female,' he said, 'and she was pregnant.'

'How sad!' cried Izzy. 'Why did she die?'

'It looks almost as if she was harpooned,' said Bill.

'Oh no! How can people do such a thing?'

They stood and looked down at the beautiful creature, torn apart and hurt by man. Another creature broken.

'I think I might cut its head off,' said Bill unexpectedly.

'What on earth for?'

'If I bury it, the flesh will rot away and the bones come clean. I'd like to have a porpoise head.'

'You like that sort of thing, don't you? Fossils and things.'

'I must go back to the house and get the knife,' said Bill. Izzy followed, but Jack stayed with the fish. Louise was still sitting far away with the little girls. 'Fossils,' Bill went on, 'I like, yes, because of the millions of years since they were alive.'

Izzy shivered. 'That terrifies me. Millions of years! Think of it! It makes us so – well, meaningless.'

'Not meaningless. Brief. You shouldn't worry about it. Especially not you.'

'Why not me?' Izzy was greedy for any pronouncement about herself, from his lips.

'Well, you're so good at living in the present.'

'Am I?'

'Of course. You know you are.'

They reached the house. It was light and still, inside. The wood ticked as wood does, quietly. They stood in the sitting room and felt the silence. Izzy caught sight of the mug of wild flowers.

'Did you put those by my head, this morning?' she blurted out.

'It was Susannah's idea.'

He smiled a slightly taunting smile.

'They are lovely. It cheered me up a lot.'

'You looked as if you might need cheering up. Sleeping on the sofa with tear-stains on your cheeks.' Izzy felt as if she was melting. Reckless impulses seized her.

'You should have given them to Louise.'

'Oh. Why?'

'Because she's falling in love with you. Just a little bit,' added Izzy. 'Be nice to her.'

He stared at her. 'I don't want to hear things like that.'

'Don't you? Most men would be flattered.'

'Don't talk in that way. It's not you.'

'What is me, then?'

'Don't be silly, Izzy. I can't be doing with anything like this.' He turned away, rather crossly. Izzy was stricken. He paused by the door. 'I have to get better first. I'm hurt.'

Izzy felt suddenly still and solemn. Something deep inside her relaxed. She had no idea why she felt soothed, but was simply glad she did.

'Come on,' he said. 'Let's get that knife.'

Days passed. Mountains were climbed, flowers picked. Somehow Izzy and Charles didn't manage their private expeditions, though Izzy hardly noticed. She watched Bill and Louise paddling with Susannah. Louise's long red hair danced around her face in a fiery flicker. If Bill did not find her fantastically beautiful, he would not be human. Izzy lost her appetite. She wished Charles would stop wearing his silly Mexican hat. It made him look like a toadstool.

LOVE IS A DEVIL

One morning, before breakfast, and a promised trip to Portmeirion, Izzy walked alone on the beach. Suddenly Louise appeared from nowhere and was at her side, crying.

'I've made an absolute fool of myself, Izzy! And now there's nowhere to go. I can't go back to the house – he's there. And Michael mustn't see me like this. Oh please, take me away somewhere today. By yourself. Not with Charles. We can go away up the coast, on the train. Anything. Only I must get away.'

Izzy ran indoors and whispered to Charles that their day in Portmeirion had to be postponed. Louise needed help. She was in a state.

'What's this, then?' enquired Charles wearily. 'Post-natal depression or some such female complaint?'

'Sort of. Sorry, Charles.'

'All right, then,' with a massive sigh. 'I'll see if I can tempt young Bill to come up to Aberglaslyn with me. And maybe Michael.'

'Oh yes, do!' urged Izzy. Life today would be much easier without those two hanging about. Dick would be useful, though. Izzy caught his eye through the window – he was on his way to the outdoor loo (Dick felt he didn't really deserve to use the indoor one, somehow). Izzy gave Dick the kind of look which demanded assistance. He faltered, turned and hung about outside the front door, waiting for Charles to leave.

'I must say, though, darling,' drawled Charles, reaching for his inevitable straw hat, 'you do deserve top marks for your collection of lame ducks.'

The moment Charles had disappeared round the side of the house, Izzy seized Dick's sleeve.

'Dick! I need help! Were you planning to go anywhere today?'

'Er, well – only a bit of hill-walking, like. But I'd much rather stay here and help you, Izzy.'

'Oh, Dick, you are – lovely! Listen. Louise is in a bit of a state. Can you take the kids off up the other end of the beach?'

'What, the baby and everything?'

'Yes. She's very good,' Izzy fastened the baby-sling onto Dick's shoulders. 'If she gets a bit fractious, walk up and down and sing "Dance To Your Daddy".'

'How does it go?'

'Oh, sing – sing anything. Bring her back if she's really hungry. Just try and keep the kids out of our hair for as long as you can.'

Dick went off. Izzy ran back out onto the beach where Louise was sitting hunched up, the wind blowing her tears round the sides of her face.

'Oh, don't cry, Louise! I mean, well, do cry, yes, if you need to. But it's such a shame. Just as you were beginning to feel better and everything.'

Izzy sat beside her and put her arm round her shoulders.

'You feel – lovely and warm, Izzy.' Louise leaned against her. 'You're so – good to me.'

'Gosh! I mean, this is nothing, compared to how good you've been to me.'

For a while they sat in silence. Gradually the sea's rhythm seemed to encourage Louise into speech.

'I feel such a fool,' she raged. 'Such a fool! I said – no, I can't bear to tell you what I said. But he made it very clear that he wanted nothing to do with me. It was dreadful. I mean, I'm sure he put it kindly and was tactful and all that, but, oh God! It was so humiliating!'

'Hush! Never mind!'

'But how can I look him in the face again?'

'You don't have to. They've gone off all day. Michael's gone, too. Dick's in charge of the children. Gwyn's gone climbing. Maria's asleep. So there's nobody here but us chickens.'

'But what about tonight?'

'We can go out to eat tonight. Just you and me. Find a fish and chippie somewhere. Come back and go straight to bed. And weren't you leaving tomorrow anyway?'

'Yes. There is that.'

'Well, then. Don't be upset. You needn't even set eyes on Bill Bailey again.'

'Thank God. I shall never forget it as long as I live. The trouble is, I'd lost touch with reality. I thought because I felt that way, he was feeling that way, too.'

'Well, he bloody well should have!' exploded Izzy. 'I mean, you are so lovely, Louise – really – I think you've looked stunning this week. There must be something wrong with him.'

They watched the waves for a while.

'Of course,' Izzy went on, eventually, 'there *is* something wrong with him, now I come to think about it. I mean, he's in such a state about his wife leaving him.'

'I know. It was so thoughtless of me. How could I be so crass?'

'You weren't being crass. Just generous and, well, you were reacting understandably. I mean, he is so very nice, and well – anyway.'

'Dear Izzy,' sniffed Louise, cuddling her. 'The more incoherent you are, the more it consoles me, somehow.'

'Oh dear. Well. Yes.'

Izzy and Louise collected shells, that day: played with the children after lunch, and swam. Maria appeared in the afternoon and sat under a beach umbrella. Izzy placed little Rose in Maria's lap.

'There!' she said. 'Practice!'

'How can something so small and soft be so frightening?' mused Maria. 'I suppose it's because she's so vulnerable.'

'Yes. But also, tough as old boots.'

'She looks like Sibelius,' observed Maria. Rose wrinkled her nose at them and sang strange baby songs upon the sound of wind and waves.

Dick volunteered to cook for the men and children that night: Lancashire hotpot with a bit of curry in it. The women drove off for the evening, and returned late and laughing under the stars. Louise slipped successfully upstairs without even setting eyes on Bill Bailey: Izzy and Maria joined the men.

'We were sorry that you absconded on our last evening together, darling.' Charles put an arm around Izzy's hips.

'Aye,' agreed Gwyn, 'forced us back on disgustin' male bonhomie and over-indulgence in alcohol, like.'

Izzy liked the feeling of Charles's arm around her. These days spent apart did seem to increase his affection when at nightfall they met again. She was going to enjoy the last day with him. The others were all going tomorrow – except Dick. He wanted to climb a particular mountain, and the plan was for him to go back with Izzy and Charles after having helped them clear up on Monday.

The next morning, Bill Bailey's old car had already disappeared when Izzy looked out of the bedroom window. A veil of cloud had covered the sun, and cold little tongues of wind whipped around her shoulders. She shivered. Thank goodness he had gone. Poor Louise could have a peaceful breakfast.

'It's not very good weather, I'm afraid,' she reported to Charles, who was lying in bed reading Ruskin. 'Cloudy and a bit cool.'

'Well, there you are, you see. I've been trying to take you off to see Portmeirion all week. I told you the weather wouldn't last. It never does, in Wales.'

'Oh I don't mind!' Izzy bounced back into the room. 'We'll have a lovely time, Charles! Just you and me! I'm dying to see it!'

Izzy's first view of Portmeirion was across some marshy meadows. It stood high on a hillside, a mile or two away, a magical collection of pinnacles and domes, gleaming mysteriously in a secret cloak of dark woods.

'Oh, Charles!' squeaked Izzy, 'it's wonderful!'

'Dear little weasel. I knew you would like it.'

He squeezed her hand.

The domes and pinnacles disappeared as the car cruised into the surrounding woods, along a drive lined with dark swaying shrubs. At length they arrived at a toll booth, parked, paid their admission and wandered under a gate house and into Portmeirion itself. It was much smaller than Izzy had expected. She was astonished to find that buildings which had looked massive from a distance were actually no bigger than garages. The building with the dome – which she had somehow imagined to be the size of the Sacré Coeur – was scarcely the size of a dovecot she had seen in Charles's parents' garden in Thraxton. Mind you, it had been quite a pretentious dovecot.

'Why, it's – it's tiny! Like a sort of toytown!'

Charles was in his element, pointing out important windows here and embellished doorways there: statues, fountains, ornate clocks, campaniles and grottoes. Izzy walked about in a daze of curiosity, like Alice through the looking glass. In some ways, it was just like Italy, which she had been to several years ago and adored. And yet – and yet, not altogether like Italy. Here, under a kind of awning, was a vast bronze statue of a Buddha glowing in the dark. Along a walk by the sea, a strange painted statue of a sailor. It was a collection of oddities, curiosities. Charles seemed to know every detail of the history of the place. She half-listened, wanting to find her own sense of the place, but wanting also to share his enthusiasm.

Izzy bought a postcard, at which Charles raised his eyebrows, slightly.

'I must send one to my mum!' she explained. Izzy felt a twinge of guilt. She had meant to ring her mother days ago. It was hard to imagine what Mrs Comyn would have made of a place like this. 'Can we go and have lunch now?' All these curiosities had given her an appetite.

They went to a self-service restaurant and Izzy pounced on some chips. Charles managed to capture a table outdoors, surrounded by flowers in tubs, and looking across to the bookshop. Though the day was cool, they were sheltered by the Italianate wall of the ice-cream parlour. Here Izzy gobbled her chips with undisguised greed.

'I say, old thing,' Charles reproached her, 'slightly piggy tendencies are emerging.'

'I must eat them quickly,' explained Izzy, rather ashamed, 'or they'll get cold.'

'Ah, well. You should have been sensible like me and chosen a salad.'

'It's not salad weather.'

Indeed as Izzy spoke, a raindrop hit her on the nose. It was only the merest tickle of a raindrop, and it was not accompanied by any others. All the same, it hinted of a summer ending.

'It's so extraordinarily Italianate,' remarked Charles, gazing blissfully at the nearest wall. 'Really, one could be in a little hill-town in Tuscany, somewhere.'

Izzy looked around. 'Well, in a way, yes. But there's something not quite right about it.'

'Not quite right, darling? Whatever do you mean?'

'Well, I miss the old ladies in black looking out of the upstairs windows. You know, with their canaries and things. The washing hanging on lines, and so on. And the bar on the corner. I mean, there's a bar on the corner in all those little Italian towns, isn't there? With old men hanging about in there talking about the war or something. And I miss the young men on their motorbikes buzzing about.'

'Really, darling! Fancy missing those frightful bikes! The silence of this place is part of its sheer bliss.'

'Well, I know they sound awful, but they're part of the life of those little Italian towns, I think.'

'You must be mad!' Charles laughed and stirred his coffee. Izzy peered up and down the street.

'Where's the chemist?' she asked. 'I need a plaster.' Her Empire pumps had not proved equal to all this up and down work, these woodland paths, these stone steps. She had a blister on her heel.

'There isn't a chemist here, I'm afraid!'

'Not a chemist? Why not? There's a bookshop.'

'Yes, but it's not the sort of place where you'd have a chemist, darling. The bookshop and the boutique and so on are for the visitors. If they need ordinary shops they go to Porthmadog. Or Penrhyndeudraeth.'

'But isn't that rather inconvenient for the people who live here?'

'Silly one! Nobody does live here.'

'Nobody lives here?'

'Only the hotel staff. The whole of the village is holiday accommodation, you see.'

'But – nobody ordinary lives here?'

Izzy felt suddenly strangely hollow and sick. No wonder she had missed the old women in black leaning over their balconies, talking to their canaries.

'No, silly. It's a folly, really, you see – on a heroic scale. A *jeu d'esprit*.'

'Oh, how weird!' Another raindrop hit Izzy on the chin. She shivered. 'So it's not real. It's not a real place, at all.'

'Of course it's real! It's a wonderful creation, a work of art. What could be more real than that?'

'But – I need to go to the bank.'

'My dear, the whole of the rest of the country is covered with banks. Besides, I have more than enough money to get us home. Don't worry.'

'Charles . . .' Izzy needed to approach the subject of money a little more closely. Her loan to Michael and Louise had left her seriously overdrawn and the bank manager was not pleased. 'I wonder if you could possibly – lend me a bit of money?'

'Of course, darling! How much?' He got his wallet out.

Izzy hesitated. She had dreaded this moment.

'About – about, well, five hundred pounds.'

'Five hundred pounds?' Charles raised an eyebrow. 'Has the little weasel been spending too much? An over-indulgence in sticky cakes?'

'It's just that – well, I had to lend Michael five hundred.'

'Whatever for?'

'He – they – their nanny left them after a row, and she demanded a month's wages in lieu of notice or whatever, and Michael didn't have a bean, because he wasn't expecting to have to pay her until the end of the month as usual, and there was this awful rather frightening man she'd sent round to collect her things, waiting for the cheque, and Michael was afraid he would punch him on the nose if he didn't give him a cheque, so the only thing I could do was lend them the money.'

Charles shook his head and smiled a thin, rather too tolerant smile.

'Dear me, Izzy,' he sighed. 'Your friends really are a prize collection of no-hopers.'

'What do you mean?' Izzy flared up. Her face went suddenly hot.

'Well, honestly, darling, I haven't liked to say anything – didn't want to complain, but really! This past week has been one bloody disaster after another.'

'What disaster?'

'Well, first Maria and then Louise going all pathetic and needing your attention. Your holiday has been completely ruined by the need to take care of your wretched friends. Patching up their egos and wiping their brows every hour of the day and night, instead of enjoying yourself with me, as you – and I – had every right to expect would be the case.'

'But Charles! I thought – I thought – you had had a good time. I mean, going off on your trips, and things.'

'My dear Izzy, the purpose behind this holiday was, if you remember, for us to get away and have fun together.

For me to show you lovely places and for you to relax and rest and gather your strength before the new term and all those ghastly yobboes you have to face.'

'They're not yobboes!' cried Izzy. 'They're just kids, very good kids, most of them – kids who have had lots of problems to contend with and – and they have to grow up in a horrible inner city, that's all.'

'There's no need to shout. Don't draw attention to us, please. People are trying to enjoy their lunch.'

'And another thing!' Izzy's voice dropped to a deadly hiss. 'I can't help it if my friends need me at an inconvenient time. I didn't mind looking after them, at all. It was nice to feel useful for once. Taking care of people in trouble is a bit more important than having fun, isn't it?'

'Oh, very noble, my dear. But I'm not sure I agree that there was any real trouble in the first place. Female hysterics is more the case, surely? I mean, what was ever really wrong with Maria and Louise? Nothing. Vapours.'

'For your information, Charles, Maria is pregnant, and that makes her feel very ill. And Louise is recovering from a very difficult birth and – and it's been hell for her, the first few months.'

'Ah! Women's troubles!'

The sun came out, and Charles put on his straw hat with a smile.

'You can't dismiss it like that! Don't you realize? They're renewing life! Making new life, Charles! How dare you sneer at them? They're doing the most important thing any human being ever can do!'

'People are looking at us, Izzy. Please be quiet. If you can't control yourself, I shall just have to walk off until you've cooled down.'

'Don't bother!' Izzy jumped up. 'I'll go myself!' And she ran off, down towards the sea.

Tears were streaming down her face, and people stared as she passed. It was as if real emotions were not appropriate here, either. Izzy made blindly for the quayside place, wanting to leave most of the village behind her. Wanting to look out across mere water. She turned her face to the estuary, looking out to more bays and promontories, darkly wooded, soothingly wild and empty.

Charles came up behind her. He grasped her arm, quite fiercely, and put on his most authoritative voice – one he'd never had to use, with Izzy, before.

'Now come on, Izzy. Be sensible, please. Let's have no more of this. Look! Here's the dear old boat. Called *Amis Reunis*. What could be more appropriate?'

Izzy looked. It did seem to be a boat, moored at the quayside, but as she stepped onto it, she realized with uneasiness that it was made of stone. It did not move. It was not buoyed up by the water, alive, dancing and ready to go. It was dead, fossilized, fixed: concreted to the land.

'But it's made of stone!' she gasped. 'It's not a real boat! It can't even go anywhere!'

More tears burst from her eyes. Charles looked very angry now. He was still wearing his hat.

'Stop these stupid hysterics!' he demanded. The hat shook furiously on his head. He looked like a toadstool in a thunderstorm. Izzy burst into appalling laughter.

'You look – you look – so silly!' she gasped, trying to strangle the dreadful waves of laughter that came tearing up her throat like sobs.

'Damn you, Izzy, stop it!' Charles was evidently unaware of the hat. 'Stop behaving like a child. I can't stand it.'

Izzy felt as if she was drowning in a sea of sobs. She summoned one last despairing whelm of strength, seized his hat from his head and flung it out to sea. Somebody laughed nearby. Charles looked aghast, bereft, bald and blinded.

'Shit!' he squeaked. 'You stupid woman! What the hell did you have to do that for? The Old Man brought me that hat – from Mexico! From Cuernavaca!'

'I hated that hat!' Izzy blurted out. 'I've always hated it! It made you look like an idiot!'

'You're the idiot!' thundered Charles, staring out across

the waves to where his hat bobbed merrily off towards Ireland. 'I'd never have believed you could be so stupid!'

'But then, you don't know me, do you, Charles? You don't know me, at all!'

'Evidently not,' Charles recovered some composure. He stared at Izzy with terrifying coldness. He said no more, but Izzy knew what he was thinking. He didn't want to know her. He wished he never had. Swiftly, she drew off her engagement ring, handed it to him, and walked back up the hill. Charles paused, shrugged, shook his head, grinned – all for the benefit of any curious bystanders, who were to understand by this that he was merely the dignified victim of an outburst of female hysterics. Then he set off heavily up the hill after her. He knew she hadn't a hope of getting anywhere from here, on foot.

They drove back to Harlech in a terrible silence. Tears flooded silently down Izzy's face. She sniffed, and sniffed, until Charles irritably thrust his handkerchief into her lap. She accepted it silently, and buried her face in it for the rest of the journey. It smelt painfully of Charles, the smell she had come to associate with being embraced. But it was getting saltier by the minute. Up above, the sky went black. A fierce rainstorm burst over their heads. Izzy was grateful for its noise. The windscreen wipers danced to and fro in a manic attempt to wipe away the sky's tears. But they seemed unending.

AWAY, AWAY!

The house in the dunes seemed sad and deserted when they arrived. Everyone had gone except Dick, and he was drinking a cup of tea and staring out at the rain.

'Oh!' he jumped when they came in. 'Er – hello. Have a lovely time? Did you – er – enjoy yourselves?'

'Yes, thanks, Dick,' Izzy immediately crossed the room to be out of his sight. He had noticed her red eyes, and he looked confused and anxious. Charles was composed, however. Having an extra person there made it easier for him.

'I think we'd better clean the place up today, if you don't mind,' he said. 'I'd like to leave first thing tomorrow. It's a long drive back.'

'Oh, yes, Charles! What can I do?'

Izzy was only too glad to point her puffy tear-stained face at the floor: vacuuming, scrubbing. Dick found relief in a series of heavy tasks: humping sacks of rubbish to the car, and thence to the pick-up point at the back of the university building, across the dunes: cleaning the shower, wash basin and both lavatories, sweeping the yard, thrusting himself passionately into the cooker in search of every last drop of grease. Izzy and Dick cleaned in companionable silence, whilst Charles fretted about, straightening pictures, counting keys, folding blankets so the edges matched exactly, and drawing blinds.

Izzy scrubbed with a kind of desperate intensity, as if to remove all traces of herself from this house: every little crumb of skin, every hair or tiny fragment of fingernail. She also worked hard as a farewell tribute to a place which had sheltered her so pleasantly and where, until today, she had been so interested, contented and absorbed. What's more, ferocious housework somehow exorcised pain. When at last it was all done, she wandered out onto the beach. The rain had stopped, though a strong wind blew off the sea and the sky was streaked with wild red weals. She sensed someone behind her, and jumped. It was Charles.

Izzy flinched. She had the absurd conviction that he was going to kill her. But his face was buckled with sorrow. He did not look like an angry thing, only pathetic.

'Dear Izzy,' he faltered. 'Please. Let's be friends again.'

'Oh Charles,' she could not find the words. The wind buffeted them both so that they could hardly stand. Huge waves crashed onto the beach, a few yards away, and the sea swept boiling up to their feet.

'Look, I'm sorry, Izzy. I – I was a bit – well – thoughtless today.'

'Dear Charles!' she cried. 'Please don't!' He must not make himself lovable, now: that would be worse than ever.

'You're the – the only woman, the only interesting woman – who's ever loved me. Please don't give up on me. Please, Izzy! I love you!'

'Don't, Charles!'

They were both crying now. But things had to be said. Izzy tried to swallow the ball of tears that was scuttling up her throat.

'It doesn't feel right, that's the trouble,' she cried. 'It doesn't, really, you must feel that. You don't like my friends or my work.'

'I do! Darling, I was only being – being jealous because I wanted you a bit more to myself whilst we were here. I was being unreasonable. I know I was. It was quite right of you to look after your friends.'

'I know,' said Izzy. She was desperately aware that she did not want him to talk like this. This man was vulnerable, lovable even.

'Please, Izzy,' he begged. 'You have to educate me.'

Izzy waited a terrible time, watching the waves follow

one another remorselessly ashore.

'It would never work, Charles,' she sighed in the end. 'I shall always love you in a way. And I hope we'll be – well, be friends, soon. Or at least in the end. But can't you see—? I feel so – so wrong, somehow. All wrong.'

'But we used to feel so right!'

Izzy sighed. She thought back to the early days. Even then she had had a creeping feeling of unease. He wasn't tempestuous and demonstrative, like her. Their love-making had never, ever been irresistible and easy. He'd started off by hating her shoes. She remembered him throwing them in the rubbish bin in his street. Silly shoes, maybe. But part of her history. Hers to throw away. Hers. She felt a pang of betrayal towards her old shoes. Why had she let him throw them away? Why had she not rescued them? She'd been paralyzed by his authority. But how could she tell him any of this? It was impossible.

'I'm not good enough for you,' she burst out. 'Your mother thinks so, and she's right.'

'That's nonsense!' cried Charles. 'When I saw you coming down the stairs at Thraxton, in your beautiful dress, it was a revelation. You could have been born there.'

'But I wasn't born there!' cried Izzy. 'I was born in Bradford Royal Infirmary.'

'But that's all right!' cried Charles into the wind. 'That's fine! What's wrong with it?'

'I never thought there was anything wrong with it–' hissed Izzy '–till I met you!'

Charles sank into a perplexed silence. 'This is ridiculous,' he observed eventually. 'You're quite sure you don't want me, then?'

'Oh, don't put it like that!' pleaded Izzy. 'It's not like that at all, you know that. It's just – we're so different – our backgrounds are different – our jobs are different – our friends, our families, everything.'

'But all that wouldn't matter if you loved me enough!'

There was a terrible pause, into which the winds leapt,

shrieking. Izzy's hair whipped around her head like a coronet of mad snakes. She nerved herself up for one final effort.

'I don't love you enough,' she concluded, and hung her head.

Charles reached inside his jacket pocket. *He's got a gun*, thought Izzy. Her mind whirled. *Or a knife. He's going to kill me here and now on this beach and Dick can't help because he's still in the house polishing those bloody saucepans*. She stared at Charles in frozen horror, knowing that she was so guilt-ridden that if he did try to kill her, she wouldn't have the heart to resist. He brought out a small piece of paper which fluttered in the wind. It was a cheque for five hundred pounds.

'Here's the money you needed,' he said. 'If there's ever – ever anything I can do to help you, I hope you won't hesitate to ask me.'

'Oh Charles!' Izzy burst into new, even hotter tears. His kindness was much harder to bear than his spite. But he was not detained by these new tears. He turned to go.

'I shall go out for the evening,' he said. 'I won't be back till late.'

And then he was gone.

Dick was cocooned in his sleeping bag in his tent. The storm outside seemed to be increasing: the wind boomed around the dunes, howling like a wild thing. Dick was scared. He was also disturbed. Izzy had been so odd this evening. After Charles had gone off in his car, Izzy had come in and said, abstractedly,

'Is there any food left?'

'But we've finished everything. I – I just threw the last biscuit away.'

'Oh God, Dick! Nothing to eat!'

Izzy's crying had left her very hungry and thirsty.

'Well – I could, er, go to the chippy, Izzy, if you like.'

'But we haven't got a car.'

'Oh. Yes.'

'Never mind. We can walk, Dick. Only just one thing.'

'What is it, Izzy?'

'I've got no money.'

'Oh, that's all right, Izzy. I've got plenty. Let me lend you some.'

'No, it's all right. I'll go to the bank tomorrow. Only Dick—'

'What?'

'Don't say anything.'

'Don't – when?'

'Tonight.'

'When, tonight?'

'Don't say anything, from now on, I mean. All evening, if you can manage it. I'm so – I can't face talking.'

'Of course not, Izzy. Anything you say. I don't want to talk either. I won't say a word. We'll have a nice quiet evening, shan't we? Not a word. I promise I – ooops, sorry.'

The whole town seemed shut up, when they got there. It was Sunday night. But there was a large hotel and Dick bought Izzy an expensive dinner which she consumed in silence. Dick was worried. Izzy must be very upset about something. He didn't dare ask what. Well, it had to be that Charles geezer. Dick hoped – but then, on the other hand – what difference did it make to him who Izzy married? He glared gloomily into his beer and hummed along with the muzak.

She had pressed his arm when they got back to the house, and slipped inside. He'd muttered about wanting to get an early night, and staggered off to this, his little refuge in the dunes. Now he lay under the storm with a wildly beating heart. The thought of Izzy being upset disturbed him greatly. He tossed and turned in his sleeping bag, and then switched on the powerful lantern he kept by his head. There was only one thing for it. Pornography.

Dick reached deep into the darkest recesses of his rucksack, where there was a convenient long zipped pocket, perfect for stashing his modest collection. His trips to Soho had provided him with a publication designed to drive away all thoughts of the storm, of Izzy in distress, of what they were going to have for breakfast, of what Charles would say in the car on the way down to London tomorrow, of where he, Dick, was going to live now that Aunt Vinny had – and other kindred worries. Dick turned hastily to page eight. A woman of staggering dimensions, dressed entirely in bits of old hot-water bottle, dog-harness and bootlaces, glowered down at him. Dick rolled over onto his back and cringed deliciously up at her.

He was halfway through his first whipping when there was a sudden sound from the real world – a gasping, plunging sound outside the tent. The tent flap was wrenched open. Oh hell! This was the North Wales Vice Squad! His dog-harness lady was about to be seized, and he, Dick, to be thrown in some mouldy cell. Perhaps in the dungeon of Harlech Castle! To fester there awaiting trial for polluting the beach – because Dick had to admit that since his eye fell on dear old page eight, a black slick of depravity had flooded out from his tent and obliterated every inch of the sands. Nay, of the entire world. With a palsied and desperate thrust he flung the magazine out of sight, over the rucksack. It stuck on top, instead, revealing part of a human thigh encased in liquorice boots.

'Dick!'

Izzy's face was suddenly there, facing him. She looked desperate.

'What is it, Izzy?' he cried. 'Is owt up?'

She wriggled into the tent beside him: or rather, on top of him, since the tent was extremely small.

'Oh Dick!' she breathed into his face. 'Can I stay here, please? I'm so scared of Charles! I don't want to sleep in the house! I was in a spare room but I couldn't sleep! I'm sure he's going to kill me in the night.'

'Kill you? Why – why, Izzy? Kill you? Surely not!'

'Oh, I expect I'm just being silly. But do let me stay here, Dick! Charles and I have – we've finished with each other.'

'Oh, I am sorry,' gasped Dick as she buried her head in his chest and threw both her arms around his neck.

'Oh, Dick, Dick!' she moaned. 'Protect me, please! Please!'

'You're safe with me, Izzy! I won't let anyone touch a hair of your head!'

Dick bound her to his electrified trunk with all the strength of his mighty potter's arms. But all the same, it did occur to him that should Charles throw open the tent flap with some instrument of death in his hand, there would be little Dick could do to protect Izzy. She, on the other hand, would provide an excellent barrier for himself, spreadeagled as she was on top of him. How could he defend her? Could he whip Charles to death with a rolled-up pornographic magazine? Especially from his present supine position? Would it be a safer bet to hurl the lantern at him? Maybe it would be safer if Izzy was underneath. Yes, Dick was convinced that it was a good idea. He was quite prepared to lie protectively on Izzy for the whole night, if necessary. Or should Charles prove a tenacious enemy, for several years.

'Oh, Dick, you're so nice!' Izzy wriggled passionately against him. Even though the sleeping bag was between them, it wasn't a very expensive one. If you held it up to the light, you could see through it in several places. And as luck would have it, one such place was in an extremely helpful position, right now. Nicely warmed up by the woman in the dog-harness, Dick now thrust himself energetically upwards, intent on protecting Izzy from below. The law of gravity may have been against him but the law of depravity was firmly on his side.

'I'll take care of you,' he panted, approaching an ecstatic crisis of protection. All that was required was to imagine that he was embracing Izzy: really embracing her, that is.

Hastily Dick's imagination clothed her in a few random bits of ripped hot-water bottle – and WHAM!

Christ! There was an ear-splitting shriek, and the roof flew off. Dick closed his eyes tight. So this was it. Death. The Bonk that leadeth to the Beyond. Uncle Norman had been right. Women bring destruction. Dick assumed he had lost consciousness, because when he opened his eyes, the tent was not there any more: only innumerable stars. Even now his soul must be streaming upwards through the galaxies, in search of a sordid little corner in which to anchor itself against the gales of eternity.

'Dick! The tent's blown away!' screamed Izzy's voice. Dick sat up. She was right. The tent, his clothes, and the pornographic magazine had been whirled away into some dark vortex of sky and mountain. Tomorrow, perhaps, the woman in the dog-harness, torn so cruelly from the side of the man who worshipped her, would stare up through sodden grass into the uncomprehending eyes of a slightly radioactive ram.

'Oh God, it's pouring! Come on, Dick! We'll have to go back to the house!'

Dick panicked. Inside the sleeping bag he was entirely naked. He fumbled at the latches of his rucksack and pulled out a pair of pants. The wind snatched them and hurled them wantonly towards Snowdon. Dick scrabbled again, but the rucksack had gone.

'I must get dressed!' he shouted above the storm. But Izzy had seized the rucksack and was running towards the house. Dick stood up, clasped his sleeping-bag round him and hopped and floundered towards shelter like a man in some mad nocturnal sack race. His last despairing thoughts were that if Charles was waiting to bash his brains out with one of those saucepans he, Dick, had so recently burnished, he could not protect himself without losing his dignity. Death or dishonour. Which was it to be?

THE WORDS OF MERCURY

As Dick hopped through the front door, his sleeping-bag skidded on the floor which Izzy had so urgently polished, and Dick fell with a thunderous crash, knocking over a small hall table and shattering the beautiful little bowl which had stood upon it. Izzy was horrified. What the hell was Dick playing at?

'Dick!' she cried. 'Why are you still in your bag, you idiot?'

Charles appeared at the top of the stairs. He was holding a heavy torch in a menacing way. Dick looked up from the floor. Through stars he heard Izzy berating him and saw Charles poised above him for what was certainly going to be a final, fatal whack. Izzy's lover would despatch him with a *Guardian* Special Offer heavy-duty car torch.

'What the hell is going on?' thundered Charles.

'Er – sorry,' Dick apologized feebly. 'I – er—'

'Dick's tent blew away,' explained Izzy in a rush. 'Just blew away, Charles, the wind's incredibly strong!'

'Was that the Doulton bowl that went just now?' enquired Charles irritably.

'Oh, that pretty bowl! I'm so sorry, Charles, only Dick slipped – I wonder – could we have it mended, do you think? I mean, I heard of a woman who can do wonders with broken china, and – oh dear.' Izzy was picking up the bits, and discovering that the bowl had shattered not so much into pieces, as powder.

'I give up,' sighed Charles sourly and walked back to his bedroom. He paused by the door. 'Do try not to break anything else irreplacable before tomorrow morning.' Then he was gone.

Dick requested a pair of underpants from the rucksack and struggled into them whilst Izzy swept up the last fragments of Doulton. Then she instructed Dick to occupy the downstairs bedroom. She would sleep on the sofa under the patchwork quilt. She begged Dick to leave his door open, so that if Charles crept down in the night with murderous intent Dick could wake up and save her. Although the wind was still roaring with such fury that it would have been difficult to hear twenty murderers, all equipped with machine guns.

Izzy covered her head with the old patchwork quilt and shuddered. The storm was buffeting the walls so violently that the whole structure shook. Perhaps the very house would be lifted from its moorings and hurled headlong against the cliff wall. It was, after all, built on sand. And the day of wrath had come. Izzy wondered if they would all die if the house was blown down, and if so, whether they would die instantaneously. Perhaps a giant tidal wave would rear up and crash down on them. It was exactly the sort of weather that could lead to disaster. *I won't sleep a wink*, thought Izzy, sticking her fingers in her ears. She fell asleep instantly.

Next morning she opened her eyes and saw the coffee table where Bill Bailey's bunch of flowers had been. Or Susannah's, rather. Today the table was bare. She had polished it yesterday and it gleamed austerely in the morning light. The wind had dropped, and the house had stood, and Charles had not murdered her in the night. But there was that dreadful journey to London to negotiate. And the Doulton bowl! The memory of the shattered bowl filled her with such guilt, she covered her head for a few moments. She had carefully put all the fragments on a white plate, just in case there was any hope of salvage. But she feared not. Dick was such a clot.

She tiptoed into Dick's room and shook him awake. He blinked, reached out for his glasses, rubbed his face and groaned.

'What's the time?'

'I don't know. But it's morning. And Charles wants to leave early.'

'Look, Izzy, I've been thinking. I don't think I want a lift back, actually, thanks very much. I think – I've decided I'll go back by train. In fact, I won't be going all the way to London. I'm stopping off at Birmingham to see a friend of mine.'

'Oh Dick! What a brilliant idea! Can I come, too?'

Dick gaped. 'But – but – I thought you were going back with Charles?'

'I think it's better if I don't, actually, Dick. Yes. I'm sure he'd prefer it, too. Much more tactful. I'll come with you on the train. To Birmingham.'

Dick blinked. This was awkward. His trip to Birmingham had sinister undertones. He was planning to stay with an old flame of his called Michelle. She had met Dick in London but had returned to her native Birmingham to help her sister run a boutique where a variety of appallingly tarty clothes were sold. Michelle had, in the past, modelled the odd synthetic tiger-skin play suit for Dick, and he was hoping that she could be prevailed upon to provide similar entertainment this time. Dick had not had an easy summer.

'What's the matter, Dick? Can't I come and see your friend? Is she a lady friend? Oh yes, I see – you're blushing, Dick, you naughty boy. I won't hang about, then.'

'Oh no, Izzy, I'd love – I'd love you to – er, if—'

'No, Dick. It's simple. I'll go straight to London on the train. I'm dying to see a few city pavements again.'

Breakfast was not attempted, as there was nothing to eat in the house and they would only have to wash up afterwards, which would, as it were, make a mess of yesterday's comprehensive spring-clean. They did drink black coffee, though, and stared out at the grey and still savage sea. Izzy put a lot of sugar in hers to give her the courage for a vital speech. A last, tactful lie.

'Charles,' she said, trying to sound casual, 'I don't think

359

I'll go all the way back to London today. Dick's decided to go by train to Birmingham, and I think I'll go along with him and then drop in at Stratford and maybe see a play or two.'

'Fine,' said Charles, finishing his coffee and standing up. 'Whatever you like. I'll give you a lift to the station, though.'

At the station Izzy deposited a brief kiss on Charles's cheek, and he smiled a strange friendly smile.

'I'll be in touch,' she whispered, wanting to soften the parting.

'Fine.' He waved to Dick and then, at last, was gone.

Izzy stood still for a moment. Up above their heads the castle towered. Birds wheeled around, black specks against the muddled clouds. Cold winds sneaked around her ankles. The summer seemed all broken up and spent. But in her innermost heart she felt a weird flicker of warmth. She took Dick's arm as they waited for the train.

Once they were on the train, Izzy felt even better. The train chugged and shuddered through beautiful green hills, stopping at tiny stations where there was not a sign of a human soul. They all had strange magical names. In the fields the cows cropped lush green grass. It felt cosy to have come inland, away from the sea.

'Izzy . . .'

'Yes, Dick?'

'I can't afford to live at Worcester Road any more.'

'Nor can I.'

'Well, Michelle – my friend in Birmingham – I was on the phone to her the other day, fixing up this visit, like – well, she used to live in Stoke Newington. Only she's gone back to Birmingham, now. Well, she says, her old landlady might have room for me.'

'Oh Dick! What about me? Would she have room for me, too?'

'She might. I'll ask. I mean – I hope Aunt Vinny won't be upset, but – I don't think it's practical, living right the other side of London from where we teach, either.'

360

'Oh no. That's right.'

There was a Septemberish feeling in the air. These were the last few days of the summer holiday.

'So you wouldn't mind – sharing a house with me, Izzy?'

'Mind? Dick, I'd love it! You've been so good and helpful to me, these past few days. Weeks. Months. You're my mate, Dick.'

Dick wished that this could have been true in a more zoological sense, but it was better than nothing.

'So it's really all up between you and Charles, Izzy?'

'Oh, yes,' Izzy leaned back and looked out of the window. 'You see, we weren't really suited, Dick.'

'I know. Difficult, isn't it? I mean – to find somebody.'

'Well, it sounds as if you've got somebody, Dick. Michelle.'

'Oh no! Not got. Not in the sense of – you know. She's just a – well, she's just a – sort of old, well, casual – er person, like.'

'I remember you brought her to Michael and Louise's party last year,' said Izzy, taking off her jacket. This compartment was warm. Nice and warm like a nest. 'Yes. I remember Michelle. Michael thought she was really sexy.'

'Oh no!' panicked Dick. He did not want to think of sexiness, not with Izzy in her T-shirt now and this train vibrating like a spin-drier. He wished he had brought that copy of *Exchange and Mart* that had been lying about in the house. He looked out of the window, concentrating hard on the trees. None of them looked yellow yet. There was still a little bit of summer left.

After Newtown Izzy fell asleep with her mouth open, and Dick watched vigilantly lest any rogue fly should presume to approach that jewelled cave. Izzy smiled in her sleep, and Dick, watching her, smiled in sympathy.

Back at Aunt Vinny's there was a letter for her. Delivered by hand. She tore it open.

Dear Izzy,

Here's your cheque for five hundred pounds. A strange thing happened. Charles rang to ask if he could buy one of my paintings – the one of the child running into the field of poppies. The one that used to be up in your room. We moved it down to the kitchen when Melanie came. Anyway Charles saw it that time he came round to supper and he rang up to say he'd like to buy it. He offered me *three thousand pounds*! I couldn't believe it. And of course we couldn't afford to refuse it. He said it reminded him of you, somehow. I think I know what he means.

He said that you and he had decided that your engagement wasn't really on. I do hope you're not feeling too bad, Izzy. I hope we can cheer you up a bit if you need it. You were so kind and understanding to me in Harlech, and so wonderfully helpful when Melanie left. We've got a new nanny now, by the way – she's an Irish girl and divinely ugly. And very clever and nice.

Izzy, you were so good to me. I can't thank you enough. The funny thing is, now I'm home I hardly ever give a thought to Mr B.B. Isn't it odd? Perhaps it was an aberration. I'm getting on quite well with old Michael and Charles's buying that picture has inspired me into getting out my things and starting to do a bit of sketching.

Could you do me a favour? I'd really like to do a picture with Susannah in it. You know I like children as subjects. Could you possibly borrow a photo of her from Bill for me, please? I don't want any direct contact with him but I'm sure you'll be seeing him so if you could ask it would be very nice.

Give us a ring when you come back. I hope you're not too unhappy. We're worried about you!

Lots of love,
Louise.

Izzy walked to the phone, to ring them straight away. But there, on the table next to the receiver, were a couple of scrawled phone messages in Aunt Vinny's wild, loopy handwriting. Izzy read the first one.

A woman called Georgie Pope rang (*can* that be right?). She said she'd met you at Thraxton and would you like to have lunch with her sometime to talk about the possibility of a job in the film business. Will you please ring her on 789 5430.

Izzy's pulse raced. The film business! She seized the phone, but as she was dialling, the other message caught her eye.

My dear, your mother is ill. In hospital. She's had to have an operation. Not sure of the details. Your brother rang. He and his wife are there at the moment. Please could you ring them when you get back.

YOU, THAT WAY: WE, THIS

When Izzy got back from Yorkshire, there was a letter waiting for her, from Charles. At the sight of his neat black handwriting, her heart lurched for a moment: with panic, with possibility, she knew not what. But there were only a few well-bred lines inside, beautifully placed on the very centre of the page, beneath his Spitalfields address.

Dear Izzy,

There are a few things of yours here at the house. As you still have a key, you'd be welcome to collect them at any time. They're on the table by the sofa. On Thursday and Friday the 1st and 2nd September I shall be out all day. It's best if we don't meet, I think. Perhaps you'd be good enough to leave the key on the hall table when you leave.

Yours,
Charles.

It was Friday already. She must go now. Go and get it over with. She'd just have a cup of coffee, first.

Dick joined her for the coffee. He had good news. His Birmingham friend Michelle's ex-landlady in Stoke Newington had two spare rooms and would be delighted to accommodate Izzy and Dick. Izzy quailed at the thought of giving her notice to Aunt Vinny. But in the event it was all right: very convenient, in fact. A French couple, friends of Aunt Vinny's, had asked her to find them a flat in London for the academic year.

'Such short notice,' fretted Aunt Vinny. 'So disorganized of them! But then, they are so really charming! I'd quite given up hope of finding anything for them! But you say you'd like to move out during the next few days? My dear – on the one hand, how very sad! But there again, how opportune!'

So that was all right, then.

'The house in Stoke Newington is – well, it's really nice, Izzy,' Dick promised. 'There are Orthodox Jewish families on both sides. One lot's got thirteen children.'

Izzy didn't really care what it was like. All that mattered was that it was available, it was five minutes' bike ride from school, and compared to Aunt Vinny's, it was cheap. Izzy wanted to move and have done with it, and was tempted to start packing right away. But first there was more tying-up of loose ends to be done. She must oblige Charles, and go stealthily to his house to remove the last traces of herself, and to return his key.

Spitalfields smelt of autumn: a spicy chill hung about in the shadows, which seemed longer these days. Izzy's footsteps echoed in the quiet street. Not the clip clop of high heels, this time, but the pounding of sensible trainers bought in Keighley market. She passed the rubbish bin where Charles had disposed of her Joan Crawford slingbacks. That all seemed years ago, not weeks. The whirlwind romance had blown itself out, leaving havoc and wreckage. Izzy put the key in the lock, turned it and went in. A deep melancholy rose up in her at the familiar smell of the hall. The door closed with a sad echo. Here, in this submarine green hall with its faintly phosphorescent chandelier, they had stood together and felt love gathering and dancing in every vein.

Izzy sighed, and walked gingerly into the drawing room. Strange how guilty she felt, even though he had asked her to come. The camelback sofa where she had planned to cuddle up to Charles for a whole winter – how lonely and empty it looked. No prospect of any more cuddles ever, and it was still only early September. It was a beautiful room. But not, Izzy realized, one in which she could ever have felt comfortable.

'Hello,' came a voice suddenly from a dark corner. Izzy blinked. She hadn't noticed anyone in the voluptuous shadows. So many oil paintings and busts: pale faces, noble faces. And here was a real face. It was Bill. He got up from the desk where he'd been writing.

'Fancy seeing you,' he said, running his fingers through his hair.

Izzy was thunderstruck. She realized that mentally she'd put Bill away on some high shelf, so she couldn't reach up for him and break him. Now she was forced to confront him, in the wrong place at the wrong time, at the moment she felt most vulnerable about Charles. She felt herself blushing. The whole room went hot.

'I'm sorry if I disturbed you,' she faltered, 'but I wasn't expecting . . . Charles asked me to come, you know. To collect my things.'

She gestured towards the table, where her eau de nil Empire pumps lay, with a few items of clothing, neatly folded, and two paperbacks.

'Oh no,' said Bill. 'You're not disturbing me. I was wondering how you were.'

Izzy hesitated. Should she sit down? It would be too rude to go straight away. And yet she hated having to talk to Bill here, like this.

'Sit,' he invited her. A nervous giggle burst from her lips. She sat down.

'You sound as if you're talking to a dog!'

'Would you like a bone or a bowl of water? Or are you all right?'

'I'm all right,' said Izzy. 'I had a cup of coffee just before I came.'

Silence fell. Why was it so hard to talk? It had always been so easy, before, with Bill. They both stared at Charles's Persian carpet.

'How are you?' Bill enquired, at length, looking up with much too brisk and defensive an air.

366

'Oh, well, you know, it's been a bit difficult. I've just come back from Yorkshire. When I got back to London I found a message that my mum was in hospital. So I had to go off straight away. I've been up there ever since.'

'What is it? Anything serious?'

'A duodenal ulcer. I think she's going to be all right. My brother and his wife are up there. She's just come out of hospital. The trouble is, I can't go up except at weekends. My new term starts on Monday.'

'Ah yes. The new term,' Bill sighed. 'So this is your last day.'

'That's right.' Izzy paused. He said nothing, and stared at his fingernails. She must go on saying ordinary things. 'And I'm also moving house.'

Bill looked up.

'Oh? Why?'

'I can't really afford it in Westbourne Grove,' faltered Izzy, shying away from Aunt Vinny's connection with Charles.

'Where are you moving to?'

Did he want her address? Izzy hesitated, and decided against offering it.

'Oh, it's a big house in Stoke Newington. Quite near the park. A friend of Dick's fixed it up for us. He says it's very nice. I think we'll enjoy living there.'

'We?'

This monosyllable seemed aggressive, somehow. Poised. His tone was odd.

'Oh, me and Dick. I seem to be doomed to share places with Dick.'

Bill went back to his papers. He picked up a pencil and started doodling.

'I think Dick's a good bloke,' he said.

'Oh, so do I! I mean, when I said doomed, I meant, you know, just that we shared in San Francisco and then Westbourne Grove and now Stoke Newington. I mean, Dick's lovely. Well, he can be a bit of an idiot at times, but . . .' Izzy hesitated. 'Not nearly such an idiot as me,' she concluded miserably. Tears were gathering behind her eyes. She must seize new, harmless topics.

'I can't decide whether to give up teaching,' she burst out, 'or get a job in the film industry.'

Bill looked up. 'Oh?' he enquired. 'How's that?'

'Well, that friend of – of Charles's—' There, the name was out, she'd said it, had gone past it, and it was all right. 'The woman at Thraxton, Georgie Pope her name is, well, her PA is having a baby next year so she'll need somebody new. She mentioned it to me when we were there. Now she's asking me to have lunch with her and discuss it. I mean, seriously. So I have to think – to decide, really, if I want to give up teaching.' Izzy gave him a pleading look. He shrugged and went back to his doodle.

'Well, don't ask me for advice.'

'I wasn't.'

There was a silence again. The room seemed to be filling up with silences, across which they threaded frail bridges of words. Or at least, Izzy did. He seemed to say less and less. She had never felt so uneasy with him. She had never felt so uneasy with anyone. It had been a disaster, his being here. She felt sick to the depths of her heart. She longed to run away, but she must first stay and complete a little more small talk. Very very small.

'That's enough about me!' she cried, clumsily. 'What about you? I mean, how are things? How's Susannah?'

'She's fine,' he sighed. 'And at least Marianne has promised not to go to the States this year. She wants a divorce, though. It's all going through. It's – well, very depressing.'

He rested his cheek on his hand. Izzy felt herself plunge into icy water. He was unreachable. But she must swim on, drowning in polite privacy.

'Oh dear. I'm sorry you're so unhappy. I mean. But. Well, what about your work? What have you been doing? Did you ever bury that porpoise head?'

'Oh, yes. In a quiet corner of the Fellows' Garden. It should be ready to dig up next spring. It won't be smelly any more, by then. Just beautiful. Yes.'

Bill smiled at her, but somehow, then, his smile cooled and he stared straight into her very soul. Suddenly everything was so still, Izzy could feel all her pulses ticking aloud. She must say something, to fill this oppressive silence.

'What else have you been doing?' she gabbled.

'I've been thinking about you.'

A tidal wave crashed over Izzy's head. Mad feelings swept through her. The tears flooded effortlessly into their ducts. Her eyes began to brim.

'M – me?'

'Yes. Charles has been talking about you a lot, of course.'

'Ah – yes. How – how is he?'

Izzy was lost. Those terrible words *I've been thinking about you*, so sweet and so frightening, seemed to have stunned her. She scrabbled away at other sentences, unable to speak what was really in her heart.

'Charles is very upset. I'm taking him off to Tuscany tomorrow. That's why I'm here.'

'Oh! Tuscany! I wish I could come!' cried Izzy thoughtlessly. Bill threw back his head and burst into strange laughter.

'Sorry! But that would really defeat the object, wouldn't it?'

'I – I suppose so.'

'He's got to get over you.'

'Will it take him long?'

'Who knows? He's never really been in love with anyone before, I think. Nobody like you.'

'Was he – so really, so much in love with me, then? Oh dear, I feel so – so terrible. But I couldn't help – couldn't help it, really.'

'I know. You did the right thing. As an impartial observer I can promise you that you did the right thing.' He produced the first genuine grin of the evening.

'Oh do you really think so?'

'Of course. It would have been a terrible mistake for you.'

'Oh. Thank God. I mean, thank God you think so. I'm glad it made sense to a – an impartial observer.'

She challenged him a little with her eyes. The silence opened up again, a great lake in which they both breathed and looked.

'Do you know what I want to do?' he asked. Izzy shook her head, dumb with longing. Every limb trembled. Her toes cracked violently in their trainers. 'I want to come across this room to you. But I can't.' Her heart almost stopped. This was it, then. The end. Road closed. No thoroughfare. No entry. Cul de sac.

'I understand,' she lied, and looked away, at the strange marble bust in the fireplace. It was this museum, this art gallery, keeping them apart. But no. It was more than the place. It was the whole history of their meetings. It was Fate. The tears took their chance and fled down her cheeks. Dimly she remembered that she must ask him for a photograph of Susannah for Louise. But all that seemed out in another life, a mundane life she had once occupied, before plunging into this abyss: where Bill Bailey could have come to her, but wouldn't.

She got up, and grabbed her clothes and books. She would have to go. Every moment in this room was unbearable, now. She lurched towards the door. He turned in his chair.

'Don't go, Izzy!'

'I must! I can't – can't stay. It's too – hard.'

'All I need is time!' He leapt up. 'Don't cry, silly thing.'

He caught her up in his arms, and the world cracked. Izzy's nose was suddenly deep in his cotton shirt. He smelt of hay and skin. He held her very tight. She felt their hearts racing together. Then he drew apart. He held her at arm's length.

'I have to have time. If I don't give myself time to get over Marianne, it'll spoil everything.'

'How long?' asked Izzy, filled with a desperate greed.

370

'I don't know. Just – be patient.'

Izzy looked at the floor. She could not trust herself to look at his face.

'Come on, Izzy. You have a lot to do. Your mum to help, and your work to decide about, and your new house. Look! Send me your new address. And then – next year . . .'

Izzy began to feel brave, and excited. She must not hurl herself into this. For once she must hold back. The months stretched away, aching, ahead, but he was right. She must. She straightened up, shoulders back, eyes level.

'Could you just . . . send me a photograph of Susannah? Only Louise wants one. She wants to do a picture of her.'

He pulled his wallet out of his pocket and gave her a photograph from it: an image of himself and Susannah embracing in a windy field. Then he placed his hand very gently on her cheek.

'I won't have one of you,' he smiled. 'I want to have fun, trying to remember your face.'

Izzy moved away, and heroically gulped down a fresh supply of tears.

'Goodbye,' she said.

'Goodbye.'

She went out. There was no kiss. Only the dear delicious evening air. As Izzy soared westwards on her magic trainers, she had never felt more alive.

EXEUNT

The first day of term. Dick arrived early, stuck his head briefly into his pottery room, noted its swept-clean, unused look, and then went up to the staff room to wait for Izzy. Maria was there. She waved to him. He floundered across to her, passing several new members of staff. There was one little woman with glasses and big teeth, who got in his way and smiled at him. Dick smiled back, and wriggled past. She must be the new geography person. He hoped she would not develop an interest in his rocky outcrops.

'Dick!' Maria beamed. Dick was encouraged. Maria did not seem nearly so frightening as before. This pregnancy business was doing her good. Apart from making her feel absolutely wretched, of course.

'How are you, Maria? How are you, erm – feeling?'

'Not so bad, now, thank you, Dick. I haven't been sick for three days. And it's rather a wonderful feeling, giving in your notice on the first day of term.'

'Have you – given in your notice already, then?'

'Yes. Just now. It was great.'

'When's the – big day? I mean, the expected day? I mean, when's it due?'

'The beginning of April. I suppose I could have gone on until the next half-term, but I thought, sod it! This is my chance.'

'Well, you're looking very – very good,' concluded Dick.

'Thank you, Dick. I'm not feeling half-bad, either.'

There was a bellow from across the room. It was a new sound. Dick looked for its source, and saw a very large fellow with a black beard and abundant curly hair. He looked like an Elizabethan explorer or swaggering pirate.

'Who's he?' asked Dick.

'The new Head of English,' whispered Maria. 'He's called Browne, with an e. He arrived last term. A very sardonic bugger. Pleased with himself, as you can see. A real lady-killer.'

Dick was filled with foreboding. The pirate Browne flashed his eyes across the room. Dick looked away. So this man was Izzy's new boss. Izzy had had to miss the staff meeting yesterday because she was travelling back from Yorkshire, so she hadn't met Browne yet.

'How's Izzy's mum?' asked Maria.

'Not too bad. Izzy rang me last night when she got back. She said they were all, you know, pleased with her progress and that. I think Izzy's planning to go up and see her every weekend for a while. Help her get back on her feet, like.'

'I thought she was moving to Stoke Newington next weekend.'

'No, we're doing it every evening this week,' explained Dick. *Doing it!* Crumbs. That sounded a bit – you know. He whipped out his handkerchief and blew his nose unnecessarily hard into it. He sometimes wished – no, he often wished – that he could wear a mask all the time. 'I've got a new van. So then she can go to Yorkshire on Friday night.'

'Poor Izzy. She'll have her hands full for a while.'

'Aye. She'll manage, though. She's very – what's it called?'

'Resilient?'

'Aye. Resilient.'

Dick tried not to think of Izzy's resilience. It was a tangible quality, with her. Springing and bouncing all over the place. It shouldn't be allowed. Dick mopped his brow. He glanced nervously at the door. If he was in this state just thinking about her, whatever would it be like when she bounded into the room?

'She's had an awful summer, really, hasn't she, Dick? That Charles business.'

'Yeah. Still, I never did think he were quite right for her,' frowned Dick.

'Nor did I. But she does rush headlong into things without stopping to think.'

'Aye. Well. I think that's part of her – you know,' struggled Dick. 'Her att – charm, like.'

'I bet she'll fall madly in love with old Browne,' sighed Maria. 'I can just see it all. Inevitable.'

Dick panicked. In his mind's eye, he saw Izzy talking animatedly to Browne: he saw Browne laughing and placing a huge hairy hand on Izzy's divine, dimpled knee. A few days later, he would catch sight of them through classroom doors, heads together after school, studying some damned book or other. Browne's arm was round Izzy's shoulder. Dick's fantasy rushed onwards like a train: Browne lurked in the bookroom with Izzy: together they counted copies of *Kes*. Browne's eyes flashed dangerously in the dark: Izzy fainted with longing at the sight of his twitching beard and masterful corduroy trousers. Browne seized Izzy: they fell into a nest of old Comprehension books, her face buried in his beard. Dick, lurking outside the bookroom, heard a horrid hairy panting and the rustle and thump of much squashed literature. Lost amongst the books, Izzy gave a delighted little cry. Dick's heart smashed into a thousand pieces, like the Doulton bowl. He flung himself out of the nearest window and was scraped off the playground by the caretaker.

Izzy would cry at his funeral, though. Her bosom would shake – under her black rubber, no wait, black silk suit. Bugger it, though! Browne would be there too, his arm comfortingly thrown round her shoulders, his monstrous hand stroking her heaving breast.

'Oh Dick, Dick!' Izzy would sob. 'I've lost my dearest friend! If only he could have told us what was wrong!'

Later, of course, they'd visit his grave. Izzy would be carrying a small posy of daisies – 'His favourite flower!' she would sob, throwing the flowers upon Dick's slumbering sod. And then Browne would seize her again, and fling her familiarly down with an erotic panache fit to wake the dead. But perhaps Dick wouldn't be dead, after all. Perhaps he'd be buried alive! Perhaps he would revive feebly in his coffin, awakened by the powerful thumps from above. It would be just like me, thought Dick, to bungle it. He could just imagine waking up during his funeral and being too embarrassed to say anything because he didn't want to upset anybody.

'On the other hand,' Maria went on, 'Izzy will have to wait her turn. Alison Rees has got the hots for him at the moment.'

Dick looked across to the dreadful Browne. Alison Rees's interest in him did not comfort Dick. Alison Rees was no match for Izzy. She had strange fat legs and no bust. Whereas Izzy – Dick lapsed into the painful but wonderful knowledge that he was sharing a house with her once more. He would have plenty of opportunities to glimpse her splendid details as she dashed from bathroom to kitchen and then upstairs, past his ever-open door, to her sanctum. Occasionally he would be invited up. Izzy would sprawl on her bed and confide in him. About Browne, if necessary. And then, when the whole affair finally blew up in some catastrophic disaster, she would hurl herself into his arms, and he would enjoy his moment of maximum pain and pleasure.

Dick was a kind soul, but he was beginning to hope that Izzy was destined to suffer a series of disastrous affairs. At least it would be better than marriage. Then he could always be around to pick up the pieces. Bearing in mind Izzy's reckless and generous heart, he might manage a comforting embrace, well, every eight months or so. And maybe gradually all this comfort would begin to, as it were, penetrate Izzy's consciousness. Perhaps one day – she would look at him in a curious way and say,

'You know, Dick, I've just realized. I've been so blind, all these years. But now I see it all and yes, Dick – it's you! You're the one! Yes, you're the one I've really loved all along! Oh come to me, Dick, come to me come come come!'

'Here she comes now,' said Maria, as Izzy burst through the staffroom door.

Yes, there she was. Dick was sorry to see that she looked more beautiful than ever. She positively shone. Her hair sprang around her face in little black crinkles. She had washed it that morning – in the shower, perhaps – Dick steadied himself on the edge of the coffee-table: he did not want to crash unconscious at her feet among piles of *The Times Educational Supplement*. Something flashed at the other side of the room: it was Browne's eye. He had caught his first sight of Izzy's back view, and his mouth actually hung open for a moment. How deeply Dick wished he could have lobbed a phial of deadly nightshade therein.

But no. It was too late. Browne had seen Izzy. It was only a matter of time before Izzy saw Browne. Izzy flung herself down in a chair opposite Dick and Maria, with her back to Browne, but he was still looking.

'God!' gasped Izzy with a grin. 'These jeans are tight! I must have put on a hell of a lot of weight recently. I'll have to fall in love or something.'

Dick winced. There it was: the whole damned scenario, all set up. Even now Browne was casting such burning looks at the back of Izzy's neck, Dick was surprised her hair didn't start steaming.

'Right, Dick!' Izzy smote him energetically on the knee. Dick jumped. She seemed in rare high spirits. 'Bring the van round tonight and we'll elope!'

Dick groaned.

'Come on, Dick! Don't look so hang-dog! Have I got time for a coffee?'

'Don't get up,' pleaded Dick, springing to his feet. Izzy must not on any account flaunt her wonderful person unnecessarily about. 'I'll get you one.'

Dick fled to the coffee machine, and burned himself on it. All around him, tides of greeting and gossip flooded and flowed. In a way it was exhilarating. At least he could teach, dammit. Well, more or less. At least he could make pots. And most of the kids seemed to like mucking about with clay. And best of all, Izzy taught here, too. He was certain to see her at home and at work. What bliss!

Why, it was better than being married – except that the proximity was always slightly too approximate.

He returned with Izzy's coffee. She was talking energetically to Maria. His ears devoured her words, mortified that they had lost some.

'Oh thanks, Dick! You're an angel!'

She stirred her coffee and beamed at him. Dick beamed back. He was not an angel. She had got it wrong. He had it on certain authority from – someone or other, someone way back, someone at school probably, that angels didn't have things. Whereas Dick – Dick was lumbered. And, as Izzy had been kind enough to say once, he was well-endowed. Had she been telling the truth? Dick wondered, often. Since he had not been to public school, he had little experience of the male person. Across the room Browne gave another bellowing laugh. A deep, thrilling sound, no doubt. Dick cast a quick, jealous look at Browne's trousers. Yes! They were baggy, of course. They needed to be. He probably had to walk around with a wheelbarrow.

Izzy turned to discover the source of that fascinating bull-like sound, and Browne spotted his chance. He grinned at her. Dick's heart shrivelled. What was the point of pumping on? Why not just stop, right now? So many heavy days to get through. Not to mention the nights – with Izzy sleeping in the room above! Dick's stomach lurched with joy and fear.

'Who's the bloke with the beard?' hissed Izzy.

'Your new boss,' explained Maria. 'Jenny Odham got a job in a Sixth Form College.'

'Oh yes. I remember you said. What's he like?'

'Fatal,' smiled Maria.

'He won't be pleased with me, though,' said Izzy, pulling a worried face.

'He'll be chuffed to his bollocks with you, my dear,' retorted Maria, who was recovering visibly from the first ghastly months of pregnancy. Dick's stomach turned. He wished fervently that no more references be made to Browne's equipment. Already it seemed to blot out the sun.

Dick lurked in the shadow of its splendour.

'No really, Maria.'

'He's a terrible old lady-killer. And he kept asking about you. Someone's obviously tipped him the wink.'

'What wink?'

'That you are the answer to a horny old philanderer's most feverish prayer.'

Izzy burst into what Dick thought was rather a crude cackle. 'Don't be silly, Maria! I wouldn't touch him with a bargepole!'

'Oh yes, you would. I give you six weeks.'

'You're quite wrong! I'm a reformed woman. I'm not going to fall in love with anybody. Am I, Dick?'

'No. I mean, aren't you? I mean, how should I know?'

'Dear Dick! One day I shall do the decent thing and fall in love with you.'

Izzy's eyes danced over Dick with a strange playful gaiety. But Dick felt he was landscape, background. Mere furniture.

'Don't you dare do anything so irresponsible!' scolded Maria. 'Dick must not be trifled with. He is a pillar of society.'

'I know – hey, listen!' Thus did Izzy abandon the subject of him, Dick, and lower her voice and – God help him – lean forward towards him with, evidently, some much more fascinating confession, some horrible confidence hanging on her lips. He yearned for it.

'I don't even know if I'll be here next term! That's why Browne's going to be angry with me.'

'But why?' asked Maria. 'Have you made it up with Charles, again? Are you going to run off and marry him after all?'

'No, silly! Why would I want to do a stupid thing like that? No, listen – there's this woman – Georgie Pope – you remember her – she was at that houseparty thing at Thraxton – she wants me to give up teaching and go and work for her in the film business.'

'The film business!' cried Dick. 'Blimey!'

So that was it, then. It was bound to happen, of course.

He could have seen it coming a mile off if he'd been concentrating. Next year Izzy would disappear into Wardour Street. Next spring he'd be getting a postcard from her, filming in Mexico with – with that smooth geezer – what was his name? Charles Dance. Or someone even, well – worse. Thingummyjig who'd had all those wives. Roger Vapid. Jeremy Irons. Oliver Reed. Errol Flynn. Clark Gable.

In his mind's eye – and how much Dick often wished that his mind was blind – he saw Clark Gable bending over Izzy on a bed. The windows were open. A Southern breeze stirred the curtains, and played with the curls on Izzy's brow. Seven vast orchestras swelled with longing. And he, Dick, sat out there in the dark, in the back of the stalls, sucking his Fat Frog ice lolly and remembering the night she'd plunged into his tent on the dunes at Harlech. Harlech! Already the place had a magic ring to it. Even if it did sound like someone clearing their throat. Dick's tent rose again among the dunes. Only it was a more majestic tent, furnished with tiger-skins and Turkish delight. Once more the door-flap parted and Izzy, clad in harem trousers and a jewelled bra, pushed herself in. But this time it was Rudolf Valentino who swept her into his arms. Dick leaned back to watch and sighed, partly with relief. At least at the back of the stalls you are out of sight, in the dark.

'What do you mean, the film business?' asked Maria suspiciously.

'Well,' grinned Izzy. 'She's some kind of producer or editor or something. And her assistant is leaving. She thought I might like to take her place.'

'What, you? But what do you know about the film business?'

'Absolutely nothing,' giggled Izzy. 'But I could learn.'

'You can't leave us, Izzy!' Maria cried.

'Well, you're leaving us. It'll all be totally different this time next term. Everything changes. I'm a bit sick of the rut I'm in. I think I may have reached the end of a—'

'Don't say *era*,' commanded Maria. 'I've already had enough clichés for one morning.'

The bell went. Dick ran off. He did not want to witness

the meeting of Izzy and Browne. Already the great man was looming up with an unpleasantly eager expression on his face.

'Ah!' boomed a voice behind Izzy. 'You must be Izzy Comyn. I've heard a lot about you. I'm Steve Browne.'

Izzy turned and shook hands with the pirate king. His hands were enormous. He came straight to the point and blazed a look of unmistakable lust at her. Izzy withdrew her hand and smiled cheekily up into his whiskers. She felt, at the moment, prick-proof.

'Hello!' she said. 'How do you do?'

'Let's go to the pub at lunchtime,' he murmured. 'Get to know each other.'

'Oh, yes! That's a good idea, isn't it, Maria? We usually do go, with Dick, don't we?' Izzy skipped aside, and tried not to look too coquettish. Browne glowered a little at the thought of Maria and Dick, but he liked the hint of resistance. It wasn't something he experienced very often.

'I must be going,' smiled Izzy. 'I have to meet my new form. The new 4C. They always give me tough fourth years because I'm a bit of a yobbo myself.'

Browne cast a last admiring glance at her as she withdrew. Izzy felt his eyes burning her edges. She was going to have a lot of trouble with him. Just as she reached the staffroom door, Pat Pritchard caught her by the sleeve and held the phone to her.

'It's for you,' she whispered.

Izzy seized it in panic. Was it something about her mum?

'Izzy Comyn?' She thrust her other finger into her offside ear.

'I say, Izzy darling, this is your tedious old ex-lover Michael calling.'

'Michael! I can't talk now! The bell's just gone.'

'Look, I know it's a bad time to ring, but I just wanted to say, any chance of a drink on Thursday night? For old times' sake, you know? Just you and me. Louise will be at her Tai-Kwon-Do.'

'I can't, Michael. Really. Sorry. I'm moving house.'

'Moving out of Aunt Vinny's? I am relieved to hear it, dear heart. And what corner of London is to be graced with your presence, may I ask?'

'Stoke Newington. I'm sharing a house with Dick.'

'Ah. The inevitable Dick. But let me assist your removal, Izzy. Remember I have a Volvo Estate. I'm a big boy now. It's very, very long, I promise you.'

'Stop it, Michael!'

'Ah, that giggle! Do it again! My eardrums are all on fire, madam.'

'Shut up! Don't be silly.'

'I shall come and help you move.'

'Dick's going to help. He's got a new van.'

'I shall come too. I simply can't not. Do you realize I haven't set eyes on you for more than a week?'

'Michael! Please don't start that!'

'Only being chivalrous, darling. No predatory intentions towards your delectable self. No, no. Perish the thought. See you on Thursday night.' He rang off.

Izzy plunged off towards her classroom and her class. She had taught them drama the year before last. They had been loathsome little second years, then. There had been a particularly vile little boy called Daniel Swayne who had insisted on impersonating a dog in a drama lesson of Izzy's at which a School Inspector had been present. Daniel Swayne had run round the drama studio cocking his leg against everything, culminating in a baroque dog-pee against the Inspector's chair. Izzy shuddered at the memory of it.

She could hear them shouting and flailing about in the room. This was the moment of truth. She set her shoulder to the door and burst in. The class paused in its mayhem.

'RIGHT!' bawled Izzy. 'I want everyone in their seat and absolute quiet and I want it RIGHT NOW!' She brandished the register. A divinely handsome young man stood up and handed her an apple.

'Here y'are, Miss Comyn,' he smiled down at her. 'Welcome 'ome.'

There was a chorus and cheering.

'We're glad we've got you Miss we're everso glad ent we Wend? Yeah Miss we was hopin' you'd be our form-mistress Miss it's brilliant ennit Sheel?'

Izzy was still looking at the young man.

'Your face is familiar,' she faltered.

'It's Daniel Swayne, Miss!' shrieked the girls.

'Sit down, Daniel,' commanded Izzy. 'You have become very tall.'

She opened her register and smiled to herself at the wonders that time could wreak. And how the past, well, passed. They all sat down, more or less, and the volume of noise thinned somewhat.

'Didjer 'ave a good 'oliday Miss? She ent half brown ent she Deb?'

'Yeah you bin to San Tropay Miss?'

'I had a great summer,' concluded Izzy, fighting to keep a real smile at bay. But it would break out, and it felt so odd, kind of cracking across her cheeks. It was as if her face was stiff with disuse: worn flat with all those tears. It seemed such a long time since she had really smiled.

'Come on! Be QUIET! If you're quiet for the register I'll tell you all about Hollywood afterwards.'

'Shush! ShoooooSH! Shut up Wilkes! SHUUUUU-UUUUSH!'

Silence fell: well, almost. Izzy felt herself bathed in friendly grins. She picked up her pen.

'Mark Ackroyd?'

'Yes miss.'

It was a new beginning. Yes.

THE END

UP THE GARDEN PATH
by Sue Limb

Izzy has problems . . . fat and spotty (too many cream cakes), she is hopelessly in love with Michael. Michael, unfortunately, is married to Louise – and intends to stay that way. Meanwhile Izzy has to contend with the assorted delights and terrors of 4C (that would have to be her class!), put up with being adored by Dick (the pottery teacher), and somehow cope with the maniacal, larger-than-life attentions of Hywel and Gwyn, two sex-mad Welshmen who force their way into her life and affections, in spite of their very obvious faults . . .

UP THE GARDEN PATH is a brilliant comic debut about men, marriage, sex, eating, love and life.

'Laugh-out-loud funny'
Margaret Forster, *Books & Bookmen*

'Enormously entertaining'
Financial Times

'A marvellous start for a new writer with such an unmalicious, bubbling sense of humour'
Elizabeth Berridge, *Daily Telegraph*

0 552 12561 X

A SELECTED LIST OF HUMOUR TITLES
AVAILABLE FROM CORGI BOOKS

THE PRICES SHOWN BELOW WERE CORRECT AT THE TIME OF GOING TO PRESS. HOWEVER TRANSWORLD PUBLISHERS RESERVE THE RIGHT TO SHOW NEW RETAIL PRICES ON COVERS WHICH MAY DIFFER FROM THOSE PREVIOUSLY ADVERTISED IN THE TEXT OR ELSEWHERE.

☐	11525 8	CLASS	*Jilly Cooper*	£3.50
☐	12865 1	LOVE FORTY	*Sue Limb*	£2.95
☐	12561 X	UP THE GARDEN PATH	*Sue Limb*	£2.50
☐	01296 8	THE WORDSMITHS AT GORSEMERE (Trade Paperback)	*Sue Limb*	£6.95
☐	12796 5	ONE MAN AND HIS BOG	*Barry Pilton*	£1.95
☐	13233 0	ONE MAN AND HIS LOG	*Barry Pilton*	£2.50

All Corgi/Bantam Books are available at your bookshop or newsagent, or can be ordered from the following address:

Corgi/Bantam Books,
Cash Sales Department
P.O. Box 11, Falmouth, Cornwall TR10 9EN

Please send a cheque or postal order (no currency) and allow 60p for postage and packing for the first book plus 25p for the second book and 15p for each additional book ordered up to a maximum charge of £1.90 in UK.

B.F.P.O. customers please allow 60p for the first book, 25p for the second book plus 15p per copy for the next 7 books, thereafter 9p per book.

Overseas customers, including Eire, please allow £1.25 for postage and packing for the first book, 75p for the second book, and 28p for each subsequent title ordered.